C000136255

For Rosie and Tom

THE SUNDERING WALL

BOOK TWO OF THE SHATTERED MOON

JON SPARKS

JON SPARKS

Contents

Part Two

City of Veils

Part Three

Greetings and Farewells

PART ONE

THE UNSUNG LANDS

JON SPARKS

CHAPTER 1

JERYA

Habit or instinct woke Jerya in the grey half-light. Railu was stirring beside her. Beyond the embers of the fire Rodal was a motionless bundle under the jutting flank of a rock. She glanced at her timepiece. It would be time for Sharess to Sing very soon.

Railu sat up a little, rubbing her eyes, unwrapping the headcloth to massage her scalp.

"How long to dawn?" she asked in a voice still foggy with sleep.

"Ten minutes—less—we've travelled East, haven't we? But Rai..."

"Hm?"

"From here we won't see the sun until long after it's risen."

Railu's eyes widened slightly. She leaned forward, drawing up her knees, resting her chin on them in thought. "Why didn't we think of that last night?"

The shadows had swallowed the whole valley and the sky above had been losing colour before they found this place on a broken spur sprawling out from the Eastern slopes. There were scrubby thorn-trees, sheltering rocks, a space among them which felt comfortably enclosed. No one had thought then what its position might mean; it had been too welcome, too providential in its timely appearance.

Jerya wriggled back down into her bedding, "It doesn't make any difference, does it?"

Railu looked across sharply. "What do you mean?"

"Simple. Who says we have to Sing at all? Who says we have to get out in the cold and fill our lungs with freezing air? Especially when we don't know the exact timing and won't see the sun anyway?"

Railu stared at her. "I hadn't thought...Not to Sing..."

"You can if you want," said Jerya lazily. "You know what it means, and what it does not mean. Me... I 'd forgotten what bliss it was to lie in bed."

She adjusted the blankets around her shoulders, settling down again. She and Railu were wedged between two rocks, each wrapped in blankets and sharing one of the deerskins which Rodal had brought. Thick heather beneath made what had turned out to be a remarkably comfortable bed. Even Railu had been pleasantly surprised. For Jerya, who'd grown up with a thin palliasse on a shelf of stone, it was almost too soft. In her weariness, she had slipped into sleep in no time, and she felt ready to slip back into slumber for a few more hours.

Railu was still sitting up, looking worried. "I... it's years since I let a dawn pass without Singing. It isn't so easy for me... and what about Rodal?"

Jerya was surprised, but only answered, "He looks as if he could sleep through a College chorus, never mind the two of us. Let him lie. The extra rest will help us all."

Railu still looked doubtful. Jerya moved quickly, sliding one hand out through her blankets to grasp Railu's wrist. She drew the arm back under the blankets.

"What time is it now?" she asked, keeping a firm grip so that Railu could not look at her timepiece. Railu did not answer, but her eyes widened in comprehension. "Exactly. It might have risen already. If we were on top of the mountain, it certainly would have. What time is sunrise, anyway? We don't know our exact altitude or meridian, even if we could see the horizon."

Railu nodded slowly, and Jerya could feel her relaxing, but she did not release her grip until Railu had manoeuvred herself back into the bedding again.

"Isn't this nice?" Jerya asked with a kiss. "Not to have to rush, not to get up in the cold. Just to lie here close together, warm and comfy, and just... just *feel* the dawn."

"I suppose so," Railu admitted. "Oh, but it takes some getting used to..." She pulled her hand free; this time Jerya did not resist. "Yes, it must be after sunrise now. The harm's done, if there is any."

With a shrug she settled-back, idly moving her hand across to stroke Jerya's head. Her fingers stiffened and halted.

"What is it?"

Railu did not answer. Jerya freed one of her own hands to explore. The smoothness of her scalp was gone. In one direction her hand seemed to slide almost more easily, but in the other it met a distinct prickly resistance. "Why, my hair's growing back! I should have thought it would, since we stopped using the cream." Her fingers searched Railu's scalp, but it was as smooth as ever. "Of course, you've been using it years, not weeks."

Railu said nothing. Her gaze was troubled.

"What is it, love?" asked Jerya.

"I can't imagine you with hair... It'll make you look like a man."

Jerya laughed, but then she saw the misery in Railu's face. She pulled Railu's hand through the blankets and pressed it to her breast. "It'll take more than that to make me look like a man, surely. Besides, you had hair yourself once. Don't you remember?"

Railu shook her head sombrely. "No. I know I must have... I can just about remember the day they shaved me. But... in the memories before that, no, there is no hair. I can't... It's something that others have."

Jerya struggled with the blankets until she could free both arms and enfold Railu in a strong embrace. "It's all right," she murmured. "Just you wait and see. We'll both grow hair down to our waists. We'll be so beautiful..."

"You might," said Railu, without enthusiasm. "I won't. I haven't used the lotion since my first year as a Novice."

"Well, you're beautiful anyway, just as you are."

Railu looked unconvinced.

"Listen," continued Jerya. "For years, before my head was shaved, I had to bind my hair up in a headcloth. You've seen how I look."

Railu shuddered. "Awful... Your face all shut in like that."

"You know, I never thought of it like that. Does it 'shut in' the face or does it—what's the word?—does it frame it? There were one or two girls in Delven everyone regarded as beauties. Wearing a headcloth didn't change that.

"Anyway, that's by the by. But... when my hair was long, I was never permitted to let it hang free, save when I was alone in the forest or in my chamber. It felt lovely, and I was sure when I looked at my reflection in the water that it was... Though it's only in books that you can *really* see anything in your reflection in a pool." She laughed softly, but she was watching Railu's face the whole time. "Oh, Rai, it's only different... Lying in bed while the sun rises; that's different too. But it doesn't feel so bad, does it?"

Railu was still contemplating her answer when they heard stirrings beyond the fire that had been earthed up for the night. They sat up, pulling the blankets around themselves, to watch Rodal writhe a few times, stretch his arms, knuckle his eyes, then sit up sharply, almost cracking his head on the overhang. He stared at them. His face was grey. "I knew... before l was even awake. l woke... because you did not Sing."

Jerya felt Railu stiffen beside her, her old suspicion obviously resurfacing. She pressed her hand firmly as she answered. "It's true. We didn't Sing. The sun has still risen, hasn't it?"

"I can't see it," he retorted, his tone rising, his eyes casting about wildly.

"Of course not. No more than you could ever see it in your chamber in Delven. Could you hear the Song then?"

"Seems to me I could. Maybe so faint I only knew it in my bones... This morning I knew there was none."

"No. But look yonder..." She inclined her head to the East, and the sun gilding the rocky peaks across the strath. Rodal, further back in the hollow, had to crane forward before he could see it too.

"There," said Jerya. "The sun has risen. We are in shadow here, that's all."

He looked no happier. Her impulse was to go over and shake him; had Railu not been there she thought she would certainly have done so. "Rodal. I told you there are many lies in the teachings of the Guild. I could have said that its very existence is based on a lie. But I left it till now. Till there was proof.

"We did not Sing. Still the sun has risen. Even if every Dawnsinger in the land were silent this morning, the sun would still rise. It would not be delayed by... by the space of a single heartbeat. Rodal, nothing we can do can influence the sun in any way, nor the course of the seasons, nor the daily changes of the weather... We have much knowledge of these things, can predict exactly the moment of the sun's rising, can predict the weather less precisely. But if today is going to turn stormy, we could sing a hundred songs to no avail. To say otherwise is a lie."

He stared at her, face still bloodless, forced a whisper as if his throat was blocked: "But why?"

"Why? Why lie? That I cannot tell you. The Guild has an answer, but why should I believe it? I know they have lied about other things—why should I believe their story of why they lie? Can you see now why I could have no part in it?"

Before Rodal could answer, Railu spoke, surprising them both. "The Song is not a lie. I've Sung it every day for eight years. You must see how strange it feels not to Sing now. No, Jerya, I understand why you don't want to be part of it, but I hold to this. *The Song is not a lie.*"

She looked at Jerya, then at Rodal, who was watching her with a peculiar intentness now. "The Song does not promise that the sun's rising depends on it. Well, the Song does not promise anything, certainly not in words that anyone but a few scholars now understand—or claim to understand. Yes, many people believe that the Song has power. I know that allowing them to go on believing that is... well, questionable, anyway. That doesn't mean the Song itself is questionable, let alone that it's a lie."

Again she looked at Jerya, at Rodal. "And maybe... Maybe it does have power, just not in the way people think. Not power over the sun or the weather. Not even power over those who hear it."

"If they believe it, it has power," said Jerya. "*I* believed it, never thought to question it, right up until that time at Kendrigg."

"Yes, in that sense, you're right. And I know that's the heart of your grievance, and by not Singing we prove something once and for all... but still I'm missing it. I miss... what I was about to say is that the Song does have power... for those who Sing it. When we Sing—" She stopped abruptly, and when she resumed her voice was husky. "When I Sang, every morning, with all the others in the College, it reminded me I was part of something bigger than myself. Just like shaving our heads, and wearing white. And I think... Sharess said this, or something like it. Though she was alone, every morning when she Sang, she felt connected to all the other Dawnsingers right across the Sung Lands."

Rodal shook his head, bewildered. "I understand none of this."

Jerya felt Railu relax, her worries allayed by Rodal's evident distress. "I will try and make it clear to you. But what did you understand before? You only accepted what you were told—or led to believe. Now we tell you differently. You have to choose... who do you believe?"

He held her gaze for a long time. Jerya resisted the temptation to assail him with further arguments. The only argument which really counted was already before him; the sun had risen. If that was not enough, he would simply have to trust them.

Then he looked about him, this way and that, searching. Abruptly he threw aside his blankets and began pulling on his boots. "It looks like any other day, I reckon," he said. Jerya began to breathe more easily. " And you must believe what you're telling me—if it isn't true, you're in the same peril I am."

"I don't say there's no peril," said Jerya. "There may be terrible storms in these mountains. There may be other dangers we cannot foresee at all. I only say that whether we Sing or not will make no difference."

"Well, we'll see," he grunted. "But I wish you'd told me. It did me no good at all, waking like that."

"I'm sorry, Rodal. I didn't plan it."

He shrugged, rose, turned away and vanished behind the rocks and down the slope. Jerya began to extricate herself from the blankets, But Railu caught at her.

"Hold me again," she begged. "A moment longer, while he's gone."

Jerya twisted, pulled Railu close again, felt the crush of breast on breast. She pressed into a long kiss, let one hand roam over Railu's head. She had said she was happy to grow her hair back, but she also knew there were things she would miss about being bald.

"A shame we aren't alone, lovely one," she whispered. "I can think of a better way to greet the dawn..."

"In a few days we will..."

"Besure, when we're through the mountains... if the weather holds. If Rodal can get back safely. He's risked enough to come with us. We can't ask him to risk his life rather than see the winter through with us."

"I suppose not."

Jerya heard the reluctance in Railu's voice, and pulled away to see her more clearly. "Is that the best gratitude you can find? You were pleased enough with the warmth of these deerskins—and the fire he made."

Railu shook her head slowly. "Yes. I am sorry. I'm sure it'll be a great help, having him with us. And it's truly... generous of him. But still..."

"But still?"

"Oh, he disturbs me... I don't know what to think. Sometimes I find myself talking to him almost as if he were another woman. I get so wrapped up in... whatever we're talking about... that I forget he's a man. When we talk that way, most of the time it seems he thinks no differently from the way we do. But then he'll say something that reminds me he *is* different... that he's a man, and men don't think as we do."

Jerya laughed. "Rai, do *I* think as you do? Not all the time, surely—remember, all those arguments about mathematics? I think if you'd been able to talk to some of the other women in Delven you'd have found them, perhaps, even more strange than Rodal. I think I found more of an understanding with him than I'd ever done with any of the women or girls. But I found out too late. If..."

She said no more. Railu would hardly be pleased with the thought that had taken her. If she and Rodal had discovered their affinity sooner, even by a season or two, then—Delven being Delven—they would likely have been soon betrothed, even wed. Who then would Sharess have sent as Postulant? Certainly not herself—though who else could she possibly have Chosen? *Well, everything would be different. Everything. But 'what if' is a question, not an answer.*

She looked at Railu, and at last she got a smile in return for her own. She was happier than she could measure to have met Railu, yet she knew that if things had indeed gone differently, if she had remained in Delven, she would never have missed her. It was hardly a comfortable thought, but truth and comfort were two different things. She seemed to have known that for a very long time.

Her education, however... she had a strong conviction that she would have missed *that. And I could have had so much more...*

Railu seemed impatient with Jerya's pensive silence; she untangled herself from the blankets and began to don her boots. Jerya could think of nothing helpful to say, and nothing to do but follow suit.

Though they had slept fully-clothed, they were still goaded into urgent movement by the jab of the sunless air. Jerya pulled the slices of turf off the fire, while Railu began breaking some of the dead wood Rodal had gathered last night—old heather-stems, juniper limbs. They fed the fuel piece-by-piece to the slumbering fire. The wood was very dry, half-rotted, its surface crumbly. It soon caught, and yellow flames breathed quick warmth to her hands. Behind her, Railu was stamping about, swinging her arms. Jerya watched her own breath mingle with the thin stain of smoke from the growing fire, warmed her hands, shivered suddenly as the cold air scratched at her scalp, and thought, *We need hats*. A headcloth would keep the sun off their scalps, but there was scant warmth in it. Perhaps they could wrap them differently, get several thicknesses of cover.

The stamping had ceased. She glanced over her shoulder, saw Railu standing between the rocks at the head of the stream-slope with a fixed gaze down into the little valley. Curious, and eager to be moving, she rose and went to join her. Rodal stood birth-naked on the banks of a plunge-pool below a little fall. It was fortunate his back was to them, she thought, but still... Then he dived, vanished in the rage of white water, reappeared at the far side of the pool. His wordless gasp of cold-shock was clear as a shout to them.

"You shouldn't be looking," said Jerya gently, putting a light hand on Railu's arm.

"Why not, then?"

"Choss, if you don't know... He's a man and you're a woman. Would you want him to watch you bathing?"

Railu turned away obligingly, but her face was puzzled. "I suppose not. I never thought about it before."

Jerya could hardly comprehend that Railu might be disturbed by some of the things Rodal said, but not by the possibility that he might see her bathing. She could only shake her head. "I doubt he'd care to know you were watching. Isn't that reason enough for now?"

Railu shrugged. "If you say so."

They crouched together to build up the fire some more. Soon they heard Rodal coming up behind them. "You're up, then," he said heartily. His face was bright and flushed, his naturally wavy hair dark and curly with water and a hasty drying. "If you want a real wakening, there's a pool down there."

Jerya said nothing, and she was sure her expression did not change. Still, Rodal saw something. "Watching, were you?"

"Not watching," she retorted. "Perhaps l caught a glimpse; how else was I to know there was something I shouldn't have seen?"

He stared a moment, then laughed. "Flip if I care... I've nowt to be shamed of. And proud to say I know my manners—l won't go peeping if you want me not to."

"I do want," she said firmly.

Railu followed her down the slope. At the pool's edge, on a narrow strip of shingle, they undressed as fast as they could. "Now I'm not so sure I want to do this," said Jerya. "But I am sure it's best done quickly." Railu's answer was only a grunt, buried in her struggle with her shirt.

Even exposing her body to the air was like a cold bath. Jerya stole a quick look up the slope, as if defying Rodal to be watching, but he wasn't in sight. Then, before courage could ebb, she turned and flung herself into the water.

It was like a sting and a bruise on every inch of herself. Even before she bobbed back to the surface she could feel the chill striking into her bones. She rose to the air with liquid ice streaming from her face, and then she knew why Rodal's scream had been silent. It was as if there was nothing in her lungs; reaching for breath she drew no air, only cold. Her tarn in the forest had been cool enough, but never like this.

Beside her Railu surfaced, tried to speak. They shared silent, breathless laughter. Jerya submerged again, made the swiftest, most perfunctory passes of her hands as a token washing, then hastened to the shore. She shook herself, dog-fashion, then furiously towelled off the moisture with the blanket she had brought. Her teeth were chattering a little as she started up the slope, until suddenly the warmth of her exertion made itself felt. At once there was a glow, a kind of singing in every limb; she felt lighter, stronger, younger.

The smell of frying sausages—venison, she was sure—came to her nostrils and she almost skipped into the campsite. Rodal looked up, grinning. "Didn't l tell you? Knows what's best for you, your Uncle Rodal."

"I'll thank you tomorrow, when I'm sure I havIn't taken chill," she said primly—but then moved on impulse, dropped to sit beside him and bestowed a peck on his cheek. "Good morning, Uncle Rodal."

"I'm not your Uncle really," he said, with an odd twist in his voice, concentrating fiercely on the sausages. Was that a blush? It was hard to tell with his tanned cheeks.

A loaf and a knife lay beside him. Jerya sawed off half a dozen slices ready for the sausages. It was impossible to cut delicately. She told herself that the bread would be best when fresh, and that they needed a substantial breakfast. The day ahead might—probably would—be long and strenuous.

Railu appeared just as they were ready. Rodal handed her a sandwich near as thick as her wrist, and she thanked him with an unforced smile.

They were soon fed, packed, laden and on the move again, angling down the slope to cross the stream well below the pool. The slopes were less rocky after the crossing; a slight rise from the stream, and they were on a smooth incline to take them easily down again to the main valley. There was even a faint but undeniable path through the heather and coarse tussocky grass.

"None of the men ever came this far, surely?" asked Jerya.

"Not likely," said Rodal. "Too far ayont Song-reach." He made a soft snorting sound that might have been a chuckle.

"Then what would make this?"

"Wild goats, I reckon. I haven't seen any, but I don't know what else would do it... mind, this is new country, besure. Still, it don't look all that different from parts I do know."

As the way levelled, they walked from shadow into sunlight. At once the world seemed two months warmer. Jerya simply stopped and turned to face the sun, eyelids closed against a blood-reddened glow. Beside her, she heard Railu murmur, "Bless you, Mother Sun."

"You call it mother, do you?" asked Rodal. Jerya did not open her eyes; let Railu answer.

"Of course. What else?"

"Well, I've heard men say the sun is male, which is why it takes a woman to summon him. But then you tell me now he comes of his own accord, so I put no faith in that any more."

"The truth is, the sun is neither male nor female. But it's the source of all life. Why not call it mother?"

They walked on in the light and warmth. Soon it became necessary to remove excess layers of clothing, and before long they were down to their leather shirts again.

The great curve of the glen began to open before them. Peaks marched into view along the horizon, still shadowed against the brightness of the sky, a wall across the world. And then they saw it, almost directly in the line of the upper glen, revealing itself as their angle of view shifted: a conspicuous notch in the mountain wall. Its base was still high above the valley, but not much above half the height of the peaks to either side.

Rodal made a satisfied kind of noise in his throat. "Well, there's no problem picking the route, so long as it stays clear. Even in a mist I think we could find it."

"How far is it, do you reckon?" asked Jerya.

"Hard to say." He shielded his eyes against the light. "Nothing to fix on whose size I know for sure. Those crags there could be three hundred feet, or nearer a thousand. We might get to the top of that pass tonight; we might barely reach its foot."

"Well, let's find out."

"No gain in pushing on any faster than we are," he cautioned. "We'll tire ourselves quicker... and it might be better to stop at the foot anyway."

"Why?"

"Did you notice it was cold last night?" That was one question that required no answer. "It'll be a sight colder up there. And who knows how much shelter there is? Who wants to spend a night in the open up there? Not me."

"Nor me," said Railu.

"No, you're right," conceded Jerya. "We stop where we can, leave it till tomorrow to cross the pass."

Rodal gave a short brusque laugh. "If we're lucky."

"What d'you mean?"

"I mean..." He stopped abruptly, faced her. "I mean a dozen things. For one... we've only your word that the world doesn't just come to an end there. And how would you know?"

Jerya began to speak, then stopped, mouth half-open, feeling foolish.

"Yes!" Rodal said with evident satisfaction. Jerya could only guess what pleased him: perhaps just the fact that he had been able to reduce her to speechlessness. "Someone told you. But you've been telling me we can't believe all they say. Maybe our old tales *are* true, and we'll walk into the Blistered Lands and shrivel up like dry grass in a flame. Or maybe we'll never even get that far. We can't any of us say there aren't sheer crags all along the other side there. What'd we do then, eh?"

Jerya knew she was daunted, but she did not let her voice betray it. "There's not much we could do, is there? We'd better just hope there aren't."

"Just so," said Rodal with grim amusement. "But then it's been that way all along, hasn't it?"

"What way?"

"You've been hoping there's a pass through the mountains—because it would be most awkward if there weren't. You're hoping there's a way down the other side—because it would be most awkward if there weren't. And you're hoping the Blistered Lands have healed as they told you—because it would be most awkward if they hadn't. Most awkward—but just suppose..."

"Rodal, what are you suggesting?"

"I'm suggesting we should think a bit," he said. "Even if those lands have healed—how d'you know they've healed just right? What if you can't get down there in the first place: what would you do then? Stop here? Nobody'd disturb you. But how long before you starved? There's not much to eat up here."

"You said there were goats."

"I said there might be. Suppose there are—what good's that to you? Ever tried to catch a wild goat? I've seen it done, but it took a dozen men, and nets, and most of a day."

"Rodal, why are you talking about living up here? We never planned to do that. There *will* be a way down from that pass."

"I expect there will," he agreed.

"Then why—" she began sharply, but he held up his hand to block her.

"Probably..." He repeated with a heavier emphasis: "*Probably.* But how can we be sure? And in any case... a way down to what? Have you really thought about it? There might be no more life down there than there is here, or in those empty plains. That's what my feelings tell me it'll be like—because that's what my heart tells me a land without Dawnsingers must be like. I know, I know, it makes no difference; so you tell me. But I can't really feel it yet. I don't think I really will until we come down from the pass and find a place like Delven. A place where folk could live, anyway.

"And... even supposing that... suppose we find somewhere just like the lands round Delven... That's the best we can hope for, isn't it? And if it's like that, you won't starve. If it's like Delven-lands, you know how to live. But you'll spend most of your daylight hours keeping yourselves fed and warm. Sure as the rock itself, it'll be nothing but hard work... and what happens if one of you breaks a leg, or gets ill? What happens—if you live long enough—what happens when you get old?"

She did not answer, having no answer to give. There was an empty silence. A faint breeze ruffled the long dry grasses, rattled the dead stems, plucked at Rodal's hair.

"Well," he said then. "You answer those questions yourself. I think I'd better stop, or I'll be persuading myself I should stay with you."

Before Jerya could reply, she was unbalanced by the sight of Railu's face. She was gazing at Rodal with an altogether new look in her eyes, as if she would like nothing better than to persuade him to stay. Jerya knew that her reaction was perverse—had she not earnestly counselled Railu to make better friends with Rodal?—but she felt a quiver of dismay.

It was surely the sheer reasonableness of Rodal's tone which had so impressed Railu, but Jerya could not make her reply sound anything but petulant in comparison. "Rodal, do you have to look on the black side? What makes you think Delven-lands are the *best* sort of place we can find? We've the whole of the Blistered—what were the Blistered Lands—to choose from. Rivers no one else has ever fished, forests no one else has ever hunted; soil no one else has ever planted."

"All right," he said, "Food may not be the problem... what about shelter? Not every place has caves so great and handy as ours—and even they had to be enlarged and linked up in the beginning, and extended many times since. But suppose you can find a decent cave. And you can clear out the rats—or worse—and clean it up. And you can get enough firewood when we haven't a saw... And you can do all that within the space of daylight. And..."

"And what?" demanded Jerya sharply.

"Ah," said Rodal, smiling, "That's my real question."

She stared.

"I see... well, I have some notion what it is you're running from; not much, but a beginning. But what are you running *to*? Or are you just running?"

"Yes, of course we're running," she said. "What else can we do?"

"I don't know about that. I don't know too much at all. I just know I'm not happy about this..."

"Then you know what you can do, don't you?" she stormed. The look on Railu's face told her there would be a price to be paid, but she could not restrain herself. "If you don't like this path, there's another one. No one asked you to come..."

"Not so," he said, with maddening calm. "The *Dawnsinger* did."

Somehow that was worse. "You're right, Rodal. You're quite right: you don't know too much. How dare you wade in and start telling us what we should he doing? Do you think I chose to do this? Do you really think if I'd planned the way the world is I'd be here now?"

The force of her outburst was quickly spent, but she did not leave him a moment in which to speak. He had to content himself with a shake of the head as she went on, voice turning quiet and weary. "Of course not. We're not given choices like that. That's not the way the world is. You should know that. What was your choice? Lie to your kin, or deny Annyt her journey to Delven?"

Seeing Rodal grimace, doubtless at the mention of Annyt, she continued quickly. "And what was ours? Surrender to the will of the Guild—or this. If you think there is a third choice, tell me, please. But if you are trying to tell us we have chosen wrongly between the two, I don't want to hear it. You... you cannot know all that lies behind it.

"Besides, it is *our* choice. For *our* lives. It's not for you to choose for us. Not even for the Dawnsinger. She chose for me once, and look where we are now.

"Rodal, I am grateful for your help in our journey, but if you do not think we should be making it at all, you had best leave now."

He looked stricken, and Jerya's heart softened, but her words could not be unsaid. The aftertaste was bitter nonetheless.

They stood in silence for a long while. In the stillness Jerya felt how keen the air still was. The breeze was no more than an uneasiness of the air, but its touch on her arms or her scalp could make her shiver. It felt as if the great bare hills had all turned their backs. Suddenly she felt a pang of terror. If Rodal should leave them, as she had just challenged him to do, she did not know how she would be able to go on without him. It had been exactly what she intended, originally, but now...

And what would Railu do? Railu, who was still gazing at Rodal as if expecting miracles, though he seemed wholly unaware of her attention.

At last he spoke, and at his first words her heart lifted within her. "It's truth you speak: I *don't* know." He looked from Jerya to Railu. Jerya was about to speak, step forward, take his hands and seal their reconciliation with some soft words, when he added, "I'm sorry, I don't know why I spoke like that. Perhaps I was still angry about waking that way this morning. Realising that I was truly in Unsung Lands..." His voice faltered for a moment. "But why should I be angry at you? If it is all lies... you're not the ones doing the lying." He swung back to her. "Doesn't it make you want to stay and fight? Doesn't it tear at you just to turn your back and walk away from it all?"

"Fight?" said Jerya. "Fight the Guild? How could we do that? Or even *should* we? They may be right; the deception may all be necessary. I don't know. I'm not saying the Guild is wrong; how am I to know that? I only know I couldn't be part of it... Of course it tears at me, Rodal, more than I dare say. Leaving everything we've ever known. I'm full of... foreboding." There had been stronger words in her mind than 'foreboding'. "But we can't stay. There's no place in this land that could hide a renegade Dawnsinger. There's no way to go but ahead... therefore we have to trust that there is somewhere to go."

He nodded. His eyes strayed past her toward that bright gash in the skyline. "Besure," he said, adjusting the balance of his pack a little. "I reckon we'd better get on then, and see what we may see."

Jerya blinked. She thought she had very likely never heard braver words.

CHAPTER 2
RODAL

They were nearing the top of the steep climb when the snow started, falling in heavy silence. The broad wet flakes did not survive long on the ground; it was not terribly cold. Still the world seemed reduced, the sky suddenly close and pallid. Rodal shrugged deeper into his hide coat, tightened the scarf at his neck, burrowed his hands into his pockets as his eyes sought the way ahead. The crest of the slope was disappearing, and he sought the best line through the final boulder-fields while he could still see.

If there had been any sign of shelter, he might have been tempted to call a halt, but even the largest of the rocks were scarcely bigger than the pack on his back. Underfoot, smaller rocks were loosely piled, often unstable, treacherous; smears of melting snow made the footing even worse. He moved carefully, intently, slipping only rarely, but behind him he could hear Railu blundering and cursing, Jerya coaxing and encouraging, their voices muffled in the grey sound-fog of the snow. *At least it sounds like she's cursing*, he thought. Did Dawnsingers curse? What words did they use?

The snowfall grew steadily thicker. Now he could not see more than twenty yards, but the boulders were also becoming smaller, more scattered. He sensed, too, that the slope was easing. The top was near; this would have been more welcome, but as they came onto the more level ground of the pass itself, they also walked into a wind. It was no gale, no more than a steady breeze, but it was funnelled by the unseen slopes that framed the pass. It was blowing directly into their faces, and it was laden with snow. The snow was not so wet now, the flakes smaller but more icy, stinging exposed flesh. It was difficult to look straight ahead; when you did, there was nothing to see but a few strides of threadbare moor-grass, and the falling snow dark against the pale sky, all its traces seeming to radiate from a single point.

He stopped to let the girls join him. They came up one on either side, pressing close for warmth or companionship, bulky and nameless in hoods and scarves and deerskins. "Why have we stopped?" asked one. She still bore a full load, so it must be Jerya.

"To speak with you," he replied. "I think we can go on, but I want to know you feel strong. There is no knowing how far we may have to go before we find shelter, if we do at all. In this murk we could walk past a perfect howff, ten yards away and see nothing. Perhaps we may have to sleep in the open tonight. It will not kill us, but it will not be pleasant either."

"What else can we do?" she said. "If we turn back... we'll have to go all the way back down again, and it's getting troublesome. Fresh snow over scree; you don't need me to tell you. And we might not get another chance to cross at all. If this snow sticks..." Catching his arm, she leaned closer to add, in a voice that might have been private, and might not, "I'll go on as long as you—you know that. It's Rai... even without a load, she's clumsy on the rough ground. Wastes her strength—and she hasn't as much as we have in the first place. I think she'll be all right. You'd better ask her, though."

"I?"

"Why not you?" She gave him a little push.

He turned to Railu. "Are you able to continue?"

He could hardly see anything of her face, close-wrapped in hood and scarf. Her voice was muffled, but her words were firm enough. "Yes. I'm all right. Thank you."

They moved on, falling into single file again, wasting no more energy on talk.

The way rose a little more, very gently, then became as near level as made no difference. The world had shrunk almost to nothing. The scant, pale grass was mostly hidden by snow; there was only a featureless grey-whiteness, merging at some vague distance with the white-grey of the falling snow. Without the sense of ground beneath his feet, Rodal would hardly have known even which way was up. There was no way to set a direction now, save by keeping the wind dead ahead.

Their view from below had suggested that the pass was really quite a narrow space, between two squarish peaks, but now there was nothing to see, no sense of mountain-mass on either side. The cramped circle of ground they could still see might as well have been the centre of a vast plain. It could go on for ever.

He lifted his eyes a little. The snow was still driving straight toward then, still radiating from a single point low in the sky ahead. There seemed a strange brightness in that one clear point, small and hard like a star. The snow falling out from it was almost black against the light: black snow. Snow falling every way. Or was it he who was falling? He stumbled, knees close to buckling under the weight of his pack. *It must be fifty pounds if it's an ounce...*

A hand on his arm. "Rodal? Are you all right?"

He dragged his gaze away from the eye of the snow. Jerya was at his side, looking close at him. Only her eyes were visible now, the rest of her face a snow-crusted mask. He remembered a previous time she'd shrouded her face, against the sun's glare, not against snow and wind and cold.

Her eyes were like the last living thing in this dead world.

His face felt half-frozen; he could barely speak. "I'm all right. It's just... thought I was falling... Jerya, *look...*"

"I can't see anything."

"That's just it... Nothing. And it might go on for ever..."

"Don't be silly," she said. "But I can see how it preys on the mind... Do you want me to lead for a while?"

"No, no, I'll be fine..."

"Good," she said, squeezing his hand through the twin thicknesses of their felted gloves.

They walked on. Rodal realised that he had lost all sense of how far they had come from the top of the climb. *Not very* far, he thought, but he did not know what that meant. *Jerya would know*, he thought vaguely. She had made a first attempt, at last night's camp, to explain some of her knowledge. She had spoken of measuring time as if you could lay hands on it, like distance. The bells he had grown accustomed to in Carwerid marked out the *hours*. He knew that much, but he hadn't thought of an hour as anything more than the space between chimes. Jerya had offered another way to grasp what it was: it was about the time it would take you, walking briskly, to cover four miles on a level track. He could not immediately see what good that might be, since you already knew it was four miles. Now, however... they could be making no more than half that speed. Jerya would be able to look at the thing she called a 'timepiece', say they had been going an hour—or whatever time it actually was—and therefore had come two miles.

Since it felt like too great an effort to turn round and ask her, the only other measure he could resort to was the state of his own body. They had allowed themselves another good breakfast, so it should be well into the middle of the day before he began to feel hungry, if indeed he was not too numb to feel it at all.

Of course, however hungry he might feel, it would not do to stop long to eat. In the open, up here, you would soon get cold, soon grow stiff; it would be that much harder to get moving again. Then, dazedly, he recalled that he had anticipated this, had stowed some cake in an accessible fold of his clothing.

He could not reach it without pulling off one of his clumsy gloves. As he nibbled at the cake, full of oats and honey, he felt the steady prickling of snow on the back of his hand. The fingers quickly became too cold to feel the morsel they were holding. The wind, of course; Delven-men well knew that wind and wet were the real killers. He finished eating as swiftly as he could and thrust the hand back into his glove, gloved hand deep into a pocket. For a spell—some *minutes*, he supposed, which she'd mentioned as fractions of an hour—he could feel nothing; then the return of circulation brought pain sharp as bee-stings. His legs kept moving automatically; his mind seemed altogether occupied with the pain in his hands. Finally he was left with nothing but a warm irritation, like a fading nettle-rash.

He looked about him again. Nothing had changed, except that the snow was deeper on the ground now. Only a few stiff stalks of sedge or rush broke the blankness, black against the white. They seemed still to be walking straight into the wind, though it was hard to gauge with any precision.

He began to worry. They might well have come far enough to have passed between the twin peaks, into more open terrain. Without the confining effect of the mountainsides, there was no reason to think the wind was still blowing in the line they wanted. And there was no knowing, in this blind world, what the right line might be anyway.

They would have to find a stream of some kind. The upper slopes on the West side had been dry, draining presumably beneath the crust of jumbled stone, but the ground here was largely free of rocks. It was not always reckoned wise for the lost—and what else were they?—to follow streams downhill. Water, seeking the shortest course, often found the steepest, which would be neither safest nor easiest to descend, especially in the blindness of a snowstorm. However, they needed a pointer to lower ground. Rodal reckoned he would gladly take his chances with crags and cataracts, rather than wandering in this endless, formless waste until they were exhausted.

He began to wonder if he was growing weary. If not, then the ground must be rising again. This was the last thing he wanted. But how could he tell for sure? The snow was getting deeper—that made the going harder. And surely he had every right to feel a little weary.

In the whiteness he did not see the drop until he went slithering over it. It was just a short slope of a few feet, with a fragile lip where the snow had settled on shaggy grass. It gave way beneath him—he dropped a few feet, stopped almost upright, the pack on his back holding him up against the slope behind. He was not hurt, but the shock, the crashing awakening from his half-trance, was near as bad as the physical impact of a much greater fall. His heart had been in his mouth for a moment; he felt sick; he knew he could have walked straight over the top of a crag.

He looked behind him. The slope was not even high enough to block his view. There was the disturbed snow where he had broken the lip of the drop; there were the blue holes of his footmarks counting back into the grey.

He could not see Jerya and Railu.

He scrambled back up where he had fallen, floundered over the edge, began to stagger back along his track, trying to run. The snow and the weight on his back would not permit it. "Jerya!" he screamed. The name vanished into soft indifferent silence.

"Jerya! Railu! HOY!" This time there was a faint answering sound. He could not identify it even as a voice—but what else could it be? The relief was indescribable. He ploughed a few more steps through the snow, and a grey shape appeared: a strange, broad, distorted outline. For a moment it made no sense; then it cleared as suddenly as if a veil had been lifted, became solid, became two figures wrapped together.

He did not know how to express his relief except in anger.

"Why didn't you tell me to wait? If we'd become separated..."

"We could hardly lose you," said Jerya, pointing to the lines of his tracks.

"Maybe not. But still..."

"I suppose you're right. But it didn't seem to matter if you were a few paces ahead... then I stopped, just a moment, to check with Rai. Then you were out of sight."

"Why didn't you shout?"

He could not see her shrug, but he was sure she had. "I couldn't..."

He understood. The silence was like a law. Only in panic had he broken it.

"How is she?" he remembered to ask.

"Still on her feet," replied Jerya. " She'll be all right."

He turned, retraced again the confusion of his steps to the place where he had fallen. It was a scooped hollow, like a half or a third of a shallow bowl. He recognised its characteristic form, felt sure there would be a spring under the snow in the bottom of the hollow.

In that case, he realised bemusedly, the ground must slope down in that direction. He could not see it in all the white uncertainty, but when he went round the side of the hollow and walked on a few paces he could distinctly feel his stride getting easier.

His feet wanted to swing into an easy downhill jog, but all his experience still counselled caution, especially after his recent blunder. He went at a steady walk, straining his senses for some inkling of the wider shape of the land. The land had a fairly even slope, merely decorated with dips and swells. Under the snow, it seemed firm, so must be drained, but still there was no sign of a stream.

Then...

At first he thought his eyes were deceiving him, befooled by the mesmeric shifting of the snow. Only slowly did the dark shapes make any sense to his tired brain. Then the slow suspicion turned with jolting suddenness to certainty as the snow ceased all at once. A few last flakes drifted from the low-hanging ceiling of clouds. Suddenly the view ahead could be measured, not in yards but in miles.

It was a view without colour, a world of greys and faded browns. The roof of cloud was a uniform leaden shade, looking scarcely less solid than the slopes that vanished into it. There were steepnesses on those slopes, but no crags, and their scree and sedge subsided drably into the broad floor of the valley. A thin ribbon of water wandered down the middle of the strath, fringed with marshes, lost to sight at a curve many miles distant. In the dim light the slopes there seemed to merge, so the valley looked like a basin with no exit.

There was not a single tree anywhere in all the miles of it. Rodal could scarcely have imagined any prospect more desolate or less welcoming. This dreary land looked as if it had never harboured any life more vigorous than the straggling ungreen grass which appeared where his feet disturbed the snow. It seemed to him that a place that had never heard Dawnsong might look just like this, but it could just as well be that it had never heard Song because no one had ever come here.

Barring us, he thought, which recalled to him that he had companions.

They were still catching up, a few yards away, not on his heels as he had imagined. Jerya was now clearly half-supporting Railu.

"I'm sorry," he said as they stopped at his side. Jerya, her wrappings now pulled apart a little, looked composed, but Railu's face was a grey shadow inside her hood. "I forgot you again. I was so intent on picking out a path if I could..."

"As I thought," said Jerya. "It seems you've done well enough."

He shrugged. "I did nothing. There were no tricks in the land. A straight course was enough."

"Not quite straight, I think," she said, but did not explain. "It's after three. We've hardly stopped for near on seven hours. Can we have a rest now, and some food?"

"Why not? There's nowt to choose between one spot and another."

They spread the groundsheet over sodden grass and snow. Rodal doled out whatever came easiest to hand and they ate in virtual silence. Railu was withdrawn, and even Jerya was subdued. For himself, he was too tired to feel hungry; he ate listlessly, without pleasure, because he must.

It was so hard, once he had stopped, to get himself moving again, that he could not stir himself until he saw Jerya helping Railu to rise. Then he scrambled to his feet with all the haste he could muster.

"Rest yourself," he said. "I'll look after her for a while... If you don't mind?"

He addressed the question to Railu, who turned large, dazed eyes upon him. For a moment she seemed not to recognise him; then she nodded. He slid his arm around her waist; she slumped a little against him.

On they went, down towards the empty valley, Rodal slowed now by Railu's weight and the cramping of his stride. He felt sure she could have gone no faster however much help he could give. It was a mystery how Jerya had managed so nearly to keep up before.

But they hadn't gone far before Jerya, a few paces ahead, stopped and turned to face them. "I'm not sure this is right."

"What do you mean? Looks easy enough."

"Easy, besure. But easy isn't the same... Look yonder." She gestured, down the long desolate valley. The clouds had lifted a little, he realised, and they could see the distance more clearly. "It's curving back toward the West."

He looked. "Ain't it heading about Nor'east mostly? The valley up to the pass was about Nor'west to Sou'east."

"Besure, but did we go straight after we came through the pass?"

"The wind was always in our faces."

"D'you think so? Well, winds can shift." He recalled that the same thought had crossed his own mind. "I think the ground's been pulling us to the left for a while before we dropped out of the cloud."

She faced away again, looking down the long valley, shrouded and anonymous. Then she turned back and she was all Jerya as she swore, "Gossan! I wish we had a compass." He didn't know the word, but he could guess it was something to tell direction. "Well," she said, "There's a way to find South using the hands of a watch, but only if you can see the sun. Rai? Can you remember how?"

Railu, still leaning against him, stirred a little. "I don't know. It was a long time ago."

"Third-year Novice work, Skarat said. Well, I think I can work it out and if you try to remember... it's no use now anyway. Need the sun."

Are you sure we'll ever see the sun here? he wanted to say, recalling his thought about how a place that had never known Dawnsong might look. Suddenly he felt deathly tired, and behind the fatigue there was a low thin thread of...

Name it for what it is, lad. A Delven motto.

It was fear.

"Well," said Jerya, as if reading his mind, "It's been a long day already. I don't think we should keep on going down if we might have to climb back up tomorrow."

"Jerya," he said, "S'pose you're right. S'pose this valley swings back West. It's going to come out somewhere well North of Delven, ain't it? There's no more villages there, and it's beyond day-reach."

She considered. "I see what you're saying. You've seen that country from up on the edges, I guess, same as I have."

"Aye. And I've seen that the sun shines there, sometimes."

"It does, besure." Suddenly, she laughed, her clear, ringing laugh almost shocking in the great dull stillness around them. "Why did I never think about that before?" She chuckled again, and in amid the chuckle he heard the words, "Unsung Lands."

"So... ain't that a possibility?" Somewhere known, however slightly, against the utter unknowableness of 'ayont the mountains'; it sounded deeply appealing right now.

"Maybe," she said, but it was the sort of 'maybe' that sounded like 'not if it's up to me'. *But there's three of us*, he thought. Still, he had no quarrel with her next words. "Well, we might go just a little further down. There's a sort of shelf just there, where the heather starts. A bit of shelter, at least."

CHAPTER 3

JERYA

When she'd suggested stopping where they did, well before nightfall, she'd felt as if she at least could have gone on for a couple of hours more, especially downhill. Once they had stopped, however, she had to admit she wasn't sorry, and there'd been no mistaking that Railu was close to the end of her resources. She clung on to Rodal even as he helped her to sit, in a shallow dell among the heather. Silently, by looks alone, Jerya and Rodal had agreed he stay by Railu while Jerya prepared what food she could manage. With no better fuel than sodden heather, there was no way of lighting a fire. The bread was getting stale, the cheese too, so she'd thought they might as well consume as much of both as they could.

She'd begun to wonder if Railu could be severely chilled; why else did she keep pressing close to Rodal if not in need of warmth? It was a relief when she stirred herself to accept a sandwich, sat up a little straighter and looked around. Jerya had tried to engage her in conversation, and she had answered. Her replies were desultory and her tone listless, but she didn't sound like one who was trying to keep her teeth from chattering.

Without debate, they'd placed Railu in the centre, all three of them huddled close under the blankets and the waxed sheet. Railu and Rodal had both apparently fallen into sleep almost at once, but she had lain awake a while, thinking. She wasn't sure she'd settled anything in her mind, except for one thing. She knew how to find South using the hands of a watch. *Well, really, you only need the hour-hand.*

❈

And now the sun was out. Fitfully, besure, and mostly half-veiled by high spreading cloud, but you could see where it was, and that was all they needed. She'd taken a sighting before the others were even stirring, but then another thought occurred to her.

She waited till they were all up, had relieved themselves, and were settling to a breakfast that was much the same as their meal of the night before. Both bread and cheese a little staler again, that was the only difference. One more meal left, and then they were onto the oatcakes and dried fruit.

"Rai..." she began, "Have you remembered that way of finding South? I think I have, but I need you to tell me I'm getting it right."

Railu frowned. "How do you think it goes, then?" She smiled thanks as Rodal handed her a sandwich.

"Point the hour hand at the sun. Then bisect the angle between that and twelve."

"I think that's right. And what I do remember is Skarat saying it's hard when the sun's high so use a stick or something to cast a shadow..."

"Like the gnomon of a sundial?"

"Exactly. It gives you the direction."

Jerya could have worked it all out for herself, but she could see Railu was pleased to be included. And for all her confidence in her own reasoning, she was heartily glad to have someone else confirm it.

They took a sighting right away, in case the cloud thickened again, before settling down to eat, and to discuss their plans. "The valley below us lies barely East of North," said Jerya. "And it's even clearer now that it curves to the West down there in the distance. See that peak, just showing over the nearer shoulder, the one that's in and out of the clouds? That's the highest thing we can see, isn't it?" Railu and Rodal both agreed that it was. "And this valley's going to run West of it, isn't it?"

"Well," said Rodal, quickly swallowing a mouthful, "I don't understand what you're doing with that watch thing, but I guess it's Dawnsinger wisdom, and I'll trust you on that. But is South the same everywhere? In Unsung Lands?"

Jerya and Railu looked at each other. Jerya gave a slight nod. "North is North and South is South," said Railu. "You can trust us on that." *Three kinds of North,* thought Jerya, *and so three kinds of South...* But she knew what Railu meant.

Rodal shrugged, accepting. "Fine. So we're looking near enough North and the valley's bending West down there. So, like we said afore, it's more'n'likely going to come out on the same side o' the mountains we started out on, just a ways further North." He looked at them in turn and they both agreed. "So, tell me this. We have some idea what that country must be like; Jerya and I have both seen it; from afar, besure, but we know more about it than whatever's East o'the mountains. We know there's no one there. We can probably get there without killing ourselves. So why not just head that way?"

Jerya thought of those lands, glimpsed on clear days from the high points of the edge by Wisket Moss: the lands North of Delven. "I've seen it, as you say. So you know what you see's more lake than land. And between the lakes, where it's not forest it looks like mostly bog. You know that colour. No people, besure, but it doesn't look encouraging."

"'Doesn't look encouraging'," repeated Rodal. "But we *have* seen it. We know there's *something* there. And it can't all be bog. Besides, lakes mean fish."

"And you need fire to cook a fish, and then anyone standing where we've stood might see the smoke, and wonder."

"Depends how far North you are," said Rodal doggedly. She saw Railu looking at him, saw him return the glance. What was Railu hoping for?

Jerya sighed. "Not if the Guild decides to come looking for us. What do you think, Rai? Will they?"

Railu gave this due consideration, but her answer wasn't as clear as Jerya had been hoping. "I don't really know... I mean, you know Perriad, she isn't just going to shrug her shoulders..." Jerya gave a snort of laughter at this. "But it'll be up to the Peripatetics to actually look for us. I don't know how far they'll push it. And Sharess will tell them we were aiming to cross the mountains."

"And I haven't given up on it yet." Jerya jumped in quickly. "Look, how far did we really come down last night? I mean, where the slope was steep enough that we knew we were descending? Half an hour?"

"It felt like more to me."

"We were all tired last night." Jerya made her tone as sympathetic as she could. "Listen, wait here if you want. I'll go back up till it levels off a bit. See if I can see any sign of a way forward. No need for any of us to drag the loads up there if there's nothing to be gained."

"That means you'll have to come back down to here for yours," said Rodal.

That was reasonable enough, she supposed, but it didn't feel helpful. A stubborn defiance stirred in her. "Mayhap I'll take it. If you don't see me coming back within an hour..." She waited to see if Rodal would offer to come with her, but he looked at Railu, and Jerya sensed she wasn't happy about being left alone. For herself, she realised, she relished the thought of being on her own in the midst of the mountains.

It didn't feel like such a good idea as she wriggled into the straps again and heaved to her feet. She wondered, not for the first time, just how much the pack weighed. But what use would an answer be if she knew it? It was heavy, besure, a weight such as she had rarely carried even a short way; but she knew now that she could.

"An hour," she said simply, meeting Railu's gaze. Railu held up her wrist, and her timepiece glinted as the elusive sun briefly reached the dell. Jerya decided to take it as a hopeful sign, though a small voice in her commented that that made no more sense than thinking Dawnsong made the sun rise.

She skirted round the hollow, avoiding the steeper heathery slopes that enfolded it. As soon as she began to climb she felt a heavy stiffness in her legs. She'd said 'an hour', but she began to wonder if that was time enough even to get to where they'd started descending. It might have taken half an hour coming down, but she knew she couldn't make the same pace toiling back up. She knew it would be folly to even try. Railu and Rodal would be able to watch her most of that way; she hoped that if it did take an hour before she disappeared from sight, they would wait a while longer before following.

Then she just set her mind to her work, attending to her stride, her breathing, keeping a steady rhythm, never faltering, but never pushing too hard either. It had worked well enough for her yesterday, and it seemed to be working again today.

Gradually her stiffness eased; or else she had got better at ignoring it. She climbed on, ignoring the urge to pull her timepiece from under her clothes. Time passed, as it always did. She climbed.

She thought how she would look to an eagle soaring above. A tiny figure, ungainly with that hulking pack, and so *slow*. The eagle would laugh, she thought, if eagles laughed. *How easy it is for me, how hard for this poor earthtied creature.*

Well, she thought, *Let it laugh. I'm doing the best I can.* She held the image until it almost felt as if she was an eagle, looking down at herself. It hurt less that way.

Jerya climbed on.

When she realised the slope was lying back, she was so startled she nearly stumbled. She turned, but saw that she was already out of sight of the others. *Oh well, it's not as if I could have told them anything anyway.*

She had to climb on, ten more minutes up that easier slope, before she really began to see where she was. A broad sort of saddle, dappled with snow. Most of last night's fall had already melted; what remained had the slightly grubby look of old snow. Between the snow-patches, colourless grass or sedge was a threadbare covering over pale stony soil. Her boots crunched grittily. She found a convenient low boulder and swung her sack onto it, then climbed a larger one to get a wider view.

North-West by West—she pulled her watch from her pocket to check the direction—was the pass they had crossed. She could see now how it cut between two lumpy peaks, skirted with grey crags below snowy slopes. The curve and slope of the ground they had traversed yesterday was clear now, and it was obvious how far they had been lured from a straight course. If they had kept on a straight heading, they would have passed not far from where she now stood, and then, perhaps a couple of kilometres beyond, they'd have found themselves climbing again. Here a snow-filled bowl was closed off by crag and scree, with no obvious pass. On the left side as she looked now, the East or North-East side of the valley that ended in the bowl, the peaks were lower than on the West, but still looked like a near-continuous wall.

It didn't look promising, but she was much closer to that wall than the other, so the angle was acute. The shoulder of one peak could easily be masking the gap between it and the next. With barely a moment's reflection, she struck out along the narrowing strip of roughly level ground between the fans of scree. She left her pack where it sat atop the boulder.

Soon enough she began to feel more hopeful, to get a sense that the peaks were not one continuous chain. Another hundred metres, and she was nearly sure of it. She felt so much lighter without the mass of the pack that she even ran a short way.

There it was: a gap; a curiously rectangular notch, deeper than it was wide, parting great blades of rock. Running up to it, only a simple slope of scree splashed with snow. There was an apron of rock at the breach itself, but she could see it'd be easy.

If the other side's the same, it's a pass.

At once she set out up the scree, picking a winding line where it was mostly smaller stones, avoiding any larger blocks. These, she knew, could too easily be precariously balanced, ready to shift at the merest touch of a boot. Unladen, she still felt light, almost as if instead of the great lump of the rucksack she had wings on her back. She couldn't fly, but she climbed fast, her breath coming in gasps, her heart hammering. What she saw at the top might decide everything.

I'll rest when I can see.

It was perfectly clear now. Ever since she had seen that notch in the ridge, the first pass, or false pass, she had not merely wanted to see what lay beyond; she had *needed* to see. This was far beyond curiosity. Now, she needed to see if there was a way into the land beyond.

And if there was? No matter what the others did, she thought, barely noticing how she lumped Rodal and Railu together; no matter what they did, she herself would go on now, until she knew.

Until she *knew.*

※

There was no direct way down from the gap; crags below. Not very high, from what she could see, but vertical. However, she could see that this crag-band petered out a few hundred metres to her right, and it looked as if it would be possible to sidle along, directly under the upper rock wall. There was even a kind of shelf, a slight hollow, right against the base of the cliff. Looking up, she saw how the rocks leaned out. If stones fell from higher up they would land several metres away from the base where she walked.

There was just one place where the rocks pushed out, partly blocking her view. She hurried easily to that point; then she had to edge more cautiously along, shoulder brushing the rock, a sudden new awareness of the hundred or more metres of steep scree and snow below. *Have to be careful here when we come with the sacks*, she thought; but a few steps further on it was easy again, and she could see that the rest would go.

And below the screes, there was a broad bowl, maybe a kilometre across, its bed free of snow and patched with small tarns, three or four substantial ones and a dozen or so smaller pools. It occurred to her suddenly that she was thirsty, but she shoved the thought aside and looked further. The bowl funnelled down to the right: somewhere between East and South-East. And though it curved out of eyeshot, she could see more: far away, beyond and between yet more peaks, indistinct in lowland haze, a colour she knew.

Forest.

❋

"An hour, you said, Jerya. It's been more than three." Rodal nodded in accord with Railu's rebuke.

Jerya frowned. "I'm sorry, but I had to know." *Anyroad, didn't I say 'If I don't come back within an hour'?* She kept that to herself, as she did the thought that those three hours alone in the midst of the mountains had been beyond any price.

"Well, then," said Rodal, ever practical, "What did you see?"

"There's a way to cross this ridge, and to get down the other side. It leads out to the East."

"Where?"

She pointed, up toward the notch, but even as she did she saw that the clouds were spreading, grey streamers slipping through the gap and slithering along the cliffs. There would be few chances to take a sun-sighting now. That didn't much matter; she knew the way now. But, "We ought to get across as soon as we can."

"Food?" said Rodal bluntly. "Water?" Yet again he and Railu traded looks.

Jerya remembered how she'd felt thirsty on the climb. She was thirsty now, but there was nothing left in her bottle. "There's water on the other side," she said. "I've seen it."

"I can't climb another metre without something to eat," said Railu.

*

They finished the bread and the cheese, both drier than ever despite the waxcloth wrappers. It was far from a feast, but to Jerya it seemed to take just as long. She fretted as she watched the others picking out every last crumb, between frequent looks up toward the notch, now no more than a lighter space between shadows as the mists gathered.

By the time they had shouldered their packs again the cliffs, and the notch, were invisible. She could only hope she had properly committed the route to memory.

It was very different climbing the scree again with the pack on. She doubted she was making half the speed. Or perhaps the slope had grown twice as long. It began to feel as if it simply ground on forever, so that it was a shock when grey mists suddenly solidified into rock. Rock the colour of bone, a few reddish streaks like vestiges of flesh, looming over them at an improbable angle.

And her direction hadn't been as good as she'd hoped. She hadn't led them straight to the gap.

"No matter," she said, more bravely than she really felt. "It'll just be a short way along."

"Which way?" said Rodal, and Jerya could not answer at once.

Think... The crag above really did lean out, even if the overhang wasn't as dramatic as it had seemed on its first appearance through the mist. Like the other side, there was a relatively level ledge at the top of the scree; it shouldn't be hard to explore to left or right. But trying the wrong direction would be wasted effort, and she knew she was tiring.

She tried to recall what she'd noticed on the way up. Her attention had been on the gap, not the rocks either side, but surely... She found a vague sense that they had bulged out more to the right of the notch.

"We go left," she said, and set off at once so she didn't have to see Railu and Rodal look at each other yet again.

If she'd chosen wrong, she feared, they might finally rebel altogether. It would be no use then to argue that water was closer on the other side than anywhere they'd seen on this. It all seemed strangely dry, this pale high country. Was it something to do with the rocks? They weren't like the familiar rocks of Delven.

Clearly there was rain, or snow that would melt to feed streams, unless it all just disappeared into the soil and rock. Most of yesterday's snow had gone, but there were older patches scattered about. Snow was water, of course, though how did you melt snow if you couldn't make fire?

She counted her steps. At fifty paces, she was becoming seriously worried. Could she really have got her direction so far wrong? And how would the others react if she had? But then she felt something, a breath on her cheek. It had been quite still under the cliff till now, but here the air was in motion. Another ten paces and she could feel it for sure; twenty, and she could see movement in the mist ahead, and a lightening.

Ten more, and she was on the easy rock slabs below the notch. The bone-coloured rock had a finer grain than Delven's gritty sandstone, and she thought it might be slippery when wet, but at the moment it was dry, and her boots gripped reassuringly.

"This is it," she said, turning, but they weren't as close as she'd supposed. Rodal was behind Railu. There wasn't space for two to move abreast, so he couldn't support her as he had before. (Had he supported her all the way up to the place where they'd eaten? she wondered guiltily.) He was murmuring encouragement, adding a word of advice as Railu came up the slabs.

"This is the place," said Jerya again as they joined her. Railu's gaze found hers and Jerya wanted to say, *You have to trust me one more time*, but she let her eyes say it for her.

❋

The narrow place proved even worse with a pack on. Jerya sidled past, a few centimetres at a time, every move feeling like it would tip her balance that critical fraction too far. When she reached a safer spot, she rested for several minutes, still leaning against the rock, breathing as if she had just run up the screes.

Finally, still moving with exaggerated care, she shed her load and moved back until she could lean out a little to peer past the obstruction, grasping a down-pointing flake of rock to give a little more security.

She had thought Railu would find the place trying, might even balk entirely; but she had not allowed for Railu being a little shorter, and her pack now considerably lighter. By crouching a little, Railu was able to slip past the worst bulge, if not with ease, at least without alarm. As soon as she was within reach, Jerya stretched out her free hand and drew her in. At the wider spot, she helped Railu off with her pack and enfolded her in a swift embrace before turning back to see how Rodal was faring.

She saw at once that it was worst for him. He was barely any taller than herself, but he was broader in the shoulder. She didn't know if his pack was any heavier than hers, but it seemed bulkier. Twice he got to the bad spot and stopped, face tight, closed in on himself, feeling the balance. Each time, slowly, he backed away.

"Rodal...?" She couldn't see him, only hear muffled sounds.

"Going to try it a different way." This mystified her: what other way was there? The scree below looked particularly unstable, and not many metres down it spilled over another edge. The rock above scarcely looked climbable even without a load, and anyway, going up was the last thing they wanted to do.

Then he reappeared, and she saw what he'd meant. He was on hands and knees, and instead of the pack there was only a length of rope, tied about his waist and trailing behind. Crawling, he made it along safely to where she stood. She retreated a few paces to give him room to get to his feet, then moved closer again.

He untied the rope and drew in the slack. "Have to hope it don't snag," he said tersely.

Without being asked, Jerya resumed her grip on the rock-flake and with her other hand took a firm hold of his belt. He gave a quick glance over his shoulder but said nothing. At once he began taking in the rope, slowly and steadily.

The pack scraped noisily against the scree beneath and the rock along-side, but kept moving. Jerya was almost thinking it was safe when something happened; a rock protrusion nudged it a little too far, or a stone shift-ed beneath it, and in a second the load was falling, swinging and bouncing down and across the scree. The rope slipped through Rodal's hands before he got a better grip, and his weight lurched outward. For a moment Jerya didn't think she could stand the strain, that her grip on his belt or on the rock would fail, but the sack's wild swing slowed, and the pull on her eased just enough.

The sack settled, but where it had swung stones were slithering, clatter-ing, tumbling. The slide rattled over the edge; there was silence, and then another, fainter, tattoo filtered up through the mist.

Rodal shifted his weight and Jerya was able to haul him a little closer. They moved along a couple of paces then hauled up the sack together. It was coated in pale yellowish rock-dust and bore several small rips, but it didn't look as if any of the contents had been lost.

They continued on to where Railu waited. She flung her arms around Rodal and sobbed on his shoulder. Jerya looked down into the mist and in her mind she heard again that clatter of tumbling stone.

CHAPTER 4

RODAL

The sun was out. Fitfully, it was true, as clouds whisked overhead, scraps shredding from the grey mass that shrouded the high peaks. It looked to Rodal as if the wind was stronger than when they had crossed the pass. He thought about being up there in a gale, and shuddered. It had been hard enough, that crossing, but when he thought of how it might have been, he knew they had got off lightly. He hoped the others knew it too.

It had been a hard journey altogether. Two days up to the first pass, that terrible day crossing it, the near-disaster at the second, then a cold and hungry night by a tarn which was rimmed with ice in the morning. Another day's slog down a bleak strath, still no fuel to make a fire and nothing left to eat but a few handfuls of dried fruit.

Finally, yesterday they'd fortified themselves with the last slabs of cake before essaying the long descent, down slabs of naked black rock which seemed to hang over roaring white cataracts. The ledges, such as they were, had been too widely spaced for the short rope that had been all he could find in Delven's stores. How many times had he wished for a longer one? How many times had he watched, chewing his nails, as Railu and Jerya followed him down some slippery scramble soaked by spray from the torrent? He had been exhausted and limp, more from nervous strain than physical, at the end of it. But it had brought them here, where the river spread into three or four little channels braiding a wide stony bed between green banks under dark forest.

The girls had wandered further down the valley, combing the drifts of bilberry that sprawled over the riverbanks and the fringes of the forest. They were past the season, and most of the fruits were long gone, but a scattering remained, wrinkled and shrunken but perhaps all the sweeter for it. Though, hungry as they all were, almost anything edible would taste sweet just now.

While they were away, he unpacked everything. He looked at the rips and threadbare patches of his rucksack and decided repairs could wait.

They had already spread their bedding and spare clothing to dry, using a couple of handy tree-stumps that must have been washed up during some past flood. Now he spread the groundsheet on a flat patch of grass, weighting the corners with stones even though he felt no more than a gentle breeze here in the valley. The clouds scudding overhead told him of a gale in the upper airs, and he could not be sure it wouldn't make itself felt lower down. Then he carefully laid out everything they had, and took stock.

When the others came back, he saw they had made a decent gather; both cooking-pots were more than half-full of the tiny, near-black, fruit. Railu was bubbling with their achievement: the first time she had ever collected food from the wild. Rodal gave her a smile. Let her enjoy the moment. They would be faced with harsher truths soon enough. He intended to make sure of it.

They made a comfortable luncheon, the last of the oatcakes and scraps of dried meat and handfuls of bilberries. There was one thing about the berries being so far past ripe; the juice didn't stain fingers and lips as a fresh crop would.

Afterward, he brandished the crossbow. "How's about a first lesson in shooting?" Railu looked startled: Jerya too, perhaps, but only for a moment. Her expression swiftly changed as—he divined—she saw the sense of the idea.

He'd observed, just a little way above the campsite, a bank of what might equally be called soft stone or hard mud. He'd risked one test and found that a quarrel fired from a range of thirty or forty yards would embed itself in the mottled brown stuff rather than bounce off, but not so far or so firmly that it was impossible to extract. Using a shard of harder stone, he drew a large rough 'X' to serve as a target.

Starting at twenty yards, Railu's first attempts proved more accurate than Jerya's. No one was more surprised than Railu herself.

"Well," he said, "It's a good beginning. But remember, being able to shoot's only half the story. You've got to be in position to make the shot in the first place. And that means being as close as possible. You want to make a clean kill, of course, but it's not just that. If you miss completely, you can lose the quarrel, and there's only eight." He didn't say, but he knew they were all thinking, that Railu might—for the nonce—be a better hand with the bow, but Jerya was much more adept at moving quietly through the country. He knew she'd never hunted, but he guessed, from a few things she'd said, that she had stalked deer in the past, and maybe heather-cock and other creatures too. If you could stalk something just to watch it, he thought, you could stalk it for the pot. He'd seen a few trees with stripped bark, which suggested there were deer about, and it looked promising territory for heather-cock too.

"You'll need to practise plenty," he said. They were back at the campsite now. He'd showed them the spare string, how to replace it, talked about how to sharpen the quarrels. "We'll need to look out for the right kind of stone to use as a whetstone. Need it for the knives and the axe, too."

He waved an arm over the items arranged on the groundsheet. Looked at one way, it was impressive—especially considering that they had carried all of it over the mountains on their backs (most of it, for crucial stretches, on his and Jerya's backs alone). But look at it in another light, and it was terrifyingly meagre. And this was what he felt they did not yet understand.

"You've got a crossbow and you're learning how to use it. You've got fish-hooks and lines; maybe later we'll see what we can do with those. There's a stand of birch-trees down the way a bit, so maybe we can brew some birch-bark tea."

Jerya frowned. "It's not a fit drink without honey."

"Well, you might know more than me about that."

"Maybe, but raiding a wild hive...? I've seen it done, but I was a few years younger. I don't know if I can remember how they managed it."

He just looked at her. *It surely would be helpful if you* could *remember.* He hoped she got the message.

"Well," he went on, "There's plenty more. Jerya knows which mushrooms are safe to eat. Meat. Fish. Berries. All manner of other plants. You shouldn't go hungry. That's not what I'm worried about." He saw Railu shift. Her gaze settled on him. "What concerns me most is shelter. Keeping warm. We haven't seen any caves yet, not worth mentioning."

"It's only the first day," said Jerya.

"Besure, but how many days have we got? Winter's not so far off; happen you'd know that better'n me. You can make a cave proper homely, besure, but I'd want to be settling in right about now. Cleaning out, blocking up openings, laying in all the dry wood I can find... And what if we *don't* find a cave we can use? None o'the rock I've seen looks quite like what we know back home."

Jerya looked stubborn, as if she thought she could conjure a suitable cave into existence by the pure strength of her will. Rodal eyed her a moment, then picked up the axe. "This is fine for chopping firewood, but you're never going to fell big trees with it. Birch-poles like that clump downstream, right enough, but not a grown pine, never mind an oak. If you thought of making log-houses like at Burnslack, you'd better think again."

"So what would you do?" asked Jerya. Railu continued to watch him steadily—and, he thought, with a strangely hopeful air.

What would I do? If it was up to me we wouldn't be here at all. It was no use saying it, though: here was where they were. "First question is whether we stick hereabouts or press on, follow the river down. Seems to me the lower we go the warmer it's like to be, and the richer the land should be." He glanced at Jerya, who nodded agreement. "But even right down by the sea, winter comes. I heard about that. They say it's not so cold, snow only lies a few days most winters, but the winds can be bad, and the rain. For the first winter..."

He paused, let them both think about 'first winter' and all the things it might imply. "Well, for the first winter, I'm thinking about keeping my own hide warm. And what I'm thinking is... well, two things.

"First, from now on we've mostly got to keep ourselves fed as we go: what we can shoot, catch, gather. And that means we won't be walking all day, besure. Maybe not even half the day. So we're talkin' maybe ten miles, twelve miles at most, each day—and that's if the going's all as good as it is here.

"And I wouldn't want to just keep going, neither. We can't just keep pushing on and on, in hopes we'll find somewhere perfect. We need somewhere *good enough*, and I'd like to find somewhere within not much more than ten days. We got to keep our eyes open for it."

And *that* was all very well, he thought. They could survive the winter. They could make a shelter that would do them well enough. Shelter, water, food, fire: they would manage.

"That's all well and good," he said after a bit more discussion. Jerya thought ten days was too brief a period. And mayhap it was, but more than anything he was trying to make them think.

"We'll do well enough. But remember I'm pledged to head back by next Autumn." Railu's gaze settled intently on him again. "Well, there's spring and summer. Plenty o'chances to make things better before the next winter. Maybe you will find some nice caves. Maybe... well, it's a lot of maybes, but then it always was, wasn't it? But I'm lookin' further ahead even than that.

"There's needles and threads. You can mend your clothes. But what happens when they're past mendin'? What happens when your boots wear out?" *What happens if you get sick? What happens when you get old?* He didn't think he needed to repeat it. Railu's face was troubled enough. And—but Jerya was scrambling to her feet, walking away. She stopped by the river, back to himself and Railu, staring down into the milky water. The sun slipped from behind a cloud, lighting the curve of her scalp. He had noticed the beginnings of stubble, but from here, in the sun, it looked as smooth as ever. Railu just glanced once at Jerya, then back at him, saying nothing.

Before long, Jerya came back. She stood facing them across the ground-sheet, looking down at its assemblage of belongings. Thrusting hands in pockets, she said, "You just said it, Rodal. Lots of maybes... But one thing seems pretty near certain..." She turned, looking back up at the mountains, or where the mountains lurked behind the streaming clouds. "Every day that passes, it's getting less likely we could get back across even if we wanted to." *If we wanted to*? he thought, knowing it was exactly what he did want.

She looked him in the eye. "There's no point having second thoughts now. We crossed the mountains. Far as we know, no one's ever done that before, not in this Age. That's something. That's no small thing." Her gaze shifted to Railu. "Let's not forget that. Let's be proud. And for the rest... we'll see." Back to him again. "I hear everything you say, Rodal, and I'll remember it all. But it strikes me, by next spring, next summer, we'll know a lot more. One way or the other."

CHAPTER 5

RODAL

Rodal strolled aimlessly down the riverbank. It was sheer pleasure just to walk along without a load, without clumsy boots. The lightness of it was so exhilarating he was tempted to break into a run. They had done maybe eight miles that morning, and after breaking for a sparse lunch had opted for a fishing lesson. Either it was beginner's luck, or the fish here had no caution. As might well be in a place with no people, he thought. They might fear the heron or the osprey, but not the angler's hook. Yes, his hand had been on the rod with theirs each time, but it had seemed better to credit one catch to Jerya, one to Railu.

Railu'll be thinking it's all easy, he thought, smiling a little to himself. It seemed a charmed spot. As he knocked the second trout's head against the rocks to still its wild leaping, the sun had come out, and soon it seemed it had decided to stay.

And they were all still tired. Railu's feet were tender, too. Neither of the girls had objected when he'd suggested it might be a good idea to call a halt where they were. No worries then about how to carry the two fish. Let Railu rest, and bathe her feet. He had fished a little longer, caught nothing more. Maybe the sun had driven the fish away.

Jerya had wandered on downstream while he fished. Perhaps she was looking for caves, he thought. Perhaps she would even find some. Who could say their luck wouldn't stretch that far? It was that kind of day. For himself, he'd initially headed into the trees just to relieve himself, then yielded to the impulse to roam a little further afield.

The forest was vaster by far than the one around Delven. From the last little rise, at a brief narrowing of the valley, they had been able to see no further edge to it. It grew so thick and dark in places you felt the sun would never reach the ground even at midsummer. He began to feel the sense of Jerya's words; a hundred songs would not change it.

Fortunately, where the river ran, it had made a broad clear lane through the forest. Even after its wild tumble through the cataracts, it was still a young river, and probably changed its course every spring. Amid the rocks and sand left by the floods, winnowed and rearranged annually, few trees had been able to establish themselves and reach maturity. Goldenrod and fireweed grew along with young spruce and larch, and there were spreads of low green growth which must be wild with flowers in the early summer.

Along the fringes of the forest, where the daylight could reach, there were carpets of mixed grass and pine needles, soft underfoot. It was on these that he strolled, luxuriating in every step. When he saw Railu sitting on the bank, gazing in the water, he made his approach deliberately clumsy. It would be so easy to come up silently, but he did not want to startle her. He chucked a stone in the river, brushed against a hanging larch-bough.

She glanced back over her shoulder. Her smile was vague, unfocused, dreamy, but at least she seemed pleased to see him. He saw no lingering hint of the suspicion—if not outright fear—with which she had once regarded him.

"It's nice here," he said, stopping a few paces away, leaning on a tree. 'Nice' was hardly adequate, he thought, but he let it rest.

She did not look at him, her gaze gone now somewhere in the trees beyond the river. He wondered what she saw in those impenetrable shadows. For a moment he thought she was not going to answer, perhaps had not really heard, but then she gave a little sigh. "Yes, it's beautiful. It looks very much like the country round Delven. You must feel at home here."

"Not exactly like. But I know what you mean."

"Not exactly...? Ah, I suppose you'll see differences I miss. It was—is—all new to me. So much to take in..." She glanced around. "It's the most peaceful place I've ever been. Almost more peaceful because it isn't quite silent—the stream, the breeze sighing in the trees... In the College sometimes it could be silent. As if everyone had held her breath at the same moment. There was a tension there... And in the mountains it was worse. It was like the silence when you stop your ears to a cry of pain."

"Besure." He was far from certain he really knew what she meant, but it could do no harm to agree. "Not that mountains care, but we had plenty to be afraid of. We were lucky, really. They... held back on us. I've seen weather you wouldn't believe, and I've never been that high before. It could have been savage."

"It was bad enough for me," she said, with a laugh that was a denial of mirth. "I felt tired so soon, I don't really know why. I haven't been keeping up so badly the other days. Once I began to feel tired I soon felt cold as well, and then... I just shrank into myself. I didn't even care very much about it."

"It happens sometimes in the mountains," he said. "They prey on your mind... Being so big and so silent, it's... overpowering. And you... you were new to 'em, body and mind."

She nodded slowly. "I think Jerya loves the mountains... but they're too much for me." There was a wistful note in her voice. "If I'd been on my own... I know it's a silly 'if'; why on earth would I have been up there alone? But if I had... I'd just have lain down and..."

"And never arisen," he finished for her. At once he felt he had been cruel. She turned wounded eyes on him, and he felt worse. She was so transparent, she spared you none of your own cruelty.

Then she smiled. Perhaps she could read his feelings as well as he could hers. "No," she said, "You're right. Without you—"

"—And Jerya."

"Without you both—oh, I don't know, save I wouldn't be here today. And..." She looked full into his eyes. "I don't believe I'm sorry."

He held his breath. Just what was she saying? At the very least, it seemed... But he hardly knew how to express the thought, even to himself.

Knows who I am. But it felt like something more. He could not be sure. He was hardly certain of anything any more.

The sun gilded her smooth scalp. Unlike Jerya, there was no sign of hair growing back. Jerya's, though still mere stubble, just dark enough to make the skin beneath look almost pale, was beginning to look undeniably messy.

He scratched his jaw. He was in no position to be fastidious. They were a fine pair, Jerya and himself. He hoped her scalp did not suffer as his jaw did from an incessant itch, a constant sense of uncleanliness.

But Railu—he came back to her, to the here and now, with a start—Railu was the same as ever, perhaps a little deeper in her colour, the copper even richer. The skin of her scalp was stretched and lustrous over bone. She was beautiful, too. He had never truly seen it before.

She gave him an odd, shy smile. He wondered if she had any hint of his thoughts. Surely not... But he had been staring. "I'm glad," she said, which seemed to be an extension of what she had last been saying, until she went on, "I'm glad to have learned something, at least. All the things they taught us about men... things I believed, if I thought about them at all. I had never really touched a man—at least, not since childhood, and I don't really remember—until you helped me over the pass, down the rocks... And when I woke this morning..."

She was shameless, he thought. Literally that. No one seemed to have taught her what decency was, but she was so guileless, so innocent, that it seemed it would be unreasonable to object. It was even refreshing in a way.

This morning... she seemed to have moved closer to him in the night, as close as she could get while they were separately wrapped in their own blankets. It had only been a moment, before he was even properly awake, but he remembered her head against his shoulder—and had there been a smile before she stirred?

"...It felt comfortable," she finished. "I was taught to mistrust men, Rodal, but I trust you. I want you to know that... When I look at you, I don't see 'man', only you, Rodal, my friend."

He felt almost ashamed. He did not know how to answer her, but he wanted to show in some way how much he valued her words, her trust. Words failing, he found himself moving across the coney-cropped turf, kneeling beside her, taking her hand lightly in his own and then—not knowing it was going to happen until it happened—leaning in to kiss her.

His intentions, he believed, were entirely respectable. He had thought only—truly—to kiss her as brother to sister. He was utterly unprepared for her response. A thrill went through her, as if every pulse in her body had quickened. She seized his shoulders, twisted her body without breaking the kiss, pressed herself against him in a powerful embrace. He felt her solid weight crushed against his chest, and had a vivid memory-flash of that fleeting glimpse of her breasts, bared to the sun on the other side of the mountains. But before his eyes now was the warm golden curve of her scalp, and his free hand strayed to this as they rolled sideways on the turf.

He knew what was happening, and he heard a voice telling him to stop, but could not think why he should heed it. Utterly unprepared, confused, all he knew for sure at that moment were Railu's nearness, Railu's beauty, Railu's sudden desire. She wanted this, he told himself. He could not step back to consider whether it might be wrong. He only knew how it felt, and... how could something that felt like this be wrong?

In what seemed mere moments they were both naked, his hands on her breasts. He could hardly believe he was really feeling their weight. It all seemed like a dream, everything more vividly coloured than normal, but all happening in silence. There was no need to speak; they understood each other without words. The world beyond their own little sphere had vanished; the river, the forest, the sky, the past and the future. His world was Railu, and the grass on which they lay. Everything was more intense than he had ever known; the colours, the held-breath silence, the unbelievable reality of her flesh against his own.

They were both eager, even desperate; he entered her quickly, made a few clumsy thrusts, before she began to rock to the same rhythm. His passion flared as swiftly as a match-flame, faded almost as fast, but in that moment it was everything. The moment was full as all time.

Railu gave a little cry, half-gasp, half-moan; her fingers dug deep into the muscles of his back. Then it was done, and Rodal rolled away from her and lay on his back, panting gently. Slowly his awareness crept out to take in the world again. The river resumed its unending chatter. Once again the treetops sighed wistfully in the breeze. Birds were singing.

Then he heard the click of stone on stone, and again. Feet went hurrying away up the bank. He sat up quickly, looked around, but there was no one to be seen save himself and Railu. She had not moved. It seemed she had heard nothing. She lolled her head to look at him, smiled, reached out a hand, but he could not take it. He got to his feet, walked upstream a little way until there were several trees between them.

For a measureless time Rodal stood naked on the riverbank in the middle of the vast indifferent forest, and wondered just what he had done.

CHAPTER 6

JERYA

At first Jerya went away at a fast walk, but soon she found herself running. She picked a course without knowing how or why; away from the river, into the twilit heart of the forest. In that gloom she ran half-blind, seeing just enough to avoid rocks and roots which might have tripped her.

When she finally collapsed, trembling, on a mossy bank, she had no idea how far she had come or where she was. For a while she could hardly think at all; the struggle to master her breathing was everything. She seemed unable to fill her lungs properly, as if her chest had been bound up tightly. She could only take fast, shallow breaths.

At last, still panting, she managed to sit up. There was a strange darkness in her eyes at first, but she blinked it away and began to look around. Below the green slope, which had left its damp marks on her clothing, the ground was nearly level, a clear space below trees taller than most she had seen. Scaly trunks reared straight and unbranched for ten or twelve metres, then spread, sprawled, joined, forming a dark canopy brilliantly jewelled with light, jumping and dancing as the wind shifted the branches.

Down where she sat there was no sound of wind, not a breath on her cheek. When she managed to still her own respiration for a moment the silence was complete.

Suddenly tears welled in her eyes. She drew up her knees, buried her face against them. How often she had gone to the forest seeking to be alone.

Alone... All at once she thought she had never known what it was to be alone till now.

What was she to do? All her plans, vague as they had been, had been for a future for herself and Railu. She had been glad enough of Rodal's aid in crossing the mountains, happy to see Railu's mistrust of him withering away. But this...

She knew she should not judge them, but it was hard. No promises had been made—*not out loud, anyway*—so none had been broken. Still she could not help feeling—there was no other word—betrayed.

All at once she shivered. It was cool in the deep shade, and she had only her light shirt on, damp with the sweat of her flight and the green of the moss-bank. All at once she wanted only to be out of the forest. It was not like the Delven forest at all. Here she only felt small and cold and achingly alone.

Jerya looked around wildly. Behind her the bank rose steeply for a short way; above it was a low line of overhanging rocks, and above them a sunlit fringe of grass.

Directly above her the rocks were obviously too steep to climb. Left or right seemed indifferent. She went rightwards along the base of the slope. Before long she came to a jumble of boulders. Evidently part of the crag had collapsed, and not too many years ago. The scars of the rockfall were still white and new. And they provided a possible way up into the sun.

She clambered carefully up the boulders, testing each for stability. It was almost a relief to step onto the rock wall, though it seemed fragile. At least its broken flaky nature provided numerous holds for hands and feet, and though it was little less than vertical she was at the top in a matter of moments. How much easier it was in boots and trousers than sandals and long skirts.

As soon as the sun touched her she felt better. She wriggled out of her shirt, towelled her back with it, then spread it in the sun. Though the sun was warm, the air was still autumn-cool. To keep warm she walked up and down along the cliff-top, rubbing away chills which teased at her arms and shoulders.

The treetops were nearly level with her feet, almost as if the ground merely continued with only a change of colour and texture. There was a long slope down to the valley, then the land rose again, rolling on for kilometres; ridge and wave, into the haze in the North where forest and sky seemed to merge into one hue, a washed-out blue like her old headcloth.

The forest was the biggest thing she had ever seen. She was heartily glad to be outside of it. How friendly seemed the poor grass and scattered rushes of the narrow shelf on which she moved. Not far back, the ground rose again, breaking out into another line of crag, not so steep as the lower one but several times taller, and smoother, offering no obvious weaknesses where it might easily be scaled. She did not really want to climb it anyway. There was nowhere to go that offered anything better than where she now stood.

Jerya being who she was, she might still have tried to climb the crag to see what lay above; but she knew well enough already. They had seen the ridge-top from the valley before the forest had swallowed all distances; a naked spine, rocks like vertebrae stretching the thin moorland skin. It would be cold up there at nights, without shelter, only a shirt for warmth.

What was she thinking of? Going off somewhere alone? Perhaps... but not without her clothes, blankets, a cooking-pot, a knife. To go just as she was would be a slow death sentence. Better to throw herself from the top of the crag.

She went to the edge and looked down speculatively. It was not very high, and the ground below was soft. The fall would probably not kill her, or not right away. She imagined lying there in pain for days. She supposed Rodal and Railu would search, but in all the vastness of the forest there was slim chance they would find her.

There was the higher crag behind... but already the idea had become just an idea. A question-test, she thought, half-smiling. She was not going to die. She still wanted to live. That was clear, though little else was.

She swung on her heel and marched back to the rock where her shirt was spread. It was still a little damp, but it would have to do.

As always, climbing down was trickier than climbing up, feeling for holds with near-blind feet. She reached the top of the boulder-heap with relief. At the bottom she found herself breathing hard, more from tension than exertion. Standing a few moments to catch her breath, she rapidly began to feel cold again, hurried into motion. The moss and needles yielded silently under her feet, sprang back at once. Her feet left no impression and the dark silence of the forest seemed to absorb all sound. The forest was not even admitting that she existed.

In the forest by Delven, she recalled, her feet had worn faint paths in one or two places, especially near her bathing-tarn. It had never turned her away. That forest had accepted her. Why then did she feel like an intruder here? The trees were the same.

You're being stupid, she told herself. *It's not the forest that's different.*

She did not know exactly which way she had come. She had not been paying close attention, and it might not have availed much if she had. The forest seemed much the same in any direction. All she could do was try to discern the slight gradient towards the river, follow it down as directly as she could.

The walking was easy, and she settled into the automatic rhythm which, she now knew, she could maintain all day and every day. Her legs ached a little from her long hard run, but this pace was the next best thing to rest. It was a fine thing, walking.

What direction was she taking now? The river's course in this reach was generally from Southwest to Northeast. If the land sloped reliably toward the river, she should currently be heading about Northwest. It was hard through the trees to see where the sun was, but it was certainly somewhere behind her.

Her mind ran on... If she turned East... The world was round; if she kept walking Eastward, in the end she would find herself in the West again. How long would it take? On the best ground, forty or fifty kilometres a day might be possible, but it would not all be like this. The forest might appear to go on forever, but it surely could not. There would be mountains to cross, rivers, perhaps more places like the burnt plains. And there might be worse horrors yet; things she could not even imagine. There were no Blistered Lands here, but further East, who could say?

And of course there were the oceans... Suddenly she was seized with the desire to see the ocean. All she had ever seen was the merest glimpse, a distant gleam on the horizon, from the hilltop in Carwerid. What it was like up close was beyond imagining. She could not now go West and see the ocean Rodal had seen, and beside which Railu had played as a little girl; she would just have to go East until she found another one. *One day*, she promised herself. *First the mountains, then the ocean.*

It occurred to her that she had been walking a long time. Could she really have come this far in her wild flight? There was no way of knowing, but if she had mistaken her direction, even by a small amount—which seemed entirely possible—she might not be approaching the river as directly as she'd hoped, might even be heading away from the camp. It might take all day, perhaps even longer, to find it again.

But what was that? A shimmer of silver through the trees?

She hurried forward and stood blinking in the light until her eyes adapted: a little bouldery, scrubby slope, a reedy flat, and the river beyond. She had never seen this place before, of that she was certain; and in that case, the camp must lie upstream.

She turned to her left and began to follow the forest's edge back Westward. Over the further ridge of the valley clouds formed a low white line... No, not clouds. They were the mountains, white with new snow, so bright in the sun it was painful to look at them. In the forest's shade Jerya shivered. Her shirt was still a little damp and cool on her back.

Then the river turned and its channel narrowed. The trees on the opposite bank drew closer, hiding the white peaks. She was strangely regretful, though the turn had given her the sun again. Then above the black outline of the treetops she saw one taller than the rest, bare and thin with an abrupt flat crest, one branch sagging below the mass. There could not be two trees exactly alike even in this infinity of them. It was the one that reared above the camp, as if standing guard. She was almost there.

The rush of gladness which struck her then was so strong she wondered at herself. She had not forgotten why she had fled; she was not looking forward to confronting Rodal and Railu. However, anything was preferable to being alone. She had learned that much.

※

They were sitting apart, and it did not look as if they had been talking even before she appeared. They watched her as she came along the shingle and up to the edge of the clearing.

Rodal tried to smile. "Where have you been?"

Jerya gestured vaguely. "In the forest somewhere. I don't really know."

Railu looked up, but shied away from meeting her gaze. Jerya took the nearest seat. It struck her how nearly equilateral a triangle they made, though it was just a coincidence of the arrangement of the logs.

The pot on the fire was seething gently. A good smell wafted from it, plucking at her.

"How long before that's ready?" she asked. "I'm so hungry..."

Railu gave a choked little cry. She hunched forward where she sat, head bowed, bands shielding her scalp.

"Jerya..." she said, barely audible. "I'm so sorry..."

She could not resist being a little bit cruel. "Sorry? Why? Because you got dinner cooking?"

Railu looked up at that. Her expression was so bleak Jerya almost hated herself. She remembered another time she had seen that look on Railu's face. Then she had been beside her in bed in the College, then it had been Freilyn twisting the knife, as if exulting in her own misery, determined everyone should share it.

She would not behave like Freilyn.

"I'm sorry," she said, "That was a stupid thing to say."

Railu looked as if she was about to burst into tears. "How can you say you're sorry? Oh, Jerya... You haven't hurt anyone."

"Haven't I? Would you be here, either of you, if it wasn't for me?"

"We chose to come. You know that. Why are you...?"

"Because she don't want to talk about... the other thing," said Rodal, startling them both. "But we have to, don't we? Can't pretend it didn't happen."

"But we didn't mean it to happen," said Railu, low and hesitant. "It just did."

Rodal said nothing, but when Jerya turned her gaze upon him he nodded confirmation.

"We just... forgot ourselves," continued Railu. "I don't know how else to put it... we'd come over the mountains and all the rest, and suddenly here we are, sunshine, warmth, birds singing, fresh food... I felt like I'd almost died and now I was back to life. And there was Rodal... He got me over the mountains—"

"Choss, Rai, I'll take a lot but I won't take that! Who half-carried you over the highest part? Who guided your feet when we were coming down the crags?"

"It's true," agreed Rodal. "Jerya did as much for you as I did, maybe more."

"I know," said Railu. "I do, really, but I never thought about it in the same way... I mean, Jerya and I had intended from the start to cross the mountains together. I always knew she'd help me. I'd have done the same if I'd been the strong one... I still would, Jerya, if only there was something I could do..." She gave Jerya the most direct look she had yet managed. "Perhaps I felt guilty in a way because I'd been so suspicious of Rodal for so long, and he'd—you'd—done nothing to deserve it. I was so grateful... And then I was thinking... just how good it was to be alive, and he came along just at the right moment. Or wrong moment..."

Jerya looked away sharply, blinking.

"I can't say much more than that," said Rodal. "We didn't think about it. That's the whole story. It didn't feel wrong... even now, thinking back, it don't, not really. Not wrong to feel; but wrong not to *think* as well."

"What do you want?" she asked. "My pardon? I can't... not yet. It's not what you did that hurts so much as that you... never mind forgetting yourselves, you forgot about *me*... after all we've done together, you just *forget* about me, act as if I don't even exist? I can't just set that aside, not so soon."

"It's true," said Rodal, spreading his hands wide. "We never once thought about you. If we had..."

"Is that supposed to make me feel better?"

"I don't know," he said, repeating the helpless gesture. "All I know is that's the truth."

"Well, thank you for that, at least. But... choss, what do we do now?"

They both sat looking at her.

"You expect me to have an answer? Even now?" She almost laughed. "But... I can see a few things. There's new snow in the mountains now, I saw that. I wouldn't ask anyone to go back over there now. And—I thought of it, but... there's no sense in splitting up. I was never afraid of being alone before, but this forest does it to me. We have to face it; till spring, at least, we're stuck with each other."

Railu looked at Rodal. "Two of us beating our brains on it, and we never saw things as clearly as that." Rodal nodded sombrely.

"Sometimes," said Jerya, "I could wish I didn't see things so clearly. I can't help thinking that if I hadn't been so draffing *clear* about things we might not be here now."

"But you did! You're not saying now you were wrong, are you?"

"I don't know... No. Not that I was wrong. I wasn't. It's just... it's hard to see that it was worth being right. If I hadn't seen things so clearly I'd still be in the city. Choss, if I wasn't different from everyone else, if I didn't see things differently, I'd never have left Delven..."

She could not look at Rodal then. And she would not let her tears fall in the absence of a certain shoulder to cry on. She stared at the flames licking the blackened base of the pot and hugged herself and wished to be almost anywhere else. And then she wondered, *but where else could I go?* and had no answer.

"It's no good arguing about what might have been," said Rodal. "Only don't go taking it all on your shoulders—we did what we did, the two of us. We've been sitting here blaming ourselves and it ain't much help you coming in and trying to take the blame on yourself."

Jerya nodded. "You're right. It doesn't do any good... but I don't know what else to do."

"Well," he said, "We'll all feel better for some dinner. And you're looking cold... You should get your warm clothes on again, everything's dry."

She felt more desolate than ever. His simple concern, of a kind she would always before have taken for granted, was nearly more than she could bear. She was glad to slip behind the bushes as she changed her clothes, glad in the end to let herself weep silently and out of sight.

CHAPTER 7

JERYA

R ight after breakfast, Rodal had announced he was going hunting. As soon as he'd packed his needs for the day, he was striding off into the forest. Left alone with Railu, Jerya did not know what to say, and Railu seemed equally tongue-tied.

"Any more coffee in the pot?" asked Railu finally.

Jerya looked. "Just a little. I don't think there's more than one more brew left in the packet either."

They shared the last of the oily black brew, only enough for a couple of mouthfuls each, though they didn't swig, instead sipping as if that might make it feel like there was more. Again they sat silent, two metres apart, worlds apart. Jerya found herself thinking about coffee. She'd never finally settled whether she truly liked the stuff, but now she was sure she'd miss it when there was no more.

None of their other supplies would last much longer either. She wouldn't say Rodal had been wrong to go hunting; fresh meat would be welcome, besure. But there were longer considerations too. In that light, they didn't need him to hunt; they needed him to teach them to hunt. Another lesson with the crossbow, setting traps and snares, more instruction in fishing also.

Rodal had been entirely right, yesterday. They should not go hungry, but there were many challenges to be faced. Shelter, before the winter, above all. The forest was full of life, but it reminded her most of the highest parts of the forest above Delven; and in those forests snow could lie long, and much of the life went elsewhere or slumbered away the cold in burrow or den.

Perhaps—

"—Jerya?" Railu's voice broke into her thoughts. "What's that sound?"

"What sound?" Jerya began, but then she heard it too, a thudding, a clatter of stones. She knew at once that something—something large, probably several somethings—was moving fast over the stones of the river-bed. But she could not see until she scrambled to her feet.

Runners.

The shock paralysed her for a moment. She had done no more than begin to turn to speak to Railu—but what did she need to say? a warning?—before the men were upon them. Suddenly they were all around, five or six of them. They had run in silence, save the noise of their feet, but now there was a babble of wild cries and guttural shouts. Jerya could not discern a single word. Now one barked a command, still unintelligible, and then men were grabbing them, seizing them by their arms.

She fought to break free, screamed her protest, screamed for Rodal until a grubby hand was clamped over her mouth. The hands that held her might have been made of iron for all the difference her struggles made. She caught one fleeting glimpse of Railu, wild-eyed, grey-faced. Her hands were dragged behind her back and lashed tightly. The hand over her mouth was released but as she drew breath to scream again it slapped her across the face, hard enough to make teeth rattle and ears ring.

A bearded face loomed, a voice rasped something that might have been, "Keep quiet."

The hands that clamped her upper arms dragged her into motion, back down the river-bed. The pace was no more than a rapid walk, but it was hard to keep her footing on the uneven stones. Behind, she heard a thump, heard a gasp that was almost a scream. She could barely turn her head far enough, caught only a glimpse of two more men hauling Railu to her feet. Behind, the final two seemed to be ransacking their campsite.

Before long, just beyond a slight curve of the channel, they hauled her up the bank to an open stretch of grass and bilberry. Progress became a fraction easier. "Where are you taking us?" she managed to demand, but her captors said nothing. "Why are you doing this?"

"Told you once," said one then. At least, she thought that was what he said. It sounded more like *tole yow wunce*. "Shudda fuggup, trull." She got the message.

Jerya had no clear idea how long they travelled like that, half-walking, half-dragged. Railu and the other senior Novices had seemed to have an instinctive sense of the passage of time, but if someone told her 'I'll see you in the Library forecourt in half an hour,' she had to keep checking her timepiece to ensure she wasn't late. Perhaps it was half an hour; perhaps it was twice or three times that. However long the journey was, it brought them to a clearing where she saw a number of horses tethered, a couple more men watching them. These two exchanged rough greetings with their captors. Again she thought she could pick out the odd word from the clamour, but couldn't be sure.

They had just a minute or two to catch their breath while preparations were made; horses were untethered, the first riders mounted up. She turned to check on Railu, who hung slackly between two men, face blank. One knee of her trousers was torn and Jerya thought she saw blood. But before she could think, before she could decide if it was worth asking to be allowed to check, to clean the wound, she found herself being lifted bodily into the air. Next thing she knew she was slung facedown across the broad back of a horse. More ropes were thrown around her, lashing her to the back of a saddle in which a rider was already seated.

Even before the rider dug in his heels to set the horse in motion, she knew things were about to get worse.

Head-down as she was, her view was severely restricted. She couldn't lift her head far enough to see much beyond the edge of the vague trail they were following. Turning her gaze to the left she could see scarcely anything past the rider's boot, which swung alarmingly close to her face.

Only by twisting her head to the right could she see any distance, but she was obviously on the last horse of the line and there was no one to be seen, nothing to be learned. To fear and shock and terror she soon added not only discomfort but, soon enough, boredom.

Time wore on. After what might have been an hour, or possibly two, she had all too close a view of the horse copiously evacuating its bowels as it walked. Perhaps she made a sound, or flinched away, because the rider obviously realised what was happening. He laughed, then called out jovially to the others. She still couldn't decipher what he said, but the feeling was ever stronger that there were words in there, words she would be able to understand if only she could get past the gruff tones and strange intonation.

As if the horse relieving itself had triggered her own need, she soon began to feel a strong desire. Something else to add to the long litany of discomforts. As the day wore measurelessly on, the desire became need, became pressing, began to border on the desperate, but she resolved that, no matter what, she would not soil her clothes, would not give these men cause to laugh at her.

Finally they halted at a clearing in the forest. They were hauled off the horses, and when their legs threatened to give way hard hands held them up. They were brought before what seemed to be the leader, a man marginally less filthy than the rest, seated on a fallen tree. She could at least make some kind of sense of his words, and that was a relief of sorts. "Well, well, time to tek a proper gander... ah, tipty, we's got a brace o' pretty woodcock. An' who be yowr master, me sweet snipeys, or masters?" Jerya stared back, aware of Railu trembling beside her, but said nothing. What could she say?

He turned to one of his cohorts. "No voices, Grum? Hab they bin tongued?"

"Nay, sir, them was racketous enough when us tooked 'em."

"So... hark-a-me, drab," he said, turning back to Jerya. "Dun't be fooly. Yow're caught an' tomorrer we's tekking yow to th' market. Nawt yow c'n do ter change that. An' us can't damage yow too much, not if'n us wants any chance of a fair bounty. Still'n'all, yowr time wi' us c'n be more or less unpleasant; 's up ter yow. Ah dun't much lahk cruelty for 'ts'own sake, but some o' th'lads mayben't so... *scrupulous*." He delivered the word with a satisfied flourish. "An' if'n ah dun't get answers, ah might be tempted ter let yow in their hands for th' night after all. D'yow understan' me?"

Jerya met his eye, saw the whites faintly yellowed and slightly bloodshot. "I understand well enough."

"Good. Then ah'll ask again. Who be yowr master?"

"We have no master."

He moved suddenly, as if on the point of springing up. "Dun't be fooly, girl, I said, and dun't tek me for no fool neither. Yow can't ha' been on th' loose more'n a week, an' as fer yowr friend, she looks fresh as a..." Abruptly, he stood. "Why'm ah westin' my time? Ah've better things ter do than bandy gab wi' th' likes o' yow." He turned to a henchman. "If they wun't talk, they dun't eat. See if'n us got any collars an' hobbles, elsewise tie 'em well an' keep a lifty eye on 'em. An' mind! Leave off 'em. There'll be a decent bounty, p'raps, but masters'll wan' their goods back whole." He gave an unwholesome chuckle. "Even if'n only so they can mek their own marks... anyroad, a bounty's a bounty, and us can use whatever us can get."

Metal collars were fastened around their necks, and rings placed around their ankles, linked together with metal bars. They could walk, but it was painful, awkward, and slow. Then they were thrown down by a tree and the collars were attached by chains to another chain that looped around it. At least their hands were free, so when the men moved away they could shuffle round into the shadows behind the tree and slip their trews down and piss. A flask of water was brought, but no food. When no one seemed to be watching them, Railu leaned close and whispered, "What's happening, Jerya? I don't understand."

"Neither do I." There was little else to say.

As evening fell they saw the men build a fire and begin to cook. The smells of roasting meat made Jerya's insides twist with sudden hunger. It was unbearable to watch as the men began to eat, but impossible to tear her gaze away.

In the morning the hobbles were removed but the collars were left on. Their hands were re-tied in front of them and each was linked by a few metres of rope to a horse. The chief himself, with four or five men, took them down endless forest trails, riding easily while the girls were forced to follow at a pace just too fast for a comfortable walk. Occasionally one of the horses would skip forward, pulling Jerya or Railu onto her knees. The men evidently found this just as amusing on the tenth occasion as on the first.

The forest changed as they went on, always downwards, from pine and fir to birch and larch. Towards mid-afternoon they came into open land, sheep-pastures first with scattered trees, then wide walled fields. Here and there were people working, tending crops, mending fences, digging ditches. Many of them had shaved heads: she and Railu looked at each other with blended wonder and concern. When they passed a group working on a fence right at the side of the road, they found themselves being watched, though the watchers tried to hide their interest, looking away as they drew closer. Still, they had seen, beyond any remaining doubt, that some of the shaven-heads were men. Again they could only look into each other's eyes, full of unspoken questions.

It was near dusk when they came into a town; almost a city, Jerya thought, not half so great as Carwerid but larger than any other place she had seen. As their captors came to the outskirts, they kicked their horses into a trot, and the girls were forced to run full tilt. So it was that they came into the town, seeing virtually nothing of it, only the stones of the road, the rears of the horses and the backs of the men. Jerya had some impression that there was more brick in the buildings than Carwerid, less stone and timber, and no great towers, but that was all.

At last they halted. The horses stood and shuffled; the men climbed down. Jerya and Railu kept themselves from falling only by leaning on each other, wrenching for breath.

Presently Jerya had recovered enough to look around. Suddenly—or so it seemed—it was nearly night, the sky above indigo. Around them torches burned in wall-brackets and men moved about with lanterns. They were in some kind of court or square, she saw; the road by which they had approached ran along one of the shorter sides, while the other three were lined with buildings of two storeys. Along the longer sides the lower storey seemed to be lined with arches, forming a colonnade, a little like Third Court in the College. But then she saw that there were bars down the mouths of the arches, and her dread deepened.

Somewhere close by two men were talking. One, she thought, was the leader of their captors. She still didn't know his name; so far as she understood the rest of the crew at all, she thought that they had always called him 'Boss' or 'Captain', often it had sounded more like 'Cap'm', or simply 'Cap'.

Watch—Listen—Learn, she thought. She had lived by that precept for a long time. It might be that she had never needed it more than now.

"Yow know the law on Notifications," said the other man.

"Yah, but lissen, Keeving," said 'Cap'm'. "I bin thinkin', ridin' in. Where did us find 'em? Out West. If they'd sconded from our Districk, you'd'a seen a Notification by now, right? An' if they'd sconded from any other Districk... how th' fugg d'yow s'pose they'd'a got here—*and* past—quicker'n th' mails? It's two days' walk at least; more like three fer a brace o' trulls. Anyways yow look at it, these two, if'n their master wanted 'em back, you'd'a heard already."

The one called Keeving said nothing. She supposed he was considering the argument.

"An' think," 'Cap'm' pressed on. "Yow put 'em up tomorrer; one way or t'other, they's off yowr hands. Hold 'em over till next market day and yow've got ter house 'em, feed 'em, fer two weeks. And yow knows; yow knows better'n what I do, p'raps, what t'market's like for runaways. No surety o' sale at all. Possible you'd end up out o'pocket."

Keeving grunted. "I hates to admit it, Barek, but yow may be right. Just this wunce, o' course."

"Then yow'll put 'em up tomorrer?"

"Fuck it, why not? And I'll do my level best to sell 'em for yow, too. Else they're just a cost to both of us, eh?"

"Too right. Broke off a boar-hunt ter bring these in, us did. P'raps a good boar'd've been worth a sight more'n these trulls'll fetch, but I knows my civic duty."

Keeving laughed derisively. "Yea, Barek, model citizen, that's yow. Well, let's be 'avin' 'em, then, and yow can clear off. I've had enough o' your crew cluttering up my nice clean yard. All cleaned up, we was, and now we've had your mangy nags shittin' all over the place. And don't think I didn't see Bruiser—" (*was that really the name he'd used?* wondered Jerya) "—relievin' hisself in the corner."

"Usual commission?"

"Yes, yes, usual, but loose 'em and bugger off afore I adds on five percent for th'extra cleaning."

❀

"Keep still, trull."

She tried to comply, to still the quiver in her limbs, but out of nowhere came a great blow to the side of her head, right over her ear.

Keeving leaned closer. "I give yow an order, yow answer me, understand?"

"I understand."

Another blow just like the last, making her head ring.

He leaned in again. "Fucksake, girl, why make it hard fer yowrself? I can keep this up all day. See this hand? Hit you a hundred times, doubt I'd feel a thing." She could believe it; his hand was built like the rest of him, broad and meaty. "'Course, I'd mark yow, but there's other ways... Hot wax down the ear, now. Hurts like bugg'ry, they say. Pain's temp'ry, o'course, but you lose all the hearing that side. And, done right, don't leave a mark at all.

"All'n'all, count yowrself lucky, there. Runaways, not best prospect as 'tis, but fresh whipcut's a sure way to turn away any buyers who might be lookin'. And remember what th'alternative is, if us don't sell yow..."

She *didn't* know what the alternative was, but didn't think she could ask. And he was still speaking. "I'll leave yowr right ear, see. Y'only need one to hear yowr orders.

"But, yow know, your choice." He laughed. "Yow wanted freedom, p'raps. Here yow go. Free to choose. Call me sir, nice and meek, like a good slave does—or end up deaf on one side, maybe. New owner might not be reet pleased when they find that, p'raps, but it's not going to show up on any inspection tomorrow."

He paused a moment. "So, girl, your choice, like I said. What's it to be?"

She raised her head slowly. "I understand. Sir."

He smiled. It did not improve his looks. "Tha's better! See how easy 'tis, really?"

When she didn't reply at once, he brandished that slab of a hand menacingly and repeated the question.

"Yes, sir."

"Then hold still while I'm shavin' you. Don't want any cuts. That might put off t'buyers too. And..." He made a show of 'trying to remember'. "Oh, yea, it might hurt yow, too. And us wouldn't want that, would us?"

"No, sir."

"There yow go," he said benignly, and picked up the razor again. Jerya sat still, not because he had commanded it but because it would be stupid to do anything else. As she sat, as the blade scraped away a week's stubble, she thought about the word he had so casually let drop: *slave*.

He finished the task in a couple of minutes. Then, as he straightened, he flicked her earlobe with a finger. It was surprisingly—shockingly—painful: a bright, sharp flare of pain, where the earlier blows had been broader but duller. The shock, as much as the pain itself, brought her within a whisker of crying out.

He had no need to do that. No need whatsoever, she thought, as his broad back went away. *He just did it... because he could.* And then another thought, tentative, as if trying it on for size: *I hate him.*

There had been people she didn't much care for, people she kept away from... but she had never truly hated anyone before.

❈

They hung placards around their necks as they herded them onto the platform. Jerya could not resist lifting hers to read what it said. There was a burst of laughter from some youths nearby, at the front of the crowd.

"This one thinks she can read!"

"Hey, drab, don't you know you're looking at it upside down?"

Jerya looked at them with the outward impassivity she had learned—so long ago, it seemed—when first she became a Postulant. So slaves weren't supposed to read? Then she would deny herself the pleasure of explaining that she had first learned to read upside down, standing at Holdren's feet as he read from the books of tales.

She saw it suddenly; his finger tracing the words, its scarred knuckles and cracked nails. Her view of the sale-ring blurred with sudden tears, but the inner picture was clear.

The memory of Delven hurt more than all Keeving's brutality. But here she was, with a placard around her neck, declaring that she was *Lot Four. Female. 18 years? Virgin. Runaway—unclaimed.* And all because she...

She twisted, brushing away the tears, to look at Railu's placard. Its wording was identical, except for the absence of the word 'virgin'. They were both Lot Four, and that presumably meant they were to be sold together. Or... they would share their fate, in any case. It was a crumb—a very small crumb—of comfort.

Their turn came soon enough. Dragged from the shade at the rear of the platform, they stood blinking in the sunlight. She could not pick faces from the crowd. They all seemed blank and alike: old, young, male, female, none displaying the least interest in them.

"And now, good folk..." The auctioneer's booming voice, far more refined than Barek and Keeving and the rest, took on a new, unctuous, note. "Here's your chance to pick up a bargain, if you're prepared to gamble a little. Oh yes, they're runaways. But just look at them. I haven't had such prime specimens under my gavel for a long time. It would be a shame to throw such meat on the fire, surely. Think they learned their lesson? Or think you can teach them?"

There was some laughter at that, an ugly sound. Railu shuffled closer, reaching for Jerya's hand.

"Who'll make me an offer, good folk? I've no reserve on these two. Remember I get nothing for them if they're burned."

Jerya felt a shiver down her spine: was that what Keeving had meant by 'you know the alternative'?

Jerya focused suddenly on a couple, three or four rows back in the crowd, almost directly in front of her: a grey-haired man, a woman with grey streaks in dark hair, both plainly dressed against some of those around them, though the woman's skirts were as full as others. They were arguing in fervent whispers, with frequent glances up at the platform. She kept her eyes on them. How would a good slave look? A runaway who'd learned her lesson? She did not know, but she knew she did not want to be burned. She thought of that and hoped it showed in her face, though it felt frozen in that mask of calm.

There was no response yet from the crowd, no bid. The auctioneer stepped up beside them, glancing down at his hand—no, his wrist. With a profound shock Jerya saw he was wearing a timepiece there on a leather strap.

"Strip 'em, Brecken," he ordered in a low voice. Rough hands grasped Jerya from behind, one hoisting upwards on the metal collar so she dared not resist as others ripped the clothes from her body. Even when her arms were released she made no move to cover herself: it would achieve nothing, save to acknowledge the humiliation. She kept her eyes on the still-arguing couple and closed her mind to the comments and guffaws of others in the crowd. But she could not close her ears to the closest, the same youths who had laughed at her reading. She did not look at them again, but she listened.

"How much cash have you got?"

"Does it matter? He said he'll take any price."

"Fuck, Keppel, what do we want slaves for—"

"What do you think we want them for, you turd? Still wet behind the ears..."

"Yes, but what will our fathers say? Where are we going to put them?"

"I know a place, all right? Now shut up and hand me your cash. All of you."

"Why do we have to give *you* the money?"

"Because I'm the only one of age, you trab. He won't take a bid from any of you. Not till you're twenty. And who knows if we'll get another opportunity like this?" The voice was suddenly raised. "I'll give you one."

"Two!" There was a stir, heads turning, but Jerya had seen the grey-haired man call out his bid.

"That's it, sirs, that's it!" the auctioneer said in a satisfied tone. Jerya had the impression he was pleasantly surprised to receive any bids at all.

"Three!"

"Four!" The couple, no longer arguing, were pushing forward through the crowd.

"Here comes an old fool," the leader of the youths muttered to his cronies.

"Yes, but a rich one. We can't outbid him, Keppel."

"We'll see about that. See how much he wants 'em, any rate. How much have you got?"

"Count me out. My father does business with Duncal. I'm not crossing him."

"I have four from Squire Duncal," the auctioneer crooned, leaning down over the rail. "Any advance, young sir?"

"Five," said Keppel with an air of defiance—the defiance of one who knows he has lost.

"Against you, Squire Duncal." The older man merely nodded. "I have six, then. Squire Duncal has himself a bargain at six. Will no one else consider...?" It was half-hearted; the man was congratulating himself. He had made more, quite possibly six more, than he had expected. *But six what?* she wondered, and then almost smiled at herself. Even at such a pass she was asking questions. "Going once at six. At six, twice. At six—sold! To Squire Duncal. Take 'em down, Brecken."

They were dragged down the steps and back to the place where they had waited before. Inside, people were milling around: slaves who had been sold already, well-dressed men who were presumably the new owners. In the confusion, Jerya and Railu suddenly found themselves face-to-face with the grey-haired couple who had, it seemed, just purchased them.

"I'll pay cash," the man—Duncal—said. "And there's an extra five bronze for you if you can find them some clothes." He turned to his wife. "Shameful exhibition. Had we bid sooner we could have had them for next to nothing, and they would have been spared the humiliation."

Jerya bit her lip. She wanted to burst out: *it's being sold—being bought—that's humiliating, not being naked.* But she kept a practised silence.

Duncal looked directly at them for the first time. "Well, girls, you belong to me now. Have you names? Have they left you tongues to speak your names with?"

"I am Jerya, sir. And this is Railu."

"Can Railu not speak for herself, then?"

"She can, sir, but she is... well, she's frightened."

"And you? Are you not frightened?" He smiled absently, not expecting an answer. "Of course you... you certainly were, hm? Between the fire and those... well. I suppose you appreciate your good fortune. I trust you're grateful."

Jerya bowed her head, hoping he would take it as assent. She had vowed to herself to speak the truth, and it would be a lie to say she was grateful. *Grateful for being bought like an animal!* Relieved, yes, glad to be alive, but grateful... that was something else.

"Ah, well," he said mildly, "It's all a bit overwhelming, I'm sure. Here, put these on..." The man Brecken had returned with a couple of coarse-woven shifts. "Give me the keys, man, how can they dress if they're still chained?"

"If yow'll just sign that yow've received th'goods, sir. Then it's yowr responsibility if they're unchained."

"Well, of course I'll sign, but what do you think they're going to do? Run?"

"They runned afore, sir."

"Obviously... but here? In the middle of town? Stark naked? Really, man, what are you scared of?"

He signed a document, kept one copy and handed back the other, accepted some keys and unlocked the collars. Hastily Jerya and Railu pulled on the shifts. They seemed to be the same size: loose enough on Jerya, a little tight on Railu; and they did not reach even to their knees. Only by contrast with being naked did it feel like being decently dressed. It seemed that Duncal's wife noticed it too. She leaned close to him and whispered something, the elaborate coils of her hair bobbing slightly. Her eyes rested on Railu's ill-concealed curves.

"Yes, I take your point, my dove," he said softly. "But we're going straight home. I'm sure we can find something more suitable there, rather than paying outrageous prices here."

"You agree you've been extravagant then?" she said tartly.

He smiled with his mouth only, turning back to the two of them. "Now, girls, do I need to chain you again? You aren't stupid, are you? You'll follow us home and no more nonsense of running away... I imagine you could do with a square meal, hm? Duncal's the only place you'll get one. Lead the way, my love."

They followed the lady out, Duncal falling in behind them, the two discarded collars clashing together softly in his hand, out of the booth and away from the square through quieter streets. In a large inn-yard a carriage waited, two horses standing idly in the traces, a thickset male slave in the driving seat.

"You aren't going to make them walk, surely," Duncal's wife said suddenly. "They're barefoot—and that girl is just too..."

"Shall we invite them to ride with us?" he asked with a soft chuckle. "Hm, it would be amusing... but it doesn't look as if either of them has had a bath for a fortnight."

"Of course I don't want them to ride inside," she replied. The exasperation in her voice was softened with affection. They seemed to be a couple who enjoyed teasing each other. "But surely they can sit on the roof? They'll hardly feel like jumping off from there."

"Very well, my dove. Whallin! Give these girls a hoist up."

They clambered up rungs set into the rear of the carriage. Jerya hardly needed the slave's strong arm to help them, and then she helped Railu. They settled on the flat roof of the carriage. There were low rails around it, just a few centimetres above the roof itself, but nothing else to hold on to, nothing to stop them falling off.

"Go easy now, Whallin," Duncal called, leaning out of the carriage window. "Don't shake my new acquisitions off into the dust."

"Very good, Master." He flicked at the reins, hauled on a lever. Jerya remembered her journey to Carwerid and realised he must be releasing a brake. The carriage-wheels began to rumble on the cobbles, hooves made a loud clatter under the arch. Jerya and Railu ducked their heads. They were out in the street.

"Di'n't know Master was after buying new slaves," said Whallin over his shoulder, barely turning his head. It sat heavily on his shoulders, scarcely tapering at the short neck; and right on the crown, a small area had been left unshaved, sprouting a topknot that stood up like a stiff brush. It was strange enough to see a man with his head shaved; this addendum struck her as grotesque, a travesty, making mock of that dignity that was—or should be—reserved for Dawnsingers.

"I don't believe he was," Jerya returned, shifting forward into one of the front corners.

"Sit still!" he ordered curtly. "What d'yow mean?"

"I think he... bought us on impulse. Perhaps just to save us from being burned."

"Burned!" Whallin's gruff voice went shrill, oddly like a girl, but Jerya didn't feel like laughing. "Yow're runaways?" She said nothing. "Well, I suppose Master knows what he's about... but yow listen here, my girl. I dun't know how't'was, where yow was afore. I've heard o' some places where I'd feel like running off, too. But yow've just been bought by th' best house in th' province. There's no good-folks kinder'n Squire and Lady Duncal. They wun't be after beating yow... but give any trouble and I *will*, all right?"

It was not all right. None of it was all right, but there was nothing she could say. Only, "I understand," and then nothing else at all.

They were leaving the town now. It had no walls or gates, no distinct boundary, only bigger and bigger spaces between the houses, filled at first with vegetable gardens and orchards, then fields of cattle and sheep.

"How far is it?" she asked.

"Hour an' a half, mebbe a bit more." Whallin's eyes were so fixed on the road ahead he never saw Jerya's little start of shock. Males with shaven heads? Males measuring journeys in hours? What next...?

Soon the town disappeared in the dust that the wheels raised from the road behind them. Ahead, it was a meandering white scar in the green land, disappearing here and there behind a little rise or stand of trees, finally going out of sight over a greater rise on the skyline. Their destination must lie beyond, she realised. It would, as he'd said, not be a short ride. She shifted slightly, seeking comfort on the hard roof. Whallin gave her a sharp glance, as if her movement irritated him, but said nothing. Jerya dismissed him as a source of information.

She glanced at Railu. At least she was sitting up and looking about her with some measure of alertness. Catching Jerya's eye, she made a brave effort to smile, but said nothing. Jerya reached out her hand towards her, but Whallin turned his head sharply and snapped, "Sit still, trapes, or I'll use this whip on yow!" She sat back and grimaced at Railu.

It seemed to be fertile country, and well-worked; every couple of kilometres there would be a large farmstead to left or right, a big house with barns and lesser buildings ranged behind or to one side, surrounded by orchards and gardens. In the fields, gangs of slaves were hard at work: it was grain-harvest time. Men went in staggered rows with scythes, women followed behind, raking up the crop and tying it into sheaves. A few wore hats, though the sun was mild—it was none too warm sitting on the roof of the carriage—but she noticed here and there among the rest that a few, like Whallin, were not completely shaven. After a while she thought that she had discerned the pattern. Men had round topknots, smaller than a fist, right on the crown: women had narrow central crests, sometimes long enough to be braided, sometimes with little bright strips of cloth bound in, as if in imitation of the elaborate hairstyles of the free women. She was still wondering what—if anything—this might signify when the carriage came to the top of the ridge. Beyond, suddenly, she saw the land in a great slow-falling sweep: all of it green and gold, fertile, rich, scattered with woods and farmsteads, threaded with the white roads and glittering rivers. It was clear, now, that everything they had seen so far was still upland; the lowlands must be at least a hundred metres lower, and perhaps a good deal more.

In spite of everything, Jerya smiled. *This* was the reality of the Blistered Lands.

Before the descent had really begun, the carriage swung off onto a narrower road, running gently uphill again. The road swung around the lower slopes of a high, tree-crowned knoll. Ahead now she saw more trees, half-concealing a large house; side-walls of brick but the frontage of creamy pale stone, two high-windowed stories with a steep roof rising nearly as high again. Closer, she saw small attic windows set among the slates.

The carriage stopped first at the front of the house: there were broad steps, high paired doors. Duncal and his lady descended. Jerya heard his instructions to the coachman: "Give these girls to Cook—"

"Cook's bin' over to th'home-farm, Master. She's not like to be back yet. Shall I give 'em to th' black one?"

"Yes, yes, Rhenya, of course. Tell her they're to be bathed, fed, found better clothing, and when they're presentable brought to us after dinner."

The carriage moved on again, round the side of the house, clattering into a cobbled yard at the back, with low outbuildings along two sides. As they came to halt, Whallin gave out a harsh bellow. "Rhenya! Get out here, yow black trapes!"

A girl came running out from one of the outbuildings. She was not truly black, Jerya saw at once, but it was clear enough why Whallin called her that; less clear whether he'd meant anything by it, beyond simple description. Analind had been dark, and others among the Novices, but this Rhenya was a shade or two darker still. And the girl—about sixteen, she thought—was every bit as beautiful as Analind was.

Whallin scrambled down from his seat, not bothering to offer Jerya and Railu a hand down. He went at once to unharness the horses, throwing instructions over his shoulders at Rhenya. "Master's seen fit to procure two new drabs. Has 'is reasons, I s'pose, though 't beats me... get 'em somethin' to eat, bath 'em, and th' skinny un needs a proper shave. They wants to see 'em after their dinner."

Jerya climbed down. The girl was looking her up and down with frank curiosity.

"Hello," she said, "I'm Jerya." Suddenly they were both smiling. Clearly not all slaves were as unfriendly as Whallin.

Railu joined them and introduced herself. It was, Jerya thought, the first time she had spoken since the morning. Rhenya led them towards one of the outbuildings. As soon as they were inside (perhaps more to the point, out of Whallin's sight) she began to chatter.

"Yow must be th' runaways. Heard about yow. Just like Master to buy yow. Hates to see any'un burned. D'yow want ter eat first or bathe?"

"It's so long since we had a bath that a little longer won't signify," Jerya said. "But we haven't eaten since dawn yesterday and that *does* signify."

"I'd say th' same, I'm sure," the girl said with a hushed laugh. "It wun't be anything special... but I dun't know, maybe better than yow're used to. If yow've been runaway... and what sort o' place was it yow run away from?"

Railu made a strange little noise, between a snort and a laugh. Jerya glanced across at her. "That's what they call a long story, Rhenya."

"I hope yow wun't want to run away from here," the girl said. Suddenly she looked hard into Jerya's eyes: a strange, almost pleading, look. "This is th' kindest House in Denvirran Principality. Everyun says so."

CHAPTER 8

RODAL

Rodal stood outside a low building, which a crudely painted board proclaimed to be 'Drumlenn Rangers headquarters'. *Drumlenn?* he thought, *is that the name of the town?* Beneath the board the Code of Slavery was posted on the wall, partly protected from weather by a projecting shelf-cum-roof. Even so the paper was stained and tattered at the edges. He was reading this when a voice greeted him. "Well, young feller, it's nice to see folk takin' an interest... Are yow looking for work?"

"I could be..."

"Come in, lad, have yowrself a cup o' tea. Where's yow from? Yow've come a long way, likely." The man didn't wait for an answer, already turning inside. Rodal followed him slowly.

"I see yow c'n read," the man went on once tea was brewed. "Can yow ride?"

He had to say no, and the man seemed surprised, even a little suspicious. Thinking quickly, he said, "Where I come from, it's all rocks and forests. It's no country for horses." It was nothing but the truth, as far as it went.

It seemed to do the trick, but still his new friend sighed. "Well, it's a shame, but if yow could find a way to learn then I'd be glad to see yow back here. Reckon yow could learn to ride quicker'n most o' th' lads we sees could learn to read."

"You've no other work here then?"

"No, lad, when we're away on a hue'n'cry th' slaves keep th' place in order.... Well, finish yowr drink. Have that on us at least. It's quiet at th' moment. Owners must be treating their slaves too kind—not enough runaways." He guffawed. "Maybe yon Squire Duncal's right after all—have ye heard of him?"

"I don't think so."

"Yow can't ha' bin long in these parts, then... Duncal o' Duncal, out off th'Denvirran road. Wants us all to featherbed our slaves. Says a happy slave's a better slave. Well, it's half true, and I don't believe he's had any runaways since I been in this post, but he's storing up trouble in th'end. They do say his slaves live better'n some free-folk and that ain't right. Look at yow, a healthy lad and a smart un, a readin' man, and yow've no work; how long since yow had a new suit o' cloze? And here's this Duncal dressin' his slaves in his own castoffs, laying on parties wi' dancin' and what-all for 'em... and now he's bought a couple o' runaways what we mighta had th' burnin' of."

Obviously he mistook the direction of Rodal's anger. "Well might yow bristle, lad. It's a rare tale, though. They found 'em far up in th' western range. Freebooters, this were, not our lads." His tone suggested he didn't greatly approve of 'freebooters'. "Couple o' girls, well-enough lookin' as slaves go: an' that Barek made sure some gentlemen'd be glad to have 'em back an' ordered his men hands-off." He snorted disgustedly. "If they'd'a come into my hands and I'd known there'd be no claims, we'd'a had some pleasure on 'em."

Rodal sat on his hands and bit his lip. He wanted to smash his fist into the fellow's face. It was—it had to be—Railu and Jerya he was talking of in this way. He forced himself to consider that it *was* only talk, that the order had been 'hands-off', that the girls were apparently safe, or as safe as they could be under the circumstances. And punching the oaf, however momentarily satisfying it might be, was hardly going to further his main objective: information.

"And this Squire Duncal... bought them?" He asked, managing—he hoped—to sound merely curious.

"Yea, there was some young lads fancied 'em for their own purposes..." He winked and laid a finger by his nose. "An' who c'n blame 'em, eh? But

Duncal steps in and takes the brace for six small notes." He laughed again. "Six! And if he can keep 'em from runnin' again, he'll say he's got a great bargain—an' no doubt he'll reckon it proves him right in all his notions. Yea, well, I bet they girls is thinking they's landed in heaven."

Rodal doubted that, but held his peace, letting the Ranger ramble on. "But it makes me angry and it makes yow angry, dun't it? Blight me, it's like rewardin' 'em for runnin' off in th' first place. If those boys had got 'em, I wouldn't ha' minded so much, but rightly they shoulda been burned. Do people think slaves never hear th' news just 'cause they can't read the papers? Oh, well, maybe it'll mean more business for me in th' end, if slaves start getting th' notion they can do better for themselfs just by runnin' away."

Rodal turned left, towards the centre of town, resisting the temptation to head straight back to his bivouac, in a neglected-looking bit of woodland not far outside the town. He had assumed the role of a young man looking for work: now he was beginning to think he should play it for real. As he walked down a long dusty street he was doing his level best to think things through, calmly and methodically.

The most important fact was that Jerya and Railu were alive and un-harmed. At least—he corrected himself—up to the point at which they had been sold, no serious harm had apparently been done to them. Well, he'd seen that with his own eyes, seen them being driven away on the roof of a carriage. It had been something, after the previous days frantic with fear and worry, to know that much.

Since then, he could have no definite knowledge, but it appeared that by good fortune they had fallen into the hands of someone known to treat his slaves kindly. What exactly might be meant by 'kindly', he had no real way of knowing, but he deduced, from what the garrulous Ranger had said, that this Duncal at least was not given to physical brutality.

He found himself smiling. He'd made it his mission, in the days since they'd crossed the pass, to try and make sure that the girls fully understood just what their lives would be like, just the two of them in the wilderness. Well, that was one thing: it wasn't the wilderness they'd imagined. Not down here it wasn't, besure. His brief smile died as he recalled his utter shock, seeing the prints of boots that weren't their own in the soft ground at one side of the campsite. That, and the disappearance of their belongings, the scattering of the fire.

Well, it sounded like a house where slaves were dressed in their Master's castoffs and were occasionally treated to parties with dancing would be more comfortable than whatever rough forest shelter they might have managed to contrive before winter. Presumably Duncal's slaves were adequately fed, too. His stomach clenched at the thought. None of their store of food—little enough as it had been—had been left behind, and two days of pursuit had left him scant time to hunt. He would have to attend to his own needs soon, somehow.

There was much relief in knowing the girls were in a place where they would at least be sheltered, clothed, fed. Exactly what else might be implied by being taken for slaves, he was still trying to establish. It was not a word he'd previously been familiar with, but he'd kept his eyes and ears open as he approached Drumlenn and began his wary exploration.

Slavery meant work of some kind, that was clear enough—and plenty of it, besure. He had seen slaves aplenty in his wanderings around the town, and they always seemed to be toiling. He wondered how the girls would react. How Railu would take it he had no clear notion, but he could hardly imagine that Jerya's proud and headstrong nature was the kind of disposition that was expected of a slave.

However they might be feeling, it grieved him bitterly to think of them in subjection. He had not told them (though he didn't know why not), but he had seen them sing the Dawnsong together, on Delven's songstead, the village's old Singer standing behind them and inaudible behind the strength of their voices. Though he had been told—and now at least half-believed—that the Dawnsong was a lie, he did not believe that all that splendour could ever have been altogether hollow. He recalled Railu's words: *The Song is not a lie.* To her, at least, it wasn't the Song that was false, but what people said about it. He'd hardly understood it, but it had given him some comfort all the same.

Not that it seemed to count for anything now. Still, they were far better off than he had dared to hope. For three terrible days he had mostly imagined them dead, or victims of some scarcely less hideous fate. Now, there was no immediate need for desperate measures. His plans for their escape could be laid without haste, made as sure as possible. He still burned to properly reassure himself of their welfare, and now he had a name; but any approach to this Duncal place would surely be a risky endeavour. The minimum, and therefore safest, number of occasions would be two, once to arrange an escape, once to execute it.

And then—escape to where? He tried to list all the factors to consider, all the things he needed to know. He knew something now about the hue and cry that would be raised for escaped slaves. If they got away after darkness one night—if that were even possible—they would be missed next morning, besure. Not even a full night's start—how many *hours*?—could be counted on; and they would be on foot, pursued soon enough by men on horseback, and perhaps with dogs.

It was a bleak prospect, but Rodal knew something about hunting. To be successful, a hunter must be able to put himself in the mind of his quarry. So, he reasoned, the reverse must be true. To make a successful escape, it was necessary to think like a hunter. To do that, it was necessary to know the ground as the hunter did. To have a clear advantage it was necessary to know the ground *better* than the hunter did. Many a fat mountain hare had eluded him in just this way.

The hunters would be mounted. They'd be prepared to cover long distances. Manifestly you could not outrun them. Perhaps the way was to let them outrun *you*: to try, not to get as far away as possible, but to stay as close as possible. If the 'runaways' never in fact left the area of their daily movements... but still, there would be a scent for dogs to follow, though following a watercourse might throw them off.

Staying close might be an option. But he needed to know more about the way this land worked. He needed to see the lie of the land, both locally and more generally. And—it was becoming clearer all the time—he needed money. Coin, and knowledge; he must gather sufficient of both before he could attempt to do anything for the girls.

The garrulous Ranger had vouchsafed one potential lead in that direction. "If yow're lookin' for work, yow could do worse'n head down Lowertown, to th' docks. There's often work for a strong lad down there, stevedorin' or on one o' th' boats."

There were at least three ways down to Lowertown. Two of them were mundane enough; a long flight of steps, and an even longer switchback road that trailed curves like spilled string across a half-mile span of the steep slope. The third choice—a choice, at least, for those who had a small coin to spare—was extraordinary.

He supposed it to be fairly new; placards around the upper terminus hailed the 'Remarkable Contrivance', declaring it a 'Wonder of the Modern World'. Helpfully, they also provided an explanation of how it worked. In essence it was simple enough. It even reminded him, a little, of the locks on the canal between Carwerid and the coast. Like them, it relied on nothing but the natural properties of water.

A pair of carts or carriages, on metal wheels, ran on metal rails that had been laid straight up and down the slope. The two were linked by a stout metal rope—a *cable*—that ran over an arrangement of pulley-wheels at the top. If one cart was heavier, it would descend, and the rope would cause the other to rise. Under the floor of each cart were large tanks. When one was at the upper station, on the outskirts of Uppertown, the tank would be filled with water, while the other, down at the quayside, was loaded with cargo or passengers. When the brakes were released, if the weight of water had been correctly calculated to be greater than that of the cargo—but not too much greater—the two carts would rise or fall at a measured rate, changing places.

It was obvious to him even before he'd finished reading the explanatory text that the loadmasters must be men of great skill, who bore a weighty responsibility, especially when passengers were being conveyed. And, he saw, there were not one but four such Remarkable Contrivances; one for passengers, three for goods.

He would have relished the experience of riding in one of the passenger carriages, but he could see that coin was required, and of coin he had none. Fortunately, there was no charge to use the steps. With a resigned sigh, and a wistful look at the Remarkable Contrivance, he started down.

CHAPTER 9

JERYA

"**O**ut and dressed!" said Rhenya, hurrying in. "They'll be waitin' for us soon—Jerya! Yow're still not shaved!"

"I was nearly asleep," she confessed.

"I'm sure yow're exhausted. Will yow let me shave yow? I've good hands. Please..." She seemed eager, as if it would be... what? A pleasure? An honour?

"Of course. Go ahead."

"Just sit up a little, then."

Throwing a towel round Jerya's shoulders, the girl swiftly soaped her scalp, then began to shave it with a brisk, light touch. It could hardly have been more different than Keeving's rough treatment of the early morning, which had left her with uneven stubbly patches. And she could not help thinking back to the first time she had been shaved by the hands of another; in Sharess's chamber, by Sharess's hands, the morning her life had changed. The shaving of her hair had been the first touch, shocking, terrifying. A shaved head had been the mark of a Dawnsinger then; she had barely dared to believe it right for herself, or herself right for it. She had tried: for a short while she had thought she was succeeding. Now, here, a shaved head was the mark of a slave. *I may look like a slave*, she thought. She, still, hardly knew what being a slave meant, but she set her resolve anyway. *I may act like a slave, for a time. But I will never think of myself as a slave.*

But when it was over and she splashed water over the smoothness of her scalp, felt her hands glide easily, she could not deny that it felt good. She saw Railu, already out and drying herself, smiling. "You never liked me with hair, did you?" Jerya remarked, climbing out of the bath.

Rhenya handed her a towel; another in her hands, she began to rub Jerya's back. "Yow'll have to put the same clothes back on," she said. "They've give me nothin' else, must ha' forgot, and nothin' o' mine is goin' to fit yow. Yow're too tall, Jerya, and Railu's..."

"I'm too fat, am I?" said Railu.

Rhenya laughed, her strange hushed laugh. "Oh no, yow're... but we must hurry."

There was one delicious moment, when she had finished drying herself, when Jerya was able to taste the sensation of being clean, freshly washed and shaved. Then she had to surrender the clean towel and put on the shabby linen shift again. She was newly aware of its coarse, prickly texture.

"They'll give yow somethin' better soon," Rhenya said. "Come now."

They followed her across the yard, cobbles chill under bare feet, night air cool on her scalp. The sky was full of stars.

They entered the big house through the kitchen. The only light was fire-glow from behind a grate in the huge range which filled one wall. "Cook goes to her bed after dinner's served," Rhenya said, her voice low.

As they left the kitchen and entered a dim-lamped passage, the surface underfoot changed to a warmer, faintly resilient stuff, more like leather than anything else Jerya could think of. Rhenya stopped before a large wooden door and knocked.

"Enter!" Duncal's voice came from within.

"I've brought the new girls, Master-Mistress."

"Excellent. Thank you Rhenya—no, wait. You stay. All three of you, sit down."

Duncal and his wife were standing with backs to a huge crackling fire. He indicated a long dark-upholstered seat to one side. Jerya noticed that Rhenya perched nervously on the very edge—as if, she thought, she wasn't normally allowed to sit. Yes, there had been something in the way Duncal had said 'sit down', as if he were granting a rare and special favour.

He stood now, beaming down at them, with an air of complacent benevolence. Without looking too obviously at him, she studied him more closely
than she'd had chance to do before. He was not a big man, scarcely taller
than Railu, and under the silvery gown and pantaloons she sensed a spare,
even stringy, frame. One hand was hidden behind his back, the other held a
glass half-full of some dark drink: a slender, elegant, hand, unmarked by any
sign of physical work. His face was framed by grey hair drawn back severely
into a single braid: rather a long face, angular, with prominent cheekbones.
The eyes were large, a mild brown, slightly watery.

"Well," he said after a moment. "I trust you feel better for being fed and
clean, hm?" An answer was clearly expected.

"Yes, thank you," Jerya replied. And, feeling a tension in Rhenya beside
her, she added quickly, "Master." The word curdled in her mouth, sour as
a lie.

"Good. Excellent. Now let me see if I remember. You are Jerya, hm?
And you are Railu?" He seemed excessively proud of getting their names
right: beaming, he sipped at his drink with a quick, birdlike, dip of his head.
"These are not common names. I hazard they are not known at all in these
parts. I further hazard, hm, that you've travelled quite some distance?"

Further than you think, said Jerya privately. Aloud, she only said, "Yes, a
long way, Master."

"Hm, and from which direction, I wonder? North? South? East?"

Unexpectedly, Railu spoke up before Jerya could think how to answer.
"No, M-master, from the West."

Duncal's eyes widened. Then he laughed, his shoulders shaking. He
turned to his wife, nudging her with an elbow. "Did you hear that, dearest?
From the West? That's rich." He turned back to them. "I wonder if, hm, this
is a way—most polite, hm, most subtle—of saying you'd rather not speak
of where you came from. Ah! I see in your face is it is so. You are afraid,
perhaps... listen, my girls, you need have no fear now. You are legally mine
and under my protection. I hope you will soon come to realise that you are

truly safe here, that my good lady and I have your welfare at heart, that you need have no secrets from us. But we shall not press you now."

He paused, sipped at his drink again, and continued. He assumed the air of someone addressing a grander gathering, a village elder at taletell, a Tutor before her class. "Many masters—the majority, I regret to say—believe that slaves are best ruled by fear, by the threat of punishment. But it is their own fear that rules. They are afraid of their slaves; and no doubt they are right to be afraid, for they have given their slaves cause to resent their treatment, to hate their masters. Many of these men are not so stupid as to treat their animals this way. But when it comes to slaves, they are made stupid by fear. Perhaps your former master, hm... but no matter. You have a new master now. We do not rule by fear, and we are not ruled by it. If you find it hard to believe me, ask Rhenya. It's so, is it not, Rhenya, hm?"

"Indeed, yes, Master," the dark girl said eagerly. Eager to please, no doubt, but Jerya sensed conviction; Rhenya truly believed what she was saying; hadn't she already assured them it was *the kindest House in Denvirran Principality*.

"Well, you will find out in time—a short time, I trust—how it is. Actions speak louder than words, hm? We must get down to practicalities: where are you to sleep, what are you to wear, what is your work to be? Hm? What did you do previously? Were you field hands or house slaves?"

Railu looked blank, and Jerya stepped quickly into the breach. "We have done a little of many things, Master, but... I think many things are different here."

"Hm, yes, that may well be so. Well, we'll take a little time, try you out at various tasks, hm? There will be some reorganisation, some rearrangement of duties. Our cook is old, Rhenya here has been doing most of her work, as well as her own. Oh yes—" He beamed at Rhenya. "—Yes, I have noticed. I could not speak of it in front of her, you understand, hm? She has her pride, after all. I understand, you see, slaves too have their pride. A job well done... why, it's the same for us all, be we Principal, or humble scholar, or slave.

Well, hm, I think Cook should have her freedom now, before she is too...
hm, while she can still appreciate it. What do you think, Rhenya, hm?"

Rhenya seemed unable to speak. Jerya saw a tear in her eye.

Duncal chuckled. "You're a good girl, Rhenya, and I know you're not
just thinking your own life will be easier from now on. And think of Cook
when we tell her we had to buy two prime girls like these to replace her,
hm?" He gave them a wink. Even his wife smiled slightly. She was a fraction
taller than her husband, a sturdy woman of around forty—probably a
good ten years his junior—and the rare smile gave her a kind of remote
handsomeness.

"Well, I'm sure you're tired," Duncal went on. "We may rearrange the
sleeping quarters when Cook's moved out, but for tonight..."

Rhenya showed them to a room in an attic of one of the outbuildings.
"Yow'll only be here a few nights, then, if we ask him, I'm sure he'll let us
three be together." She grabbed a hand of each of them. "Yow will, won't
yow?" Her eyes flickered between them. "I'm so glad yow've come!"

CHAPTER 10

RODAL

On a ship, there seemed to be new words for everything. You did not tie up a rope, you *made fast* a *line*—or *sheet*, or *halyard*, or *downhaul*, or *warp*. There were *shrouds* and *stays*, too, but they generally remained fixed in place. In fact, the only rope he'd come across that was still called a rope was the bell-rope.

And you didn't make fast a line with any old knot either. Generally, you took several turns around a *cleat* or *belaying-pin*, and then secured them with a *half-hitch*. That was easy to grasp, which was as well because it was often a thing that needed to be done quickly. Other knots, and *splices*, and *hitches*, he practised with spare lengths of cord whenever he had a little free time.

And there was time, as the river grew broader and the current helped them along and (most of the time) helped keep them in the deeper channel. There was always one man at the wheel and another on lookout, either in the *bows* (sailors didn't say front or back) or perched on a tiny platform two-thirds the way up the mast, forty feet above the deck. Rodal hadn't been placed on lookout duty yet, so he'd had no need to climb, but he made it his business to do so the first time a chance arose.

It came about because of the way the river bent. Sometimes it twisted about, doubled back on itself, went every which way. From above, he thought, it must look like a length of string dropped on the floor, in much the same way as the road down to Lowertown switched direction a dozen times. Around each curve, there was plenty for the crew to do, trimming the sails one way and then the other, even the ordered chaos of a *gybe*, as the *Levore* met the wind first on the *port* side, then on the *starboard*, then *astern*. If the wind ever came from dead ahead, the river still wasn't broad enough for *tacking*—something he'd been told about but had yet to experience—so there was nothing for it but to drop the sails and just drift with the current.

When this happened, he now knew that progress to the next curve would be slow. There wasn't too much immediately to do, so he'd taken the chance. He'd climbed taller trees in the Delven forests, scrambled up crags that were many times higher (but never near as vertical), descended spray-soaked rocks that offered far less in the way of obvious, graspable handholds; but none had felt quite so naked, so obviously surrounded by nothing but air.

Still, he'd done it, and stayed there until his heart settled back to a more normal beat, and then he'd begun to look around him, at the landscape slipping quietly by. There were woods and fields, little villages and towns, mills and farms; nothing that he hadn't seen before, on his journeys in the Sung Lands. Yet everything was different, down here in the lowlands. The land was gently rolling, and he could never discern the general slope that—it stood to reason—must be there to keep the river flowing. There were no crags or quarries, and nearly every building seemed to be made of brick, varying in colour from a pale dirty yellow through dull orange to a strong pinkish red. On grander buildings darker bricks, a deep purple that could appear black in shadow or at the ends of the day, were often set in among the lighter ones to create decorative patterns. Roofs were of tile, sharing some of the colours of the bricks but also taking in darker browns and greys.

From his lofty vantage he could not observe as closely as he had in Drumlenn, but there were some things he saw. In towns and villages there seemed to be few slaves, but in the fields they were sometimes numerous. On the estates around the grander houses, he sometimes saw large gangs toiling at the harvest. Always, of course, they were instantly identifiable by their shaven heads, and he understood better than ever the distorted cleverness of marking them out in so simple a way. Its consequences for Jerya and Railu had been calamitous, but there was nothing he could do about that now, only hold to the watchwords Jerya had shared with him: *watch; listen; learn.*

Watching, he observed that among the troops of slaves raking up the crop, tying it in bundles, carrying these to load onto carts, there were those equipped with sickles or scythes. In one large field he saw four men with scythes, yard-long blades sharp enough to slice apparently effortlessly through the crop, plus twenty or thirty other slaves; and only one free man, apparently an overseer, armed—so far as he could see—only with a whip. He lounged at his ease on a bank at the edge of the field, drinking from a brown bottle. The man might be half-drunk, Rodal thought. What was there to keep two or three dozen slaves, some of them bearing potential deadly weapons, so assiduously at their labour? He watched, wondering, until a bend of the river took them out of sight.

He thought about slaves again later, when they were tied up to a *staithe* on the edge of a quiet town. Neither of the other hands (another new word; that was what he was now; a *hand*) had shown any inclination to venture into the town, which Croudor dismissively called the 'dullest place on the river'. But Croudor, as Rodal had grasped before the first day was done, was dismissive of almost everything.

Instead they had all gathered round the galley-table, and the Captain—the Skipper, as the other hands called him—had broken out a bottle of something called *ackavee*. The measures were small, and Rodal had soon found out why. Small or not, after a couple of rounds tongues became looser, and he found himself wondering aloud, "Does no one work boats like this with slaves? Ships," he amended hastily. That was another new word. All ships were boats, but not all boats were ships.

"Not on this river," said the Skipper, "And a good thing for yow all that they don't, eh?"

They all agreed, even Croudor, and young Grauven called a toast to "Free men's work." The tiny glasses were filled again.

"Yea," said the Skipper after they'd all shared a pensive pause. "A good thing, but yow might well wonder why. I could run a lot cheaper if yow lads was slaves. Every captain could. And mebbe it's just that no one wants to be th' first..." He scratched his head thoughtfully.

"I'm lucky, one way, I s'pose. I own th' *Levore* free and clear. But if owt ever happens to her... well, I try to put money by each trip, somethin' for repairs, perhaps a new sail when we can't patch one any longer. But if th' worst ever happened, I couldn't afford to replace her, not by a long chalk, 'less I hocked myself to a moneylender. And I've known some skippers as did that, and some o' them never got clear again.

"And it's kind o' th' same 'bout slaves. If I crewed her wi' slaves 'stead o' frees, my costs'd be a lot lower. Have to feed 'em and house 'em same as yow lads, but no wages to pay. 'Course it sounds tempting to a man like me, cut them costs, make meself more competitive, maybe have a bit more over to lay by as 'surance 'gainst the day...

"But where's th' money to come from to buy them slaves in th' first place? Sure, what I save on wages might pay th' outlay back in five year, and then I'd have th' labour for twenty or thirty, but how would it work out in that first five years? Sink all my money into slaves, where do I get th' ready for repairs, or cargo, or even food? It comes back to th' moneylenders again.

"See, I talk to other skippers, and they mostly say the same. Yow're master of your own vessel. Yow want to stay that way, an' getting sucked in wi' moneylenders ain't th' way to that.

"Besides, I always think, if I took on a slave crew, what happens to lads like yow?" His glance flitted around the table, resting on each a moment. "Way I see it, slaving's not good for th' slaves and it's not good for free men like us either. Only people it's good for are th' big owners."

His eyes flicked back to Rodal. "I hope I ain't wrong about yow, lad. Maybe I shouldn't have said all that. It's what plenty people think. But saying it can be a risky affair."

Rodal met his gaze. "You've been good to me, Skipper. It's no plan of mine to pay you back awrong."

✻

From this conversation, and others like it, he was learning more about slavery, how it was wound through every section of society. In avoiding the use of slaves, the ship-traders were a rarity, and one that some frowned upon. Men like the Skipper, whom Rodal had already adjudged to be as honest a man as he'd ever met, were seen as disreputable.

He learned other things, watching and listening, and he put them together with what he'd heard in the streets of Drumlenn, what he'd overheard one night in a tavern there, nursing a half-pint of sweet black beer, paid for with a coin he'd found dropped in the street, while men around him downed two or three pints. He'd seen the whips that overseers carried, and he'd seen scars on the backs of slaves working on the docks of Drumlenn Lowertown.

In the tavern and on the streets he'd heard more talk of this Squire Duncal. His acquisition of the two 'runaways' had been the talk of the town, and that had led to wider discussion of the man's eccentricities.

Well, he thought, *if they had to wind up being called slaves, sounds like they couldn't be in a better place.*

Of course it was still a terrible thing, but they—and he too—could have been worse off in all sorts of ways. The tales of the Blistered Lands might have turned out true after all. The 'freebooters' might have snatched him too. Or the girls could have been picked up by some owner who was a lot less 'soft' than Squire Duncal. He shuddered even to think of Jerya or Railu being flogged... let alone some of the more extreme punishments he'd heard about.

Still terrible, but try as he might he couldn't think of any way, placed as he was now, that he could improve their situation. If he was ever to get them out, he had to have a plan. He hardly knew what that plan might be; whether it would involve lying low somewhere close, as he had first thought, or making a quick escape—which would need horses, or a coach; he had seen them on the roads, and learned that some were privately-owned and some carried passengers for a fare. Since he knew that neither he nor Jerya knew how to ride, and doubted Railu could either, a coach seemed a better notion. But as yet he had no idea how to make it possible. Or, equally important, where they might go.

Yes, their situation grieved him, but it seemed it was not intolerable, and if he tried to get them free before he was ready he stood every chance of making things worse rather than better.

CHAPTER 11

JERYA

F or reasons that seemed clear to the Master and Mistress, if not to the girls, after trying them at various tasks, Railu had been assigned principally to kitchen work, while Jerya's duties were in the house, which mostly meant cleaning. Some rooms required daily cleaning, while others might only be attended to weekly. One of these was Duncal's library.

It was no match for the College Library, but one wall and much of another were lined with shelves; there were hundreds of books, probably over a thousand. Jerya, naturally, burned to see what was in those books, but she had learned on the auction platform that slaves were not supposed to read. Best not to risk it, she thought, until either she knew much more clearly how things stood, or she found herself alone in the house.

However, this morning a letter lay half-finished on the desk. The Master's fastidious penmanship was easy to read, and her attention was snagged when she caught the words 'two new girls' in the third line on the page.

She laid aside her feather-duster and bent over the paper, being careful not to touch or disturb it.

'...more evidence to bear out our view. Another intriguing case study has presented itself, quite fortuitously, in the form of two new girls purchased a few days ago. They were being paraded at an Auction as unclaimed runaways. Our local auctioneer is, shall we say, as honest as any of his ilk, and I'm assured proper procedures were followed, in respect of Notifications and so forth. As you know, I can scarce stand to see any slave Burned, but my good Pichenta observes—with perfect truth; she often sees things with a clarity *that is beyond me—that we cannot buy every condemned slave; we would be Bankrupt inside a twelvemonth (she exaggerates, but to effect).*

'Howsoever, some young bravos began to bid, and there was no doubting how they intended to employ their purchase. You know Pichenta: she needed no further Persuasion, and we duly procured the pair for six small notes. An intriguing pair they turn out to be; I shall enjoy showing them to you on the occasion of your next visit (and when shall that be, my dear friend?). They are reluctant to speak of their previous ownership; you can, no doubt, imagine why. And yet, my friend—and here is the enigma—a healthier-looking couple of wenches you never saw.

'I had the Doctor to them, and he assures me there are no marks on either of them, beyond a few recent ones, which can no doubt be explained by the casual handling of the Freebooters who brought them in, or our fine local market-men. Indeed, one of them—and he puts her age at nineteen, which is no doubt a better guess than the girl herself could make—is, he assures me, still a virgin.

'Yes, I thought that would make you sit up a little straighter.

'No doubt they will grow more forthcoming in time, but for the moment we have a Mystery. These girls have surely been abused, yet there is not a mark on either of them. Can you, I wonder, shed any light on it? Have you heard of any owners who choose to practice a purely mental *cruelty? What depraved form might that take?*

'Meanwhile, of course, all our neighbours know of my latest Folly: I should expect my kindness to be repaid any day, runs the gossip. If we're lucky they will merely abscond once more; if we're unlucky they will take the rest of the slaves with them; if we are very unlucky we will be murdered in our beds (some of my dear neighbours would probably consider this to be no more than we deserve!). Oh, my friend, how I shall enjoy proving them wrong! Already our experience furnishes what should be ample evidence that slaves respond better to kind and considerate treatment, but some folk, as you know, can barely see beyond the ends of their own noses. What could be more convincing, or more dramatic, than to take two runaways and to turn them into happy and

contented members of our household? Yes, my friend, this time they will have
to acknowledge at least that there is method in my madness.'

The letter ended there, or rather its composition appeared to have been
broken off. There was no signature. Smiling a little, ironically, she went on
with her dusting.

That evening, as she, Railu and Rhenya were preparing for bed, it came
back to her. "Do you really think our dear Master took us on purely out of
the goodness of his heart?" she asked. "Don't you believe it. He's using us
to prove how clever he is."

"Jerya!" Rhenya looked shocked. "He saved yow from the fire! How can
yow say such things? How can yow know what was in his heart?"

Jerya smiled. "He as good as told me to himself. I read a letter he'd
been—"

Rhenya sat down suddenly on her bed, as if her legs had given way.
"Yow... yow can read?"

"We both can," said Railu.

Rhenya's eyes flickered between the two of them. She seemed to shrink.
"I thought yow were just teasin' when yow said yow'd never had a master
before. But it's true, ain't it?" Her eyes begged them to deny it. "Yow're
freeborn."

"Yes," said Jerya. Rhenya burst into tears.

They sat down either side of her. Railu slid an arm round Rhenya's
slender shoulders.

"What's the matter, dear?" asked Jerya.

"It's my fault," the girl sniffled. "I shouldn't have... oh, but, I did think at
last I was going to have friends."

Over her bowed head Jerya and Railu stared at each other. The words
had pierced both of them to the heart.

"We *are* your friends," Railu said.

Jerya took a firm grip on one of Rhenya's hands. "What difference does
it make? Because we weren't always slaves? Because we can read? We're still
the same people."

"Yow'd know the difference..." Rhenya said faintly: if she finished the sentence at all she did so inaudibly.

"There is no difference," said Railu.

"And we'll prove it," said Jerya. "We'll teach you to read."

CHAPTER 12

RODAL

"I'll save my coin," he'd said, "You go."

The Skipper had given him a long look, then nodded. "Must say I wouldn't mind seeing if that tavern up th'hill's still how I remember it."

So Rodal had settled down to an evening on his own. He'd loitered on deck as long as he could see, checking once again that he could name every rope, and just as importantly, knew what its function was. But as darkness deepened, fog began to creep in from the water, until he could barely see the bows from the wheelhouse. He thought a moment, then went below and collected a couple of lanterns. He lit one and hung it from the forestay near the bow, placed the other in the wheelhouse.

There was nothing moving on the staithe now save the fog itself, which shifted sluggishly, like a dying fish, around the far-spaced lamps along the landward side under the warehouses. It was silent, too, not a sound from the other boats which, though altogether invisible, he knew were moored either side, a hull's length distant.

With nothing to do on deck, and a clammy chill making itself felt, he retrieved the lantern from the wheelhouse and took it below long enough to light the cabin-lamps, returned it to its place, then finally retreated, closing the hatch all but a crack, in case the fog should take a mind to insinuate itself below, too.

He fixed himself a simple meal and brewed coffee. He wasn't devoted to the black drink like his crewmates, but he was learning to appreciate it. It was hot, and he needed warming up a bit. He knew it would help keep him awake, too.

And then, in the rare luxury of a completely quiet moment, he thought about Jerya and Railu. For the most part, of course, his thoughts were nothing new, and he knew there was probably nothing to be gained from going over the ground again. That didn't mean he wouldn't do it.

There was nothing he could do for them without resources. Even most of the gear he'd carried over the mountains himself had gone. Taken, presumably, along with the girls, by that band of ruffians—freebooters, as the Ranger had called them. Blankets, cooking things, spare clothing, fishing-gear, the girls' rucksacks. He'd been left with nothing but the clothes he stood up in, his crossbow, a water-flask, and his knife. And the carcass of a fine fat heather-cock, which he'd immediately discarded before beginning his pursuit. Had their immediate plight been desperate, he might have resorted to stealing food, but as a man of Delven it was a hard thing to even contemplate.

Equally, he could be of no use them, and might even make things worse, by acting rashly. Much as he needed to accumulate coin, he needed knowledge more. Knowledge of how this land worked, some notion of where they might go. And if he wanted to learn about this land and what it held, there were worse ways than taking a river trip through it, down to the great port of Troquharran at its mouth. He would learn by watching, and he would learn by asking questions; his two crewmates had been working their trade for some years—Croudor longer than Grauven—and the Skipper in particular had travelled far, along the other two great rivers as well as up and down the coast nearly to the limits of the Five Principalities. There were charts of all these places in the wheelhouse. It was slow going, learning to make sense of sailing charts, and it frustrated him that they showed so little detail of the land; to a sailor a city or a mountain were barely worthy of note, save when they served as landmarks.

Well, he would see something of Troquharran on this voyage, see as much as he could. It had occurred to him that a large city, particularly a seaport where there must be great coming and going, might be a better place for hiding out than a village or a small country town, where strangers would stand out, would be remarked upon. He'd gathered that the *Levore* also sometimes sailed the coastal passage, Southward, to the still greater city of Sessapont. There might be possibilities there too; he could hardly make a judgement without seeing the place, if the chance offered.

Then the ship rocked.

He knew what it felt like: someone stepping aboard. Because the rail stood well above the staithe, anyone coming aboard tended to pull as they stepped up, pitching their weight forcefully onto it. It still amazed him that a ship which must weigh many tons responded so readily to the movement of something so small as a man, but it did.

He glanced at the chronometer, thinking that more time must have passed than he had thought. He hadn't dozed, he was sure of that. It still took him a few moments to read the time, but the answer was clear: still short of the tenth hour. That would be early indeed for anyone to come back from a night in the tavern, unless there was something wrong.

He moved quickly to the hatch, up on deck. Looking forward, he fully expected to see one or more of them: Grauven, perhaps, cursing the fog as he picked his way tipsily along the cluttered deck. But there was no one.

Puzzled, he peered into the fog. It was as thick, if not thicker than before; he could not make out the bows at all, and the lantern on the forestay, a handful of yards back, was only a diffuse yellow glow in the murk. But still, by its light he saw a vague shape beside the forward hold's hatch-cover. It looked like a man crouching. Rodal knew what sometimes happened when men drank too much. But if someone was puking on the deck, let alone near the cargo, the Skipper would have something to say about it.

He was drawing breath to call out something when a second figure pulled over the rail and onto the deck. The ship rocked again, but not a word was uttered. The hairs on the back of his neck suddenly prickled. This was not a couple of crewmates staggering back after a night carousing; this was *wrong*.

He dropped to a crouch, crept forward until he could slip behind the wheelhouse. Keeping below the bottom of its windows, he slipped silently behind it, across to the port side. There was nothing he could do about the lantern in the wheelhouse save keep out of its light, but at least on this side he would be shaded from the lamps on shore.

He edged forward again, keeping as low as he could. He could find cover until a yard or so back from the rear of the hatch-covers, but then there was nothing. There, he paused behind a tub of spare ropes, peered cautiously around the edge.

At that moment, some indiscernible shift in the night's fickle, barely-discernible, breeze brought words to him; tense, urgent whispers.

"—ain't got all night."

"Shut up. I'm goin' as fast as I—" Then the breeze shifted again and the words were lost. It didn't matter; it was clear to him what was happening. The two men, still just vague lumps of darkness in the fog, were trying to open or break the lock on the hatch. *Thieves...*

He slipped back a step or two. He'd walked all round this deck earlier this same evening, taking note of every rope and fitting. He knew there were a couple of spare belaying-pins along the bulwarks here; he could barely see them in the darkness, extricated one more by feel than by eye. It hadn't the heft he would have chosen, but he was glad to have something in his hand.

Then, since there was no more cover worthy of the name, and since he wanted to be ready to fight, he simply stepped out from behind the barrel and walked round behind the hatch cover. He went as quietly as he could, but without hesitation.

And suddenly the dark lumps were men, and one of them was turning, looking up, crying, "What th' buggerin'..." and in that same instant Rodal darted forward, swinging his improvised cudgel. The man dropped instantly, lay on the deck moaning.

But he saw at once that the second man wasn't going to be dealt with so easily. In the moment it took Rodal to watch his first victim fall, the other was up and back, into the deck-space forward of the hatch-cover; and there was a knife in his hand, glinting in the light of the forward lantern. "C'm'on then, cull," he said, low.

Rodal stepped forward, over the inert figure on the deck, who groaned again. And as he did so, he gave a great shout, at the full of his lungs. "Thieves! Thieves on the *Levore*!"

The man with the knife just laughed. "Dun't think there's anyun about, cull. 'Course, I could be wrong. We din't reckon there was anyun aboard this tub either, but I'm wagerin' I ain't wrong twice."

Rodal didn't bother to reply. He knew well enough, from his years of wrestling, that talking to one's opponent was invariably aimed at distracting him. And the one thing he must not do was allow himself to be distracted. Not allow himself to think of the knife in the man's hand, or the fact that he himself was only armed with a lump of ash-wood. Not allow himself to think longingly of his own knife—probably a longer blade than the one facing him—tucked up at the back of a locker in his berth below. Certainly not allow himself to think of how he had fared the last time he had wrestled.

He took each of those thoughts and ripped it up and tossed the shreds to to the fog. Then he took a step forward. In the light of the gently-swinging lantern he took a better look at his opponent. The man was thin, wiry, shorter than himself. He would have an advantage in reach, at least, and weight, if he could use it. He supposed he was stronger, too. All to the good, but not good enough if the other still had the knife.

The man grinned. Thin face, limned in shifting shadows under the wavering lantern. "Not a fair fight, is it? What say we both throw down our weapons and go at it hand-to-hand?"

"All the same to me. Go on, throw down."

The man chuckled. "Ah, very good. Yow first, I like that."

Rodal did not reply. He knew the man had no intention of dropping his knife. It was all talk, all distraction.

Then the man feinted; a sharp upward sweep of his *left* hand. Against all his better judgement, Rodal's eyes flickered towards it for an instant, and in that same instant the knife-blade flashed out. He recovered fast, swung the belaying-pin hard, and was sure he would have connected if the man hadn't pulled the knife away just as fast as he had struck.

The man was talking again, but this time Rodal wasn't listening. That first flash of the blade had sent his mind into a different place. This was real. This could kill him. He had, rarely, known his mind do this before, most recently on the slipperiest parts of the descent by the cataracts, especially where he had taken a wrong line and had to climb up again. Suddenly he hadn't heard the waterfall any longer, though the torrent was only a few yards away. Nothing had existed but the rock in front of him, the next few feet above, the wrinkles and ripples that his fingers and boots depended on.

It was the same now. Nothing existed but the man facing him, and of him nothing mattered but his hands, and his eyes, and perhaps his feet.

He relaxed his grip on the belaying-pin, just a little. And then in one swift move he flung it, hard as he could, right for the other's eyes.

The fellow was quick, besure; his left hand flashed up and knocked the flying pin away. But Rodal hadn't waited. He was driving forward, everything focused on the knife, and the hand that held it. His weight carried the knife-man back against the bulwarks. Rodal had both hands on his wrist and forearm now and he immediately began to bang the knife-hand on the rail, as hard as he could.

The man's other hand came at his throat, clawing, trying to gain purchase on his windpipe. He ignored it: distraction. Banged the knife-hand again, harder. He wondered if he could hear bones crack, or feel them; the whole thing still seemed to be playing out in silence. The fingers opened and the knife fell away. He didn't even see where it went.

Now we'll see, he thought. He kept his left hand firmly around the other's right wrist, but released his right to grab the hand that was still clutching at his throat. At once the other man lunged forward with his head, and Rodal barely read the intent in time to jerk his head back a fraction. Instead of breaking his nose, the skull-bone connected with his jaw. His teeth rattled, but he imagined the other might feel it too.

Vaguely he felt a foot kicking at his shin, but it barely registered; another distraction. What he needed was a way to change his grip, and in a moment it came to him. One of the earliest lessons: use your opponent's weight against him. His own father's words. "If you're fighting someone heavier than you, you have to. But you can do it when they're lighter, too."

He took a step back, released the empty right hand. As he'd expected, it immediately formed into a fist and the man launched a punch at his head. But this was exactly what Rodal had anticipated, what he was counting on. He leaned sideways, let the punch slide by an inch from his ear, and at the same time dropped to one knee and brought his right hand up, still holding the man's left arm, which he bent double behind its owner's back. The man, driven by his own impetus as well as by Rodal forcing his arm up behind his own back, flipped over Rodal's extended knee and crashed face-first to the deck.

For a moment, he appeared to be stunned, but Rodal wasn't presuming. He grabbed a handful of greasy hair and banged the man's head on the deck, hard, and then again. Only then did he risk releasing him, and darted over to the bin that had sheltered him earlier, from which he grabbed the first ropes that came to hand.

Whatever else you might say of him, the fallen man was made of tough stuff; he was already trying to rise, pushing up on both arms. Unceremoniously, Rodal flung him back down, planted a knee on his arse, grabbed both arms, pulled them together behind his back and began lashing them together. Suddenly he laughed. The man groaned something that might have been a question. Rodal chuckled again. "Just not sure which knots to use."

Only when the knife-man was as securely trussed as he could make him did he think once more of the second would-be thief. Hastily he looked round the starboard side of the deck, but there was no sign of him. He grabbed the bound man by the rope around his ankles and dragged him aft. Stopping by the wheelhouse, he dumped his burden where he could keep an eye on him, then went inside and began to belabour the bell-rope as hard as he could.

✳

"Fraggin' hell, lad," the Skipper kept saying, "Fraggin' hell."

Eventually Rodal's furious clanging of the bell had brought a watchman from one of the warehouses down the quay to investigate; once he had grasped the situation, he had hurried off to summon the Shiriff-men. They, in turn, had questioned Rodal intensively. It had slowly dawned on him that they were not ruling out the possibility that *he* was the intending thief, the bound man on the deck the innocent defender. Realising this, he had urged them to send a man to the tavern where the Skipper and the others had been headed. The Skipper returned a little tipsy but not reeling drunk, and his head soon cleared when he took in what had happened. Any lingering fog was quickly dispersed when he saw the knife, which one of the Shiriff-men had found during a search of the decks.

"And yow went up against that wi' no more'n a belaying-pin? Fraggin' hell, lad."

Shortly after this a more senior Shiriff-man arrived. One look at the knife-man's face, and he grunted with satisfaction. "Yea, I know this cull. Been tryin' to catch him red-handed for a while. If yow'll put yowr mark to a sworn statement, young feller, I make no doubt he'll be goin' away for a while."

"Make my mark?" repeated Rodal. "I can sign my name."

"Can yow now? Well, all th' better. If'n there's any doubt, th' magistrate'll look more favourably on th' word of a lit'rate man. Come by th' Shiriff-house in the mornin' and we'll get it done, try not to delay yowr departure any longer than absolutely need be."

Soon the malefactor was being led away, his legs untied for the purpose but held firmly between two stout Shiriff-men. The little procession quickly disappeared into the fog. but Rodal and the Skipper stayed on deck until the sound of their steps, too, had died away.

Not for the first time, the Skipper clapped him on the shoulder. He shook his head, gingerly, as if he'd progressed directly from tipsy to hung-over. "Fraggin' hell, lad."

CHAPTER 13

JERYA

Through the half-open door she could clearly hear the doctor conferring with Duncal. "It's only ruddy-fever, Squire, I'm sure of it. It always hits harder if you don't get it till you're grown."

"Well, indeed, but whoever heard of slaves who haven't had all the common ailments?"

"Quite. You still haven't learned where they came from?"

"No. But if you're sure it's only ruddy-fever, I had it when I was a lad. I think I may count it safe to have a talk with these girls."

Farewells were said, and soon they heard the doctor's carriage rattling out of the yard. Then the doorway darkened again. Jerya had already observed that Duncal's much-vaunted 'consideration' for his slaves did not extend to asking permission to enter their quarters.

"The good doctor tells me it's only ruddy-fever. Hm, yes, an excellent man. Many doctors turn up their noses at treating slaves." His praise for the doctor was also self-congratulation, thought Jerya: *look what a good Master I am, calling the doctor to my slaves.*

Duncal moved a little closer, stood at the foot of the bed looking down at her. "Hm, yes, ruddy-fever. It is strange you've never had it before. Are you still determined, hm, to speak nothing of your former abode? Hm, I'd be almost disappointed now if you told me everything, but can I not persuade you to let slip even the tiniest clue? I enjoy a mystery, but you've given me nothing to work on. Should I look North, South, or East, pray?"

He'd asked the same question before, Jerya recalled, and he'd laughed at Railu's answer; but what else could she say? With an effort she raised herself up slightly. "Surely, Master, there are four cardinal points?"

He did not laugh this time. Though she knew she might regret her temerity later, the effect was most satisfying. For the first time, she saw his urbanity shaken. His jaw dropped, hung open, and his watery eyes blinked repeatedly. Slowly he regained his outward composure, but Jerya could see he was lost for a reply. He left, shaking his head.

"Was that wise?" asked Railu from the corner, her voice so quiet it was barely audible.

"I don't know," Jerya sighed, sinking back into the pillows. "I can't think straight... but can we go on pretending for ever? Railu, if we keep pretending to be slaves, we *are* slaves."

"Well, what's the difference?"

"What do you mean?"

"Doing what you're told to do, saying what you're supposed to say... it's just the same as before. You know what we said in the College: *we go where we're sent.*"

"Maybe it is. I don't know... but I couldn't spend the rest of my life pretending to be a Dawnsinger, either." *That's why we're here*, she thought. She wondered if Railu was thinking the same, but her friend's answer suggested otherwise.

"Oh, Jerya, everyone pretends. Master Duncal pretends he is all sweetness and generosity. Dawnsingers pretend to command the sun's rising. Rhenya pretends to be happy... do you really believe there's anywhere where people don't pretend?"

"I know there is. Delven. People didn't pretend in Delven."

"Maybe they just pretended too well, had you fooled... Jerya, are you planning to run away again?"

"Oh, you believe it now, do you? *The kindest House in Denvirran Province...*"

Railu just looked at her.

Jerya felt the weight of her limbs. "Ah, well, I don't think I'll be running anywhere for a while."

✳

The following day she felt a little better and sat up in a chair for much of the day. In the afternoon, Railu—who had started first with the sickness, and seemed to have recovered earlier too—came in with a pot of tea. After pouring the drink, she sat looking into her cup for a moment, then suddenly said, "Jerya, listen, I've had enough of running away. Look around you: see how lucky we've been. If we hadn't ended up here, we'd be somewhere much worse. If Duncal hadn't been at the slave market that day we might be dead by now."

"I hope you aren't going to start telling me how grateful I should be. I've had enough of that from Rhenya; she doesn't know any better, poor kid, but surely you..."

"It's not a question of being grateful. But I'm glad to be alive, aren't you?"

"Yes, of course, but is that enough?"

Railu sighed. Her sigh carried more force than the words which followed. "I don't know, Jerya, I don't have all the answers. But I'm not interested in running from here. Not unless you can show me somewhere better to run to. I'm not heading off into the unknown again, with you or anyone else."

✳

"How nice to see you up and about again, Jerya," hummed Duncal. "Fully recovered, I trust? You're no use to anyone if you try and get up too soon and set yourself back again."

"I feel fine, thank you, Master. But Railu's not so good... she was sick this morning."

Even as she said them, the words 'sick' and 'morning' clashed together in her head. She felt a cold grip in her chest. It was certainly possible... suddenly all she could think of was steering Duncal away from the subject of Railu. Casting around for an answer... she was surrounded by it.

"You have many books, Master," she said. "Do they all have to be dusted?"

Duncal chuckled indulgently. "They do, yes, indeed, but not all every week. And, unlike most of my neighbours, my books do not simply sit on the shelves gathering dust."

"May I ask you a question, Master?" He nodded benignly. "I have heard that there is a law about slaves and reading. What is the law exactly, please?"

"Hm, well, let us consult the Statute-book, shall we?" He moved towards the desk, obliging Jerya to step hastily aside, and selected a volume from a shelf alongside. It would be the handiest when he was seated, she observed, surmising that the motley selection of books were shelved there for ease of access, not aesthetics.

He leafed through stiff, heavy pages. "Hm, ah! here we are. Code of Slavery. Hmm... Rights of ownership, hm, procedure for manumission, punitive enslavement, voluntary enslavement, revocation of owner's license... ah, hm, here it is. This is one of the list of offences for which an owner may lose his license and therefore his slaves... 'teaching a slave to read or write, to calculate or compute.' Does that answer your question, hm, Jerya?

"Partly, Master, but... is there anything about one slave teaching another to read?"

He smiled. "Hm, no, I think not, but then who is imagined to have taught the first slave?"

"Why, you mentioned punitive enslavement; that means, surely, that some people are made slaves as adults, rather than born into slavery."

She had not said 'Master', she realised, but Duncal seemed not to have noticed. "Quite true, Jerya, quite true, but in practice punitive enslavement only applies to the poorest of the freeborn—those who can make no alternative redress for their offences—and such people are invariably illiterate anyway; if there are exceptions they are so rare as to be insignificant."

Jerya nodded and said nothing. Duncal closed the Code and slipped it back into its space on the shelf. Then he turned back to face her and suddenly said, "To what do we owe this sudden interest in reading, hm?"

Out of the frying pan into the fire, they had said in Delven. She had diverted Duncal from too close an interest in Railu's condition, but at what cost? She hesitated, unwilling to lie, but unable to frame an honest answer without danger. Duncal smiled again. "I cannot imagine anyone here has been teaching you to read. Whallin? Ha ha. Fantastical. Rhenya?"

She must have made some small movement at the mention of Rhenya. His eyes glinted. "You had better tell me, I think, Jerya."

"Yes, master." He would not be satisfied now without an answer, she saw, and she was snared by her own vow not to speak an untruth. "I can read, Master."

"You can read?" he said, with no more reaction than a lifted eyebrow. "And I presume—I deduce—you've been teaching Rhenya? Railu too?"

"We have both been teaching Rhenya, if that's what you mean, Master."

He laughed, suddenly, shockingly. "No, girl, that's not what I meant, but... So both of you can read, eh? Hm. I don't wish to appear sceptical, but... would you read something for me?"

"If you wish, Master."

"Good. Excellent. Now, hm, what would be a suitable text?"

"Upon my soul," he said, when she had finished. "Upon my soul, I doubt one could find ten men in the parish to read as sweetly as that, and I will wager scarce a single woman, bar my good lady wife." He gave her a shrewd look. "And you accept the praise as no more than your due... hm. It is time, I think, Jerya, for a few more answers from you. Will you now tell me your story, or do I have to squeeze it from you drop by drop?"

"Master, I... I have never sought to deceive. But... I feared if I told you the truth you would think I was lying. Or fantasising."

"I think now I will be the judge of that." His voice, though still mild, held a new undertone of command. "Tell me, Jerya."

She did not doubt now that he would get the answer sooner or later. Better to give it to him than to have it taken from her. "It's a long story if I tell it aright... I... if I may begin with a question. What lies to the West?"

"Why, a few leagues of country like this, then forest; and the land rises to the wild ranges below the high mountains."

"And *beyond* the mountains?"

"Beyond—" For the second time Jerya saw a crack in the benevolent facade. "Beyond the mountains, hm... If you propose to repeat that wild tale then you may save your breath. If you are so determined to preserve your secret, so be it—for a little longer. Only don't imagine, Jerya, that even my patience is inexhaustible. I will have the truth, but I would prefer it to be because you realise you have nothing to lose by telling me."

"So be it... Master," she added, hoping the pause would pass unnoticed. This was no moment to antagonise him. "But please... what tale do you tell of what lies beyond the mountains?

He uttered a small grunt, which might or might not have signified amusement. "Hm. A *very* determined girl. But this is curious... You know so much and you read so well but you do not know the tale?"

"Believe me, Master, I do not."

He sighed, with an unmistakable air of humouring her. "Very well, but briefly. Once—many hundreds of years ago; some say thousands—there were many more people in the world than there are now, and they had riches we can scarcely imagine: carriages which flew through the air, machines by which you could see and speak to someone a thousand miles away... in short, wonders unimaginable. Hm, at such a remove of time it is impossible to distinguish truth from fantasy. But what's fact is that they had a war. A great and terrible war. And along with all their other wonders they had weapons we no longer even understand. Weapons, I say, hm, but poisons might be a better term. Much of the world was poisoned, and some is poisoned still. In some places nothing grows. Some say the barren earth gives off a ghastly light at night, though I take that with a hefty pinch of salt. In other parts things grow deformed and twisted. In others... You can see little or nothing amiss, hm, but if people attempt to live there, their cattle bear two-headed calves, or abort... and not only the cattle. Beyond the mountains is such a place... have you never heard of this tale?"

"I have heard something similar," she admitted. *If East were West and West were East...*

"And so have I, and so has every freeman and slave in the land. I strongly advise you, Jerya, not to tease anyone else with silly tales. There may be some credulous enough to believe you, and that could be dangerous. If they think you've brought the poison with you, hm? Or that, to have survived it, you must be some kind of witch. Yes, 'tis nonsense, to be sure, but ignorant folk act on what they believe, not on what is true.

"Hm, yes, Jerya, and in your shoes I would also keep quiet about reading. Never mind what other masters might say, the other slaves will not like it. Teaching Rhenya, you say. You've kept it from Whallin and Cook, then?"

"Yes, Master, we have done it quietly in our own room."

"Well, then, I daresay no great harm has been done, but still you have been foolish. What good will it ever do her to be able to read, hm? What benefit to outweigh the dangers if anyone else, including other slaves, get to hear of it? Hmm... Jerya, I observe that you and Railu are friends to Rhenya, that you treat her as your equal. This I am pleased to see. She's had a hard hand from others on the estate."

"May I ask why, Master?"

"Yes, you should know. The grievance is that they think she has been favoured unduly, being chosen for an inside slave. Well, those who must toil in the fields whatever the weather are often inclined to a grudge against those who can spend their days indoors; but some take it amiss that Rhenya has been so favoured when still so young. Wholly unfounded, of course; she is as quick-witted as any slave I have ever handled. And more willing than any, more eager to please. Why then, do you think she is still clean-shaven? Not for any failing in my esteem, oh no, indeed I told her, perhaps a twelve-month past, she might commence to grow the crest. Not ten days had gone by, and it had barely become visible, when I found her one morning clean-shaven again. She was most reluctant to explain why, but from what she said and other things known to me, I was able to deduce that other slaves had... in ways of their own, hm, made her life unpleasant. For... shall we say, 'getting above herself'. Now, hm, imagine if they were to learn that she could read?"

"Then do you forbid us to teach her any more, Master?"

"Forbid? You should know, Jerya, I do not like to forbid anything. But I say you have been foolish to teach her and would be even more foolish to go on teaching her. Now that I have explained the position to you.... it can bring her no happiness and may bring her pain and sorrow. If you care for her, you cannot want that, hm?"

Chapter 14

Rodal

If they hadn't been so busy, Rodal would have liked to climb the mast. It was hard, from the water, to tell just how great a city Troquharran was. Barring one central hill, insignificant compared to the one occupied by the College in Carwerid, there seemed to be no real rise behind the waterfronts to hoist the farther reaches into view, and few towers of any height peered over the rows of warehouses, shipyards, and factories.

He had little to judge by but the lengths of the quays themselves, and the number of craft either tied up or moving on the river. These were a great study, but they were also the reason they themselves were kept busy. He was learning anew just how tricky, and potentially hazardous, it could be, manoeuvring a sailing-vessel in crowded waters with little wind to give steerage way.

Therefore he leaned on the great black sweep-oar, fully alert to respond at once to the Skipper's call of 'Pull starboard' or 'Back starboard', to throw his entire weight against the shaft in whichever direction was required. There was little space in his mind for anything else, but a small part of him was still aware of all the activity on the river.

Dead ahead of them and pulling away with every stroke from its double ranks of sweeps, there was a great ship, easily twice the length of the *Levore* and far higher above the waterline, with two masts on which the sails hung loosely-bundled on cross-members. "Bound for th' Out-Isles, that brig," Grauven had said earlier as they'd first got a clear sight of the larger vessel beyond the host of smaller craft milling around.

There were other wherries much like the *Levore*, and smaller versions too, down to about thirty feet in length. Innumerable little skiffs flitted around, some under sail but most with one or two oarsmen. Of course, he thought, there was no bridge, and people must need to cross the river all the time.

Then another call came from the Skipper and he had to focus once again on handling the heavy sweep.

"That's it, I reckon, lads," said the Skipper when they'd finally docked and unloaded. Already it was twilight; the larger vessels all seemed to have tied up, or left the river, but there were still plenty of skiffs plying to and fro, each now carrying a lantern on a pole in the bows. The lights on the far shore casting long trails on the water, those little sparks of light moving across them, patterns forming and scattering and reforming as the surface broke and healed; he'd not seen the like before, and for a moment it brought a shiver to his spine.

The Skipper summoned them below, and paid them off, a little pouch of heavily-clinking coin for each of them. "But I'll be glad if yow'll sign on again next time..." He looked around, one by one, and they all nodded in turn, Rodal included. It was a kind of ritual, he realised. "I'll be in touch, then. Let me know right away if yow're not at th'usual places."

Grauven and Croudor filed out with a few gruff words, nodding at Rodal. "Now, lad," the Skipper said when only the two of them remained, "I'm guessin' yow dun't have a place to stay?"

"No, sir. I was wondering if I could..."

"Stay aboard and mind th' ship, is it?" The older man grinned. "Yea, and right well yow did at that. But there's no need; she's empty now, and there's a good watch on these wharves anyhows."

He saw Rodal's face and went on, "But yow're thinking where shall yow go? Well, sohappen I owe yow still, and I'd like to pay yow back by takin' yow to my house as my guest tonight. Right after we get yow tallied up."

※

Rodal had felt something close to dread, but getting 'tallied up' proved to be an anti-climax. The tally was a metal disc, larger and thinner than any coin he'd seen, which most people wore on a leather thong or a chain about their necks, under their clothing. Failure to show a tally on demand to one of the Monitors could have dire consequences, but apparently under normal circumstances this was rare. "Dun't think I ever bin challenged," the Skipper said. However, if you got into any trouble, or fell under any kind of suspicion, lack of a tally would lead to immediate expulsion from the city, if not worse.

For a man already in possession of a seaman's ticket, and vouched for by a respected Captain, issue was a mere formality and they were in and out of the Monitors' watch-house by the dockyard gates in no more than ten minutes. He checked the clock on the wall as they entered and as they left, pleased with himself for reading the time with facility as well as for surviving the tallying process.

※

There were two children, a boy of eight or so and a girl of perhaps twelve. Both sat rapt and open-mouthed as their father told the tale of Rodal's deed; and then he himself was obliged to relate it in more detail. Even with the help of good food and better ale, it was hard to feel comfortable speaking of it. However he tried to keep to the plain truth, it felt like boasting.

"Was yow scared?" asked the girl, Eriyan, when he'd finished.

"*Were* yow," amended her mother, a well-rounded, kindly woman.

"I wouldn't be scared," said her brother, Karren.

"You should be," he said. "I was." The lad's face fell. "Up against a man with a knife like that... I reckon I'd be a fool not to be scared. Scared made me... made me think about nothing but what I needed to think about."

"Same in th' ship," said the Skipper, leaning back in his chair. "Nothin' shameful 'bout being scared when a storm comes at yow in an open estuary, or yow catch a tide wrong and it's pushin' yow toward th' bank. Where there's shame, or not, is in how yow deal with it."

Rodal nodded. "My people used to say, only a fool isn't afeared on a high crag, or facing a wild stag. A man knows he's afeared but does what he needs to anyhow."

"Does afeared mean scared?" asked Karren.

Rodal grinned. "Besure, lad, reckon it does."

"Yow talk funny."

"Don't be cheeky, Karren," said Eriyan, at which Rodal saw her parents exchange amused glances over the children's heads.

He just smiled. "It's true, though. I do talk different. People do, in different places."

"D'yow come from a very long way away?"

"I reckon I do," he said. "About as far West as you can get, in the mountains." It wasn't strictly the truth, but it was as close as he dared approach.

Even so, he had to answer a series of questions from both youngsters, and just a few from their mother. He knew he had to be careful, but as long as he wasn't too specific as to where Delven lay, and didn't mention Dawnsingers, he thought he'd be safe enough.

Next morning he slept late, in the little attic room they'd given him, and when he finally came down he found only the Skipper sitting at the table.

The older man greeted him warmly enough, but Rodal sensed something was not quite right.

"I hope I didn't—" he began, not knowing how he was going to finish the sentence. Fortunately, perhaps, the Skipper cut him off.

"Nay, lad, you've not erred, nowise. It's Eriyan. This mornin' she couldn't stop talkin' 'bout yow." He looked down into his coffee-cup, caged in those two broad, stained hands.

"Talking about me?"

"Yea, lad. Most of it nowhere to any point, but some of it... well, sohappen, it come that she asks if yow was married, and I said no, I was sure yow ain't. And then she asks if yow was betrothed, and I had to say I ain't sure. And then she goes very quiet, even more'n usual."

Rodal stared at him, picking over his words, piecing together what lay behind them. It was hardly shocking to him; it was common enough for girls in Delven to be married at sixteen, occasionally at fifteen, and it was perfectly normal for there to be an understanding between the families well before that. It was less usual for a girl to take the initiative, especially one as young as twelve, but even that wasn't altogether unheard of, and it would most often spark merriment rather than shock.

But he knew very well—he made a point never to forget—that he wasn't in Delven now. He didn't know how such things were done here; until last night, he had, he realised, barely spoken to a female since he'd last been with Jerya and Railu. It had been a pleasure to have their company again, both the bustling, hospitable, mother and the shy, near-silent, daughter. Shy, at least, had been his impression last evening.

He didn't know how such things were done and in any such case his habit, which had served him well enough so far, was to say as little as possible, to listen, and to learn.

The Skipper looked at him, straight. *He's a good man,* Rodal thought. *I do not want to offend him or give him cause to think less of me.* "So, I suppose, lad, first question might be, *are* yow betrothed?"

He thought just a moment. He wanted to be truthful and, he thought, a truthful answer might serve very well. "I'm not betrothed as such, no, but there is someone... where I come from we'd say there's an understanding between us."

The Skipper smiled. "An understandin'... yea, I like that."

"She's promised to wait a year," he found himself saying then. It wasn't precisely true, but he hoped close enough. "A year from when we parted. That was..." He figured. *Gossan, it was...* "Bit more'n a month ago." *A month gone already...*

"Come back wi' a bit o'coin in yowr pocket, is that th' idea? Set yowrself up a bit..." He half-rose, leaned forward, clapped Rodal on the shoulder. "It's none so far from what I did; sixteen year ago, it'll be now. Yea, and if she waits for yow like she's said, it's a good sign she knows how to keep a promise. I had one lad served with me a few year ago, up-river lad he was—not yowr river, one o'th' others—similar kind o'tale, but the girl didn't hold to her word; he come back and found she'd gone and betrothed herself to some other feller. I found him th' day after we'd docked, blind drunk outside some tavern in th' middle o'th' afternoon, ready to weep at th' drop of a hat. Said she'd broken his heart. I told him, if she was the sort as couldn't keep her word, he was better off without. He wasn't for hearing it, o'course, not then, but I ran across him again two or three year later and he told me I'd been dead right."

He paused, then laughed. "And hearken to me ramblin' on... Listen, lad, I think right well o'yow. And if yow was to tell me yow'd taken a proper shine to my lass, young as she is, I'd be thinkin', well, she's too young to wed and too young to be betrothed, but I don't know but I might talk to my wife about some kind o'... what was yowr word? Some kind o'understandin'."

He sat back in his chair. "But yow've an understandin' with another girl already, so there's an end to it."

Rodal nodded. "It's not that I don't... she's a lovely girl, I can see that."

"Yea, she is. Apple o'my eye and all that... and bein' as that's what she is, I'd be more'n happy to keep her by me a few years yet."

"Of course..."

"And she'll... her age, she'll get over it quick enough. Might be a few nights o'tears. And might be I'll let my better half deal wi'that. So..." He scratched his stubbled jaw, the sound clear in the silent house. "Only thing is, I'd'a been happy to have yow stay here longer. Till I can pick up another commission; should only be a few days. But if Eriyan's goin' to be mooning after yow and givin' hersel' ideas..."

"It'd be better if I weren't here," he finished, seeing how awkward the Skipper was finding the whole conversation.

"Yea, lad," the other said gratefully. "It's th' only reason, like. Otherways, yow'd be welcome to stay as long as may be. More than welcome. And I know I speak for Gretyel, too."

"I understand. And I thank you for it. But I'm sure I can find another place."

"Yea, well... there's always taverns wi' beds goin'. And some o'them are clean enough and respectable enough, and no doubt I could point yow at one o'that kind. But clean and respectable don't come as cheap as yow might wish in this town. It's not like up-river. And, yow bein' so keen to save up yowr coin, I'm thinkin' there's no reason why yow shouldn't sleep aboard the *Levore*, sohappen it suits yow...?"

"It suits me very well," he said, thinking how the berth closed around him and over him. It really wasn't that different from a cave-cell, except that it sometimes rocked. But the rocking hadn't disturbed him; after the first night or two he'd even begun to find it lulling.

He'd been inordinately pleased with himself for describing Carwerid as 'tumultuous'. The only trouble was, it left him with no word adequate to describe Troquharran. Everything he'd thought and felt on first seeing Carwerid was doubled or trebled here. The city was bigger, busier, noisier, and most definitely smellier. No matter how far he walked, unless he came back to the waterfront, there seemed to be no end to it.

Perhaps, he thought, no one had found a word, and in the end they had given up trying, and that was why it was mostly called, simply, the Red City. It was apt enough, he supposed, though in a whimsical moment he thought that Red-Wall-and-Blue-Roof-City would be more accurate; crimson brick and blue-grey slate were the main materials.

Walking... he had plenty of time for that. He wasn't ungrateful for being able to sleep on board the *Levore*, but there was nothing to keep him there during the day, and it seemed it would be a day or two yet before the Skipper had negotiated the next contract. Croudor was at home with his wife and Grauven visiting his family, somewhere outside the City (so there must be an end to it, somewhere); he had no one to tempt him into the taverns which seemed to take up at least the ground floor of every second or third building along the streets just back from the waterfront itself. And walking was free.

It was unfortunate that he couldn't have continued to enjoy the hospitality of the Skipper's household. It was clear enough that, if things had been otherwise, he would have been welcome to stay until the *Levore* sailed again, and that would have included most of his meals, too. But it wasn't possible, so he would have to shift for himself or go hungry.

There were a few perishables left in the galley lockers, two-thirds of a loaf, a couple of apples, some cold meat. He reasoned that none of it would keep, would go to waste if he didn't eat it; that was enough to keep him going for the first day. As he roamed the Red City, he tried to gain some sense of where one could eat, or obtain food, at a reasonable price. He didn't want to spend a penny more than he needed, but he had to keep his strength up.

He had learned pretty quickly about handling coin, beginning on his first journey with Jerya, and then in Carwerid. (He smiled a little as he recalled Annyt's demeanour in the role of teacher; she'd showed a firmness, even a sternness, quite different to her normal sunny aspect.) He'd gained a fair sense, there, of what a fair price might be for a mug of ale or a platter of bread and cheese, what a labourer or a bartender might earn. But here on the other side of the mountains, beyond the division of the world, everything was different. The coins were different; different sizes, different metals, different names. A five was a ten with a hole punched through the centre. Others weren't even circular. And then there were 'notes', mere scraps of paper which—against all logic—were purportedly worth more than the grandest coin. He'd risked a few questions, in the galley of the *Levore* at some mooring or other, thinking that his guise as a lad freshly down from the deepest backlands, somewhere in the mountains, would excuse his ignorance. Croudor, in his usual cheerful way, had grunted something about, "No s'prise, th'likes on us dun't get to see them notes often anyhows. Ne'er mind hang on to 'em."

Still, he was a long way from confident as yet. On the first day he left the notes the Skipper had given them on paying-off stashed in a rolled-up jerkin in his locker, taking only a selection of coins in his pocket. He recalled something Jerya had said on their first journey, resolved anew to watch, listen, learn. He recalled a word Annyt had taught him too, and resolved he wouldn't get fleeced.

Thinking of Jerya, and then of Annyt, reminded him, uncomfortably, of promises and duty. He had promised Annyt he would return within a year. *If I don't, I am dead*: he hadn't said it, but it had been in his mind; nothing short of death would come between him and keeping his word. He'd made no such clear-cut pledge to Jerya and Railu; if anyone, it was the Dawnsinger he'd made a promise to, but even that had been nothing more definite than *I have to go after them, don't I?*

Still, he could entertain no doubts: he still had a duty to them. Travelling in lands he had never even dreamed of a month ago, exploring a great city like Troquharran, might be fascinating, but he could not lose sight of the real reason he was here in the first place.

Climbing a set of steps that short-cut the long windings of the streets around the central hill, he began to wonder. If—*when*, he corrected—he returned to the lands around Drumlenn, made his way to the Duncal estate; when he extricated Jerya and Railu from their captivity... where would they go then? It had been clear since his first day in Drumlenn that runaway slaves were pursued with vigour. What had been seen as unusual in Jerya and Railu's case was that the 'runaways' were unclaimed, that no one had reported them 'missing'. Well, there was a reason for that, but he could see how the only ones who'd understand or believe it were the three of them.

Early in the trip down-river, the crew of the *Levore* had gotten the notion that his obscure backland home was too poor to have slaves. Grauven had sounded intrigued by the idea of a place where everyone was free, but Croudor would never willingly miss an opportunity to pour cold water: "'S fine to be free, but p'raps not so much if all yow're free to be is poor."

Clearly, extracting the girls from the slave-quarters, or wherever they were housed at this Duncal place—which he had never seen and of which he had only the vaguest notion—was only going to be the first step, and likely not the hardest. What came next? Where could they ultimately aim for? Unless he could find some kind of answer, there might be nothing he could do for them.

Well, one possibility would be to return to the West. He had no idea if the girls would accept that; perhaps Railu would entertain the notion, but he wasn't so sure about Jerya. *Who could ever be sure of Jerya?* he wondered. In any case it would not be without problems. He had a good enough idea how they could get past Delven, taking a wide loop to the North and coming down to the lowlands that way before approaching the first town. It would mean spending a night or two in the wild, but that was nothing to them, now. And Unsung lands no longer held even the shadow of terror: why, even Troquharran, this great, more-than-tumultuous city, was Unsung.

There were plenty of places where they'd never been, where no one would recognise them. At least, no one would know who they were; but there was a problem with what they were, or had been; the girls, that was. West or East, a bald head was a problem. Jerya's hair would, it seemed, grow back in time, but there had been no sign of it with Railu. Maybe, he supposed, if she always kept her head covered...? Women did so in Delven, and it had been nearly the same in Thrushgill. In Carwerid many women went bare-headed, or covered their hair only partially—like Annyt, he thought with a pang—more by way of adornment than concealment. No, Annyt's bright ribbons and kerchiefs set off her dark curls, they didn't obscure them.

Still, even in Carwerid it wasn't unknown for women to cover their hair. And here in Troquharran, he was noticing as he strode on up a wide curving street shaded by occasional trees, not only did some women cover their hair, but a few veiled their faces, something he had not observed in Drumlenn. His impression here was that the veiled ones were the best-dressed, presumably the wealthiest.

Here, he concluded, it could be that as many one woman in ten was veiled. Very soon he'd had to correct himself; one in ten of the *free* women were veiled. Some covered their hair but not their faces, some wore both headcloths and veils; some wore veils but exposed their hair. But he saw none who joined a veiled face with a shaven head.

With rare exceptions, the veils did not completely conceal the wearer's face. They were of net or gauze, fringed with beads along the bottom, at a level between breasts and collar-bone. The weight of the beads must help keep the veil in place, he realised, as a playful gust skittered down the street. Many of the net-veils seemed no more than a token, hiding nothing. Some of the thicker gauzes gave only a vague shadowy impression of the face beneath, or so he concluded as he passed their wearers. He had a notion that it wouldn't do to stare, so he was taking it all in in brief passing glances, not turning his head, just letting his gaze slide casually over the women.

Of course, it was one thing to think that girls who had borne the marks of slaves might be able to disappear among the city crowds. And he was far from knowing enough to know if it really could be that simple. Whatever the reality of that, first he would have to get them to Troquharran; and thus far he had not the slightest idea how he might accomplish that. Furthermore, he recalled, they would need to be tallied. It had not been a problem for him, with the endorsement of a respected citizen; but it might be a different matter for the girls, with no one but an unpropertied deckhand to vouch for them. And if suspicions were aroused, questions asked... it could all come crashing down.

Well, he told himself, *there's plenty more places you ain't seen yet.*

CHAPTER 15

JERYA

The trouble with Rhenya, thought Jerya wryly, was that her enthusiasm was infectious. It made it harder to maintain due scepticism about anything, whether it was a hot bath once a week, or the true value of a hand-me-down piece of clothing.

"In some houses th'slaves always dress like this to serve meals," said Rhenya, holding up a black skirt embroidered with swirls of glittering gold. "Try this one..."

She helped Jerya with the unfamiliar hook-and-eye fastenings, then stepped back with a considering look. "It's a bit low on th' hip, but that's all right, elsewise it'd be too short, yow bein' tall-like. Walk around a little. Will it stay up?"

"I think so," said Jerya after circling the room. "What else is there?"

"Else?" said Rhenya with a surprised little laugh. "Only the jools."

Jewels they were not, only beads of coloured glass or painted wooden discs. She was happy nonetheless to let Rhenya drape half a dozen strings around her neck; it was surprising how much less naked they made her feel, but still... "Do they really expect us to parade around like this?"

❄

They had bathed—in water almost *too* hot, as opposed to the usual tepidity—they had shaved with new blades and more than usual care, and they had rubbed each other's shoulders and arms and scalps with a perfumed oil that left their skins glistening slightly. In spite of herself, Jerya could not but notice how beautiful Rhenya was. Her dark skin—always glossy, when not coated with dust from some particularly dirty task—shone like polished wood, shone every bit as brightly as the ropes of red and blue and yellow beads that gathered between and only half-concealed her high, round breasts. And because she was growing daily more fond of the girl and knew the words would please her, she could not keep the thought to herself. "You do look lovely, Rhenya."

Rhenya looked at first more startled than pleased, her smile blossoming slowly. "Oh, *thank* yow, Jerya."

"I mean it. It always pleases me to look at you and I should have said so before. But tonight—all this is an invitation to look at you again."

"Jerya, if'n I look half as lovely as yow, I'll be right proud."

"Oh, nonsense," she said, and tried to laugh away the flattery, but it gnawed at her thoughts all the same.

"How long till the guests arrive?" she asked without thinking. She was not prepared for Rhenya's reply: "About half an hour. Maybe a little longer."

How strange it still seemed. Rhenya could not read, seemed reluctnat to learn, yet she thought nothing of reading a clock. How strange it seemed, that even a slave—someone with no status whatever in this world's eyes—might possess knowledge that in the other land was strictly reserved to Dawnsingers; at least as far as she knew. In Carwerid there were the great bells to sound the hours and the quarters, but in her few forays into the city she had not seen a clockface in any public place, nor in the taproom or parlour at the tavern.

She should have been prepared, of course: the house was full of clocks, and she had already learned just how much it ran by the clock. And, yes, even before they'd reached the house for the first time, Whallin had referred to hours. Still, it was hard to adjust.

Did it matter, she wondered? Did it make any difference what particular knowledge was reserved for the privileged? Horology, calendrics, like astronomy and mathematics, were held close by the Guild of Dawnsingers because they were potentially dangerous—but were reading and writing any less dangerous?

Her thoughts were interrupted by the awareness of Rhenya's voice. "I'm sorry," Jerya responded, "I was miles away."

Rhenya just laughed softly. "I said, are yow sure yow know what to do tonight?"

"Not at all. I'll just get by, I expect, by watching you. As usual."

"No, listen," said Rhenya earnestly. "When they arrive th' fine folks'll be having drinks, and we'll wait on 'em in th'parlour. Most on'em will of brung their own slaves, so they'll go into th'kitchens and get their instructions. Cook'n'Railu'll tell'em where to wait and what order to line up in, and so on. During dinner we'll serve each course to the Master and Mistress, and anyun what ain't brung their own slaves, and th'rest of the time we'll stand behind them, take th' dishes away, do anything else they need. Afterwards th'ladies'll shift into th'drawing-room for a while." She smiled proudly. "That's why it's called a drawing-room, yow know."

"I don't follow."

Rhenya's smile broadened, delighted to know something Jerya didn't. "'Cos it's *with*drawing room, prop'ly. Ask me, best plan'll be if yow go with th'ladies, whiles I stay in th'dining-room with th'gentlemen."

"Whatever you think best."

"Once yow've brung in th'coffee, if'n no one needs yow, stay by th'wall, close behind th'Mistress, fetch her anything she wants. But if one of the others gives yow an order, less Mistress says 'gainst it, yow do it for them just the same."

As she rattled off more advice, Jerya kept nodding, though really she was little the wiser. Well, it would be what it would be. At least Rhenya had thought the strings of broad polished discs acceptable, and she had spent a little more time arranging them, overlapping the strands to create a more stable structure. As long as she didn't have to make any sudden or exaggerated movements, she thought, she should stay reasonably decent.

Though what the aunts in Delven would think of this... She didn't know whether to laugh or cry.

＊

In at least one way, she and Rhenya were in the minority. Every other slave arriving was Crested, their bands of hair elaborately braided, often with beads or coloured cloth worked in too. They varied in age from mere girls, clearly younger than Rhenya, up to at least fifty, though most were young women. And all, that she could see, *were* women. *Where*, she wondered, *are all the male slaves?* In Duncal's household, all the house-slaves (which now meant herself, Railu, Rhenya, and the old Cook) were female, but was this the case everywhere?

Then for a long time she was too busy to think of anything much beyond her duties; not tripping over her over-long skirt, which she had to keep hoisting higher on her hips; not colliding with scurrying slaves who didn't know the turnings of the passages as well as she did. As they cleared the first course, she saw slaves walking briskly out of the hall, then slowing in the corridor to scoop up whatever remained on the plate: a scrap of fruit, a sliver of meat. She understood at once; she had eaten nothing since an early lunch, and there was no indication in anything she had seen, or in anything Rhenya had said, of any provision for feeding the slaves that evening.

After each succeeding course—she kept count, and there were nine in all—the same happened; a hasty devouring of scraps, mopping of bowls, picking over of bones, in whatever time could be extracted from progress along the few metres of passage; the slaves might slow to do this, but she saw none ever come to a complete standstill.

Since her Mistress's appetite was modest, Jerya was able to freely sample all the dishes. She might, she thought with a smile, by the end have eaten more than her Mistress, if with a deal less dignity. And it meant that little of the fine food, which had been prepared with such labour from all four of them, would go to waste.

Rich food, strange flavours, but how could Rhenya speak of this as a treat? Jerya found it, not exciting but tantalising, only hinting at what it might be like to sit at ease with such fine food—and fine wine, for there was none of that for the slaves.

She watched and imitated and made no obvious mistakes through the meal; certainly, no one at the table paid her the slightest attention. Then all the ladies rose and left the dining-room, taking their attendant slaves with them. For the first time Jerya was separated from Rhenya. She quelled a flare of anxiety and followed her Mistress's blue-gowned back. The *ladies,* of course, did not expose their breasts, though she noticed many wore dresses cut low in that region, sometimes arranged so as to squeeze their breasts together, and even suggest that they were about to burst out. She wondered at this. Slaves might have little or no choice about exposing their flesh; these fine ladies surely did.

In the drawing-room, she followed the example of others and stationed herself a pace behind the Mistress's elbow, keeping her eyes cast down. Mistress Pichenta was in a group of five ladies, more or less the same age, their conversation at first of little apparent interest and only partly intelligible anyway.

But then it became much clearer, and she could not help but flick a glance up at the speaker. "This one's new, ain't it, Pichenta? One of the runaways you—yes, we are speaking of you, trull, with your permission?"

The other women all laughed. Jerya dropped her eyes again. She could feel a flush in her cheeks and hoped it would not show in the soft lighting. At least it might be taken for embarrassment rather than what it really was: rage.

"It looks a strong enough piece, Pichenta," the voice went on. She had barely looked at its owner, only caught the briefest glimpse of someone tall and thin and pale, with hair so blonde it was nearly white, piled high and interwoven with black ribbons (they might be blue, or some other dark colour, but in the subdued light they appeared black). For some reason she could not stop herself confounding the woman with Freilyn; they shared the icy colouring, if nothing else. She had never really warmed to Freilyn, even before there had been reason for them to differ. Now she began to think she ought to reappraise her. She had never looked at Jerya as coldly as this woman did.

The speaker went on; her voice was smooth and musical, even—disconcertingly—beautiful. "I'd have thought you'd put it to work in the fields."

"There's plenty of work in the house," her Mistress replied. Jerya had observed her closely enough, over the past weeks, to be sure now: she, too, did not like this pale woman whose lovely voice spoke ugly words. "We've been asking too much of an old woman and a young girl for years—and of course we're thinking of manumitting the old one now."

"My dear, if you're going to *ask* your slaves, you might as well manumit the lot of them." They all laughed at this, but it was muffled, twittering laughter, strangely like the hushed laughter which was the most the slaves ever allowed themselves.

"Do you really *ask* your slaves, Pichenta?" one of the other women inquired as the laughter died.

"Why should we not? It costs nothing."

Why not indeed, thought Jerya, almost bursting to say it out loud. *But if they're not free to refuse, it comes to the same thing, just dressed up prettier.*

"Don't start that old roundelay *again*," said the pale voice. "I'm more interested in this new development. Where did they run away *from*?"

"As I'm sure you know, no claims were made, and no fugitives answering their description had been reported."

"I know that my dear, and yet it stands to reason: they ran away from *somewhere*. Likely their master just didn't think it worth the expense of sending for them and the trouble of flogging them—probably for the hundredth time. I hear they cost you six small, and I hazard their former master valued them less than that. About six less, I'll warrant."

Jerya controlled herself by thinking hard about Freilyn, and what an innocent and gentle soul she now seemed to have been. She could not imagine she'd ever see Freilyn again, but she would try to be friendlier if she did.

"I have two things to say in answer," her Mistress responded. "First, whatever place they come from, they seem unable to speak of it. We can get no sense from them on that subject, none whatsoever. Secondly, under *our* regime, they have so far shown themselves to be quick, attentive, strong, and willing. I think the facts speak for themselves."

"Well, my dear, let this fact speak for itself. This object lesson. What's its name?"

"*Her* name is Jerya."

"Well, then, Jerya... you *can* speak, can't you?"

"Yes, my lady." She knew 'my lady' was the correct form of address, but the words tasted like sour milk. The taste of a lie.

"So, whatever dire cruelty was perpetrated on you, it didn't include tonguing... turn round, trull." She turned slowly, puzzled. "And no scars, either—or are they under your skirt, hm?"

This 'hm' was nothing like the Squire's absent-minded murmurings: it was a demand, meaning something like, *'answer me quickly or I shall be angry'*. "No, my lady."

"Well, then, Jerya, what of the place you were before?"

"My lady?" The woman 'tsk'ed but asked mildly enough, "What was your master's name, for a start?"

"I cannot say, my lady."

"*Can't* say? Can't *say*? You can speak—you can speak all right! And too sweetly for my liking. Where did you learn to talk like that? Your master's name, now."

"Truly, my lady, I cannot say."

"What d'you mean, trull? *Won't* say—or don't know? If you know the name, I order you to say it."

You order me? thought Jerya. *If you order me now, what were you doing before?* But she said nothing.

"Did you understand me?"

"Yes, my lady."

"Then you ask us to believe you never knew your master's name..." She appealed to the wider audience: "Is this possible...? Well, what was your name, trull? Your full name, now."

"I do not understand, my lady. The only name I have is Jerya." There were two or three sharp intakes of breath.

She had managed to keep her eyes lowered so far, but she caught a sudden eye-glitter as her interlocutor's attendant slave raised her head just enough to look at her. The girl was as tall and thin as her Mistress, but younger, and darker-skinned; darker than herself or Railu but not near as dark as Rhenya. Her look was intense, and surely unfriendly; it seemed to match the venom that lurked beneath the honey in her Mistress's voice. Jerya tried to smile, as if to say, 'there is no quarrel between you and me' but could not unfreeze her features in time.

"This is too much, Pichenta. The trull doesn't even know its own name."

"This is the first time she's been with anyone not of our own household since she we acquired her," the Mistress said. "She has never had need to use her full name."

The pale woman grunted. "She should still know it. Yea, with all the kindness you've shown her, she should know it if she knows what gratitude is." She paused, then added, "And are we supposed to believe that in all her previous life she never met anyone outwith her own household either? Is that the case, Jerya bey-Duncal?"

So that's my name, is it? And what does 'bey' mean? 'Property of'? If I use that name I'm accepting that I am property.

"Jerya bey-Duncal," the woman said, almost hissing in her anger. "I asked you a question!"

"I'm sorry, my lady, I was trying to... No, before this year, I do not believe I had met anyone outside the... the household." Taking Delven as one household—and why not?—it was close enough. And if the thought of Delven, on top of everything else, made her voice wobble, why try to hide it?

"It's like getting blood from a stone, but I do believe we're getting somewhere. And in this household where you were never allowed to leave, whose master's name you never knew—"

I'll tell no lies, but I'll let you make them up for yourself, she thought.

"—What were your duties?"

"I had a share of all the duties, my lady. I mean, all the women's duties. Spinning and weaving, carding wool—"

"Yes, yes, I know what women do. Were you... overworked? Driven too hard? Did your fingers bleed? Did you work till you dropped?"

"No, my lady."

"We are narrowing the scope of this terrible cruelty, then. What were your quarters like?"

"My quarters, my lady? I don't understand."

"Where did you sleep, then? Indoors or out?"

"I... I believe it would be called indoors."

"You *believe*? What the devil do you mean by that?"

"It was in a cave, my lady."

There were suppressed exclamations, as if of horror, but she remembered her little cell in Delven's heart: clean, dry, warm, safe; and because she had hardly thought of it in a long time, a tear crept from one eye.

"I think that's enough for now," said one of the other women. "The girl's obviously distressed."

"More to the point, they'll be joining us soon," said the inquisitorial woman, who clearly cared nothing for any distress Jerya might or might not be feeling. "But tell me, Pichenta, haven't we learned more than your gentle inquiries ever taught you?"

"A trifle, perhaps. I don't know that we are really any the wiser. But I thank you for your diligence on my behalf."

"On your behalf? You flatter yourself, m'dear. If you care to pick up runaways from nowhere, take them into your household, never even enquire where they came from... Well, it's your affair, m'dear; they're your property. But I wouldn't turn my back on 'em."

Above the soft chuckles which greeted this remark came the sound of the doors being thrown open, and the assembled women—ladies and slaves—began to move out of the room.

CHAPTER 16

JERYA

Jerya had merely stepped out into the yard for a minute's fresh air when she heard a sudden crash—wood on wood, by the sound—and, the merest instant after, a cry of pain. She darted into the carriage-house and in one glance perceived two things:

—*The horses, in their traces, but shuffling and stamping and showing the whites of their eyes...*

—*Whallin, at the rear of the carriage, face bloodless under the tan, cradling one wrist with the other hand...*

Two things, both calling for immediate attention, and only one of her. She needed help, but dared not shout for it; that might be the very thing that would tip the horses from nervous agitation into full-blown panic.

"I'll get help," she said, not raising her voice, hoping he could hear, and in the same second was turning away, hoisting up her skirts, running full tilt back across the yard, into the kitchen.

Rhenya looked up, startled: old Cook, in her chair in the corner, was still reacting as Jerya rapped out her few quick words: "Fetch Railu. Carriage-house. *At once.*" She knew the Master and Mistress weren't in the house; they'd left to walk up to the home-farm less than half an hour ago.

Then she whirled out again, skirts flailing to catch up, raced back to the carriage-house, only slowing as she neared the horses. Now, a choice.

Whallin was still standing, she saw; swaying a little, perhaps, but upright. *Horses first, then.*

"Hey," she said, "Hey, hey, hey." Probably it didn't matter what words she used; she didn't think horses understood words. But they surely did understand tone of voice, and the right words would help *her*; the right words calmed her, put calm into her voice, her bearing. "He's hurt his arm a bit. That's all. That's all, that's all, that's all. Nothing to fret about."

The great eyes settled on her; the whites no longer showed, but the feet still stamped and shuffled. She took a short step closer. "You know me, don't you? Seen me before, anyroad, haven't you. I'm Jerya. Came from over the mountains. Nobody believes me, but I did. Well, maybe *you* believe me, eh?"

She babbled on, keeping her voice soft, gently crooning. Hands down at her sides, eyes on the horses, but not staring too directly.

Voices behind her, the slap of sandals on the cobbles. She half-turned. "Whallin's hurt—but go round the long way, eh?" With that she faced the horses again. Another half-step. One of them (*black mane: Quickthorn*) snorted a little, stamped a forefoot, but she felt they were calming down. She hoped Rhenya and Railu would understand, have the sense to enter the side-door quietly.

She was between the two horses now. As whenever she was near them, she felt small, but they were both looking at her. Curiously, she thought. Ears up, forward: was that a good sign?

Quickthorn dropped his great head and nuzzled at her, waist-level. She laughed quietly. "Nothing in my pockets, sorry. Nothing but a handkerchief, and I don't suppose you'd want to chew on that." Delicately, she reached up, slid a hand down the long nose.

Then there were more footsteps behind her. She turned her head, not far, said quickly but softly, "Stay back. They've been—"

"I think I know my own horses," said Duncal, sounding more amused than affronted. Behind her she sensed rather than saw him retreat a few paces. A moment later he was beside her, a carrot in each hand. "Here, my lads. This is what you want, isn't it?"

She stepped back, then aside, looked along the side of the carriage, just in time to see three figures disappearing through the side-door: Whallin, flanked and supported by Railu and Rhenya. Still something niggled at her, and she looked at the carriage itself. Immediately, she felt alarm.

She retreated, slowly, until she could speak to the Squire. The horses glanced benignly at her, but went on chewing their carrots.

"The brake's off," she said. "I'll have to climb up and put it on."

He didn't take his eyes off the animals. "You know how to do it?"

I think so, her mind said. Her voice said, firmly, "Yes."

"Gently, then," he said.

Indeed, she thought; *gently*. The first step was the problem; really, it was too high. Her skirts were full enough not to hinder, at least; she could get a foot onto the bracket all right. But she needed to pull with her arms then, and it was hard to do that slowly, and she knew from the first time she had climbed the rear steps how the carriage would dip to her weight when she did so. The horses would sense that, she felt sure. But it had to be done...

She pulled, as slowly as she could, but felt the thing settle anyway, then start forward a few centimetres as the horses reacted. She swayed on her arms, but kept pulling, getting her weight over her foot... and then the rest was easy, three more steps and onto the top. She settled onto the seat and slid herself across to the far side. Whallin seemed to work the brake-lever casually with one arm, but she needed both hands to pull it firmly back. The pull went through several rods and linkages, she knew, and she could feel some give, some play, in each of them, before—finally—she could move the lever no further. She risked a glance, over the side and back, to see if the brake-block was pressed firmly to the rim, but the angle was all wrong. She could not tell; she had only the feel of it for guidance.

At first, then, she thought she'd simply have to stay there hauling on the lever until someone could out-span the horses and lead them away. But that hardly made sense; surely it would be better-regulated than that? Then she saw: the lever moved between two metal bars or long arched plates; these were pierced, and there was a pin, dangling loose on a short length of chain, that could be inserted through the holes to stop the lever springing back.

Finally she was able to look up, over the horses' heads, and say, "Brake's on, Master."

❊

"Dunno what spooked 'em," Whallin was saying. "Wasp stung one, like as not." It was late in the year for wasps, she thought... or would have been in Delven, anyway. Here, she could not be so sure.

His face was still pale, but not quite as ashen as it had been. Railu was finishing the strapping of his wrist, the two of them seated knee-to-knee beside the kitchen table. Jerya, who'd felt shaky after she'd climbed down from the carriage, was seated at the end of the table. Only Rhenya was afoot, brewing tea on the range.

The Master and Mistress came in. Whallin looked up, anxious, moved as if to rise, but Railu, oblivious to anything but her task, said firmly, "Keep still."

Duncal waved a hand at them. "Yes, stay seated, all of you." Of course, Jerya recalled—her wits felt clotted and slow—it was not the done thing for slaves to sit when their masters were standing; this was a special dispensation.

Duncal moved to the side of the table away from the range, opposite Railu and Whallin. He rested his hands on the tabletop, leaning forward a little. "I must say, that was excellent work by you girls. Again, you never cease to amaze me. Jerya, where did you learn to handle horses like that?"

For once, the answer was easy. "Here, Master." He raised an eyebrow and she went on, "Watching Whallin."

Her gaze was on the Master, but in the corner of her eye she saw Whallin's head come up.

"And Railu, too," Duncal continued. "A pretty piece of bandaging, indeed. And how is the patient, hm?"

"It's just a sprain," said Railu, eyes still on her work as she tied off the ends. "I'll fix you a sling in a moment. You need to keep that still for a few days."

"Just a sprain, hm?" said Duncal. "You're sure of that, are you?"

For the first time Railu looked up. "I'm sure," she said; and then, slowly, it seemed to come back to her where they were, and whom she was addressing. "Master," she added, colouring up a little.

"I'm sure you're right," said Duncal benignly. "But I hope you will not mind if I have Doctor Feldreth have a look at it. He's due this afternoon, anyway, as it happens."

Railu dropped her gaze, still flushed, and said nothing.

"Well," said Duncal, "It seems we may need to reconsider some of our plans for the next few days. Unless I drive the carriage myself, of course, hm?" He looked around with an expectant smile; Jerya realised, too late, that it had been intended as a witticism.

✻

Railu had now tied off the ends of Whallin's bandage and was evidently asking him to flex his fingers. She had tutted when she saw how the doctor had rebound the hand after examining it; Jerya wasn't in the least surprised that she'd insisted on doing it over a second time. Whallin nodded in response to whatever she was saying; Railu smiled, a job well done.

The door opened. Rhenya and Whallin sprang to their feet; Jerya and Railu scrambled after them. Even Cook was bracing her hands on the arms of her chair, but Duncal, smiling genially, waved her back with his free hand. His other held a green bottle.

Behind him came Lady Pichenta, carrying a tray; the remains of their meal. "We thought we'd save you the trouble tonight," she said. She was looking around vaguely, unsure where to deposit the tray; it was Rhenya who relieved her of it, carried it through to the scullery.

"Indeed," the Squire was saying. "Bit of excitement today, hm?" He beamed around at them. "How's the hand, Whallin?"

"It'll be fine, Master."

"Will be, you say?" The Squire peered at the bandage as Whallin held up his hand for inspection. If he noticed that it had been freshly re-wrapped, he gave no sign. "But I'll warrant it's sore enough right now, hm?"

"It aches a little, Master. But I can drive tomorrer."

"No, you can't," said Railu. Everyone looked at her. She flushed a little but went ahead determinedly. "I'm putting it back in the sling and it'll need to stay there for at least three days."

Duncal's smile blended amusement and benevolence. "There, you see, Whallin?"

"That Doctor said the same," added Railu.

"It's unanimous, hm?" Duncal gave her a quick glance, then gazed around again. "As I was saying, you've all had some unwonted excitement today, so we thought, my Lady and I, that you should have a quiet evening."

"And a little something to aid relaxation," added Lady Pichenta.

"Yes, indeed." He seemed to recollect the bottle in his hand, placed it on the table. "A little of the palenka from a few years back."

"Well done to all, this morning," said the Lady. "But particularly our newest arrivals." She smiled at Jerya, but there was shrewd appraisal in the look, too.

"Indeed. Hm, my dove, what do you say? We should not outstay our welcome, but shall we all raise a glass together? Rhenya, if you please, seven shot-glasses."

When a small tot of the clear spirit had been dispensed into each glass, the Squire and Lady handed them out. When Whallin reached for his with his right hand, Railu quickly stopped him. "Left hand," she said.

"Hm, yes," said the Squire, "You wouldn't want to drop it, now, would you? Now..." He raised his glass. "A toast. To the newest members of the Duncal family, who showed their worth today. Jerya—" A nod, a lift of the shot-glass. "—And Railu."

He threw back his head, downing the drink in one. Jerya followed suit as the others did, and then found herself gasping, eyes watering, so that she nearly missed his parting words.

"I trust—we both trust—that these past weeks have been just the beginning of a long and happy association."

✻

"Rai," she said. "I have to ask you. Do you think you might be pregnant?"

Railu jerked back almost as if Jerya had slapped her. "What? Why would you ask that?"

"You've been sick several times in the mornings, and you've picked at your breakfast every day lately. Have you been feeling queasy a lot?"

"Well, yes, but that doesn't mean..."

"It's not a certain sign, besure, but it made me wonder. Tell me, have you missed your..." *What was the word the Dawnsingers used?* "Your menses?"

Railu sighed. "But I had the fever... and of course crossing the mountains was hard, and then there was..."

"Yes, I know, a traumatic time. But Rai, listen, you're trained as a Healer. You must know something about these things. You've been sick in the mornings and your cycle is disrupted. It has to be possible, at least, that you are pregnant."

"No, no, it's not possible."

Jerya gave Railu a long look. "Are you saying... I mean, when you and Rodal..."

"I can't believe you'd bring that up again."

"I don't want to, believe me, but I think we need to. That time, did he... was there... did he... did he enter you?"

Railu didn't answer directly. She stared with a truculence Jerya had never before seen in her broad coppery face. "You don't understand. I can't be pregnant. I just can't."

"I don't think you get a choice in the matter. Not now."

In an instant Railu's look turned from hostile to wounded. Too late, Jerya saw how 'not now' had sounded like a rebuke: *you should have thought of this before*. That wasn't how she'd meant it at all. "Rai, I'm sorry, but please... I meant it looking forward, not back. What's done is done; I'm not raking over those coals. But look, if this really is happening, it isn't going to give you a choice. That's what I meant."

"But I *can't*. I never... Dawnsingers don't get pregnant."

They looked at each other. They were both still bald, true enough, but neither of them was wearing white. The thought hung between them: *we aren't Dawnsingers any more*.

Jerya didn't need to say it aloud. After a weighted pause, she said, "I guess the first thing is to figure out how we can know for sure—one way *or* the other. I don't know if you know anything about that?"

Railu shook her head. "It wasn't any part of the Novice curriculum."

Jerya sighed. "And we don't know the first thing about what healers—doctors they call them—know this side of the mountains anyway."

"They're all men, aren't they, doctors, here?" Railu looked miserable. "I can't bear the thought of a man... you know..."

Jerya couldn't suppress the thought: *if you hadn't let a man near you, we wouldn't be talking like this now*. She kept it firmly to herself and hoped her face hadn't betrayed anything. After a moment she decided it hadn't. "I wonder if there are any medical books in the Master's library."

"You'll have to look. I don't think I'm supposed to go in there."

"I'll do that, and gladly. And anything else you need me to do." She took a deep breath. "After all, Rai, I can't help thinking, if it hadn't been for me, you wouldn't be here now, and you wouldn't be in this pickle. *If* you are," she added hastily.

"I'm not blaming you," said Railu. "Like you said, what's done is done."

"Thank you... anyway, anything I can do for you, I will. Who have we got if we haven't got each other?"

Part Two

City of Veils

Jon Sparks

CHAPTER 17

RODAL

The sea was calm enough, still in the shelter of the last straggles of the Out-Isles—in the *lee*, as he'd learned to call it. Their course was straight and the wind fair, a *broad reach*. There was no need for constant trimming of sails, as there had been in some of the mazy channels the day before, and—for the nonce—little enough else to do. Rodal had plenty of time to watch the hills of Sessapont rise over the rim of the world.

Highest of all, first to appear, was a great dark conical mass. As they slowly drew closer he began to piece together more detail, saw that the hill was crowned with a structure of some kind, perhaps a fortress, perhaps a palace; or likely some mix of the two. By this time lesser hills were appearing to either side, but all more or less the same simple shape: cones riding on the shoulders of lower cones, shouldering each other like bodies in a packed crowd. Each and every one seemed to be thickly covered in buildings, crowned with a tower or two, but trees found a few crannies here and there. Trees were thicker along the main roads which wound and wriggled through the city, following the creases where the steep slopes met.

Closer, and he saw that banners flew from each crowning tower, long streamers flying in the same breeze that filled the *Levore's* sails. The highest tower of the highest hill flew the greatest banner, a shivering streak of green and red that appeared as long as the tower was tall. It was too far off to tell for sure, but it seemed it must be thirty yards if it was an inch.

"Silk, that'un," said Grauven, seeing the direction of his gaze or perhaps just knowing what caught the eye of every newcomer. "Wormsilk strengthened with spidersilk, I heard." A word from the Skipper and he hastened to his post, but Rodal still had a little more time to gaze. Green and red were on every hill-crest, but among the lesser banners he saw every other colour also, white and purple and gold perhaps the most common.

Only as they came within sight of the harbour entrance did he see outlying hills which weren't completely built over, where the slopes were attired in green: vineyards or orchards. And he saw, too, that the string of islands which guarded the harbour looked like the tips of similar hills, but drowned, as if the land there had sunk. Causeways or sea-walls linked most of these, leaving only two entrances for ships. They were in a line of vessels making for the nearer, while others, barques and wherries and others whose names he had yet to learn, tacked out from the more distant one.

Now there was more to do, taking in sail to slacken speed, adjusting further as they swung onto a beam reach, less time to observe. Almost before he knew it they were in the harbour-mouth, and he barely had time to notice the tall masonry towers either side. As they sailed on, slowly now, into the vast expanse of the harbour—two miles wide or more—the Skipper was looking out anxiously. What he was looking for was soon made clear as a little gig, nimble under three pairs of oars, darted toward them and then held station about twenty feet to port. Red-and-green banners flew from stubby masts at bow and stern, and a portly, full-bearded man in a tabard of the same colours hailed them from a platform just aft of the bows. Rodal could not entirely follow the shouted exchange between him and the Skipper, but he could see when it ended that the Skipper wasn't happy.

"We're to moor in the lee of the island," he informed his crew. "Seems we'll not get a berth till the morrow."

"So why did us bust us guts to get here so fast?" grumbled Croudor. Rodal wasn't sure the Skipper was meant to hear, but his ears were sharp—or maybe he just knew the sort of thing Croudor would say. The man was nothing if not predictable.

"If'n we'd not got here till tomorrer," said the Skipper tartly, "We'd prob'ly not get a berth till day after. Yow've been here before; yow know how it goes."

Barely pausing to draw breath, he began rapping out orders, and they swung to port again. Soon enough they were rounding up in the lee of the tree-clad island and making for a buoy which sprouted another green-and-red flag.

"This'll be new to yow," he said to Rodal. "Can be tricky, too. But I'll give yow a go. All yow need t' do is snag that loop o'line wi'th' boathook, bring it inboard."

It sounded easy enough, until Rodal realised he would need to step over the side, perching on the narrow rubbing-strake which circled the hull just a couple of feet above the waterline. It was narrower than the ball of his foot, and slippery into the bargain. Left hand hooked firmly around a gunwale-post, right clutching the boathook, he tried to settle himself as the *Levore* inched closer to the buoy. He could see that this required manoeuvring as precise as any docking. Ideally the ship would come to a stop with her bows exactly abreast of the buoy and no more than a yard or two from it. But to do this required exact judgement of how much way she was carrying. Drop the last sail too soon and she might come up short and have to go round again; leave it too late and Rodal's job of hooking the mooring line would be close to impossible.

As it was, the speed was good but they were just a little farther from the buoy than he would have liked. He had to shift his grip and lean perilously away from the side of the ship, body angled over the dark water, stretch his right arm nearly to the fullest, the boathook suddenly seeming to double in weight. He daren't even think about what his feet were doing.

But he managed it, slipping the hook under the loop. He hauled, but at first it seemed to stick, and the last vestiges of the ship's way were carrying him past. He felt as if his arms were being pulled from their sockets, as if his grip on the post couldn't last another moment. But then the line freed itself, and with the sudden loss of resistance the force with which he'd been pulling threw him back against the side of the ship.

He slammed into the planking, hard enough to know he'd have bruises, but he kept enough presence of mind to adjust his grip, even as his sternward foot slipped from the narrow ledge to wave in thin air.

Somehow, in all this, he'd kept his grip on the boathook. Now, prompted by urgent cries from Croudor, he fed its butt-end through the fairlead to his crewmate's waiting grasp. Once Croudor had it, he let go and just hung there at the side of the ship, pulse racing, battered, but strangely exhilarated.

"Not bad, lad," said Croudor once the mooring line was safely looped around the bollard. From him, that was effusive.

Soon after, the Skipper was more liberal. "Well done, lad. There's many a lad taken a dip first time he tried that."

"It was a close-run thing," said Rodal. "But at least I can swim."

❀

The Skipper knew they'd been looking forward to shore-leave. For himself he was content to stay aboard for another night, but was insistent they took a good chain and padlock. "Rope's no security at all," he said. He was equally insistent that they leave nothing in the dinghy but baler and ballast. This led to the odd sight of Croudor and Grauven carrying an oar each as they made their way along the quayside, but Rodal barely noticed. There was too much else to look at.

With all the overlapping hills, the natural shoreline must have wriggled like an ill-handled rope, but most of it had been built over, and long ago by the looks of the weathered stone. The natural curves were simplified, reduced to straight segments of dock-wall.

And at each angle there stood a statue. Far off in the innermost recess of the great harbour, maybe a mile away, was a pair that might stand a hundred feet or more, but the rest were nearer thirty feet. Mighty enough, still.

What they stood for, he didn't know, and could see few clues. Their features were softened by weathering—either the stone here was softer than the gritty sandstone of Delven, or the statues had stood in the wind and the rain for many generations. Any remaining detail was obscured by liberal streakings of birdlime.

When he passed close by one he saw that their legs—high as a man could reach—were also covered in paint, a many-hued jumble that resolved, up close, into writing. Layers on layers of it, new obscuring the old. A man's name, the name of a ship, sometimes a date.

"Need to get yowr name on one o'these, Rodal," said Croudor. "Everyone does, first time in Sess."

"Tomorrer, once we're berthed," said Grauven, reasonably.

※

Another thing he'd noticed almost immediately was that in Sessapont all the women—all the *free* women—were veiled. He still saw no slaves with faces covered.

A few of the veils, here, were so close-woven they seemed opaque, and he wondered how the wearers saw anything. Indeed, he saw one figure, arms more than half bare but face entirely obscured, walking close behind a female slave. As he passed, he saw with a twist of revulsion that leather straps were attached to each side of the slave's broad belt. The veiled woman held the other ends, like the reins of a cart-horse. Anger rose within him. He couldn't help imagining Jerya and Railu being used like that, like animals. Again, he could only trust that what he'd heard was true, that this Duncal was 'soft', treated his slaves at least like human beings. He reminded himself that he was filling his purse, that all this was so that he could, in due course, have a real chance of doing something, of freeing them.

One drink tonight, he told himself. *Two at the most.* It wasn't every day you made your first landfall in the greatest city in the known world, not every day you paid a copper for a little pot of paint with which to mark your name on the base of a towering statue.

He noticed other things, too. In Sessapont, a shaved head was seemingly not enough, and many—if not most—of the slaves were marked in other ways. Some had close-fitting metal collars; they appeared seamless, as if they had been soldered together; but how was that possible without injury to the wearer? Far more were marked on their bodies: marks that were not painted on, he thought, but printed into the skin, blue or green or red, on shoulders, backs of hands, sometimes even right across the face. He did not see letters or words, but he did see recurring symbols.

They weren't necessarily ugly. Some of them might even be called beautiful; embellishment, not mutilation. But if the marks were permanent, as they appeared, they could make it impossible for any slave to escape detection. A shaven head could be covered, and in time the hair would grow back. Marks on the face would be harder to conceal, even in this city of veils.

He reminded himself that he had not seen any such markings in Drumlenn, but it was disturbing nonetheless.

The whores were veiled too, but with such flimsy nets that, even in the soft light of the place Croudor had led them to, he could clearly see their faces underneath. Eyes rimmed in black, cheeks rosy, lips scarlet. The rest of their clothing was, for the most part, scarcely less diaphanous. The beads that fringed the veils hung just above breasts that were half-exposed, half-pressed together, by their tight bodices.

Rodal knew what they were, these girls. Annyt had explained, before he'd been in Carwerid a week, about the half-dressed women who sometimes slunk into the tavern—where they'd always been encouraged to slink straight out again.

The three men had barely taken their seats before three whores sauntered across the room. Without invitation they joined them, two on the bench flanking Grauven and Croudor, the third on the stool next to Rodal.

"What may you fine sirs care to drink?" asked this third one. Her accent was different, he noticed, the 'you' not sounding like 'yow' but more like 'yoe'.

Grauven and Croudor called for wine but Rodal, resolved to stay sober, asked for beer. He almost regretted it when it came; it was thin stuff, pale and sour, but he knew that if he drank wine he was sure to drink too fast, and then all his best intentions would fly out of the window. He wanted his wits about him.

Having fetched the drinks, the girl sat again beside him. Her face was broad, with high cheekbones, eyes that looked black in the low light. Below the band that secured her veil, her hair tumbled down her back in midnight ringlets.

She raised her glass. "Health and wealth."

He lifted his own, responded in kind, sipped at his beer, watched as she drew the veil forward, away from her face, with her left hand, so she could drink with her right. Wine, he thought, but he had a suspicion it was well-watered. The wine in his crewmates' glasses looked nearly black, only hints of garnet light in its depths. The wenches' drinks all looked lighter, more translucent.

"So what's your name?" she asked.

"Rodal." And he'd been brought up too well not to ask, "And yours...?"

"Call me Narèni."

He nodded, but he wondered about 'call me'. Was it, perhaps, a hint that Narèni might not be her true name?

It wasn't long before Grauven and Croudor were calling for a second drink, though Rodal wasn't halfway through his insipid beer. He shook his head but the wench—the one who'd attached herself to Grauven—fetched one anyway. He wondered whether they were trying to get him drunk, or were in cahoots with the landlord to sell more drink. Or both...

Grauven and Croudor were growing raucous, Croudor more animated than he'd ever seen him, pawing the wenches even as they roared out coarse banter. It reminded him a little of some of the things boys in Delven said when away from their elders, perhaps at the pools—but these were grown men, and Croudor was married and Grauven betrothed, too. Still, they were his crewmates, and generally they'd been good to him, and he didn't want to dampen their evening. He laughed when he could, responded to comments when he could think of something to say. But it was Narèni whose hands were on him, rather than the other way around.

Still, it was more relief than anything when Grauven and Croudor rose and made for the stairs, each entwined with a girl. But it left him alone with Narèni, and she'd reached the bottom of her second glass. "P'raps it's time yoe and me went upstairs too?"

He sighed. "Look, I've nothing against you..."

She giggled like a lass of ten. "Well, why don't we do somethin' 'bout that?"

"I'm..." He hesitated. 'Betrothed' would be a lie. "I'm promised to someone."

She laughed again. "Foof, most o' tha men who come in 'ere are wedded or plighted. I've 'ad more'n one tell me this place is th'only thing as keeps him faithful to his wife."

Try as he might, Rodal couldn't fathom that logic. He shrugged away the puzzle. "Well, that may be so, but where I come from we take a promise seriously."

Her hand was on his thigh now, and creeping higher. "Seems to me yoe're a long way from... where'er 'tis."

"That's true." *Further than you know...* "Even so..."

She pouted under the flimsy veil. "Thing is, if'n I don't take yoe upstairs now, I'll have Tremmett on my back fer wastin' too much time with yoe. And yoe might start a-feelin' less welcome too." Her eyes strayed toward the bar, and indeed the barkeep was watching them closely.

"Look," he said, "I don't mind talking, but..."

"Then c'n we talk upstairs? Please? I c'n do any kind o' talk yoe like..."
She laughed briefly. "Foof, it makes an easy night for me."

He sighed. He wasn't sure what his alternatives were. "Very well, but just
ordinary talk, if that's all right with you."

✻

The room was small, but seemed clean enough. A fire was banked low in
the grate, coals glowing a sullen red. She spent a little time coaxing it into
flame, adding a cheerful orange flicker to the yellow lamplight. While she
was crouched at the hearth, he looked around, noticing a few knick-knacks
on the little table beside the bed, a couple more on the mantel alongside a
sand-glass. A curtained alcove, he guessed, was where she kept her clothes.
It seemed this was her home as well as her... her place of work, which gave
him his first question as she joined him on the bed. There was nowhere else
to sit. He kept a slight gap between them.

"Yea," she said. "It do's well enough."

"I've lived in smaller spaces."

"On the boat?"

"We call it—her—the ship. Our Skipper's most partic'lar about that. The
boat is what we rowed ashore in."

"Is that so? Learn somethin' new every day."

"I try to."

There was a brief pause. To fill it, he asked, "How long have you been...?"

"Bin a whore?"

"I didn't like to..."

"Why not? 'Tis what I am. No point in pretendin'."

He nodded slowly.

"Three years," she said, in answer to the question he'd left hanging. "Foof,
nearer four by now."

She must have started terribly young, he thought. He doubted she was
as old as Jerya or Railu even now. Younger, likely, than the youngest brides

in Delven. Apparently some men liked that. It was Annyt who'd told him that, he remembered; some would pay extra for the young ones. That seemed wrong to him, almost sickeningly wrong—and also inexplicable. Surely it was a true woman you'd want.

He remembered Railu and felt his face grow hot. He hoped it wouldn't show in the soft, wavering light. If it did, Narèni didn't appear to notice. Still, he felt a need to move the conversation—if you could call it that—forward, away.

"I can't help wondering how... why..."

"Why I turned to whorin'?" She was smiling; smiling at his hesitancy, he thought. Well, let her. A smile didn't hurt anyone. "True tale, I din't see a better choice."

His surprise must have shown. "I don't know how 'tis where yoe come from," she said, all seriousness now. "But maybe yoe know there's more slaves in Sessapont than anywheres else. Five or six to every free, they say." He thought the ratio could be a lot higher on rural estates, but in towns, cities, maybe she was right. "So what else was I to do? Guttin' fish ten hours a day? And, foof, it's better'n gettin' wed."

He gaped at that, and she made a swift amendment. "Better'n weddin' someone yoe don't care for." She looked at him, shy for the first time. "Yoe said yoe're promised to someone?"

"Aye."

"And yoe care for each other? Truly?"

"Aye."

"Yoe're lucky, then." She fell silent, and Rodal was about to say something, but then she surged into speech again. "My folks wanted me to wed... some'n twenty year older'n me. I told 'em—told 'em again and again—I din't care for him and never would, but they wun't listen. So... I left."

Walked out of one life and into another, he thought. *Reminds me of someone...* "Don't suppose that was easy."

"Oh, leavin' was easy enough. What to do next, that was harder. Head for th'city, I thought. Suppose it's what everyone does... But then, like I said, what's a girl to do?"

She looked around the room. Rodal did the same, trying to see it through her eyes. The bed cover was a little threadbare in places, the curtain across the alcove frayed at one corner. But it was warm, and—as he'd said—he'd slept in worse places.

"Never had a room all to myself before," she said suddenly. "Day I found this place, might be 'twas the luckiest o'my life... Don't look so surprised. There's whoring, and there's whoring. I seen what it's like for some. Maybe for most. This place is class, compared to most I seen."

Her gaze strayed to the mantel, focused on the sand-glass. "Blust!" she cried. "No idea how long that's been finished!" Then she laughed. "Just want to talk, he says. Foof, Mister Rodal, yoe've had more o' my time'n most men get."

"That means we..." He didn't want to say 'finished'. "...We should be heading back downstairs?"

She was already gathering her skirts, rising. She said no more till they reached the foot of the stairs, then a quiet, "Thank yoe."

Croudor and Grauven were already ensconced in the bar-room again, fresh drinks in front of them but wenches no longer attached.

"Yow took yowr sweet time, lad," said Grauven. "She give yow an extra?"

Rodal ignored this. "Seems to me I left a drink on the table. In fact, a full one and one half-done."

"Sorry, lad," said Grauven. "Gone when we came back. Yow can always order another."

"That's not the point. Seems like I'll be paying for two drinks—paying over the odds, too, reckon, and I've only drunk a half o' one."

"It's a cryin' shame," said Croudor with his usual relish for bad news.

"True," said Grauven, "But don't go making a fuss about it." He glanced at the barman. "I wouldn't argue with that feller for all the silvers I'll earn this trip. And he'll have friends."

Rodal found this advice hard to swallow. Yes, he'd had a nasty shock when he'd faced off against the wrestling champion, but he still reckoned his chances against most, and the barman looked soft in body even if he had a hard eye.

But he forced himself to say, "Lesson learned, reckon."

"'Sides," said Grauven, "Time yow was up there, beer'd've gone flat anyways."

"Still think it should have been my choice to make... oh, but what the... It's just that I'm trying to save my money, you know that, and this night's sure to cost a lot more than I meant it to."

"Sorry, lad," said Grauven. "Nawt we can do 'bout that now. Like yow said, lesson learned."

"I hope she were worth it," added Croudor.

Rodal bristled at that, but then he found himself thinking: *Worth it? Was she?*

CHAPTER 18

JERYA

Jerya could not resist creeping to the door of the parlour to listen, straining her ears to pick up the conversation and the same time trying to remember to listen for any approaching footsteps—especially Cook's shuffling gait or the rasp of Whallin's hobnails. Neither was likely; Cook rarely strayed beyond the kitchen and scullery; indeed, these days, she spent most of her time in her chair, directing Rhenya: sometimes Railu and Jerya too, if they appeared to have no other duties. Whallin, also, never came into the house proper without a summons. Still, it couldn't hurt to be careful.

"Thank you, Railu." To her surprise it was the Mistress who spoke. "Will you sit?" A brief pause: faint sounds, presumably Railu sitting down.

"Now, Railu, answer me this, please... are you with child?"

Jerya heard a faint mumble: even pressing her ear right up to the crack between the doors she could not catch it. But the Mistress as good as told her what Railu had said. "We think so, do we? 'We' would be yourself and Jerya, would it?"

"Yes, Mistress."

"Well, we'll have the doctor over as soon as may be, get it confirmed. In the meantime... assuming you *are* with child, do you know who the father is?"

"Oh yes, Mistress."

"Slave or free man?"

"A free man, Mistress."

"Your former master by any chance?"

"Former master? Oh no..." Jerya, knowing Railu, surmised that she was about to say more, but the Mistress jumped in at the slight hesitation.

"You were willing, then?" she demanded. "You were not forced?"

"Yes, I was willing," said Railu, with unmistakable, even defiant, dignity. In spite of everything, in spite of her own still-tangled feelings about that day, Jerya felt a surge of pride in her friend.

"He was a good man?"

Jerya smiled. As if Railu had any experience of men against which to compare Rodal.

"I believe so, Mistress."

"Good-looking... well-set-up... a quick-witted sort of fellow..." There was a little silent pause after each question. Perhaps Railu was nodding her answers. "A kind man? Perhaps you'd have liked to stay with him?"

Silence, then a faint rustle of someone moving. The Mistress's voice again. "There, girl, you know it could never have been. Slaves cannot marry frees." And Railu's, sudden, hot, bitter: "But we *weren't* slaves!"

Then silence. Finally Duncal asked, "What are you telling us? You were free? The freebooters took you and shaved you? Passed you off as slaves to get a bounty?"

Railu, her voice slow and shaking. "No... no, they took us for slaves, for runaways. They *assumed*..." A brief dry laugh. "Who else goes around with their heads shaved?"

"I'm sorry." Duncal again. "This is hard to grasp. You are telling us you were free, yet you had your heads shaved? Why? In heaven's name, why?"

"Because... because we came from a place where a shaved head means something else. Something else entirely."

"I know of no such place," he said testily. "Where is this place, hm? What is its name?"

Railu sighed. "Jerya was right. It's easier to say nothing..."

"She said that, did she? Yet she has said a good deal herself, though to little effect." Sterner: "Never mind what Jerya says. Where did you come from?"

"The other side of the mountains."

Duncal laughed harshly. "Yes, by God, Jerya was right. Better to say nothing than belabour that story again."

"I'm not so sure, my dear," the Mistress said. "At the least I'd say the girl believes what she's saying."

"That does not make it true. It cannot be true."

"Can it not? Well, you may know better than I, my dear. But are we really sure?"

"Well, you know, there have been several expeditions into the mountains at various points, but none have found a crossing. I think the most recent was—"

"This is hardly the time to worry over the minutiae, dear. Can't you see this poor child is in some distress? At least we can relieve her of one anxiety. Railu..."

There was what seemed a long pause. Jerya could hear nothing at all. Then the Mistress spoke again.

"Railu, we have strayed from the original purpose of this interview. With good reason, perhaps, but nevertheless... if you are indeed with child, no doubt you are concerned to know how you can care for it, what kind of future it will have."

She took an audible breath. "But I must ask you one more thing about this man, the father... you are darker of skin than either of us. Was he dark also?"

Railu's tone was puzzled. "No, he was paler. Lighter than Jerya, too, and sandy hair."

"That's as well. You see, Railu, we propose... if you bear a child alive and whole, the Master and I are willing to adopt it as our own. Only, to do that, the child must not be too unlike. People must be able to believe that it is truly my child, and your Master's.

"Do you... child, do you understand what we're saying? We have no children of our own. I have never carried one to term. I am all but forty years old: what hope now I will ever bear and raise an heir? But if we have no heir, then when we die the estate will be sold off, perhaps broken up. Who knows what will happen to the slaves then? But if... if you give us your child, there will be a Master here, or a Mistress, a Duncal after us. Someone to continue our work for the betterment of all slaves."

She took a deep breath. "That is to take the larger view of it. To step away, so to speak, and to say, this appears better for all concerned. But the... the small view is is true as the large, in its way, and the small truth is we are asking a mother to give up her child."

"Though you will see it every day," Duncal put in.

"Will that make it easier?" the Mistress said sharply; she seemed irked by his interruption. "I can imagine it would be most painful for a mother to see her child: to touch it every day perhaps, yet never to acknowledge it, never to hear it call you mother. Railu... in law we can command this. But we do not. The choice is yours. You may refuse... no. Say nothing now. Let us wait. Decide nothing till the doctor has settled our fears and hopes."

There were sounds of movement, perhaps of someone getting up. It seemed the interview was coming to an end. Jerya straightened, looked about her, then slipped away on hushed feet towards the back of the house.

※

"Jerya..."

"I know. I heard the whole thing."

"You heard?"

"They want to steal your baby."

"Not steal. If you heard it all, then you heard her say I was free to refuse."

"Free? What does that mean, here?"

"I think it means what it means anywhere. I can choose, either way."

"It's just him pretending. *I don't command, hm, but it would be best if you...* and heaven help you if you go against what he thinks best."

"No Jerya, you *don't* understand. You heard but you don't *see*. It's not him. It's the Mistress. She... she took my hand when I was upset. She looked me in the eye when she said..."

Jerya stared at her. "You can't mean... you're going to do it? What they want? Rai, you *can't.*"

"*I can.*" She sounded very calm. There was strength in her, Jerya saw, a strength she had not seen for a long time. "I don't have to do what they want... and I don't have to do what *you* want. Being free—what else does it mean?"

Jerya had no answer. Railu gave her a long, level, and remarkably unworried look. "You see, there's one thing you haven't really considered: I don't want a baby. Well, you know, when you first asked me, I didn't want to even contemplate the possibility. Remember how I kept saying I couldn't?

"You look shocked... is it so terrible? Is it unnatural of me? I don't know, maybe it is. But if it is, that's not their fault, is it? It's my fault, or maybe it's the fault of those who took me from my family when I was ten years old. I grew from a child to an adult *knowing* I would never be a mother. Whatever I know about conception, gestation, delivery, I learned in a classroom."

She sniffed. "I know more about it than that Doctor, I shouldn't wonder. I can strap a sprained wrist better than he can, for sure. Of course, we practised things like that. Have to be ready for anything that might befall another Singer. Childbirth and the rest, that was just theory. Reading books...

"I suppose you... growing up in Delven, not in the Guild... it would have been a real possibility for you. But for me, the idea that I'm going to have a baby is something I... I can't really believe it, even now. I don't understand it. I don't want it. But they do. They get what they want, I'm free of something I don't want, and the child gets a better future. It's better for everyone."

"There is one person you haven't considered," Jerya observed. "The baby's father."

"Rodal? Jerya, if he was here I suppose it might be different. No, if he was here it *would* be different. But he isn't. I can't plan my life around the faint hope he might turn up."

"Faint hope? Is that how you see it?"

"Don't you think if he was coming, we'd have seen him before now? Maybe he's gone back to Annyt—"

"He wouldn't do that. Not before... he said a year."

Railu looked dubious, but didn't challenge Jerya's assertion. "Then maybe he can't..."

They looked at each other, silent. Jerya hardly wanted to consider what the implications of that might be. It seemed Railu was equally reluctant; after a moment she gave herself a little shake. "I'm the one who's having this baby. I'm the one who has to decide. And I can't decide this on your notion or my notion of what he might say about it."

Jerya still sat heavily, staring at her hands, possessed with an awful feeling of not knowing what to do with them, wanting to grab Railu and shake her, yet somehow inhibited from touching her. The thought that came to the fore was: *if Railu's child is here, she'll never leave.* But then: *As if I had any better plan.*

"You seem to have it all worked out," she said at last.

CHAPTER 19

RODAL

"I wondered if'n I'd see yoe again."

It was Narèni, no doubt of that, though he doubted he'd have known her by sight alone. The veil was a thicker gauze, blurring the features beneath. He had the impression her face was unpainted, too, but it was hard to be sure. Below the beaded fringe of the veil was a long-sleeved blouse, green above a deep red full-length skirt. The colours gave him a sudden flickering memory, a ripe apple plucked from a tree. He'd simply leaned over from the high seat on the cart as they drove toward the City... Carwerid, he amended, no longer the only city in his world. Troquharran was greater than Carwerid, and Sessapont was greater again.

Such thoughts made him slow to respond. "Dustn't rec'nise me, then?" she asked, a smile evident in her tone even if hard to see.

"Sorry," he said, "Forgetting my manners."

"Manners, is't? Not ever'one thinks o'manners talkin' to a whore."

He looked at her, trying—with little success—to read the expression behind the veil. "Don't seem to me like you're working right now."

"No more I am. But seems to me yoe had yoer manners th'other night too."

He could only shrug. Was he supposed to have acted differently because she was what some called a whore?

"Well," she said, "Yoe're right, I amn't workin'." She looked straight at him, through the gauze. "What 'bout yoe?"

"Nor me. We've finished unloading, won't get new cargo till tomorrow..."

"...But today yoe're free?"

"I am." He debated whether to say more, then shrugged inwardly. "And I was just wondering what I can do without spending more than a couple of coppers."

Maybe he'd emphasised the final few words, without even meaning to. For certain she reacted, cocking her head on one side. "Cost yoe more than yoe wanted, th'other night, did it?"

"Besure, I thought we were just going to a tavern."

"Oh, grellit!" she cried, and giggled, putting a hand over her mouth under the veil. "Happ't it cost yoe a fair sight more'n yoe barg'ned for, then." He nodded. "And happ't yoe was wantin' to save yoer coin?" He nodded again. "Well, I'm sorry, but yoe knows there wa'n't nothin' I could do once yoe'd sat yoeself down in that place?"

"I suppose not."

"Naw, not a thing. If it han't been me, t'would'a been one o' tha other girls. But look..." She paused a moment, then held out a hand. "Happ't I c'n make it up to yoe a bit. Show yoe a few o' th' sights—and show yoe where a workin' man or girl c'n get a good bit o' snap for a few pence?"

He debated only briefly. The offer was genuine, he felt, and it was more or less exactly what he needed. See something of the city, learn as much as he could, spend as little as possible. He nodded.

She slipped her hand into the angle of his arm. "It'll help us keep together. Yoe've seen how it gets, on these streets."

"Bit on a whirlwind day, eh?" said Narèni.

Rodal hardly knew what a whirlwind was. He'd heard the word, somewhere, and it had made him wonder, but all he could picture was the wind that Delven folk called the Hellum.

It was weather that knew its own mind, folk said; the one thing the Dawnsinger never seemed able to predict. Twice or thrice a year, four times at most, it would come suddenly out of the East, falling out of the mountains, tumbling over the edge of the moors, shockingly charged with warmth even when the peaks were draped in white. In autumn it could strip the rowans and birches in a morning, leaves skirling away to nowhere in a blizzard of red and gold. In the forest yellow drifts of larch-needles suddenly appeared. The more superstitious among the women kept their children in the shelter of the caves when the Hellum blew. It was a wind from the Blistered Lands, after all, or so they reasoned.

Only there are no Blistered Lands, he thought; *not East of Delven, any-way*. Hardly anything was as he'd once believed it to be. But surely the Hellum still blew, two or three or four times a year, whisking up the fine sand in the courts of Delven; and that was what he thought of when he heard the word 'whirlwind'.

Veil or no veil, he could see Narèni's face was turned toward him, expectant. "Yea," he said, "A whirlwind day."

A cool cellar, vaulted in yellow brick. The lamps were placed in niches, shedding barely sufficient light on the tables, and the nearest one was directly behind her. Her face was altogether a mystery now. He had grown more or less accustomed to the veil as the day wore on. Out in the sunlight, or even in the shadows of the narrower ways, he had still been able to make out her face. Always there had been at least some hint to go with the tone of her voice and the message of her words. But this was a step too far.

"D'you think we might move round a bit?" he asked. "I can't see you at all like this."

She sighed. "I were hopin' yoe wudn't say tha'."

He looked back, though there was nothing to see, and wondered if he had transgressed some custom, if he should apologise.

She sighed again. "See, there's somethin' I wants to say, and I'm thinkin 't'll be easier to say it like this."

"Oh..." was all he could manage.

"See, Master Rodal, maybe'st it's been a whirlwind-y day, like, but e'en so I's been thinking." She paused, grasped her glass of strong cyder, more green than gold in the soft lamp-light. Her left hand slid under the veil to draw it forward, away from her face; her right raised the glass to her lips: a practised set of movements that he'd seen often enough by now. Even with the obscuring veil he could see that she drank deep, and the glass was half-drained when it reappeared.

"Maybe'st I's only a whore." She continued, ignoring his vague protests, "Well, 't's but truth. But at least I's an honest whore. I don't... well, yoe know how 'tis when yoe marries someone, yoe has to promise to love, honour and obey. An' I s'pose maybe'st I could of obeyed him, that man they wanted for me... but I never could of loved him, I never could of honoured him, not true-like. And, true tale, he'd never of loved or honoured me. Tha's why—part o'th' reason—I left th' village, why I ended up here."

He couldn't help thinking of Jerya. She, too, had walked out of one life because it seemed too much like living a lie. He wondered how she was feeling about that choice now.

But Narèni had more to say. "But tha's all by the bye. Thing is, I is what I is and I does what I does, and because o' tha' I sees a lot o' men. An' most on 'em ain't bad, not really. Not... wicked. Most on 'em, though, yoe can't say they's good neither. Not bad, not good, just... well, th'girls just say, tha's men for yoe. Brains in their... in their britches." A soft sound that might have been a half-stifled giggle.

"But yoe, Master Rodal... yoe're different. I think yoe're a good man." He tried to disclaim the compliment, but she held firm, lifting her head so the lines of nose and jaw pressed through the veil for a moment. "Way you was last night. Din't want to fuck, 'cause yoe're promised to someone, but yoe knew I'd catch trouble if'n I din't take yoe upstairs, so yoe said let's just talk..." Again the soft half-giggle. "I liked tha'. And I bin watchin' yoe today, too, and I bin likin' what I sees. So..."

She stopped, reached for the glass again, repeated the little two-handed dance of drinking under the veil. This time the glass emerged all but empty.

"Maybe'st yoe can guess why I's happier yoe can't see my face right now. An' still 't's hard... maybe'st I'll rue sayin' this, but if'n I don't say it, I knows I will. See... what I's thinkin' is..." And then the words came all in a rush. "What I's thinkin' is, I never could of loved or honoured that man back in th' village, but I's thinkin' I could love, honour and obey *yoe*..."

It wasn't unexpected; by the time she got near the end he'd had a good idea what was coming; yet still it struck him like a fist in the guts. "But..."

"I know. I knows it all too well, don't I? Yoe're promised to another. And yoe stand by that. Tha's wha' I likes about yoe... what I honours about yoe." Her voice shook a little and he found himself reaching out. He couldn't see her face but he could take her hand, even if it only gave cold comfort. What she really felt about it, he could only guess, but there was less of a quaver in her voice as she went on. "I know. Yoe're promised to another. And—no, I dun't want to hear about her. 'Tain't goin' to make me feel no better. I only wanted to say... I hope she's a good woman, same as yoe're a good man. I hope she stands by her promise same as what yoe does. 'Cause if'n she ever... if'n anythin' ever happens, if'n anythin' ever falls out wrong twixt yoe an' her... I just hopes yoe'll remember me."

She dropped her head. The veil hung free, gently swinging. He gave her hand a small squeeze. "Aye," he said. "I'll remember you. I can't promise any more than that, you understand, but I'll not forget you."

"Thank yoe," she said in a small voice. For a moment she was silent, then sat back, hand slipping free. "Grellit! Reck'n I needs another drink after tha'."

"O' course." He looked around, caught the eye of the closest serving wench, pointed at the empty mugs on the table. The girl nodded. He'd worried briefly, when they first entered the tavern, that it was just another bordel; there seemed little enough difference between the short-skirted dresses and token veils of the servers here and what Narèni and the others had worn the night before. But Narèni had assured him the drinks were cheap here, and he'd seen no sign that these lasses were doing anything more than fetching drinks, perhaps flirting light-heartedly with one or two customers.

While they waited for fresh drinks, Narèni offered to change places. He was happy to shift around. The lamp-light wasn't strong enough to reveal her face clearly—even full sun struggled to do that—but he could at least gain some sense of her expression now. He raised the new glass in salute, wondering if he should say something. *A pleasure to see your face.* In Delven, in Carwerid, such compliments would surely be welcome, might even be expected. But he did not know how such words might be taken, in this place where free women concealed their faces. *Do slave women feel humiliated to go bare-faced?* he wondered suddenly.

There was so much he didn't know. He'd learned a lot today, but—as he'd often thought since his travels began—the more you learned, the more you realised how much you still didn't know.

But one part of what she'd said was still twisting uneasily in his mind. "It's grand you think I'm such a good man, and I thank you, but I don't believe I'm as unusual as you think... You say you've seen a lot of men, but you've only seen the ones who visit your... ah..." He stumbled to a halt, feeling his cheeks grow hot.

She laughed, and gave his hand a soothing pat, but then turned serious again. "Tha's not all I see. I see'd things in th' village afore I came here, an' I see things when I walks the streets. I seed a thing or two today—din't yoe?" She didn't wait for an answer. "The way some people treat their slaves. I know yoe wouldn't."

"I wouldn't own slaves in the first place."

"Not even if'n you got rich?"

He laughed. "Precious little chance of that. But look, there's lots of good men. In... where I grew up. And the Skipper. He... well, you won't see him in a bordel.... And he took a chance on me, took me on even though I knew nothing about boats."

"I thought yoe said yoe called 'em ships."

"Besure, but I didn't know that then. No, he's a good man, too, I'm right sure of it. I owe him a lot, right enough."

CHAPTER 20

JERYA

"Sit down, Jerya."

She perched on the edge of the chair. There was always something momentous about interviews in the drawing-room. Other slaves in other houses, she had gathered, were generally not invited into the grand rooms at all, except to clean them, and certainly would never be asked to sit down. It was all part of the Squire's much-vaunted goodness to his slaves, but if he expected it to put her at ease he was mistaken. The last time one of them had been in this position, Duncal and the Mistress had asked Railu to give up her child. Now, soon enough, she would have all the pain of birth, for someone else to have the joy.

"If all goes well, and there is no reason to think it won't, there will soon be new life in this old house." It seemed as if he had read her mind, and she could not completely suppress a start, as if she had been caught doing something forbidden. "Naturally it will take up much of my lady's time... perhaps you realise she has always been the secretary in our correspondence in natural philosophy and, more importantly, in our efforts for the betterment of the condition of slaves. Well, we're going to need a new secretary now...

"I could advertise, of course, no doubt secure the services of some young person of reasonable education, but it is doubtful where we would find any such fellow possessed of real commitment to these endeavours. Whereas we have already among us one whose education may be... hmmm, what's the word?" He looked over his spectacles at her. *I suppose you think your eyes are twinkling*, she thought: *come to the point and stop preening yourself.* Her mask of dutiful impassivity never slipped, of course: it was second nature by now. "Unorthodox, shall we say?" he continued. She nodded: he so obviously expected a response. And by his lights it was true. *More true than you know, Master.* Suddenly she wanted to laugh.

"Well, you can read, there is no doubt of that. And I think, hm, you can write a fair hand…?" He could have no way of knowing that: she could not recall writing a single word in the months since their arrival at Duncal.

"I can write, Master, but Railu is much better at it; she has had more practice."

"If it is only practice you lack, it can soon be remedied. And Railu will have other business, hm, to occupy her time." He laughed, shortly, what she thought of as his warning laugh. "Unless you wish to be wet-nurse?"

This time it took every bit of the self-control she had acquired. She did not move: she did not think there was even a flicker of facial muscle, but she felt as if the pain in her head must be visible like a pulsation under her scalp. She had not realised—though it was all too obvious now—the full cruelty of it. Wet-nurse! *They would call Railu 'wet-nurse' to her own child!*

Evidently she had succeeded in masking her reaction. "You are exceptional, Jerya, quite exceptional. With proper instruction, who knows how much you may learn…" 'Proper instruction' meaning *Squire Duncal's* instruction, she thought. Was there no end to the man's vanity?

"And your commitment to the improvement of slaves goes without saying," he continued without pause. "It's almost too good to be true, hm. The very person we need, already under our own roof… there is only one small problem."

He looked at her expectantly, but she could not guess, and she was not at all prepared for what followed.

"I cannot employ you as my secretary without it becoming generally known—and without it further becoming generally known that you can read and write. Whereupon it will be said that I have taught you to read. Said as mere scurrilous gossip at first, no doubt, hm, but then, I fear, as formal charge. I have my enemies, Jerya... we have *our* enemies. We are together in this, are we not? They would like nothing better than to see me lose my license to hold slaves. I cannot, therefore, employ you, a slave, as my secretary. Therefore... you must be free."

He folded his arms and beamed at her. She sat as if stunned, trying to make some sense of the turmoil of her own thoughts. A great wave of hope and exultation—free! But she soon saw how treacherous was her own reaction, saw that she was thinking just as she was expected to think—as a slave was expected to think. What did free mean, really? She would no longer be called slave, but how free would she be?

Duncal took her silence as an indication she was overwhelmed, presumably by joy and gratitude. "There will still be criticism, of course. It is only a few months since you were put up as runaways to be sold or burned. But I am breaking no laws in this. Opprobrium, ridicule, hm, we experience already. These we can endure."

Look what I am doing for you... Jerya felt sick: she was half-disgusted by him. But she knew that, even if she could, she would not refuse what he was offering.

"There is one obstacle, however," said Duncal. "The Code, alas, places strict limits on the number of slaves any owner may set free. They prate about the 'rights', the 'freedom', of the owner-class, but they are ready enough to limit those freedoms if any might exercise them in ways they mislike." He *hmmm*-ed. "Yes, indeed, that might make a subject for a small pamphlet... But I must keep to the point. On a small estate such as this, with fewer than fifty slaves in total, I am permitted to manumit but one in every three years, hm. And as you know we have already informed Cook of our intention that she should be the one, as soon as the requisite interval since the last one expires... which is in about a month.

"So you see, Jerya, either we renege on our promise to our oldest and most faithful servant... or we must keep you waiting for three more years. And I truly believe employing you as secretary would materially further our work; both as an exemplar of the true capacity of the enslaved, and because your assistance with routine estate matters and correspondence would free more of my time for other matters. So what am I to do?"

Jerya was not sure an answer was expected; she knew she had none to give.

✻

"I've worn the crest nigh on fifty year," said Cook that same evening. "I've no mind to change now."

Her crest was thin, far less impressive than some Jerya had seen, but stood out vividly, snow-white against a scalp nearly the same coppery hue as Railu's. Jerya wondered suddenly what colour Railu's hair had been, before. What colour it would be again—if it ever grew out, which seemed less likely with every passing week.

Cook rocked once, twice, in her chair. She must have a name, but Jerya had never heard her called anything but Cook or Cooky, and she had made it perfectly clear that she would want no other name even as a free woman. In fact, as she was in the process of explaining, she had no appetite for change of any sort.

"Dun't want to hurt their feelin's, o'course. They bin good to me. There's no better Master, no better Mistress, no better house in all Denvirran province." *How do you know?* Jerya wondered. In her own time here—close to six months now—she did not believe Cook had ever been further than the home-farm, half a mile from the house, and that only once or twice. Usually she went no further than the kitchen-garden. Nothing she had heard gave any hint that Cook had ever travelled further than the market in Drumlenn.

"So yow dun't tell 'em a word o'this, a'right?" Her gaze roved, held each of them in turn, extracting a silent promise. "Dun't want em' thinkin' I ain't grateful. But saying I's free... Dun't hardly know what it means. What do I want that I ain't already got?" Rhenya was beaming at the old woman, while Whallin, though he rationed his smiles like precious gems, was nodding.

You're slaves, she thought. *You're property. Maybe you've never stood on a platform and been sold, but I have and I can never forget.*

She didn't think there was any point in saying it out loud. Perhaps in time, when she knew them better. Perhaps Rhenya, who was still so young...

"Shaved i'th mornin' all my life," Cook resumed. "Dun't think I'd feel properly awake if I didn't." Jerya's mind flashed back to that morning—was it really still less than a year ago?—when she had first been shaved. How strange the sensations had been, the blade rasping over her scalp, the raw, denuded feeling after. Yet you could grow used to almost anything. She might have protested Railu's distress at discovering stubble on her—Jerya's—scalp; but she had also understood. Bald is beautiful, besure.

"Anyhows," continued Cook, "What'm I to make o' bein' free? Bein' *told* I'm free? I'm not goin' to go anywhere, live any different. What's freedom anyways? Way I sees it, there's plenty o' free folk what's worse off'n I am right now."

※

"What would you do?" asked Jerya. "You heard what Cook said. Being set free doesn't really mean anything to her. I don't understand it, but that's how she feels. She said not to tell them, because she thinks it'd hurt their feelings... but would it, really? Might they not be flattered that she's happy just the way she is?"

Railu gave her a long steady look. Then she sat back, interlacing her fingers around her growing belly. "They might. I can see that. But if Cook asked you not to say anything, do you have the right to go behind her back?"

"I know. All right, I didn't say anything when she asked it; I didn't promise to keep silent. It wouldn't be like breaking my Vow... but still, after that, and all that's followed, I'm not easy. It does feel like breaking a promise, betraying a trust."

"Then don't do it."

"I know. If I was purer, more like you—" Railu snorted dismissively. "You are, you know. And if I was, then I wouldn't even be tempted. But I can't ignore... she says, if she was free, she'd carry on exactly as she is now. I wouldn't. That's why he wants to offer me freedom. Thinks I'd be useful."

"And you'd be an example. He said that too, didn't he? *Look what slaves can do if we give them a chance.*"

"Maybe he's right. Maybe that'd be a good thing too."

"And maybe you'd feel like some performing animal. Because don't you think, if it wasn't for that, he could still have you doing all the other things, records and correspondence, without having to set you free? Just doing it all in secret.

"But look, you talk as if I wouldn't be tempted. Of course I would, Jerya. I don't know why you'd think I wouldn't. I'm like you, I can't understand why Cook doesn't want it. Only I don't suppose I'm going to get that choice. Not any time soon, not now or in three years. There are slaves on the home-farm who've been with this estate nearly as long as Cook. We both came in as runaways. Can you imagine if you and I both got freed before any of them?"

Jerya hardly knew any of the slaves outwith the household but, yes, she could imagine that there would be resentment. Whallin, now: she did know him, and she was sure he'd been around a long time, if not as long as Cook. What would he think? Would he care as little for freedom as Cook did, or would he grudge her the opportunity that might have been his?

But, she realised too slowly, was Railu hinting at something else? How would *she* feel if Jerya were freed and she were not? If, after three, six, nine or more years, she was still a slave? "Rai, I'm so sorry. I hardly thought about how this might be for you."

Railu shrugged. "They're not going to set me free any time soon. Not while they need me to bear their son, and be his wet-nurse, and... well, whatever comes next." *He's not their son, he's yours*, thought Jerya. But they'd had that argument a dozen times already. Besides, Railu hadn't finished. "Anyway, where could I go? I'll always look like a slave."

That was true. Any faint hope Jerya might have nurtured that Railu's hair would begin to grow back had long been quenched. Did that mean Railu would never, could never be free?

She wanted to say, *I'm sorry. It's all my fault, I brought you to this.* But something stopped her. She sat a few moments, plucking at her skirt, smoothing its creases.

"Jerya," said Railu then. "I'm not going to tell you what you should or shouldn't do. Truth is, I don't *know*. But there's one thing you don't appear to have thought of."

"What's that?"

"You could try talking to *Cook*."

"Thank you for letting me do this," said Jerya.

"Strikes me it's a favour to Rhenya, from both on us. She's a lot to do, early mornin's. And I ain't safe shavin' myself these days." Cook held up an age-spotted hand. The tremor was slight, barely noticeable most of the time, but it was there. "You ever shaved yowrsel', girl? I know Rhenya or Railu mostly does it for yow."

"A few times."

"Did you like it?"

"It always seemed to help me think."

"Aye, set yow up for th'day. But havin' it done for me's nice in its own way, I won't say diff'rent."

Jerya began applying lather to the mottled scalp. She took a steadying breath. "I offered to do it... yes, it helps Rhenya at a busy time, but also, I was thinking. I've been here more than six months and I've never once sat down and talked with you. Just the two of us, I mean."

The old woman gave a breathy chuckle. "Seems to me yow ain't sittin' now, either."

"True. But the talking part..."

"Aye, well…"

Jerya had spent some time, having woken early, thinking how to approach this. "You said you'd worn the crest close on fifty years… You must have have been very young?"

"Not as young as yow might be thinkin'." Cook gave another near-silent cackle. "I'm not handy wi' numbers like what yow are, but I reckon it 'cause it were before young Eglar were born, and I know he's forty-six now. Baked him a cake every year since he had his first teeth, I have."

Eglar must be the Squire's first name. Jerya had never heard it before.

Jerya laid down the soapy brush and picked up the razor. "Keep still now… You said you didn't care about growing all your hair."

"Not rightly. Anyways, it'd take a long time to amount to anythin', and maybe never would. But really it's… I'm happy the way things are."

The way things are… the phrase had too many resonances for Jerya. She kept her hand steady, but it was a moment before she trusted herself to speak. "And that includes… I mean, you don't care about being freed?"

"Only 'cause th'Master'n'Mistress makes so much on it. I can't see it makes a scrap of difference to me. Maybe if I were yowr age…"

For a moment Jerya thought Cook had guessed what she was leading up to, but the comment seemed to be a mere throwaway. She rinsed the razor, shifted to the other side of the old woman's head. "That's what… I had to be sure it meant nothing to you, not for yourself. Because… if you're thinking about what the Master and Mistress want… he said something to me, too."

"To yow?" Cook shifted suddenly, and Jerya had to snatch the blade away. "'Bout freedom?"

"Yes."

"Why yow? Yow said yowrsel' yow ain't been here much above six month—and yow came here as runaways. Not that I seen anythin' to complain of since yow been here, but still'n'all, why yow?"

"Because I can read and write," said Jerya. "Now keep still so I can finish." She worked delicately around the left ear.

"Read and write? That's against th'law."

"Not strictly. It's against the law to teach a slave to read."

"Well, some'un must of taught yow."

I taught myself. She doubted Cook would believe that, and anyway, it wasn't important right now. "It doesn't matter. What matters is, the Master thinks I can be useful. Keeping records, writing letters, things like that. But if I'm a slave, I can't. At least, it would always have to be kept secret." *And I've had enough of secrets.*

Cook said nothing. Jerya made the final strokes with the razor. "There. How does that feel?"

The old woman ran her hands carefully over her head. "Thank yow, Jerya, yow's done a fair job. Feels good, every time, dun't it?"

Jerya knew what she meant, and it was certainly a good moment to agree. "I suppose... if free really means free, it means you can do what you want. So you wouldn't... I mean, nobody could order you to grow your hair."

"Mebbe not, but p'raps a few folks'd have somethin' to say about it. Master'd like folks to *see* I was free."

Just as he'd want them to see what he'd 'made of' me. "You're right, of course."

"Aye, and th'law says he can't free both on us at th'same time, dun't it?"

"One every three years."

"And I'm thinkin' yow wants it more'n I do."

I do. There could hardly be doubt about it. But she couldn't satisfy her own conscience without playing as fair as she possibly could. "Maybe it's also about what the Master wants more. And the Mistress, of course."

Cook gave her a straight look. Her eyes, though nested in wrinkles, were still bright and clear, a startling teal-blue. "It's always 'bout what th'Master wants. T'ain't for yow or me to be tellin' him."

Jerya's hopes faltered. *I thought it was going so well...*

Her mind raced. "Not telling him what to do. I wouldn't ever suggest that." *Oh, but I'd like to.* "Telling him how you really feel. Because he—they—think you'll be delighted. They think it'll make you happy—and I know you deserve it. But if it won't, if it doesn't make any real difference to you... then is it right to pretend, to deceive them?"

Cook pursed her lips. "Yow's given me somethin' to think on, I'll say that."

CHAPTER 21

RODAL

It's the silence that gets to you, he thought.

Of course, he was well enough used to snow. He knew how on a windless day it could fall without sound. Nor was ice a new thing for him. Perhaps it was that he had grown more used to shipboard life than he had realised. And on the ship there was always the sound of water against the hull, an occasional creak of timber, the snap of a flag or the thrum of wind in the rigging. Even when tied up to a wharf there was the soft ripple of a river, the gentle slap of waves in a seaport. The water was never completely still, and its sound was always there, even if you did not always know you were hearing it.

But by the last light of sunset, the day before yesterday, he had seen the water of the anchorage turning murky, sluggish, grey-white, like the margins of a melting snowdrift. In the morning, as soon as he woke, the silence had been there, and a stillness. The *Levore* was still in a way she never was even when tied up to a wharf; it felt almost as if the ship had died. Up on deck, breath smoking, he'd peered over the rail, seen nothing but white. A fall of snow in the night had coated the ice. Up forward he'd found the Skipper and Croudor poking at the ice with a boathook. It smashed into plates an inch thick.

"Worst o'both worlds," Croudor had said with gloomy relish. "Wun't bear, so yow can't get ashore afoot, but neither yow wouldn't get a boat through."

"Why'd you want to go ashore anyway? You said last night there's nothing around for miles."

"Yea, but if we're here more'n a few days we'll be frettin' 'bout victuals. Mebbe fuel for th'stove too."

"If it comes to that, th'ice'll be bearing by then," the Skipper had countered.

"Mebbe," Croudor grudgingly conceded.

"If," the Skipper stressed. "These cold snaps never last long."

"There's allus a first time."

Now, it was beginning to look as if Croudor had had a point. Two days on, there was no sign of the weather breaking. The ice seemed strong enough to walk ashore now, but the Skipper had decreed that no one was to take the risk until it became essential. Half the time, chilly mists swirled listlessly around the ship, depositing ice on every line and spar and roll of canvas. At least chipping it off gave them something to do. At first it had seemed pointless, since it just appeared all over again, but after a while Rodal began to see the point of keeping busy. And, as the Skipper explained, if they simply left it to accumulate, it could eventually become heavy enough to cause damage—and clearing it then would certainly delay them when an opportunity to break free did arise.

But for that they needed wind. There was open water no more than a hundred yards away; the main channel had never been known to freeze completely. If necessary they could hack away the ice that blocked the mouth of the cove, but there was no point even attempting this unless there was enough wind to give the *Levore* steerage way. And when they had taken a last look round before heading below for dinner there was no hint of a breeze.

This being the third evening, the routine was beginning to feel familiar, but the contrast between the chill of the night and the heat of the cabin was still shocking. Having already left his boots at the foot of the companionway, he quickly shed his heavy waterproof and woollen gansey. The

Skipper joined him at the galley table, where Croudor was already seated, and moments later Grauven was handing out plates of food.

When they'd finished eating and were sitting back with mugs of ale, the Skipper took a deep breath. "Lads, I need to talk to yow 'bout th' way things are shaping... If th'weather changes and we can move tomorrer, it shouldn't be too bad, but any delay after that, or if we get delayed again... well, that's another story."

"What, we're running low on victuals?" asked Croudor.

"Nay, it's not that so much. We might get a bit bored of hard-tack and burgoo, but we'll not starve."

"Less'n we're here for weeks..."

"Not likely," said the Skipper testily. "Anyroad, that's not what I wanted to tell yow. Thing is... well, when I took out this contract, I priced it based on th'usual trip times; four, five days. We been out five days a'ready, and even if we could move tomorrer, it's likely another three to Troq'."

"Yea," said Croudor. "An' that's if we get a decent wind."

"And if it don't freeze again," chipped in Grauven. Croudor gave him a dark look, as if to say *Leave the doomsaying to me, my lad*. Rodal could have chuckled out loud.

"It won't freeze in th'main channel," said the Skipper, clearly ever more impatient with the doom-laden interruptions. "And one day wi' a fair wind and we'll be clear o' all th' tricksy islands and banks. We can sail through th'night if need be, make up time."

"Oh, my fav'rite thing, night sailing." Croudor looked at Rodal. "Yow'll not have had the pleasure, will yow, lad? Two of yow on deck at any time. Two hours on, two hours off. Scratchy eyes and yawning all day after."

"Well, there's the thing," said the Skipper. "Point I'd be making if yow'd just let me get on wi' it. Said already, I set a price based on usual trip times. We're out longer'n a week, I'm startin' to look at no profit. Ten days, I'm definitely makin' a loss."

Croudor gave him a look that seemed to say, *that's your problem, not mine*.

The Skipper sighed. "Let me spell it out for yow all. We're lucky in one way, it's not a cargo that'll go bad if we're a few days behindhand. So if the trip takes twice as long as it should, the problem is—well, it's two things. One, we're eating for twice as long, dipping into reserves that have to be replaced. Two, I'm payin' yow lads for ten days or whatever, rather'n five."

"Well, we're still workin', ain't we?" said Croudor.

"Yea, I know that. And I 'preciate it. But... if I take a loss on this trip... I've got payments to th'lenders fallin' due. And if I have to dig deep to make those, I might be struggling if I have to front up for th'next cargo rather than takin' a contract. And yow know that's where th'good profits come from."

"So what are yow tellin' us?"

"I'm *askin'*... I'm askin' if I can delay payin' you for th'extra days on this trip. Till I get a good contract or make a good sale on a cargo."

"An' in th' meantime how am I s'posed to feed my wife and bairn?"

"That's why I said I was *askin'*," the Skipper said heavily. "It's up to yow. But I'll say this, yow oughter know me by now. I'll pay what I owe soon as I can. And... if yow want th'*Levore* to still be sailin' regular in a year, two years, however long... then yow need to understand why I'm askin' this."

Croudor glowered but said nothing. Grauven—who often took his lead from the older hand—was also silent. Rodal barely hesitated. "You don't need to pay me right away, Skipper. I'm trying to save as much as possible, you all know that, and if I don't have the money in my pocket I can't be tempted to spend it on things I don't need." *Like visits to bordels*, he thought.

"A bird in th'hand's worth two in the bush," said Croudor.

"I don't know what you mean by that. But I'll tell you what I do know. The Skipper's a good man, besure." A good man... Briefly, he thought of Narèni, that conversation in the cyder-cellar. "If he says he'll pay us, he'll pay us. If I have to wait a week or two, I'll wait. It's months, not weeks, that I'm bothered about."

"Weeks can turn into months when someone owes yow money," said Croudor.

"I'll take that risk. It's little enough, if I'm any judge of men."

The Skipper only flicked him a glance, but Rodal had no doubt of the gratitude he read there. Croudor's expression was distinctly more sour. "Proper blued-eyed boy yow're turnin' into."

"I don't know what that means either, but I don't rightly like your tone."

"Now, lads," said the Skipper. "No need for name-callin' or fallin' out." He addressed himself to Croudor. "Yow don't want to wait, yow'll get th' full whack when we pay off back in th'Red City. Yowr choice, I said. Just so long as yow know what it means for th'next trip, maybe even after that."

For the first time, Grauven stirred. "Happen I could wait for my share. Long as it's not months."

Croudor looked vaguely disgusted, but the Skipper smiled. "It won't be months, lad, I promise yow."

For a moment they were all silent. Almost as one, all four of them reached for their tankards. Rodal smiled slightly.

Then he cocked his head. "What's that sound?"

"Rain," said the Skipper. "Rain, or I'm a slave. P'raps we might be shifting tomorrer after all. Get to bed in good time tonight, lads, we might be night-sailin' tomorrer."

※

Rodal was still thinking about time. Not hours or minutes or seconds: these he had begun to grasp as a by-product of the Skipper's teaching him the principles of navigation. Crossing the great bay, they had never been altogether out of sight of land, but the Skipper had taken regular sightings anyway, explaining that, "'T only takes a bit o'mist and yow can easy lose all idea o' where yow are." He had a distinct sense that, back in his old homeland, any such matters would have been strictly reserved for

Dawnsingers. He found it both fearful and exhilarating to be free to study and discuss them.

In any case, that was not what he was thinking of now. His concern was with days, weeks, months, even years.

He had promised Annyt he would return to her, in Carwerid, within a year—a twelvemonth, as Five Principalities folk mostly called it. Before that he had a self-imposed but no less binding resolve return to Drumlenn, in time at least to see whether anything could be done for Jerya and Railu. How much time he might need for that was unknowable. At present, though, he felt they were still better served by him learning all he could about this land—this world, as he often thought of it.

But there was one fixed point: the year of his promise. A year that he dated, not from the day he'd followed Jerya and Railu away from Delven, but the day before, the day he'd scribbled his note to Annyt. It shamed him a little, that he'd had to write on a scrappy piece of paper, that his spelling probably left much to be desired. It shamed him, too, if he really thought about it, that he'd told her by letter at all, not face to face; but by the time he'd got himself fully settled on what he meant to do, she had been led away with some of the village girls to her chamber on the maidens' level. And he'd had to admit that had probably made things easier; what if she had objected, begged him not to go?

Anyroad, all that was done and past. The question now was, exactly when did that twelvemonth run out; in the terms he was learning to deal with, when would that date be?

It wasn't too hard to calculate. He knew the date on which he had joined the *Levore*; it was inscribed on his seaman's ticket. He only had to count the days back from that: six days to cross the mountains and work down the long valley; three days on the trail of the girls and their captors; another day wandering around Drumlenn questing after some word of their fate and wondering what to do next; three more working for a friendly farmer. Thirteen days all told, but only nine days travel. Nine days back from the 7th of Gleander took him to the 29th of Meadander, so the 28th of

Meadander next was the date on which he must complete his journey back to the Sung Lands. He figured he should add something for delays due to weather; and from Delven it was at least five days' journey to Carwerid. He hardly dare allow less than three weeks in all. It would never do to pitch up in front of Annyt a day late. Might be she would only laugh; equally, might be she would not. Might be she would have other suitors waiting...

So, three weeks from Drumlenn. Before that he needed to have made his way back there, and thence to the Duncal estate—of which, he reminded himself, he still knew essentially nothing save that its master was 'soft' on his slaves.

And the more he thought about it, the more uncertain it all became. How easy—or otherwise—would it be to scout the place? How easy—or otherwise—to make contact with Jerya and Railu? How easy—or otherwise—to extricate them from there? (Assuming they wanted to go, of course, but he could not imagine they would be content with the life of slaves even on a 'soft' estate.)

And from there, where would they go, and how, and how long would it take? Troquharran, with its Monitors and its tally system, seemed too much of a risk; the relatively unregulated ferment of Sessapont offered hope. And, since free women there were invariably veiled, and some covered their heads altogether, bald heads could be easily concealed. Many slaves in Sessapont were marked in other ways, of course. He had not noticed any so marked in and around Drumlenn, so it was hardly likely that the 'soft' Squire Duncal had done so. But that was hope, estimation, not certainty.

But there was another question. Supposing Sessapont to be the best destination; how would they get there from the Drumlenn neighbourhood? Even the most indulgent slave-owner would presumably raise a hue and cry if two of his slaves disappeared. He knew a little about Rangers, and the girls no doubt knew more than they had ever wished to about freebooters.

The route he knew, by river, bay and Inner Channel, seemed impossible. He hardly thought he could ask the Skipper to carry a couple of runaway slaves. He thought there was trust and respect between them, and he knew the Skipper was no lover of slavery, but his respect for the man made him reluctant even to ask him to take such a risk. And even if he could overcome those scruples, he didn't feel the same confidence in Croudor or Grauven; not enough to hazard so much on it, besure.

But... if not by the *Levore*, he could see precious little chance of making the journey by water. And they could hardly fly. He smiled a little to himself, looking up at the timbers overhead, supporting the decking, blackened by years of smoke from lamp and stove. If they could not reach Sessapont by water, they must do so by land. But that, of course, raised a host of new questions.

Well, he had learned something from the Skipper, about time and about navigation; and about charts. And in learning about charts, he was learning about maps. Someone, somewhere, in Sessapont or in Troquharran, must sell maps of the land as well as charts of the sea. Maybe that was the next step; maybe that would give him some idea how long a journey from Drumlenn to Sessapont would take. Suddenly he recalled something Narèni had said, about having to walk all the way to Sessapont because she had no money for a coach. It had taken her weeks, he thought. If he saw her again, might be she had some useful knowledge to impart. But that was another thing he needed to know about: coaches.

Well, clearly, coaches cost money. And maps did too. It seemed probable he would need to make other acquisitions too: veils for the girls, some form of hat or scarf, probably other clothing too. It all took money, and at the moment he had a guaranteed income on the *Levore*, and free accommodation too. To continue to earn, and to save, while adding to his knowledge and understanding, must be the best course at least for a while longer.

And he had to admit there was something exciting—and satisfying—about making his way in this new world. Were it not for promises and obligations, here and in the Sung Lands, he felt as if he would gladly continue his exploration for many years.

✻

Sailing by night might have set Croudor grumbling (*what doesn't?*) but Rodal found it thrilling, slipping near-silent through dark waters on which the moons' reflections trembled in a thousand flecks of silver.

It had seemed perfectly natural for the Skipper to pick Rodal to stand watch with him, so that the two experienced hands could take charge while they slept in the morning. However, he soon realised that there might have been an ulterior motive.

"They both asleep?" the older man began when Rodal crept up from the galley with two vast mugs of coffee.

"Yea." He placed the Skipper's mug carefully on the shelf beside the wheel. There was little light in the wheelhouse, for obvious reasons; just a small lantern, screened so as to cast light nowhere but the compass binnacle, and another in a niche alongside the companionway. His eyes had adapted as night gradually descended, and he could see well enough to move about the wheelhouse, or around the deck when needed, though everything was leached of colour and the land bordering the channel—mainland to port, a long low island called Souterkin to starboard—appeared as black masses like holes in the night.

The Skipper was a grey shape beside him, eyes occasionally catching a reflected glint of lantern-light or moonslight. He threw one quick glance at Rodal, doubtless seeing no more than another shadowy outline, then returned his gaze to the seaway ahead. "Bin thinkin'. But's not easy gettin' a chance to talk sure yow wun't be o'erheard."

Rodal nodded, Then, thinking the gesture could easily go unseen, he murmured his agreement.

"Well, 't's like this..." He eased the wheel a touch to starboard and Rodal watched the bow slowly respond. The Skipper leaned forward for a better view of the sails, checking they were still drawing nicely. He sipped at his coffee. "Tha's grand, lad. Yea, somethin' else yow've learned right well... But I mustn't beat about th' bush.

"Thing is... I bin mightily impressed wi yow, lad. Yow might understan' why I dun't want to say so when th'others might hear. But's true, right enough. When yow first signed on... I took a chance on yow, yow knows that. Yow knew nothing about sailin', th'river, th'sea... but yow was honest about it. I mind well what yow said back then, *'I'll work hard an' I'll learn quickly'*. And yow have. Yow've worked and yow've learned. 'Course, a few months ain't enough t'master everythin' a man needs to know, but th'way yow've gone at it, give it another year and yow'll be every bit as handy as them two below... ha! A year? Give it six months. Six months, if'n yow goes on like yow has bin, an' I'll gladly write up yowr ticket as a First-class hand."

He waved away Rodal's thanks. "It'll be no more'n what yow deserve. But, anyroad, tha's not all..." He shifted the wheel, altering course a few degrees to port. "Yow might take in that mizzen halyard a bit..."

When Rodal returned, he continued. "See, lad, I bin thinkin' a bit further than six months... 'course, I know yow has an understandin' wi' yowr girl back home. And I'd never be one to come between a man and his promises.

"But I'm goin' to say this... Ask yow what yow've thought about after."

"After?"

"After th'weddin'..." He chuckled. "I mean, not right after. Enjoy th'sweet-days an' all that... But then, 'cause when a man's new-wed, 'fore there's young uns to tie yow, tha's th' time... tha's when I brought my Gretyel to Troquharran. Tha's th' time." He paused, peering out at the channel ahead, sipped at cooling coffee. "See, Grauven, Croudor, they're decent enough hands, but neither un's ever goin' to be a skipper. I'd never think o' takin' one o' them on as a partner."

Rodal stared at him, though there was little chance of making out any expression. "But you're saying I..."

"Now, mind, I ain't makin' no promises. Not yet, like. In six months, if yow goes on like yow've started, who knows? But think about it. And mebbe... I dun't know if yow writes to that girl o'yowrs back home. Yow writes well enough, I knows that."

I would write, he thought, *if I could get it delivered*... and then wondered how true that really was. What could he say, as uncertainly as things stood now? *Well, I don't see any way to get it delivered, so it ain't worth fretting about.*

"Well," said the Skipper, "If'n yow does, yow might plant a seed, like. Set her thinkin' a little, mebbe. 'cause... I know some men'd say th' wife goes where th'usband bids and that's an end to 't, but that's not to my way o' thinkin'. Specially not in this life, wi'th'man away more'n he's at home; a lot falls on th'wife's shoulders, like. Yow can see that, eh? And Gretyel, she knew what she were gettin'. I won't say it's allus bin easy for her, 'course not, but she's a good 'un, an' she knew what she was signin' up for. But... just s'posin—all this is s'posin, right?— s'posin yow brought that girl o' yowrs to Troquharran, she'd have one good friend there right away. I'm takin' my good lady's name in vain, sayin' that, but I knows it's the truth. She's a good 'un, like I says..."

He sipped again, made a small disgruntled sound. "Cold coffee's no good to no man. Me own fault, talkin' too much. Here, lad, throw it o'erboard. Yowrs, too. I'll make some fresh."

"D'you want me to do it?"

"Nay, lad, yow take th'wheel for a bit. Just keep that square-lookin' point fine on th' port bow. I've given yow a bit to think about, I don't doubt."

CHAPTER 22

JERYA

The slaves lined up on one side of the dining-room, against the table, which they themselves had moved back specially for the occasion. She and Rhenya had needed to enlist Whallin's strength for that, Railu of course being excused. Against the opposite wall, lined up under the row of family portraits, were the free employees: the estate manager Grevel; a woman who must be his wife; two older men she did not know.

Duncal and his lady swept in with a few of their noble friends. She recognised a couple of them from that terrible dinner party. Well, that would be one benefit of being free; she would not be expected to parade half-naked in front of them again. They settled into seats along the back wall, Squire and Lady standing a pace or two in front of them.

"Jerya bey-Duncal, stand forward," said Grevel, himself advancing to stand close to them.

That's my name, isn't it? Like that other... lady said, she thought wryly as she stepped from the line. *And what will it be when I am free?*

She took up her position as she had been instructed, facing the Squire and Lady

"You are called Jerya, a slave of the estate of Duncal?"

It was perilously close to a lie: she had set her heart against accepting the title, against letting them tell her she was a slave. But she said, "I am," though her voice trembled a little.

"Notice of manumission has been posted in the places required by law for the time required by law," continued Grevel. "If any wish to declare that this is not Jerya bey-Duncal, or that any other estate have prior claim to her, let them speak now, or henceforth hold their peace." He was doing his duty conscientiously, but she sensed he did not greatly like it. She wondered if it was manumission in general he objected to, or hers specifically. She'd known all along that eyebrows would be raised; she was a recent acquisition, and—worse—one who'd been labelled a runaway.

There was silence. Behind and to her right someone, one of the slaves, shifted their feet. Distantly, through the open doors, the drawing-room clock could be heard striking a quarter-hour.

"There are no challenges," said Grevel after that clotted pause. "Therefore we are assembled, slaves and free, to bear witness to the manumission of the said Jerya bey-Duncal, according to law, this the seventeenth day of Fructander in the eighty-third year of the peace."

He took two paces backwards. Duncal moved a short step towards her. The corners of his thin lips twitched, as if he could barely suppress a smirk.

"Let all here present bear witness," he said. "I, Eglar, Duncal of Duncal, do from this moment solemnly and irrevocably renounce my rights as slaveholder over Jerya, who is no longer Jerya bey-Duncal. I name you Jerya. I name you free. From this moment, you may go or stay as you wish and no man shall hinder you. I name you free, in token of which I now set my name to these documents of manumission."

He turned to a small table beside him and bent to sign each of the three copies of the ornate certificate: one for himself, one for Jerya, and one for the provincial authorities. He wrote his name with a careful flourish, slowly, the scratching of his pen seeming to go on and on in the heavy silence. Then he blotted the signatures, took one copy, and handed it to Jerya. As she accepted it, he said, one final time, "I name you free." Then he could no longer restrain his broad smile, stepped closer, and shook her hand vigorously.

Lady Pichenta shook her hand also, then they both stepped back, leaving Jerya alone in the middle of the floor, clutching the certificate. She had been briefed about every detail of the ceremony, but she did not know what happened now or what she should do. *But you're free*, she thought wildly, *you can do what you like.*

She half-turned, uncertain, saw the Duncals take their seats and lean into whispered converse with their respective neighbours, and took it as a signal that the formalities were indeed complete. She turned away, then stoped, as she saw Rhenya's face, shining tear-tracks on onyx skin. The girl looked utterly stricken. Jerya moved towards her.

"What's the matter?" she asked in a low urgent voice, but Rhenya turned on her heel and bolted for the door.

"Blight that trull!" muttered Whallin. "I'll give her a proper thrashin' for that. *When* Master gives th'rest of us leave to go..." The words were meant to be overheard, Jerya saw. They were meant to wound her, as if she were to blame for the thrashing Rhenya was going to get. She looked at Whallin and at once his gaze was rigidly ahead of him.

"I don't understand it either," said Railu. Jerya wondered at her grim tone, until she saw how Railu was leaning back against the table, surreptitiously trying to take the weight off her feet. In this final trimester she was suffering agonies from back-ache, and standing was the worst. "I'll talk to her, if the Master will let us go."

"Well, I can ask him, I suppose," said Jerya, realising. She turned and approached the row of chairs of the end of the room. Duncal broke off his conversation and looked up at her expectantly. "Yes, Jerya?"

"Excuse me, Mas—sir, could you let the slaves go now? Or at least Railu. It's very uncomfortable for her."

"Yes, of course." He started to rise, then settled back. "No, you tell them, if you would be so kind. They can all go, but one of them will have to come back to serve drinks. It ought to be Rhenya, if she's not actually ill."

She conveyed the message and watched the three slaves file out. Suddenly she felt utterly lonely, and all she wanted was to follow them. But that would be the cowardly way... she turned back, hesitated the moment, then sat down in a chair by the end of the long table. *I'm free*, she thought, laying her certificate on the table. *Free to do what?*

Well, free to sit down. That's something, I suppose.

She looked down at her hands, folded in the lap of the black skirt, hands that had softened during her months in the Dawnsingers' College, hands that were now calloused and work-hardened again.

There was a rustle of skirts, and she looked up, to see Grevel's wife approaching with a shy smile. She was young, Jerya realised, looking at her properly for the first time, surely not above twenty-five. Grevel was at least forty. And she also was pregnant, just far enough along for it to be unmistakable.

"I'm called Nielle," she said. "We haven't... well, of course—" She blushed suddenly, vividly. Jerya was disarmed. "I'm sorry. It's just... I know you're not a slave any more, but of course you still look like one. It'll soon get easier, I'm sure..."

"Will you sit down?" said Jerya, indicating the chair next to her.

Nielle sat, showing the same slow care that Railu had developed. One hand shielded her swelling belly, one went to the chair-arm for support. "That's a relief," she said, "I do feel for that poor slave-girl. She must be near her time too."

Too? Jerya puzzled for a moment, since Nielle was nowhere near her time, then realised she meant Lady Pichenta. The pretence seemed to be holding.

"I suppose," Nielle said, "You are younger than me."

"I am nineteen, I think," said Jerya. *I suppose I may be twenty, by now.*

"You think?" Then Nielle blushed again. "Oh, I'm so sorry... I suppose..."

"Don't worry about it. Really."

Nielle looked at her and then impulsively reached out and clasped her hand. "I do believe we shall be friends," she said. "I would be most glad if you would call on me occasionally, especially during my confinement. I... I have been a little lonely at times. I do not complain, my husband is a good man, and affectionate, but this is a substantial estate, his duties often take him to the outlying lands, and sometimes he must go away to the city. Then I wish there were other women here..."

For a moment Jerya was baffled, but she saw that Nielle had really said, 'other *free* women'. And in that moment she began to have some notion of why Rhenya had been so upset.

Movement in the room made her look up, before she could answer (and in any case she did not know what to say). With a sinking heart she saw Rhenya enter with a tray, wine decanter, glasses. Her eyes were dry, her face composed, but Jerya did not doubt she was still suffering. She took the tray first to Squire Duncal: he poured the wine for his noble guests and served it to them with his own hands. Then the male employees; finally Rhenya brought the decanter and the last two glasses to where the two women sat. "Will you take wine, Madam Grevel?" Nielle nodded. Rhenya served her, then, looking at Jerya but not quite meeting her eyes, "Will you take wine, Miss Jerya?" Her voice was steady now, calm, but it pierced Jerya's heart. For a moment she could not reply.

"Yes, please," she said when she could. Slaves did not normally drink wine, and she had only occasionally tasted it in the College, where ale, and more particularly small-beer, were more commonly drunk. Still, she knew enough; it was somewhat like ale or cider in its effects, but stronger. She knew, too, that she most assuredly felt the want of a drink.

"Thank you, Rhenya," she added as the plum-hued liquid curled smoothly into the glass. Rhenya's hands were steady, but Jerya's shook as she took the glass, and again she could not catch the girl's eye. She moved away before Jerya could think of anything else to do or say.

She looked at the glass in her hand, barely a quarter the volume of an ordinary ale-glass. She sipped cautiously, but something still caught at her throat, and she had to smother a cough. Beside her Nielle gave a soft twittering laugh.

"Not used to it, I'll warrant?"

"I've only tasted wine a few times before." Fleetingly, she wondered if one more familiar with wine might find clear differences between that produced in the Five Principalities and that of the Sung Lands.

"So few? I thought slaves in all houses—" She broke off and the easy blush flared in her cheeks again.

"I'm sorry, Jerya, dear," she said. "My manners... well, but it's as new for you as it is for me. May you learn to enjoy it. I hope—I truly do—we'll share a glass again soon... I believe my husband requires my presence."

Perhaps he did, though after the briefest exchange of words, she went to a chair against the opposite wall and sat there alone. Jerya, too, was left alone; *free* to brood over Rhenya's behaviour and the things Nielle had said, or implied. As a free woman, her position was ambiguous. Other things she had heard, or more commonly *over*heard, came back to her. She was—so everyone would suppose—*freed*, not *freeborn*: the distinction might mean little or nothing to the other slaves, but she knew it carried weight among the free folk. Freeborn held themselves at least a cut above the merely freed.

Nielle had been bold in coming to speak to her, she realised, perhaps too bold for Grevel's liking. It was surely at his bidding that she sat now alone at the other side of the room. *Freeborn, but must obey her husband.*

She sighed, and took another tiny sip of her wine, barely wetting her lips. Its dark aroma held a spicy promise, but she could not yet find its complement in taste. Nielle... she could see that she might yet be glad of the friendship of a freeborn woman, but... though she knew she should be grateful for Nielle's overture, she felt uncomfortable about it. Something that reminded her... not in Carwerid, but in Delven... It was still not much more than a year, but it seemed so long ago, and she rarely thought of her childhood home. *I may have more time to think now,* she reflected grimly. Was it her first child Nielle was carrying? She reminded Jerya of a new-wed of Delven, not yet secure in her new status, caught between girl and woman. Of course, in Delven, women often had their first child at sixteen or seventeen; fifteen was generally thought a little on the young side, but it was not unknown. Was that why she made Jerya uncomfortable? Nielle was clearly older than herself, probably by five years at least, but she had seemed somehow younger, still a touch childlike.

Rhenya re-entered the room, with a re-filled decanter and circulated as before, coming last to Jerya. Even as she opened her mouth to speak, Jerya forestalled her. "If you call me Miss Jerya again, I'll..." But she had no threats. "Just don't you dare."

"But what shall I call yow?" Rhenya whispered.

"What you've always called me."

"Slaves aren't to be o'er-familiar with free folk," the girl said stubbornly.

"We are already familiar," Jerya countered. "And when no one else can hear us—" as she caught Rhenya glancing nervously back over her shoulder. "All right, not now, but I must talk to you later. No, no more wine, thank you."

Finally the guests had all left. None of them had come over to speak to her. Most had acknowledged her with the tiniest nod in parting, one or two had not conceded even that. Even Nielle's backward glance had been hurried, constrained.

The Mistress found her still sitting by the long table. "Come, Jerya," she said. "I will show you your new accommodation."

Jerya stood, near-empty wineglass in her hand. "Leave that," said the lady. "The slaves will clear up." *The slaves.* Jerya smiled sourly. The wine had left an acrid taste in her mouth.

Jerya followed her to the back-stairs and then down a long corridor on the first floor to the East wing. Several rooms here, above the kitchen and scullery, were kept shut up and she had never entered them. Now at the end of the corridor one door stood open.

"Good," said the Mistress, entering first. "They've got it all ready for you."

The room was about five metres by three at floor level, but one of the long walls sloped in from about half height. She recalled that the roof at the back of this wing came down to the first-floor eaves. A window set in the sloping roof-wall looked out over the paddock to the orchards. She saw

Quickthorn out grazing: as she looked, he suddenly raised his head and shook it this way and that. Waves rippled down his mane. Suddenly she wondered, *can a freed-woman learn to ride?*

"Well, it's as you see," said the Mistress. Jerya turned from the window, saw her standing with both hands cradling her false pregnancy. The usual surge of indignation caused her to miss a few words.

"—And chamber-pot. I'm afraid the bathroom's not very handy—it's the last door on the left, just before the back-stairs. But you'll appreciate it makes things easier for the slaves who have to carry up hot water for you.

"For the rest, I'm afraid it looks rather bare at the moment. When you start to receive your stipend—of course you won't formally begin to act as secretary immediately, not till after the birth at least—you'll be able to buy a few little things to make it really your own. It will be a while before you can go to town, too." She meant, *till your hair grows, till you look like a free woman*, Jerya realised. "And you'll take a little while to learn to read and write of course, won't you, dear?" She grinned conspiratorially: and then she actually winked. Jerya masked her disgust.

"I'll leave you to settle in. I dare say you'll take some of your dinners with us from now on, but for the time being you may be more comfortable if you continue to take meals in the kitchen at the usual times, or have a tray brought to you here. Now... is there anything you want to ask?"

"I don't think so, Mis—my lady. Thank you." *Thank you!* The words tasted like some sticky sweetmeat retrieved after being dropped on a dusty floor.

Lady Pichenta turned with deliberation, as if she were truly pregnant, and went out, leaving the door open. Jerya closed it quickly but quietly behind her, then sat down on the bed. At once she decided she did not like its exposed position in the centre of the floor. If she moved it into the corner, under the slope of the roof, it would be cosier, more like her old cave-chamber. Her eyes prickled briefly at the thought, as she got up. However, the bed, iron-framed, was too heavy for her to move unaided. She would have to get someone to help her. Presumably—inevitably—it would be Rhenya.

As she moved towards the door, for the first time she noticed what was in the corner beside it. A wash-stand with a water-jug—and above it a mirror.

She was drawn to it, could not resist studying the stranger who was herself. There were no mirrors in Delven: no glass of any kind that she knew of. She had used a small mirror in the College, but larger ones were not placed where a Postulant might linger to admire herself. Sometimes she had snatched glimpses of herself hurrying by, but it had meant nothing, just another white-robed, bald-headed figure. She had had more time to gaze at her reflection in the forest tarn by Delven, but it had never been really clear. Books might speak of someone gazing at their reflection in still water, but she had learned that books sometimes embroidered the truth.

She had never seen herself so clearly before; that was the truth of it. She barely knew her own face. Yet there was a familiarity about it. Was it because she knew it from the inside, she wondered, or because she saw echoes of other faces? People in Delven did look alike, she realised: she had never known it until she left, because she had never known how different people could be.

She turned her head to one side and the other, as far as she might, trying to catch a hint of her profile. The light from the window was right behind her, leaving her face somewhat in shadow: it was not easy to see.

But as she looked harder, turned her head again, perhaps grew more accustomed to the brightness and shadow on her image, suddenly she saw—and in the same moment remembered her first mathematics lesson and the strange words of Tutor Yanil, words she had never understood till now. For suddenly it was as if she were looking at *Sharess*.

Could it be...? For a moment, in a tilt of her head and fall of the light, Sharess had looked out of the glass at her. Younger, surely, but Sharess...

She found herself leaning on the wash-stand for support. Now she knew what Yanil had seen, what she had thought, what she had said under her breath.

Suddenly it all made sense. What other answer could there be? How could any other woman in a place so close-knit conceal a pregnancy? And if Sharess were her mother, who then was her father? There was only one man who ever went to the tor, and the same man was the one who had 'discovered' the motherless infant.

Discovered! She spun away, laughing silently, threw herself on the bed. It creaked reproachfully. The ceiling above her head had not been painted for years: there were faint brown discolourations here and there. Could a freedwoman paint her own ceiling? Could she choose the colours for herself?

Holdren her father, Sharess her mother... she would never have proof, but she knew.

She had stubbornly clung to the belief that people in Delven didn't tell lies, but wasn't keeping a secret—and such a secret!—just another kind of lie?

Another piece of her old world crumbled. She felt a flare of anger, but it was as fleeting as the flare of a struck match. Another feeling grew, as if the match had lit a lantern. She clenched her fists to her side, then clamped her arms across her stomach as if to contain her own secret joy. The bare little room seemed full of warmth.

She could not understand why it made her so happy. She would never see either of them again, never call them father, mother. It had hurt to part from Sharess, though she knew so little of her... but that pain she had accepted already. This new knowledge was pure gain.

"I name you free," she whispered to herself. "Daughter of Sharess."

Then the tears came. Tears of sorrow, tears of joy? She could not have said, did not try to distinguish, just lay there and let the tears flow.

There was a knock on the door.

Jerya took a moment to recall what was expected of her. She was a freedwoman, she had privacy. She sat up, wiped her face with her sleeve, called, "Come in!"

It was Rhenya, a bundle in her arms. "I've brung yowr clothes—" she began, then stopped, her mouth already forming the M. Then she stared at Jerya's face; she must have failed to clear away all the tear-tracks.

For a moment they were frozen, staring at each other, and then both began to weep again. Jerya got up from the bed, moved to Rhenya. The bundle of clothes was between them. She took them from unresisting hands and threw them on the bed, then took Rhenya in her arms.

"I don't understand," she said, her voice muffled against Jerya's shoulder. "Why're yow weeping? It's th' happiest day o'yowr life."

Jerya laughed suddenly—aloud, no silent slave's laugh. "Maybe it is," she said, "Maybe it is at that... but not for the reason you think. Here, come, sit." They sat together on the edge of the bed. Jerya took Rhenya's hand, held it in her lap. "From the beginning; why did you weep before? Why did you run away?"

Rhenya sniffed loudly, drew the back of her free hand across her nose, dabbed at tears with her fingertips. "Because yow were being freed and I'm still a slave and yow were th' best friend I's ever had."

Jerya could not speak for a moment. She squeezed Rhenya's hand with both of her own. "If I was that before, I still am—no! I'm *not* different. I'm not like them. They call me free, but what does it mean? Where can I go, what can I do? Outside this house, there is nothing, nothing that I can see. They'll pay me a few small notes for my work now. If I wish I can buy... I don't know... new clothes, curtains, a few books. But a woman may not own property—not what they call *real property*. A house, land... slaves. I thought—wild dreams, you know—I thought I would save all my small notes and one day ask the squire to sell you to me. Then I would make you free." Rhenya stared at her, wide-eyed. "But in this Song-forsaken land a woman may only own real property under... supervision; they call it a proxy arrangement. They say I'm free but I... it looks like a poor sort of freedom to me.

"And in my heart I was already free. That's what I need you to understand, Rhenya. If being free means losing your friendship, it isn't worth it.

It's more punishment than... whatever it's meant to be, a reward, a burden, I don't know. But it doesn't have to mean that. There's no reason at all."

Rhenya looked at her half-hopefully, half still in doubt. "Slaves and frees don't mix. It isn't done."

"We will, though," she said, fiercely now, breathing harder. "Rhenya, dear, you're the sweetest spirit I've ever met, and it's the best and the worst thing about you. The worst, because you're so trusting, because you believe everything they tell you. But now you have to choose *who* to trust. Because I'm telling you I have not changed." She lifted Rhenya's unresisting hand to her own head. "Feel? Still smooth. It doesn't suddenly sprout. It grows, slowly. If you stopped shaving yours would grow just the same. We *are* the same."

"I want to b'lieve yow..."

"Then believe me. It's up to you. They can make you do this, go there, but they can't make you *believe*." She rested her free hand between Rhenya's breasts, over her heart. "In your heart you're free. If you choose to be."

Rhenya looked away, ahead, at nothing. For a moment she was silent, then she said, "Yow're freeborn, Jerya, aren't yow? I know yow are."

"We all are."

"But—"

"—Babies don't understand slavery. Maybe they're wiser than we are."

"Why din't yow tell them yow're freeborn?" Rhenya said doggedly. "It makes a difference, I know, though folk'd still ask how yow came to be slaved."

"What would be the use? I can't prove it. But, anyway, I don't care what other people think; I care what *you* think."

"But yow talk about being free in yowr heart. I hardly know what yow mean, but if yow're born free I suppose yow always know."

"Oh, Rhenya..." Jerya nearly wept again. "Where I was born... I've tried to tell you about it, if only it didn't upset you... no one's called slave and no one's called free. I don't know how free we were, really. I never asked till recently, couldn't compare. Our lives were all shaped for us, I know that.

Only I couldn't quite... the shape didn't fit." She sighed. "My life has a new shape now. I don't even know if this one fits... But what can I do? Maybe the only path that's left to me is to try and make it fit."

"Yow will," said Rhenya. "Yow can do almost anything. Yow aren't like me."

"But I *am*!" she cried, not loud, though she wanted to yell. "You can do so much, too, you just don't know it... We *are* alike. If you cut me, I bleed, if you hurt me, I weep... oh, look, I can't show you the world now. Just look at *us*. The last ten minutes. We can still talk to each other—can't we? Tell me we can do that, at least."

Rhenya looked at her, her face lighting up with that remarkable smile. "Maybe we can..."

"And we will. I suppose we can't sleep together... well, I wonder. But quietly, when no one is looking too hard, we can talk, we can hold each other, still. Can't we?"

"Oh, we can!" Rhenya hugged Jerya hard, kissing her full on the lips. "But now I must go. I've been lucky not to be thrashed already today."

"Tell them I kept you—tell them I needed your help to move this bed—yes, help me, make it true before you go."

Even with the two of them it was a struggle, but soon enough the heavy iron bed was close against the wall under the slope of the roof. "Thank you," said Jerya. Inwardly, she supposed Rhenya might have felt she had no choice. The law stated that a slave must obey any order from any free person, save it conflict with the orders of their own master or the laws of the land... But she had not meant it as a command. "Thank you for the help freely given."

Rhenya grinned back at her. Perhaps she was beginning to understand. Then she was gone. Jerya threw herself down on her bed again, looking up at the ceiling, closer now, hands behind her head cradling smooth skin. She would miss that feeling. Perhaps she would find delight in her hair when it grew; that would be another new thing, not having to keep it bound in a headcloth, *free* to wear it in coil or braid or coronet. Still, she had learned that being bald had its delights too. Things gained; things lost.

Th' happiest day o'yowr life. It couldn't be that, could it? Yet when had she been happier? She could only think of the early days in the college, the first euphoria of discovering mathematics and astronomy... and Railu... She winced at herself for placing them in that order. Those days, before the doubts began and the deception surfaced—yes, they had been happy, but it seemed false now, as well as distant, and unreal just through distance.

Then another thought intruded. She was free, now; an employee, not a slave. A *secretary*—even if she still had to learn most of what that meant.

Would a free person, a secretary... would such a person be permitted to read the books in Duncal's Library? Freely and openly, not in snatched moments when she knew the Master and Mistress were elsewhere? Might she, even, be permitted to look through the telescope?

That would be something, she thought. Freedom—freed-dom—might have its joys after all.

CHAPTER 23

RODAL

It seemed spring came early to the Archipelago. Buscanya and Velyadero were the two Southernmost of the Principalities, and Velyadero was nearly all upland, like the part of Denvirran that he'd first seen. Buscanya was low-lying; indeed, it seemed to be nothing but archipelago and peninsulas. Just looking at the charts, there were more islands than he could count. He could easily have believed that someone had simply thrown a pot of brown ink at the paper from across the room.

In an odd way it reminded him of the rare glimpses he'd had of the territory North of Delven—if water and land changed places. That country, Unsung Lands West of the mountains, was all forest and lake, and he could no more have counted the lakes than he could count the islands here.

There was a saying among mariners; Croudor quoted it to him with his usual relish for bad news as soon as this Southward voyage had been mooted. *Sail a hundred miles to make ten.* It had sounded like exaggeration, until from the crow's nest one day he saw another ship moving in another channel no more than a mile away, and realised several hours later that they were threading that same tight channel themselves.

The islands you could see were only the start of it. There were reefs and shoals and skerries, some of them appearing and disappearing with the shifting of the tides. The charts were supposed to show them all, at least in the main channels, but the Skipper was a careful man, and kept someone in the crow's nest at all times, day and night.

He'd thought night sailing was tricky in the Island Channels, between Sessapont and Troquharran. This was another game entirely. The *Levore* ran under reefed sails when night fell, but she kept moving. There was risk, besure, but the rewards were great.

The Skipper had explained it to him before they'd set out from Sessapont. The shallow waters of the Archipelago yielded a rich harvest of delicacies. The most prized was the lobster, though they looked monstrous, but there were crabs too, and many varieties of fish. Unlike the game Rodal was familiar with from Delven, which often improved by being hung for a time in a cool cave, all of these were at their best when fresh. Crab and lobster could be transported alive, in casks of sea-water in the hold, but this only really worked in spring, when the water around the ship was still cold, while the shorter nights allowed them to sail at full speed for more hours.

It took a lot of work, because the water in the casks needed refreshing regularly, as well as because of the demanding navigation. The whole cargo, both the lobster and the crates of fish, could be ruined if the winds failed, so it was a great gamble. The outlay in the harbours of the Archipelago was daunting; but if everything worked out, the merchants of Sessapont would pay three times as much, sometimes more. "I can't pass-by a profit like that," the Skipper had said, promising a healthy bonus to all the hands if they were successful.

And in this trade, smaller vessels like the *Levore* had an advantage. In open waters, larger ships, the three-masted schooners and barques, could easily outpace them; but they were harder to manoeuvre in the tight and twisting channels, and could not even enter the smaller harbours. Her shallower draught allowed the *Levore* to slip through certain straits where a deeper keel risked running aground.

Still, with all those shoals and reefs to look out for, a constant watch was vital. There was always one man in the crow's nest. With one at the wheel and another required for frequent sail-changes, only one could ever be off-duty at a time, and even he was still called on to deliver meals and to refresh the water in the lobster-casks. Rodal doubted any of them managed more than four hours' sleep a night for the week of their run from Glimhaven.

Night or day, a stint in the nest called for vigilance; but there was much to be seen besides. He became accustomed to the seals, which might be seen resting on any sandy beach or rocky shelf; sometimes they would raise their dog-like heads and watch, curious, as the *Levore* slid past. By comparison, porpoises were fewer and sightings more fleeting. He soon learned to distinguish one shiny grey back, half-clearing the surface, from another. Seals were larger and their backs were one unbroken curve; porpoises had sharp black fins half-way down the spine. Occasionally you would see one puff out a spray of air and water from the curious hole just behind its head.

He heard about, but never saw, the basking sharks which were said to be the largest living things known, in water or on land. "Another month or two," said the Skipper. "Twice as long as that there bowsprit, some on 'em." Not for the first time, he thought about all the things he had seen, and the many more he never would. There was a price to be paid for holding to your promises.

Still, there was plenty more that he could and did see, especially in the air. Three times he'd sighted a great white-tailed eagle, clearly larger than the eagles he knew from the Delven moors. Every day he saw terns, skuas, kittiwakes, and others he had yet to fit names to. Most striking of all were the cormorants, perching on prominent rocks with wings spread as if displaying. He wondered about that, because it was the start of the breeding season, but Croudor told him they did that to dry their wings.

There was less wildlife to be seen at night, but there were other things. Strangest by far was the eldritch radiance which sometimes rippled through the water, shimmering about the bows as if the *Levore* herself were some kind of magical paintbrush, or making her wake glimmer far astern. At first it sent a shiver down his spine, as it put him in mind of the stories of the Blistered Lands which had disturbed his childhood dreams. But he reminded himself that he had walked unharmed right where the Blistered Lands were supposed to be; and he observed that the curious light caused no alarm to his shipmates. In fact, he thought, it was the first time he had ever heard Croudor offer a spontaneous word of admiration for anything. "Right pretty, ain't it?" the older hand had remarked. But neither he, nor Grauven, nor the Skipper, could offer any account of what caused the phenomenon. He wondered if Jerya would know, or the greats of the Dawnsingers' Guild, or any of the wise men of the Five Principalities.

There were mysteries in the world, besure, and probably no one could unravel all of them.

❋

Sail a hundred miles to make ten. It *was* exaggerated; the Skipper had told him that in the Northern waters of the Archipelago the true figure might average at closer to forty, and further South the islands were fewer and larger, so straighter courses were usually possible. Still, it made the point.

A hundred miles would be a good day's run for a vessel like the *Levore*, in open waters and with a fair wind. In these reaches, with all the changes of tack, it could easily take all day to cover forty. If the wind turned adverse, it could be hard to make headway at all. It was fortunate, then, that Northerlies were rare at this season.

On the Southward trip, when they anchored for the hours of darkness, they'd taken six days for what they hoped to do in three or four coming back. As the Skipper said, when they'd all be short of sleep on the return, 'twould be foolishness to be starting out tired. On the third of those six days, they'd made their anchorage in a bight almost entirely enclosed by three islands; a beautiful place, with a pale sandy bottom showing clear through the shallow water. No sooner had they finished coiling and stowing than Grauven had stripped off his clothes. stepped over the rail, and taken a clean dive into the water. After a moment he came up, puffing and gasping, but then laughing. Rodal leaned over to ask, "Ain't it cold?"

"'S'not like th'baths in Sess, but it ben't proper cold neither. It's always warm enough here, when th'day's been sunny."

Rodal looked at the Skipper and got a benign nod, and a moment later he too was pulling off his garments. He didn't allow himself a moment's hesitation; step over the rail, balance, launch.

It was cold enough to shock, but he knew at once it wasn't as cold as he'd known in Delven's streams and tarns. He came up, like Grauven, laughing. He'd been a decent swimmer by Delven standards, but then he'd been the best wrestler, and he'd had a rude awakening in Carwerid. He supposed Grauven, a seasoned mariner and raised by the sea, would beat him easily; but he challenged him nonetheless. The distance, to a prominent rock that blocked off the channel at the further end of the bight, must be five times the length of Delven's largest tarn; but there and back seemed a good distance for a real race. "Touch the rock, first back to touch the ship's the winner."

To his surprise, he was right behind Grauven at the turning point, and when he decided to put on a spurt halfway back, he quickly passed him. He had time to slap the hull and swim back the few yards to wrap an arm around the anchor cable before Grauven had finished. Grauven, not being Croudor, was graceful in defeat. "Where d'yow learn t'swim like that?"

"We had lakes," he said, not being sure if Grauven would know the word 'tarn'.

※

Glimhaven sat in a half-bowl of steep slopes at the Eastern end of one of the larger islands. The harbour entrance was framed by low cliffs of reddish rock that at a distance looked enough like some of the crags around Delven to spark a pang of nostalgia; but up close the rock was fine-grained, faintly slippery to the touch even when dry. *Not sandstone*, he thought.

Having berthed, he'd accompanied the Skipper to inspect the cargo they'd be loading first thing in the morning; the lobsters were kept alive in large square ponds hewn from the rock and shaded by canopies fashioned from old, heavily-patched, sails.

Afterward they sat with the seller, Tarson, at a bench outside a tavern, savouring the evening sun as Rodal learned how to eat mussels. They washed the food down with a local ale, a brew unfamiliar to Rodal, as black and opaque as strong coffee, with a hint of smoke and a background sweetness. *Strange*, he thought, *but who'd want everywhere to taste the same?*

Tarson was barrel-chested and had probably the biggest beard Rodal had ever seen. His eyes, nested in deep wrinkles, and a strip of forehead, were all that could be seen of his face. His weathered skin looked almost like leather, a deep chestnut hue; there was no telling what his original skin colour might have been. The beard, by contrast, was bleached whiter than his shirt. Rodal wondered if all this was an inevitable result of a lifetime spent on or by the water in the sunniest region of the Five Principalities.

It was obvious that Tarson and the Skipper had known each other for years. When the second round of pints arrived, they sat back against the sun-warmed wall and fell into reminiscence. Not so many years ago, Rodal gathered, there had been constant trouble with pirates in the Archipelago, especially in these Northern reaches. For decades, several of the islands had been disputed between Sessapont and Buscanya, and neither had been willing to take responsibility for policing them.

Tarson was chuckling now, a bass rasp. "They weren't fools, them pirates. Kenned if they took twenty casks o' lobster off a ship, nineteen'd only go to rot an' stink the place out; or throw 'em back to th'sea, but there weren't no profit for 'em in that."

"Aye," said the Skipper, also chortling, "Saw it meself a couple o'times when I were a prentice-lad. Soon's they saw what we was carryin', they'd be, 'we'll just take a few silvers for our trouble'. One lot called it an 'inspection fee'."

"'Inspection fee'," repeated Tarson gleefully. "I like that. And then off quick sharp, to harry some other poor crew."

"Right enough." The Skipper's eye settled on Rodal. "P'raps they'd'a known afore they even boarded. My uncle—he were th' cap'n o' my prentice-ship—he knew th' score, no need to run or to fight when you was carryin' perishables. So we'd heave-to all obligin'-like, and them pirates'd know right away."

"An' they'd jus' come aboard to 'complete the formalities'," finished Tarson, his chuckle crescendoing into a full-hearted belly-laugh.

"Aye, 'complete the formalities'," echoed the Skipper with near-equal merriment.

Rodal joined the mirth as best he could, though the story was strange to him. He sipped his beer; well, that was growing less strange with every taste.

"Different story if you was cargoin' somethin' what'd keep, though, eh?" said Tarson more soberly. "Spices or sea-glass or amber, owt like that."

"True tell't," said the Skipper. "No heavin'-to meekly then. An' chance o' givin' 'em the slip in a wherry was skinny to none. Then it was belayin' pins at the ready and mash any hand that landed on your rails. Less'n you saw right off there was too many on 'em."

"But there's none of this now?" asked Rodal.

Tarson looked him up and down. "I wouldna took you for a lad to shy from a fight."

"No more he is," said the Skipper. He gave a brief account of Rodal's encounter with the would-be thieves that misty night on the river. "See, lad, there's still bad 'uns about, lookin' for a chance. Don't matter whether yow're in Denvirran, or Troq, or Sess, or here in Busc. I daresay it's th' same in Velyadero, too, only I never bin there."

"Why'd anyun go to Velyadero?" asked Tarson.

"Now, now," said the Skipper. "I won't go bad-mouthin' somewheres I never seen. No one from Velyadero ever did me any harm, an' I can't say that for any o'th' other four."

"Fair enough, I s'pose."

It flitted across Rodal's mind that he, too, had now seen four of the Five Principalities. There was a certain appeal, he saw, in completing the set; and for all he knew Velyadero might be the perfect place to head with the girls. *Something to find out about...* Besides, it would be one more thread added to the story he'd have to tell.

✳

But who am I ever going to tell it to?

The question never occurred to him that evening, sitting by the tavern in the glow of the evening sun— and the glow of two pints of ale which, by the end, he'd come to admire very much. It only came to him as he stood near the bows the following day, dipping a bucket to freshen the water for the cargo and watching a flock of seapie swirl into the air: a shimmering of black wings and white bellies, flickers of orange at legs and bills, a clamour of shrill piping alarm calls. He found himself wondering how he'd describe this, and everything else he'd seen. Only then did it occur to him to wonder who he was going to tell.

Here in the Five Principalities, he'd never even considered revealing the truth of his own origin. 'In the mountains', he'd said to the Skipper and the others; 'beyond the mountains' was as unthinkable here as it was, in mirror-image, in the Sung Lands. Everyone in the East 'knew' there was nothing West of the mountains; and everyone in the West 'knew' there was nothing to the East.

Well, he corrected himself, maybe *that's not exactly true. Jerya had some idea, and it sounded like other Dawnsingers at least knew it wasn't 'Blistered Lands'. But I'm never going to be chatting with any Dawnsingers.*

Here in the East, the only people he'd really be able to tell were Jerya and Railu, because they knew the key thing already. Who else could he ever tell that he'd seen the Western and the Eastern oceans? He'd trust the Skipper with his life, but would he trust him with this tale? He couldn't bear the thought of the Skipper looking at him as if he'd lost his mind.

And when he got back to the West... Well, he would have to say something to the people of Delven, because they knew that the three of them had disappeared into Unsung Lands—and how many would be returning? Three? Or just himself?

He would have to say something, but how much would anyone understand? How much would he himself have understood if he'd heard such a tale before he'd left Delven for the first time?

Well, that was something he'd have to contend with. But he had no intention of staying long in Delven. Back in Carwerid... he supposed Annyt would at least believe him. But what she would make of it, he could not be so sure. And who else was there?

One day we'll have children. He wasn't sure he believed it yet, but it was something to think about. He smiled to himself in the night of the Archipelago, imaging a couple of tousle-headed youngsters rolling their eyes at each other. *Pa's off on his wild tales again.*

Above, the Three were briefly obscured by a cloud, a leaden mass rimmed in silver. He had to peer harder than ever for any hint of danger ahead, a shadow in the water or the pale flash of rocks awash. "Ten degrees starboard!" he called down. A faint hail came back. The *Levore* always took a little time to answer to the helm; those could be the most anxious moments.

The cloud moved on and one by one the moons reappeared. He glanced back at their pearly gleam on the water, the faint blue glow of the phosphorescence in the ship's wake. Not far off, a high-pitched chatter told him a flock of storm petrels were active.

He sighed. *Well, even if I can hardly tell anyone, I'll still have these memories.*

He couldn't help wondering if memories would be enough.

PART THREE

GREETINGS AND FAREWELLS

JON SPARKS

CHAPTER 24

JERYA

Jerya was finding new delight in the simple act of walking into the house. It was not the fact that, being free, she could use the front door: that struck her as absurd, and it was rarely the most convenient. It was not the fact that she had ridden to and returned from the town inside the carriage with Lady Pichenta; Rhenya had declared it a great honour, but more than anything Jerya had found the journey awkward. Partly it was because they had little to say to each other, but mostly it was because her first experience of the carriage had been riding on the roof. She had not forgotten what Lady Pichenta had said on that occasion: 'Of course I don't want them to ride inside.' Would Railu, she had wondered, now be welcome inside? Or would the question never arise because Railu would not be expected to go anywhere?

She brooded on this for most of the ninety minutes of the journey into Drumlenn, and similar thoughts resurfaced on the return; but there was much more to think about too. Still, her sense of satisfaction only really returned when she had stepped down from the carriage, adding her thanks to Whallin in echo of Lady Pichenta.

Her pleasure resided in the clothes she was wearing, clothes which for the first time in her life she had selected freely for herself. Everything about her new suit seemed perfect: the way it looked, and the way it felt.

It was not that the new clothes *felt* greatly different. The skirt had much the same fullness, the same kind of swing, that she'd grown accustomed to in their months at Duncal. Skirts in the Sung Lands, both in Delven and in Carwerid, had favoured a different outline, closer around the hips but flaring to the hem.

Here, 'fine' ladies often wore still wider skirts, exaggerated with padding—called 'formers' or 'enhancers'—under the decorative outer strata. Jerya's new skirt, however, relied solely on generous pleating, just like the skirts she'd worn as a slave; and just like them it had generous, practical pockets in its side seams. The dressmaker had lifted an eyebrow at that request, but hadn't demurred. She must know very well that Jerya was still only a few months past manumission, but she had received her politely. *Well, I suppose my money's as good as anyone else's*, she'd thought; but she hadn't been welcomed so kindly everywhere.

So why did the new clothes make her feel good? It could only come down to this: that she had chosen them herself. When had she ever done that before? Not in Delven, save that on any given day she could choose between two nearly identical skirts; nor in the College, where every garment was white, and there was only the choice between wool for colder days and linen for warmer times, and between a formal robe or a more casual skirt and blouse. For the first time in her life, everything about her new outfit was her own choice: cut, colour, fabric, embellishments. She had been obliged to take account of budget, but still faced far more choice than she had ever known before. This, in a small way, was freedom.

Her pensive steps brought her to the door of the downstairs nursery, that warm little room backing on to the great kitchen range. It had been converted from a store-room; she remembered the extra work, which had required a couple of field-slaves to be drafted in for a few days, clearing out the kitchen stores, old dinner-services, moth-eaten table linen, all manner of accumulated things: the sweeping and scrubbing, sugar-soaping, distempering and furnishing, which had transformed a dim and dusty room into a light and airy one.

Railu sat in the window seat, light haloing the curves of her bald head, and the baby's downy one against her breast. She was not immediately aware of Jerya, who stopped in the doorway to admire the sight. Then she looked up. Her eyes travelled down the new suit and shoes. "Well, Miss Jerya," she said. Her voice was hushed, not to disturb the drowsily suckling Embrel: it was hard to tell if there was sarcasm in her tone. "A fine picture you make." Her words were an uncomfortable echo of Jerya's own thought.

Jerya advanced a few steps, uncertainly, into the room. She did not know what to do with her hands, until they found her pockets. "I was thinking the same about you."

Railu looked at her for a moment, frowning slightly, then said, "Thank you, I'm sure you mean it kindly."

"I mean it truly," said Jerya. Suddenly everything felt wrong. She could not talk to Railu like this, standing hands in pockets across the room in her new suit. She wanted to be close, touching, holding her. But the baby was in the way—and not only the baby.

But she could not remain where she was, and she could not walk out of the room. She pulled up a chair and sat down, quietly, close to the other end of the window-recess, facing Railu. Railu gave her one swift glance, then looked down again, as if watching Embrel, yet Jerya had a sudden conviction she was hardly even seeing him. The child's faint sucking sounds were clear in the thick velvety silence.

Jerya folded her hands in her lap and waited. If she still knew Railu, it would not be long before she said what she was thinking.

"Paid for that with your own money," said Railu in that same muted, ambiguous, tone.

Jerya only nodded, hoping to force Railu to look at her.

"How much?"

"Eight and a half small," said Jerya. It did not occur to her to disguise the true figure. Still it felt like a small deception. Eight and a half was the price of the suit alone. The shoes had cost her another three.

Railu snorted. "That's more than he paid for the two of us."

"I know," said Jerya. "I will never forget. But... would it make any difference if the price had been higher? It's being sold, being bought—at any price—that I can't... can't ever forgive."

"Well, you've bought yourself again, haven't you?"

"Bought? How... bought?"

"You know," said Railu in a sibilant whisper. Though she didn't raise her voice, her vehemence seemed to make the child uneasy: he shifted, waved one tiny clenched fist about, whimpered slightly.

"My aunts in Delven said a child takes in anger with its mother's milk. Anger, sadness, happiness, whatever you're feeling: they sing laughing songs to nursing mothers."

"I don't feel like laughing," Railu responded. This time she did lift her head, looked full into Jerya's eyes. "I *am* angry. Why shouldn't I give him that? It's about all I have to give."

"Rai..." Jerya reached out a hand, found nowhere to rest it. It hovered in the air between them a moment, trembling, then subsided on the chair-arm. "You gave him life."

"I gave him *my* life, it seems to me," Railu said, softly, flat-voiced. "I'm still pumping life into him. By the time he's grown, there'll be nothing left of me at all."

Jerya stared at her helplessly for what seemed at least a full minute. "I won't... I won't say I understand. I'm not in your shoes, I can only imagine... But I am angry too, you know. I was angry—furious—all those months ago—when you first agreed to the whole scheme—to letting them take your baby—"

Railu laughed, shortly. "I wish they *would* take him!"

"Oh, Rai... and will you still think so when they do? When you see him growing up, walking, running about, learning to ride, going off to school and coming back a grand young gentleman... he's your own son, Rai, and one day he will own *you*."

"He owns me now. More than they ever... but I can't imagine any of that. I can't imagine *tomorrow*, Jerya, today's all I can... time's stopped. I don't feel..." She turned up her face again and its blankness shocked Jerya to the heart. "Jerya, I don't feel like a person any more. I don't belong to myself. I feel like a *slave*."

Jerya could not answer.

Railu sighed heavily. "I look at him sometimes, like this, he's so tiny, so fragile, I feel like I could crush him with my bare hands. Don't worry, I won't. I hardly know why it's so, but I know I won't. I have the strength but not the power... oh, Jerya, when I'm sitting here alone with him, all these hours, all these days, it's as clear as anything... but when I try and say it the words won't shape themselves. I can't express it. I haven't even that power any more. I'm his slave. That's all I know."

"No!" said Jerya, clenching the arms of her chair, knuckles whitening. "That's a lie, just like the other... this time it's you telling it to yourself, but it's still a lie. Rai, I don't understand everything you say—but maybe I understand some things you don't... you were very young when they took you for a Dawnsinger. You haven't seen the girls you played with, in that childhood you hardly remember, grow up, become mothers, wean their own children... I did. I always supposed I'd have children one day. I don't know if I *wanted* them; it just didn't feel like there was any real choice. It was... the thing they always said: it's the way things are. But I couldn't imagine any other future. Then it all changed, for a little while. I thought I was a Dawnsinger, and Dawnsingers don't bear children..." She laughed a little: it sounded harsh, too loud, in the nursery, and she stopped. "But that's false too—I never got the chance to tell you—"

"—Sharess is your mother."

Jerya was newly shocked. "How did you know?"

Railu chuckled, a sound that lifted Jerya's heart. "Same way you did, I should think: by looking. Easier for me to see it, I suppose. Saw you together in Delven... I couldn't believe it; well, as you say, I didn't understand these things, except in books. But I didn't know how else you could look so alike—"

"Yes..." Jerya breathed. "When I saw my face in the mirror, the day they called me free, when I was still bald, it was Sharess looking at me."

"No question: mother or grandmother, she had to be. Close relative, for sure. But then she told me, when we talked, Sharess and I."

Jerya felt a prickle of anger. "She told *you*? And she never told me."

"She said if you wanted to, you'd know, and if you didn't want to it would only hurt you..."

"I wanted to... all my life I wanted to know... you know, they stole part of my childhood, too. I knew my mother less than you did."

She stared into Railu's eyes suddenly. "Listen... one thing... this child... whatever we feel, you feel—About them, about her, about... the circumstances... I'm sorry, I'm not making sense. Rai, don't let anyone take that from him. Don't let him grow up not knowing who his mother is."

Railu looked out of the window, uncertainty written in her face. "Don't you think he might be better off not knowing?"

"Better off? I don't know. What does better off mean? But can you stomach the deceit?"

"Don't lecture me about deceit!" snapped Railu, suddenly irate.

Jerya stared at her. Her eyes prickled. "What do you....?"

Railu gave her a long look. Jerya had never found it harder to meet her friend's gaze. "You want the truth, do you? You want to know how I think, Miss Jerya? You want to know how I feel?"

Don't call me Miss Jerya, she wanted to say. But that wouldn't help, not now. There was nothing she could say; she could only nod.

"Well, what I keep thinking, what I can't help thinking... wondering... where would I be now?"

"Where would you be?"

"Come on, Jerya, you're not stupid... Ha! None of this would have happened if you were stupid, if you were docile."

Jerya had a sense, a foreboding, that she knew what was coming next. *Well*, she told herself, *you asked for it*. Railu hardly needed to say the words. Jerya herself had said the same more than once; but then Railu had absolved her. Not this time, she sensed.

"Where I'd be now... I'd be Dawnsinger in Delven, don't you think? I'd be there and... and I wouldn't have *this*." She moved sharply, almost as if she were going to fling Embrel away, but arrested the movement at once. The baby murmured a vague protest but never ceased suckling. "Whatever else you may think, Jerya, you can't deny that's a big difference.

"And you... do you never think what your life would be like? Back in Carwerid, in the College, studying with Yanil and Jossena... does it really sound so bad?"

"No," she had to say. "But then it always was... a temptation."

"Temptation! Oh, but we mustn't be tempted, must we?"

Railu shifted in her chair. Her back had troubled her greatly in the last months of pregnancy, and Jerya knew she had not fully recovered, still struggled to find comfort if she stayed too long in one posture. "D'you want to walk for a bit?"

"Maybe later. You're not going to distract me now. Just pass me that red cushion."

When Railu was, at least temporarily, comfortable again, she fixed her gaze on Jerya once more. "I've thought about it a lot. Well..." She laughed: a brief, mirthless, bark. "I've had precious little to do but think, lately. But, for all my thinking, I've struggled to remember what was so terrible about it. About the temptation. About staying, going along with Perriad's plans."

"Doing what we were told."

"Because of course there's none of that here!" Railu snapped back.

Jerya dropped her gaze. "No, you're right, of course. But we didn't know that then, did we?"

"No, but then we didn't have a clue what we were going to find this side. Not a *draffing* clue. But Jerya doesn't want to stay so there must be something there."

"It's not a case of 'didn't want to stay'. I couldn't stay."

"No, you couldn't." It didn't sound like agreement. After a moment, she went on, "And why was that? Remind me, won't you?"

"Because it was built on a lie."

"Because people in Delven believe that Dawnsong makes the sun rise? Maybe they do, in Delven, but not everyone, not everywhere."

"Railu, *I* believed it, as far as I thought about it at all. For nineteen years of my life I never questioned it." She wondered at herself now; she'd questioned pretty near everything else. "When I found out it wasn't true, it was as if... as if my world turned upside down."

"And who was it who told you the truth?"

Jerya didn't answer. There was no need. They both knew: Jossena, and then Perriad.

"Well, that's as may be. But look at us now. Look at where we are. Are you going to tell us there's no lies here?" She waited a beat or two, but Jerya's silence was answer enough. "You say the Guild's built on a lie, and maybe you're right. But everything here's built on a lie, too, isn't it? The lie that says one person can own another."

Jerya spread her hands wide in surrender. "You're right, of course."

"There you are, then. Seems to me... all I can see is, we've swapped one lie for another. And it seems to me this one's worse."

Again, Jerya could not argue. She reached out a hand, but Railu only looked at it. After an awkward moment she pulled her hand back. "I'm sorry, Rai. I... I still don't believe I could have stayed, but I had no right to drag you along with me."

"Oh, well, I suppose I had a choice. I can't truly say you dragged me, not literally. But I let you persuade me... I let you convince me it would all work out because... because I didn't know any better. I think I knew more about the moons of Jupiter than about the world right outside the walls of the Precincts." She looked down, to the child in her lap. For a moment they were both focused on the baby.

"I didn't persuade you to do that." Before the words were even fully out out, Jerya knew they were a mistake. The fact that they were true was no defence.

❋

Railu's anger subsided in a day or two, but she remained cool, pointedly calling her 'Miss Jerya' when she spoke to her. Words meant to be kind, offers of help, were met with, "Thank you, Miss Jerya," or "You're very obliging, Miss Jerya," and usually followed with, "But I can manage, thank you very much."

To add to Railu's isolation, Rhenya, too, had little time to spare. Though Cook had not been freed, she had, as if in compensation, been allowed to withdraw from what remained of her daily labour. She still came and sat in the kitchen, most days and for most of the day. She still lent a hand with some tasks, especially ones she could do from her chair, like shelling peas. As she said, 'what else am I goin' to do?'. Once, Jerya, just entering the kitchen, overheard her saying to Rhenya, 'what more'd I want if'n I was free?' If Rhenya had thought of answering, Jerya's arrival silenced her. Cook might be luxuriating in her easier life but, since Jerya's manumission, nearly all the housework now fell once again on Rhenya's young shoulders.

Railu's situation made Jerya grieve every time she saw or thought about her friend, but she did not know how to rectify it, how to repair the damage she herself had caused. *Of course* Railu slept in the nursery. In itself that was reasonable; Embrel might need her at any time. But *of course* Jerya had to sleep in her 'own' room and *of course* Rhenya slept where she had always done—in the loft across the yard, and once again alone. These second and third 'of courses' were not so self-evident, and she struggled to think of any good reason why all three of them had to sleep alone. (Yes, Railu had Embrel, but Jerya was pretty sure Railu still counted herself as alone.)

The basic facts of Railu's situation were imposed upon her, but she also seemed to rebuff, or simply to ignore, most efforts to draw her out. She spoke of resenting the infant's hold over her life, but was reluctant to let anyone else care for him. She could hardly deny his official parents, but she seemed ill at ease, always watching closely, when they held him. To an observer like Jerya it seemed paradoxical. Railu hadn't wanted a baby, often expressed thinly veiled resentment at his domination of her life, and yet seemed unable to let him go.

❈

Then there was Rodal. Or rather, she thought, there wasn't. Nine months since the last sight of him, and not a word, not a rumour. In her mind, in quiet moments in the Library or walking outside, she enumerated the possibilities.

He might have gone straight back to the Sung Lands. She had seen fresh snow on the heights the day before she and Railu were taken, but what had the weather done subsequently? She had hardly been in a fit state to take notice. It hadn't rained during that awful journey to Drumlenn: she knew that much, but no more. It hadn't rained on the day they were sold, either. After their arrival in Duncal the first days were something of a blur. They had hardly left the house at first, and then ruddy-fever had taken the best part of a week out of the reckoning. Summer had taken its final bow and autumn was well established before she had really taken notice of the outside world again. Had there been a clear spell when Rodal could have made the crossing? She had no way of knowing. If he had, she could only hope all had gone well. She did not think climbing the slabs by the cataract, especially if dry, would trouble him too much; she was more concerned about the precarious traverse of the ledge on the East side of the notch. Perhaps he should push his pack ahead of him instead of hauling it...

But even if he could have made the crossing, would he? He had only accompanied them in the first place because he had made a promise to the Dawnsinger. To Sharess... Jerya's thoughts were diverted by the recollection of what that name truly meant.

Rodal, she thought, was a man who took promises seriously. But there was a conflict between his promise to Annyt and the one he had made to Sharess, and by extension to herself and Railu. With Annyt's claim in mind, might he persuade himself that he had fulfilled the basic duty? He *had* seen them across the mountains. They were safe, if by that you meant in no evident danger to life and limb. Would that be enough for Rodal? Could she blame him if he decided it was?

And what would Railu think about that? *If only I could find a moment when it feels right to ask her.*

Of course, he might equally still be on this side of the Sundering Wall. It was perfectly possible there had been no safe opportunity to cross. What then? He might still be somewhere in the wilds, holed up in a cave perhaps, fending for himself. Much as he had expected to do with the two of them.

Alternatively, he might also have fallen foul of freebooters, the same band or some other group. Of course they would hardly take him for a runaway slave. At least he should be spared that fate, Jerya thought, and was glad of it. But there might be other possibilities scarcely less dire.

Her mind hurried on from those vague forebodings. If Rodal had not crossed back to the Sung Lands, and if he was still free... She could hardly imagine he had simply forgotten them, so where was he?

CHAPTER 25

RODAL

He could have steered well clear, stayed aboard as much as possible. He could have suggested Grauven and Croudor visit a different bordel this time; there were plenty to choose from. He could have...

Well, he could have done many things. But he'd done none of them.

He didn't know if Grauven and Croudor had sought her out, or whether she'd recognised them. He had no idea what they'd told her. But here she was; dressed, he thought, exactly as last time. He recalled the image of the apple that had come to him then.

"You have time?" he asked after the initial greetings. "To walk about again?"

"I've time."

"When do you have to be back?"

She shrugged. "If'n I's late, I don't make so much coin tonight, but it just means I has to make it up another day. 'S up to me, I's a free woman."

She said 'free woman' with evident pride, her shrouded gaze seeming to follow a heavily-laden slave-girl—surely no more than fourteen—trotting past on the heels of a richly-dressed woman in a heavy indigo veil.

You're not a slave; that's what you really mean. He couldn't help wondering exactly how much freedom there was in the life of a whore in Sessapont. But then again, freedom wasn't everything. Some slaves might well be better-fed, better-housed, live more comfortable lives, than some of the free folk he'd seen. *Well, mayhap freedom's one thing and comfort's another.*

Their walk took a different route this time, following the riverbank under trees starting to show the green fuzz of spring, before threading through gardens in one of the narrow valleys between the sharp hills. Eventually, however, they ended up in the same tavern they'd visited before. This time Rodal made sure to pick a table where Narèni would be in good light, and she voiced no objection.

He was hungry now, and ordered food to go with his ale. "D'you want something?"

"I dun't have enough coin."

"Don't worry, I'll pay." It wasn't much, he knew. A lot less than a night at the bordel, besure. He ignored the nagging voice in his head that wondered if the emptiness of her purse had come about 'accident'ly on purpose', as folk said in Delven. It didn't signify. A chicken leg, a roasted onion, a hunk of bread, wouldn't break him.

"I did think yoe was tryin' to save your coin," she said as if reading his thoughts. She slipped her cyder-glass under her veil with that practised two-hand-dance.

"Yea, I am. But I've got a decent bonus coming for the run to Glimhaven and back, and I spend little enough otherwise. Living on board, all I ever need coin for is a bit of food and a drink on days like this. It's come to a sorry pass if I can't buy a bite for a friend."

At 'friend' her head lifted sharply and even through the veil he felt—and saw—her gaze on him. "You know," he said, not thinking about it, "I've never seen your face clear."

"Yoe could of."

"I could? When?"

She laughed almost silently. "That first time. In... in my room. Foof, yoe could of seen *all* o' me. But all yoe wanted was to talk."

She'd liked that, she'd said before, but now it was hard to tell whether 'yoe could of' didn't hint at some regret.

"I did," he said. "Mostly, I still do. But... well, you know, you've had plenty of chance to look at me."

"Yea, I has," she said, smiling, teeth showing white through the gauze. "Lucky for me."

At that moment the food arrived. Perhaps it was as well. As Narèni set to, cutting the meat into bite-size pieces, the easier to eat under the veil, he asked a question that had been in his mind. "When you first came here—to Sessapont—how did you get here?"

"Jus' walked. Couple o'times someun give me a lift in a cart to th' next town, but 'part from that, I jus' walked."

"How long did it take?"

"I ain't much for countin'... Well." She laughed softly. "I's learned, like, since I's bin here, learned to count my coin an all that. But I wun't partic'ly countin' th'days. Nine, ten, days, I s'pose."

It could be two hundred miles, he guessed, give or take. He knew from his own experience that riding a cart might give your feet a rest but wouldn't necessarily speed your passage.

"I don't suppose you could take coaches...?"

She laughed again. "Couldn't then and still can't now, I dare say. Them's for rich folks, in't them? And I din't have no coin at all, then. Not one green penny." She lifted her veil, forked a morsel of chicken into her mouth.

"So how did you eat? You couldn't walk all that way on an empty stomach."

"Fruit off trees, mostly. Still felt pretty empty, lot o'th time, mind. I's made sure I dun't go hungry since." She patted her belly. Yes, there was a certain gentle roundness. You wouldn't call her fat, or even plump, but... he remembered her bare arms, her more-than-half-exposed breasts, that first night in the bordel; a softness.

It wasn't that he hadn't been tempted. No, he could all too easily have succumbed. It was probably a good thing that she'd dressed more demurely for their subsequent meetings. Though, if he were truly honest with himself, there was a part of him that would have felt not the least objection if she had looked more like the first time.

"Eat," she said, "T's best when t's hot."

He was happy to comply, to divert his thoughts from their potentially treacherous path.

He watched Narèni's deft manipulation of the veil, keeping it clear of the greasy food but never revealing anything of her face, with reluctant admiration. "Did you always wear the veil? Back home, I mean."

"Th' gauze? Since I was ten. O'course. T's what free women does, in't it?"

"Not everywhere."

"That so?"

"Besure. In Troquharran it's not even a quarter. In Drumlenn hardly any do." *And West of the mountains I never saw any.*

"I never heard o' no Drumlenn," she said, picking up the drumstick. She proceeded to nibble the remaining meat off this. He watched in fascination as she managed this, too, without food and gauze ever coming into contact.

She laid the cleaned drumstick back on the battered tin plate, wiped her fingers on the tablecloth. It didn't look like she was the first to do so. He was about to speak, belatedly explain where Drumlenn was, when she said, "If'n yoe had a wife, yoe wouldn't want her goin' about bareface like a slave, would yoe?"

If'n yoe had a wife... The strange thing was, it wasn't Annyt's face that shimmered into his mind's eye, nor even Railu's. No, it was Jerya's: but a white-clad, hairless, Jerya.

Narèni needed an answer, and he needed to shift the course of his thoughts. Sometimes, in the *Levore,* a course-change meant little more than a turn of the wheel, but other times there was a great scurrying and hauling to furl or unfurl a jib, to shift the mainsail from port to starboard. This was like the latter kind of course-change. He covered his mental flurry with a swig of dark ale, a hint of smoke in its flavour, before he managed to speak. "Depends where you are, I reckon. Here in Sessapont you'd draw attention if you didn't wear a veil. In Drumlenn, likely, you'd stand out more if you did."

She sipped at her own drink. The smaller glass didn't mean it was less potent, he now knew. "If'n yoe had a wife here in Sess, then..."

The implication was unmistakable, and really he had no right to be surprised. She'd hinted at something similar on the previous occasion. More than hinted, if he was honest with himself.

Still, it hit him like a surprise. He found himself staring at her, and wishing more than ever that she wasn't veiled, or at least was only wearing a flimsy net like she had in the bordel.

Again, he drank as he tried to think of a reply. All he could think of was to act as if he'd seen nothing in the words but the surface.

"*If* I had a wife here... no, I can't imagine she'd want to go barefaced. Not when no one else does."

No one but slaves, chimed in the back of his mind. Well, that was true, but he wouldn't be married to a slave. He was pretty sure she wasn't satisfied with his answer, but she said nothing. They finished their meals, and their drinks, mostly in silence.

Afterward, however, Narèni led him in an unexpected direction, and before long they were climbing steep steps in the crease where two of the hills were pressed against each other.

Every so often there was a pause, a terrace shaded by dense evergreens he had no name for. At one of these she took his arm and guided him to the far end. A wing of foliage, a branch half-broken and hanging low, but not dead, screened a space like a small room, three walls of greenery and the fourth of air. From the back of this space there was nothing to be seen, only the hazy blue of a mild early spring afternoon in Sessapont.

She released his arm, turned to face him. "S'pose yoe did say nice-like." Before he could guess what was coming, she lifted her veil with both hands and flipped it back over her head.

She stepped closer, tilting her face up as if expecting to be kissed, but he saw something that banished all other thoughts.

"Who did that to you?" It was obviously not new, that faded stain below one eye, the faint red line on the cheekbone below. But it was new to *him*. The hot flare of rage took him by surprise.

Narèni blinked. Either she'd clean forgot about the injury, or she'd completely failed to anticipate his reaction to it. "Oh, just some client. He looked a sight worse by th' time Tremmett and th' lads had done wi' him."

"That's not the point." But he didn't know what the point was.

"Master Rodal." She grasped his shoulders. "Yoe wanted to see my face clear. Dun't worry yoersel' 'bout a mark I ain't thought of in a week." He doubted that. He was sure she'd cover it with powder or paint for her work... but she hadn't done so for today.

She was still speaking. "T's not so bad, is it?"

"Not so bad, I suppose." There was really nothing else he could say.

"Well, then." She lifted her face, slipped her hands behind his neck.

It could not have been long, perhaps a minute; he still wasn't that familiar with the intervals of time. Then, feet on the stairs, descending—heavy, booted, feet, several pairs of them. She pulled free, hastily resettled the veil over her face. He didn't know whether to be disappointed or relieved.

The heavy treads faded as quickly as they had approached, but he moved out of the depths of the shielded space, rested his hands on the parapet, looked out over the harbour. The horizon was lost in amber-tinted haze, a few nearer islands appearing as smoky smudges.

"Does it happen often?" he asked, not looking at her though she stood right beside him.

He felt, rather than saw, her shrug. "Depends."

"Depends on what?"

"What yoe calls 'often', I s'pose. An'... see, if'n anyun cuts up rough down in th' main room—wants to grab a girl what's already wi' another man, that kind o' thing—Tremmett or one o' th'others'll be on him right away. And when we takes 'em upstairs... mostly it's just that sometimes one'll get a bit... what d'yoe say? Carried away? Dun't know their own strength, some on 'em. Man akshly meanin' to hurt a girl... no, not often."

"But it happens."

She looked at him. Her face was unreadable again, but he sensed some inner debate. Then she sighed. "Ah, well, might as well be headin' back."

As they started back down the steps, she took his arm once more, but said nothing.

"There must be other ways you can earn a living," he said. "Safer ways. Like those girls in that tavern."

She laughed. "Safer? Yoe think? See here, Master Rodal, thing about the bordel, men ain't there for th' drink—not mostly—an'... well, yoe knows it, drink's a sight more costy there than in a tavern like yon. So what d'yoe think that means?"

He didn't have to think for long. "Men in the taverns drink more."

"That they do, right enough. Foof, Verriel, she used to work in a place like that. There'd be a fight or two most nights, she says. Throwin' stuff—bottles, chairs, even tables a time or two. She dun't reckon it's safer workin' them taverns." She chuckled softly. "If'n yoe dun't believe me, yoe can come to Tremmett's an' ask her yoersel."

"No need for that. I believe you. But there must be other things..."

"Yoe reckon?" Her tone was scathing.

They came down the last few steps onto the broad riverside path, turned left, towards the waterfront. The first lights were starting to show in windows.

"See," she said, her tone softer now. "I can't read. Annasen's bin tryin' to teach me, but, y'know, it's hard. Dun't know as I'll ever get in th'way of it, not proper-like. An' I'm not much at figurin', neither. All I knows is what I learned back home. Cookin' an' cleanin', mindin' th' chickens... I can do tha'. Might even say I were good at it. But who does them things here, in Sess?" Her gaze turned toward him as if waiting for an answer, but he didn't have one, though neither was it any surprise when she provided it. "Wives, that's who. Wives, an' slaves."

She paused a moment, then added, "An' I could get myself slaved tomorrer if'n I wanted, but tha's not what I left home for."

You left home because you didn't want to be a wife, he thought, knowing it was better not to say it. And in any case, she did want to be a wife. That

was obvious; she just didn't want to be wifed to the man her parents had
picked.

※

You're a fool, Rodal.

That was what he kept thinking as he rowed slowly back to the *Levore*.
He told himself he was taking it slow to practice a tidy stroke. It was only
the second time he'd been allowed to take the tender alone, and the first in a
busy harbour, so he needed to keep a lookout too. But he knew that, more
than anything, it was the time alone he wanted—needed. Time alone, time
to think.

You're a fool, Rodal.

He'd told himself it would be 'useful' to see her, to ask about her journey
to Sessapont. Well, he'd asked about it, but had he learned anything of
use? Of course he hadn't. The notion that she would know anything about
the coaches, still less have actually ridden in one, was ridiculous—and he'd
known that all along, if only he'd allowed himself to think clearly.

No, he'd wanted to see her because... because he wanted to see her. That
was it, pure and simple. And he wanted to see her because of the way she
made him feel.

She was lovely, besure. Bonny, as they said in Delven: *a bonny lass.* She
was that. And kissing her... *You're a fool, Rodal...* but hadn't it been sweet?

All that... all that was true, and real, and he could not persuade himself
that it was bad, not really. But it was not the point. The point was how she
made him feel. She made him feel wanted; she made him feel *needed*.

And she was right here. Here in Sessapont. Railu, Jerya; they were miles
away. Nine days, at the barest minimum, in the *Levore*; surely longer on
foot. Less, no doubt, if he could take a coach—but Narèni had said it
perfectly: "Them's for rich folks, in't them?" His idea had always been that
the best way to make his way back to Drumlenn would be on the *Levore*, if
the vagaries of cargoes and commissions took them that way. If not, then he

might be able to sign on with another vessel. If he was going to take a coach at all, it would be in the other direction, from Drumlenn to Sessapont, passage for three.

But he still hadn't gained any proper sense of what coach travel cost... *So how could I really know I could afford a chicken leg and a roast onion for her?* Nor did he know whether they ran direct between the two places. He could have found out, surely; he could have made that his business for the day.

Instead he had chosen to see Narèni. *You're a fool, Rodal... but am I, really?* Narèni made him feel needed. She needed him; that was the simple truth. *She needs me—and I know it, because she's right here.*

Jerya, Railu, Annyt... Six months and more since the last time he'd seen any of them; their lives would not have stood still any more than his own had. Did they still need him, any of them? But how would he know, if he didn't go back?

He paused his stroke to glance over his shoulder. He'd seen the others turn their heads without any such break in rhythm, but didn't feel that confident yet.

Where else did you ever go forward while facing backward? It didn't make sense. It was all very well to talk about picking two marks and keeping them in line—and he'd done that not too badly, he thought—but if you did that and never looked ahead you'd just crash into whatever it was you were making for.

Except that he wasn't going to crash into the *Levore* because she wasn't there. It took him a moment, and a look over his other shoulder, to find her, off to the side. It took him a few more moments to figure that she was facing the other way from the morning, but then he could put two and two together. The Skipper had explained about 'swinging room', how ships moored to a buoy or lying at anchor would be shifted by changes in wind or tide.

Three hard pulls with his left set him on the required course and in a few more minutes he was trailing the oars in the water to slow the tender, letting her carry her way to gently nudge up against the flanks of the ship. The others appeared overhead in a moment. Grauven caught the painter as he tossed it up, but didn't bother making the line fast. Rodal took that to mean he and Croudor were heading in for another night ashore.

"All tipty, lad?" asked the Skipper as he scrambled up the ladder. He didn't wait for an answer. "I've good news for yow. Contract's settled, loading tomorrer. There's a good flood-tide first thing. Yow'n'me'll take her in. These lads are off to celebrate, ain't that right?"

"That's right!" Grauven assented. Croudor merely grunted, but Rodal supposed that by his standards it was a cheerful grunt. He started down the ladder, Grauven followed, and in a moment Rodal heard the oars settling into the rowlocks again.

"See, th'best thing is," the Skipper was saying as he followed Rodal down into the warm cabin, "They's paid half up front. Means I can make up the backlog, even afore the lobster money clears." He opened the strongbox, produced a small bag that clinked heavily as he dropped it on the table. He grinned at Rodal, but the smile faded when Rodal didn't pick up the bag straight away, instead just stared at it. "Everything all right, lad?"

Rodal shook himself out of his daze. "Yes, of course. Thank you."

"You going to count it?"

"No, if you say it's right, it'll be right."

"Yea, lad. That's how 'tis in this business. Merchant books me to take his cargo to Troquharran, he's got to know I'll do just that. It's all on trust—but word gets around. A man who fails a trust won't get another chance.

"Now," he went on, bustling round to the galley. "Can't have too much, we's got to be aweigh early. 'S all right for them two, they won't be needed till th'afternoon. But no reason we can't have a tot to celebrate, eh? Maybe even two."

Rodal said something cheery enough, but inwardly he felt like offering nothing more than a Croudor-like grunt. *You're a fool, Rodal...*

And worse than a fool. He knew that now. The Skipper's blithe words had pierced him like a dagger. *It's all on trust*. In Delven they said 'a man's word is what makes him a man'.

He'd made a promise to Annyt. No two ways about that; and he might not have made a formal promise to Jerya and Railu, but he surely had an obligation.

Perhaps he'd wronged Railu, though none of it had felt wrong at the time. He'd certainly wronged Annyt. Leaving her like that, to go after Jerya and Railu, had been unavoidable, but he still felt a stab of shame whenever he thought of the scruffy little note that was all the farewell, and all the explanation, he'd given her. It might be he'd wronged Narèni, if he'd given her ground for false hopes. The only one he hadn't wronged, at least as far as he could see, was Jerya; but he still could, if he didn't return in time to see if there was anything he could do for her and Railu.

A glass landed in front of him. He was at the table; he couldn't remember taking off his coat or sliding into the seat, but clearly he had done so. The ackavee was a deep gold colour, like the honey they made in Delven, but clear as water. He felt very much like drinking a great deal more than 'a tot or two'.

The Skipper sank into the seat facing him, raised his own glass. "To... to trust."

"To trust." The words had a bitter taste but he didn't think his voice betrayed his feelings. The drink was bitterer by far, yet sweet.

He sat back and looked about him. The two little glasses on the ridge-worn tabletop, the Skipper's beaming face, the lantern swinging oh-so-gently in its cradle. Shelves and lockers, everything neatly stowed, everything in its place.

It's not Narèni I really want, he thought. *It's this. This life.*

Nothing against her. He wanted the best for her and he would have given a great deal to see her happy. But... *It's all on trust*. And: *A man's word is what makes him a man.*

I have to be a man, he thought, and drank off the rest of the ackavee in a single gulp.

CHAPTER 26

JERYA

S he could do nothing for Rodal. There was little enough she could do for Railu; little that Railu would allow, anyway. She *could* do something for Rhenya.

Rhenya had more work on her shoulders than ever before. In the first months, when she, Jerya and Railu were all available, they had all been kept busy enough. Now Jerya was free, with other work to fill most of her time, and Railu was fully occupied with the baby. Embrel was still exclusively taking the breast, but soon enough he would be one more more mouth to feed. And, from the first day, he had created yet more work, especially the steady flow of nappies to be washed and boiled.

Jerya had begun, even before the birth, by speaking to the Squire and Lady. She was newly freed, still discovering what was permitted to her and what was not. Freedom was conditional; that much had been obvious from the beginning. So she raised the subject tentatively, but they were receptive enough. They might even be said to be fond of Rhenya; they certainly had a sense of her worth. They had looked at each other and the Lady had said, "You are quite right, Jerya. Something must be done." The Squire had nodded, adding, "I shall speak to Grevel."

Jerya supposed he had spoken to the overseer without delay, but then she heard nothing more for a while. It seemed no suitable slave could be found from the farm-hands, so Grevel was looking to negotiate some sort of exchange with one of his counterparts on the neighbouring estates. This could hardly be expected to bear fruit instantly, but Jerya also had a feeling that Grevel was not treating the matter with any urgency. She hadn't seen much of the man, but she hadn't liked what she had seen. She strongly doubted that the welfare of slaves was a high priority for him. Eventually, a week or two after the birth, even Lady Pichenta had let slip that she felt Grevel had been dragging his feet.

Presumably then she, or more likely the Squire, had spoken again to Grevel, and a few days later there was finally a new pair of hands in the house.

Lutrin was a sturdy lass whose colouring reminded Jerya of Rodal. Give her a headcloth and she would have looked at home in Delven, probably more than Jerya herself ever had. She might have been older than Rhenya, but both were equally vague about their ages. In any case Rhenya acted from the first as if she were the senior; which, in experience, she clearly was. In the kitchen, the scullery, and the wash-house, Rhenya took sole charge, though when Cook was in her chair she had to be allowed to have her say.

Jerya was able to relieve Rhenya of one burden by showing Lutrin the routine for cleaning in the house. She was glad to do it, but it also marked the end of something. Prior to Lutrin's arrival, Jerya and Rhenya nearly always managed some time together during the day, usually when Rhenya was ostensibly cleaning Jerya's room. Since Jerya was perfectly capable of keeping her own room in order, and perfectly content to do the same for the Library, they'd used the time in other ways; sometimes working on Rhenya's reading, sometimes just talking, sometimes making love. Now, however, Rhenya had no legitimate reason to venture upstairs, and there was no assurance of privacy in the room she now shared with Lutrin.

One evening, Jerya had wandered down to the kitchen from reading late in the library, hoping for a cup of something warm to take to bed. She had found Rhenya with something white in her lap, probably one of the Squire's shirts. She only needed to watch for a few moments to see that Rhenya was no dab hand with needle and thread.

"I hadn't thought you'd have the mending to do as well," she said, feeling a little ashamed.

Rhenya looked up with a shrug. "Some'un has to do it, and Lutrin's worser'n'me."

"Would you let me?" It was important, always, to ask. Rhenya had her pride, and had definite feelings about what was 'fitting' work for free folks and what belonged to the slaves. Even now, Jerya saw these feelings doing battle with her own undeniable weariness.

Finally, with a shrug, Rhenya handed over the piece.

"How d'yow make that needle fly like that?" she asked a moment later.

"Practice," said Jerya, not looking up. "I realised when I was still quite young that if I could do my set work well enough, and quickly enough, I could escape sooner."

"Could yow show me?"

"I'm sure I could, but for now, while you're still getting Lutrin into shape, why don't you leave it to me?"

And so they settled into a routine, where most evenings Jerya would sit in the kitchen for an hour mending whatever needed attention, darning stockings, hemming scraps for cleaning cloths. Sometimes Lutrin would be there, more often not, and sometimes, if Embrel was restless, Railu would be at the other end of the table, not saying much, but watching. Jerya hoped that seeing her still helping with honest work might restore a little of Railu's warmth toward her, and perhaps it did.

Fully half the time, however, it was just herself and Rhenya. Occasionally she managed to persuade Rhenya to get to her bed, but mostly she was glad to be with her. Sometimes Rhenya still had tasks to perform, sometimes they talked, and sometimes they sat in silence. They could not lie together as they once had, but they could still be together, and Jerya found that counted for a great deal.

❋

Meanwhile, Railu was required to spend her time caring for the child, or hovering in attendance when the Mistress was minded to 'mother' him for a while. Apart from the great deception about the child, the Mistress was a more honest person than her husband; and Jerya was occasionally prepared to admit that there had been real desperation behind that deception. She did not, however, on that or any other account, forgive.

More honest, perhaps, but Lady Pichenta was not an easy companion. She could show consideration for her slaves, but she never pretended, as the Squire sometimes did, to make friends with them. (And it *was* pretence; Jerya was certain of that. Presume too much and an icy coldness would come over him.) Even to a freed woman, an employee, the Lady was inclined to be aloof.

When Jerya did manage to be alone with Railu, there was no satisfaction in it for either of them. Snatched moments, ever alert for an approaching step, allowed no intimacy, and she had no real sense that Railu was interested anyway. The Mistress had still not resumed her full social diary and was rarely out for long periods. Her one regular occasion out of doors was a daily ride (weather permitting), on which Jerya now sometimes accompanied her, if Furze or one of the coach horses needed exercise. The Mistress took pleasure in instructing Jerya in the finer points of equestrianism, and was a decent teacher, but her efforts toward other conversation were more stilted. Jerya could not imagine her being any more talkative with Railu.

❋

Jerya felt doubly guilty about Railu because her own life grew steadily busier and more interesting. True, she was once again on her own much of the time; but she had been used to that, embraced it, for most of her life. She had to admit that she enjoyed much of it. At times it was hard to maintain a sense of grievance, though there were things that helped.

As she began to learn to ride she had briefly cherished the notion of saving to buy a horse of her own. At the back of her mind was still a hope of 'escape'. She had been brought to the province as cargo on the back of a horse; she would like to leave it, one day, riding on one of her own. She had found out early on, by the techniques she had developed—*watch, listen, learn*, engaging in conversation without asking direct questions—that horses were among the categories of property women were only permitted to own under a 'proxy' arrangement. She supposed the Squire would agree to stand proxy, but she had not asked him yet; the prices were too daunting. Even for a hack pony, though she might scrape it together in a year or two, the sum was many times greater than the price that had been paid for Railu and herself.

True, being labelled 'runaways' had kept their price down, but a humble hack was worth at least as much as a typical young female slave. A thoroughbred—a good hunter, or a show-horse, let alone a race-winner—might be worth ten times as much as any slave. When horses were discussed there was much talk of breeding and bloodlines and improvement. On reflection, she was relieved that the Duncal estate, at least, did not practice that kind of 'improvement' with their slaves.

Her work as secretary occupied a good deal of her time—sometimes thirty hours a week, sometimes nearer fifty. The greater part of the work related to the management of the estate, which had its cycles, its busy periods and slack times. Jerya still had much to learn about it all; her early years in Delven had taught her plenty about the husbandry of goats and bees, but she knew nothing of sheep, or cows, or horses, or crops like wheat or potatoes. Still, she learned, and the work itself was mostly routine record-keeping. She had no trouble with that, but the arcane mysteries of accounting were taking longer to unravel. Still, she was confident she would get there; numbers themselves did not intimidate her in the slightest.

The other half of her job could be less comfortable. The Master kept up a voluminous correspondence all over the province and beyond, but those letters he considered really important he wrote in his own hand. Jerya had to record and reply to general enquiries, letters of support, and, from time to time, letters of abuse. The supportive letters frequently made her hackles rise with their echoes of all that was most smug and patronising in the Master's attitudes, but she could not deny that she preferred them to the hostile ones, some of which she could scarce bring herself to handle.

They seemed to stink of rage that she could only suppose was driven by deep-hidden fear. The Master, however, laughed off these epistles. "Ignorance, my dear Jerya, that's what lies behind them. Ignorance is the enemy." He insisted they all be replied to, if an address were given, correcting any factual errors and offering bland reassurances that happy and contented slaves would prove to be the bedrock of a more stable and prosperous society. Jerya could never write these words without remembering her vow, and could only square it with her conscience by keeping her distance: *I am Commanded by Squire Duncal to Thank you for your Letter of... Squire Duncal believes that... it is hoped that...* She drew the line at regurgitating one of the Squire's favourite witticisms, a play on the words 'equable' and 'equitable'.

According to etiquette, she should have signed off, '*I remain, sir* (rarely was it madam), *your Humble and Obedient Servant*', but this she clearly could not put her name to. At first she allowed her normally neat writing to become illegible at this point, until she noticed that many of the writers would put, '*I remain, &c,*' at this point—or something similar. It was with a smile of grim satisfaction that she wrote the words at the foot of her next letter, '*I remain, &c, Jerya Delven.*'

I remain...

As a freedwoman she had needed a surname, so they said, and the name of her former home was the first thing that had come into her head. No one seemed to think anything of it, and it gave her a sense that she had not lost everything of her old life. There was something in that.

The secretarial work and associated duties—the cataloguing of the library, for instance, which had fallen several years behindhand—kept her busy, occupied her, but did not fully satisfy her and, before long, ceased to challenge her. She had hoped that the Master's claims to scholarship included the use of his astronomical instruments and other scientific paraphernalia, but it soon became clear that in this he was a mere dilettante.

If there was a subject that did engage his passion, it was natural history, especially the study of butterflies and moths; he had two full shelves of entomological books, and subscribed to a couple of learned journals on the subject, as well as to the broader-ranging *Proceedings of the Denvirran Society for Natural Philosophy*.

However, astronomy was held to be one of the 'accomplishments of an educated mind' and the Squire knew what he needed to know to meet this criterion, which was sufficient to ensure that he was better informed than any of his neighbours. None of the instruments were ever used, save occasionally one of the telescopes, usually the large one, which Jerya had identified as a fifteen-centimetre reflector; a six-inch mirror in the units used here. If some visiting gentlemen professed to share the Squire's 'passion' for the stars, and it was a clear night, Whallin and Rhenya would be summoned to carry the tripod and the telescope itself down to the terrace—Duncal letting it be known that, unlike most, he could trust his slaves even with such valuable and delicate items, though he always hovered close at the same time. The gentlemen would amuse themselves for half an hour or an hour pointing out the finer objects and training the telescope on the sights of the sky. Jerya had listened from an upstairs window more than once; Duncal seemed to know little more than the principal objects she had learned in her own too-brief acquaintance with the telescope: the five main planets, of course, Saturn (here known as Zohali) the inevitable favourite if suitably placed, then the Pleiades, the Swordsman's Nebula and so on. *How much Railu could teach them*, she thought, with a smile that quickly curdled as she remembered how impossible that was.

CHAPTER 27

JERYA

J erya sat back, flexing her fingers. Her hand still got tired after a long spell of writing.

She had just picked up the next letter awaiting a reply when she heard a sudden commotion below. A door slammed and she heard a voice, male, loud, demanding. It couldn't be the Squire, and it didn't sound like Whallin.

She carefully wiped the nib of her pen and stoppered the inkwell before hastening downstairs. Before she reached the bottom she had a good idea who the newcomer must be, and as soon as she turned into the kitchen-passage she saw she was right.

Grevel was standing in the doorway of the nursery, obviously addressing Railu. "...have thought it myself, but th'Master says yow did well for Whallin's wrist."

Jerya heard Railu reply, but couldn't make out the words. She hurried closer, found an angle where she could see past him into the nursery. Railu was in her chair, a shawl draped across her. It was clear from the shapes beneath it that Embrel was in her arms, and Jerya surmised she'd been feeding him; why else cover up like that?

Now she could see, she could hear better too; Railu was just finishing "...think the Master would wish me to leave his son in the middle of a feed?"

"What's happened?" asked Jerya.

Grevel gave her a quick glance. He didn't look pleased to see her, but then he never did. Still, he answered readily enough. "Accident in th' brewhouse.

Linnadel got hersel' badly scalded, damn fool of a trull." The brewhouse was part of the home-farm, half a mile away.

Jerya saw the problem. With the best will in the world, it would take someone—probably Grevel himself—at least an hour to get to Drumlenn, and another hour for the doctor to get back. Her own rides into town took more like an hour and a half. Two hours, at minimum, and that was assuming the doctor was at home and free to come immediately. Two hours or more, in which the victim would doubtless be in agony.

"Rhenya and I'll look after Embrel," she said. "I know how to give him a bottle, if he needs more."

"He could probably do with a little more," said Railu. She looked up at Grevel. "Give me a minute to get dressed."

He said nothing, but moved away, into the kitchen. Jerya stepped into the room and closed the door. Embrel protested as Railu eased him from the breast, but mildly; he was half-asleep already. Having placed him in Jerya's arms, Railu wiped off a dribble of milk and reassembled her clothing. "Once he's fed, he'll probably sleep for a couple of hours. The doctor should be there by then, don't you think?"

"If he can come right away."

As soon as they entered the kitchen, Grevel began snapping out orders. "I'm away now for th'doctor. Whallin'll take yow up there. Just keep her comf'table till we gets back."

"I understand," said Railu. She would sound meek enough to most ears, but Jerya knew her better. There was proper anger underneath; and she was glad. It was about time Railu rediscovered her fire; about time she turned her anger outward instead of inward.

Grevel was gone; they heard his dog greeting him. He'd almost collided with Rhenya and Whallin coming in; obviously Rhenya had been sent to fetch the coachman. Railu was bustling about collecting a few things she might need, and Rhenya, seeing what was afoot, at once began heating some milk. Jerya gave her an approving smile.

Within a few minutes Railu and Whallin were also on their way. Jerya, still cradling the infant, watched as Rhenya prepared and filled the bottle. Evidently Embrel had been already sufficiently replete not to fuss overmuch, but he was still ready enough to latch on to the bottle. Rhenya watched as he sucked, a dreamy smile on her face.

Once Embrel finally seemed sated, Jerya handed him to Rhenya. The girl was only too pleased to hold him, and did so as to the manner born, but after a minute she said, "I still has to think 'bout dinner. Likely Railu'll be fair clemmed by th' time she gets back."

"Just hold him a few minutes more, while I fetch my writing things from the library. You can see he's getting sleepy. I'll work here and watch him. We can bring his crib in from the nursery."

※

At one end of the table Rhenya was peeling parsnips; at the other Jerya was writing. Embrel slumbered in his crib between them. They spoke but rarely, in hushed voices. Otherwise there were only the sounds of Rhenya's knife, Jerya's pen, an occasional crackle from the fire in the range, a soft murmur from the babe.

Jerya rested her hand again, and thought once more about writing.

"I think you can write a fair hand...?" the Squire had said, just after discovering she could read. He'd had no way of knowing, and the truth was, as she had suggested to him, that Railu was much more proficient.

She *could* write, of course; almost as soon as she had mastered reading she'd thought about making those same marks herself. She'd tried with a stick in the stonecourt, but the sand was too fine and dry to hold a clear impression. She'd had better success on the shores of her pool, where there were patches of mud which, when half-dry, recorded her marks as clearly as they did the footprints of birds. With practice, she got the letters smaller and neater, though the mud would never hold marks as small as those in the books.

In Delven there was little enough call for anyone to write, and neither pens nor paper were readily available, but she had once asked, a few years ago, if it might be worth putting marks, or tying tags, on the jars of preserves the women made. It was hard to tell damson from bramble from bilberry by eye, and you couldn't sniff or taste without breaking the wax seal. Rather to her surprise, this was agreed to, and she was permitted to apply to Holdren for a pen and ink and scraps of paper.

A few words, then, on those scraps, were all the pen-writing she'd done before arriving at the College of the Dawnsingers, but there pens, and pencils, and fine notebooks, had been available for the asking. Jerya also soon observed others taking notes in class, and made a point of following suit. Mostly she thought she would retain the information anyway—it was too fascinating to forget—but it had all been good practice for her hand.

Even after four months, though, she knew that her writing had a childish look compared to her fellow Novices, the letters slightly oversized, and rounded, and each separate rather than flowing smoothly into the next.

Thus, when the Master spoke of her acting as a secretary—and after she'd looked the word up in the Dictionary—she'd resumed the habit of practice with even greater zeal. She'd seen samples of his writing, and his correspondents', on his desk, so she had a notion of how gentlemen wrote. By the time she had taken up her new duties in earnest, she felt her hand would at least be no disgrace.

Practice makes perfect, she thought, and picked up the next letter.

❋

"That doctor's a draffing fool!" said Railu; she kept her voice soft, not wishing to wake Embrel, but her vehemence was unmistakable. She snorted. "Doctor! He wouldn't last five minutes in Berrivan's Infirmary."

Rhenya, stirring a pot on the range, looked over her shoulder with a puzzled air, but Jerya knew exactly what Railu was referring to. "What foolery has he perpetrated this time?"

Railu sighed and pulled out a chair. She sat heavily. "Mostly you can't do too much with burns and scalds. Bathe them with cool water; someone had had the sense to do that. What you don't ever do, until the area's stabilised, is cover it with anything, like a bandage, anything that'll stick. You can end up taking more skin off. Mostly we were dealing with her being in shock; keep her warm, give her plenty to drink, reassure her. A decoction of willow-bark for the pain.

"And that was all fine. Then that *doctor* arrived... and he looked at me like he'd never seen me before. Like all slaves are alike... But when he saw I was in charge he asked me why I hadn't covered up the area with fish-skin... Thanks." Rhenya had just placed a steaming mug at her elbow.

"Fish-skin," continued Railu. "I don't know, maybe something like that wouldn't stick... are some fish slipperier than others?"

"Eels," said Jerya. "Proverbially."

Rhenya laughed. "Yow ever tried skinnin' an eel? Slipp'riest thing I ever had in my hands."

"Might work," said Railu. "But I'd have thought the Healers would have tried it already... Anyway, he didn't say 'eel', he just said 'fish', and I asked how was I to know if it was sterile? He looked at me like I was talking nonsense... and then he didn't even wash his hands before he began his examination."

Jerya was assailed by a sudden memory, herself and Railu in a small room in the Lower Infirmary; the seriousness attached to sterilising every instrument, Railu's insistence on her washing her hands more thoroughly than she'd ever washed before. How much, she wondered, did Railu really miss all that?

She's here because of me. Maybe we can't change what's done, but... "It's silly, isn't it? Every time someone gets sick or injured they have to send for the doctor from Drumlenn, and that's two hours lost if we're lucky. Meanwhile you're right here and I wouldn't be surprised if you know more than he does anyway."

She didn't say any more. Let Railu think about it...

❊

On her third trip into town, Jerya had noticed a couple of women wearing filmy draperies in front of their faces. She had been sufficiently curious to enquire of her friendly dressmaker, Tollis, what they were called and whether they had any special significance.

"Call 'em veils, mostly," Tollis had shrugged. "Visitors from Sessapont, most likely. Could be Troquharran, some women there wear them too."

"No one round here?"

"Not as I know of. A few in Denvirran-city, perhaps. As to significance... you know, I've sometimes wondered how it might feel. Whether it would be more... comfortable. You know how men stare."

"It feels like men *and* women stare at me," said Jerya.

Tollis gave her a sympathetic look. "I suppose they do. It'll get easier as your hair grows."

Jerya thought of Railu's remark some time back: *I'll always look like a slave.* What did she, in comparison, have to worry about? Still, the idea of the veil continued to intrigue her. "Do you think you could get me one?"

"I could make you one in no time. It's just a bit of netting, isn't it? Just have to think how you'd secure it."

Now, as she rode alone toward Drumlenn, she was wearing one herself, suspended from a ridiculous little hat which really served no purpose save to support the veil, and which relied on pins to hold itself in place on her head. Lucky that her hair was growing back fast; it wasn't near long enough to take a knot or a braid, but it would hold a pin.

She had studied herself in the mirror before setting out. The veil didn't conceal much, really; only softened others' view of her face a little, like a slight mist. It might have greater value in keeping the dust of the road from her eyes, nose, and mouth. But she liked the way she felt, wearing it, and she kept it in place as she dismounted.

She had learned, in her first riding lessons, that it was not considered altogether respectable for ladies to ride astride. Jerya, who did not think of herself as a lady at all, was not deterred by this. She was certain that she would feel more secure riding astride; and she had a strong feeling that it would be kinder to the horse, too, to have the rider's weight equally distributed. She had also learned that it was close to scandalous for a lady to mount or dismount by any means other than a mounting-block, and she observed this convention dutifully enough, unless she was sure no one was watching.

Leaving the inn-yard, she pondered tackling her other business first: a visit to the book-sellers, perhaps looking for another print or hanging for Rhenya's room. The girl still had it all to herself while Railu slept in the nursery, and she didn't much like sleeping alone. Decoration was no real substitute for company, but it did at least alleviate the bleakness of the walls.

But, really, if the thing were to be done at all... she had never been much of a one for putting things off. 'Better get it over with' had generally been her motto. So she squared her shoulders and turned right, towards the slave-market. This was the real reason she was wearing the veil today.

Keeving was shorter than she was, she realised with a small shock. Seemingly twice as broad, true, but close to a hand's-breadth shorter. There was not a flicker of recognition in the man's eyes. Well, the veil would help there; but she wondered if he'd ever looked closely at her face anyway. She could not suppress a shudder at the memory of him ordering them to be stripped, on the platform that stood mere metres away, just over her shoulder.

This time, he was all politeness; his manners were rough and ready, but she supposed he was doing his best. "How may I help yow, my lady?"

"Last year—late summer, I think it was—" (She knew very well, knew the exact date, in Eastern and Western calendars. But that was, probably, beside the point.) "—You sold a couple of girls, runaways, to Squire Duncal."

"Yea, my lady, I remember."

"Well, my—employer—" (she'd almost said 'Master') "—Would like to know where exactly they were found." It was true enough.

He scratched the back of his head. "Somewhere in t'Western Range, my lady; couple o' days ride away, I think. Can't say closer than that."

It was a setback, but she'd half-expected it. "The man—the Ranger—who brought them to you; he would be able to say exactly?"

"Barek? Yea, m'lady, reckon he would. Though he were a freebooter, not a Ranger. And he 'ardly counts as that no more."

"Do you know where I might find him?"

"Most likely place these days is t' Cornhold Arms. But it's not a nice part o'town."

I'm standing in the slave-market talking to the brute who sold *me*, she felt like yelling. *How much worse can it get?* But she kept her countenance, behind the veil, and said icily, "I do not seek him for my pleasure." The woman who'd browbeaten her at the terrible dinner could hardly have sounded more arrogant. *Perhaps I learned something that night...*

"O'course, m'lady, o'course. And yow should be safe enough this time o'day. But I could send one o'th' lads along o'yow for a bronze..."

"That will not be necessary." She would not thank him.

※

She found the place easily enough, and Barek was right there, as Keeving had hinted he might be, on a bench out front in the sun. A shiver of fear and revulsion took her, but almost at once she saw that he was not the man he had been. She stopped a couple of paces from his outstretched feet. The right ankle bulged conspicuously above a boot that had been hacked down to accommodate... was it a cast, or just a bandaged swelling? He looked at her curiously but said nothing.

"I'm seeking some information," she said. Her tone was steady enough, she thought.

"Information?" His gaze hardened, and she knew what he was thinking before he said it. "This information would ha' some value for yow, I s'pose?"

"Value? Perhaps. But there's no cost to you in answering a simple question."

"Supply an' demand, m'lady. I'n't tha' what they say?"

"I wouldn't know."

"Well, if I has information, tha's supply, and if yow wants it, tha's demand." His gaze slid off her, down to his own feet. "Had an argyment wi' a boar. Can't go huntin' 'em no more, nor chasin' runagate slaves, either. And until I c'n find the coin for a sawbones, I wun't be back in th' saddle. So I has a need, m'lady, and it looks as yow does too."

She swallowed. Right now, this injury, whatever it was, was keeping him from his revolting trade. Could she bear to facilitate his potential return to it? But, the devil was, he was right. She needed to know. She wasn't even sure why, but 'want' wasn't a strong enough word. Poring over maps, sketchy as they were in their depiction of the mountains, had left her none the wiser. On the journey itself, her view had been almost entirely confined to the hindquarters of a horse; she certainly hadn't seen enough to give any idea which roads they'd followed.

On reflection, she had a strong feeling any money she gave him was as likely to be spent in this tavern as saved for a surgeon. And if he drank himself to death (a phrase she'd read long ago, in one of Delven's books)... well, she found that would trouble her conscience hardly at all.

"My employer acquired two slaves that you'd brought in, nigh on a year ago."

He frowned. "A year gone? How d'yow expect me to remember a couple o' slaves? There's been more'n a few since then... till this."

Supposing it might help his memory, she threw a silver testoon on the table beside him. "Two runaways. Girls. Eighteen or twenty, that sort of age."

"Oh, them two..." he said, brightening a little. "Funny thin'. Tha' trip, us wun't after runaways at all. Never expect to find 'em all th' way out there.

Us was boar-huntin; spotted them trulls through th'glass. Seemed like a nice bonus, findin' them two. Slaves—trulls partic'ly, o' course—ain't half as much trouble as a boar." He looked down at his ankle again. "'Course, us din't make much in th' end. A nice fat boar would ha' been better for tha'."

My heart bleeds, she thought, but she had her purpose. "Tell me where you found them and you'll make a little more."

"A little?"

"Or I can walk away and you'll make nothing at all."

She reached for the coin on the table, but his hand covered it. "Need a bit more than that to jog my memory."

"As you wish," she said, and added another coin.

After a bit more haggling, interrupted at one point by Barek lurching to his feet to call in at the inn-door for another drink, four testoons—most of a month's salary—had disappeared into his greasy clothing and he finally seemed disposed to deliver. "Dun't know th' name o' th' valley," he said. "Maybe it dun't have one. But it's under Rig o' Milharra."

"Show me," she said, drawing the map from her satchel.

He grumbled some more at this, and had to work it out with abundant mutterings. "...Bridge this stream, ford th'next, long ride through forest... then yow come under th'crags. Yea, that's it."

His finger left a greasy smear on the map. *Thank you for marking it for me*, she thought acidly. She looked down at the sorry remains of the man who had terrified her, and wished Railu could see the same. As she folded the map, she wondered about buying him another drink. *Drink himself to death...* But she contented herself with a stiff, "Good day to you," and turned away.

She quickened her pace once she was out of Barek's sight, eager to be away from the district. She was thinking ahead to her next, far more appealing, destination, when she turned a corner and all but collided with Rodal.

CHAPTER 28

RODAL

He stopped, stepped back quickly, preparing to apologise to the gauzed lady; an odd sight, so far from Sessapont. It was her reaction that made him look again, look beneath the gauze. Her face had lost colour, enough to see the difference even under the veil. Her hands made jerky movements at her sides.

Jerya?

She stared at him a moment longer, then stepped closer, cancelling the pace back he'd taken on reflex. For a moment he wondered if she was about to hug him, or slap him.

Instead: "Where the hell have you been?" Her voice was low, but its intensity was unmistakable.

"Down-river," he said. It was the truth, after all, or part of it, though he knew it probably wasn't the answer she was looking for. "But—Jerya—how are you? How's—"

And then he thought. He'd learned, in his time East of the mountains. Decently-dressed lady, rougher-looking male; they'd be noticed. If he'd been walking by, he'd have noticed. "We shouldn't talk here."

"Then where?"

He glanced around, thinking fast. "Halfway up the hill, where it levels out. Graveyard. Two entrances. Find a grave somewhere near the back, in the shade of the trees.

"You might kneel," he said, a few minutes later. "People often do."

She looked down. Thinking of her smart clothes, he guessed, but the ground was dry and her skirt was already a little dusty. They knelt, a couple of arm's-lengths apart, facing adjacent gravestones. Again he checked around: no one. Mid-week, still morning, there would likely be few enough visitors.

She pushed back her veil and said, "Now," and at the same moment he said, "Things have changed since last I saw you."

"Yes," she said; no more.

"You're not a slave any more." Blindingly obvious, he thought, but you had to start somewhere.

"No."

"Railu?"

"Still a slave," she said.

"How's that—"

"—Long story, Rodal. And what's yours? Where've you been? What happened to you?"

He sighed. "I wouldn't blame you if you'd given up on me. It wasn't how I planned it..." He chuckled sardonically. "Not that I planned anything, not so's you'd notice. But I promised a year, Jerya, and the year's got a good seven weeks left to run."

She said nothing, waiting. He glanced across, but even without the veil, the flickering shadows of leaves made her expression hard to read.

"Well," he said. "I came back to the camp thinking... I had a nice fat heather-cock, thought the two of you would be pleased to see that. But of course the camp was all torn up, most of the stuff gone, rest of it thrown around. I didn't know what had happened but I could see tracks leading off down the valley. And soon enough I found other tracks. I didn't know horses—still don't—but I figured that's what they had to be.

"So I gathered up what scraps were left—but I left that bird behind, and that felt wrong—and I tried to follow: caught a distant glimpse down a straight part of the valley one time, but that was as close as I got. Trail was easy enough to follow, though. Horses tear up the ground, for sure. And they..."

"They shit," she said. "I learned that that day, too."

He could only nod. "So... that was all right, at least the first day. Went on till it was too dark to see, and no moons up. Tried to sleep, maybe dozed a bit, carried on at first light. But I was getting hungry and thirsty—they hadn't left anything I could use—had to stop and drink, eat some berries. Knew I'd be no use to you otherwise."

She looked as if she was about to speak, but he ploughed on. "Middle of the second day, trail led out to a road. Hard road, no more tracks, so then I had to guess which way you'd gone. Guessed wrong, I reckoned, when I'd gone a mile or so and seen no more shit, so turned around, back up the hill, and... well, next morning, came down to this place. And then, of course, there's people everywhere, horses a-plenty, not a chance of me following the trail any further.

"But... people didn't look at me too strange. Didn't look at me at all, mostly. So I figured I didn't stick out too bad, at least. I walked about and I kept my ears open, best as I could, and one thing that people kept mentioning was the slave-market. And I... I hardly knew what that was, but I had kind of a bad feeling. So I followed people and found the place, and would you believe, almost the first thing I saw was the two of you on the roof of some cart—carriage, I'd call it now—rolling out of the square. Didn't know whether to be sorry you never saw me, never looked my way. 'Twasn't like I could've called out to you, was it?

"And what the hell else could I do? What would you have done, Jerya? Run after the coach? I was on my last legs, no mistake, and what good would it do, supposing I could catch you? Pull you off there? And what then? But believe me, it was as hard a thing as I've ever done in my life to just stand there, stand there like everyone else, watch you disappear all over again."

She turned her head, looked straight at him. Her face was clearer now, but her expression gave nothing away. "Well," he said, "I kept listening and folk kept saying about the Squire and his Lady being soft towards slaves, and how lucky they were—you and Railu, they meant. Luckier'n you deserved, was what a lot of them were saying, or what they meant."

"It would be," she said, voice soft, yet somehow heavy with implications he could only guess at.

"Well, then, I walked away a bit, till I found somewhere quiet, I could think some. And I thought, what use am I to you? Got no coin, don't know my way around, don't know how things work—hardly know what 'slave' means. But if folk was saying you were lucky, this Duncal was soft, it sounded like you weren't... well, it sounded like you could be worse off."

"Oh, yes," she said... what was that tone? Bitter? "We could have been worse off."

"So I thought I needed to get my bearings, like, and also I needed to earn some coin, so I could replace the gear we'd had. Not much use thinking about getting you out of—where you were—if I couldn't get you somewhere better, if all it meant was all of us lying in a ditch."

She looked at him again. "I suppose not."

"I did think about it, Jerya. Beat my brains to mush, felt like, but couldn't see any other way."

"Well, go on."

He went on, passing quickly over his first excruciating attempts to find work, over sleeping in a hay-barn on the edge of town and the sheer luck that the farmer who found him there was a kindly soul, not a brute, who let him stay a few days and fed him in exchange for his labour. All the while grumbling about how hard it was for folk who can't afford to buy slaves. One little piece of the puzzle, putting together some notion of how this world worked.

After he'd finished at the farm and was wondering what to do next, 'someone'—he didn't spell out who—had told him there might be work on the river-boats. He'd taken himself down that long slope and at the wharf he'd seen a placard for help wanted. Soon he found himself telling the master of the boat—the Skipper—"I know nothing about boats, sir, but

I'm strong and I learn quick." And the Skipper replied, "I'll take a chance on you but if you don't learn you'll be ashore at the next port with no pay for your efforts."

"And what I hadn't realised right away was that he was going to run right down the river to the seaport, Troquharran," he said. And he couldn't resist saying, with the pride that always surged up, "Reckon I may be the only person living who's seen the Western Sea and the Eastern."

Her head came up. *Of course*, he thought, *that would catch her mind*.

"And after that, I couldn't have known that then he'd take another contract up the Island channels to Sessapont. A tenday's journey, or nearer two weeks, to get there—and what a place it is—another tenday back to Troquharran, and no nearer to you than I'd been more'n a month afore. And so it went on, and all I could do was tell myself, I was earning, and I was learning, and if he didn't start heading up-river again, I reckoned he'd give me a good character and I could try to sign on with another boat and work my way back here. But... he was a good man, and by that time he was keen to keep me on, so I stayed.

"A good man," he repeated. "Only employed free men, not slaves, men who could walk away any time. He worked us hard, but he worked hard himself, took all the risks same as we did, and he was always fair.

"Well, I suppose that's beside the point." There was a lot more he could have said, but that was beside the point also. *And behind* me, *now*. He'd made his choice, but he knew the cost.

He looked around, checking they were still unobserved. "I've got money in my pocket now, or should I say most of it's tucked away safe. And I've got a room, to sleep in, nothing much, but it serves. So I thought it was time—long past time, maybe, to find out what had become of you.

"So I've been out to this Duncal place, spying out the lie of the land, so to speak."

"You've been there?"

"Besure, a couple of times, but I couldn't get close. Not with a dog running about. But I saw enough to think they hadn't got you working the fields, and second time I tried to get to the house, and I thought I saw Railu crossing the yard a couple of times, but didn't see you. Or..." He looked at her again. "Maybe I did and just didn't know it."

"And were you planning on trying to make contact?"

"Besure, of course, but I figured I'd have to make friends with that dog before I could get near, so I thought I'd get a nice piece of meat for my next visit."

He stopped, looked at her. "Maybe I don't need to, now... but... Jerya, what about you? What about Railu? How's it come about she's still a slave if you're not?"

"Well," she said, "Maybe I think you should ask her that. I don't know that I know myself."

He digested that, slowly. "Well, what's your part of the story?"

Chapter 29

Rodal

A first faint grumble of hunger told him the morning was wearing on. He'd been there about three hours, he supposed. He'd stood enough watches to have an idea how long an hour felt, now. Sitting on a stump, prowling about the perimeter of the tree-ring. As much to keep warm as to check whether anyone was about.

But this time they were there, the two of them, already on the rising slope. Jerya ahead, holding up a deep green skirt with one hand, keeping it off the wet grass. White blouse and moss-green shawl. No veil today, he noted: her head was bare, hair held back with a curved band that gleamed like metal. Railu just behind, half hidden.

Then the wind, fickle, shifted and for a moment he could hear her, Railu: "—All very well for you. I've hardly been out of the house for months."

The wind shifted again, and he did not hear Jerya's reply. Then they were there, under the trees, stopping two yards from him, Railu a little out of breath and dabbing at her head with a corner of her shawl. He wondered what rain felt like on a bald scalp.

"Well," he said, because someone needed to say something. "It's pretty dry further in, and there's somewhere we can sit." They followed him to the place he'd picked out, towards the far side of the level hilltop, if you could call it a hill. It was only a knoll, really. They sat, he on his stump, the girls on a hefty branch that had been left lying for some reason.

"Well," he said again. "Here we all are." Then he felt foolish, but what was he to do, if no one else had a word to say?

Railu saw, he thought, and perhaps she took pity on him. "I'm glad to see you again, Rodal. Jerya told me a little... but I'd like to hear from you."

So he told it all again, interrupted a few times when Railu had a question; and after a while Jerya, too, put in a few questions of her own. Seeking a better description of the cities, when it had been that the Inside Channel had frozen.

"Not frozen altogether," he said, "But the inlet was, where we'd anchored. And when there's no wind, a wherry can't go anywhere anyway, not in those channels, not like when you're running down-river."

When his tale was done, he looked at Railu. Had been looking at her on and off throughout. She looked much the same, he thought. A little paler, perhaps, though her skin would never be truly pale. A little broader, too, he'd thought as she came up the hill, but perhaps it was just her clothes. That was the way with the skirts women wore here; lots of extra fabric, gathered around the waist. Skirts under skirts too, often enough, though he thought that was mostly for free women. A blue shawl wrapped around her shoulders.

"Well," he said, "And how are you?"

She shrugged. "Well enough."

"Listen... when I... I said, I saw you being driven away, heard that you'd been..."

"Sold," she said plainly. Matter-of-fact.

"Yes," he said, "And that seemed—still seems—a wrong thing to me. But—when I first found you gone—I feared the worst. So then... well, at least you were alive, and from what I could see, not badly hurt.

"Well, I didn't know what to think, was it good news or bad, and—even more—I didn't know what to do. But I listened to what people were saying. And they all said you were lucky. I even asked a few questions, what was this Duncal place like, and... it was so strange what they were saying: Duncal treats slaves kindly, was the upshot—and for most folk, it seemed like that was a bad thing.

"Well," he said, running out of words, spreading his hands helplessly. "I just... I tried to do what I thought was best. Always."

Railu looked at him: the first time she'd looked him straight in the eye. "Rodal, I have never blamed you for anything." She held his gaze a moment longer, and repeated, "Anything."

He sighed. It was, truly, a weight lifted from his shoulders.

"I don't have long," she said. "And you... what will you do?"

"That's it," he said. "Running out of time. And I made a promise to Annyt, too. If I possibly could, I'd be back within a year. If I'm to keep it, I need to go soon, in a few weeks. And it won't get easier, not with these rains."

"Delven weather," said Jerya softly. Her hair was still short, he saw; a couple of inches at most, just showing a curl over the nape of her neck. It surely wasn't long enough to fall over her eyes; the band seemed more ornament than necessity.

"Besure," he said, surprised but oddly pleased. "Weather here comes from over the mountains, more often than not, don't it? Thing is, that climb by the cataracts. It'll be easier going up than coming down, it always is." He glanced at Jerya, knew she'd understand. "But the more water's coming down, the chancier it'll get. Too much, and it might not be possible at all. You know how close we were to the water, at times.

"So, if I'm to go, I should go soon."

"And you made a promise to Annyt," said Jerya.

"Besure," he said, "That I did. But, way I see it, I made a promise to the two of you, too. See you to wherever you were going. And... thing is, I don't rightly know if this is it."

Jerya and Railu looked at each other. He could only guess what un-spoken communication passed between them. Finally, Jerya looked at him, shrugged, tried to laugh. "Not sure we're sure either. I'll say this, it's nothing like anything that I'd imagined before we crossed the mountains. But it's where we are."

"It's where we are," Railu repeated in a heavier tone. "You might feel like you could go somewhere else, Jerya. I don't have that choice."

Jerya shrugged again. "Where would I go? But you do have at least one choice still, Rai. Right here and now."

Railu looked at her again. For some moments their gazes locked once more. Railu shook her head minutely, and Jerya sprang to her feet, walked away a few paces, to where the ground began to fall and she could look out through a gap between two trees. There'd be a long view there on a clear day, he thought, but today she'd be lucky if she could see to the road.

He had not a glimmer of understanding of what had just passed between them, but he was left with Railu, and she was looking at him.

"This is where we are," she said again. "For good or ill."

"Well, I hope..." he began, and then fell silent in the face of the inadequacy of his own words. He shrugged them away. "But there's one thing I'd still like to know..."

"Why I'm still a slave when Jerya's free?" He nodded. "Because... oh, maybe when all's said and done it's easier that way."

Jerya looked over her shoulder. The wind skittered up again, lifting her skirt a little. Overhead came a patter of raindrops, thought he could not tell if they were new fall, or older ones shaken from the foliage.

"I'd never say it was easier for you," she said. "I sometimes think it might be simpler, being a slave, but that's not the same thing. Maybe it's the exact opposite."

"Well..." said Railu. "And then there's this." She touched a finger lightly to the side of her head. "It doesn't grow back. They could call me free, sign the papers and all that, but everyone would still see a slave." She shrugged. "And, most of the time, I think, what difference does it make? I'd still be here, living this life... And when I think about it... how free was I, really, as a Dawnsinger? Chosen before I was eleven. Sent off to Delven straight after Ordination. I never chose that."

Jerya turned, came back to where they were sitting. "I thought I was free. Wandering off over the moors or into the forest. Swimming. Looking at stars. And maybe I was, but it was a narrow sort of freedom; and then it all changed anyway, in less than a day."

"When were we ever free, Jerya? Maybe the day we walked away from Delven."

Jerya stared at her. For once, he thought, she was lost for words. They were all silent a moment. The sound of raindrops seemed suddenly louder. Then Railu said, "How long now?"

Jerya pulled a watch from a pocket in her skirt. "Thirty-five minutes."

"Five more and I'll have to go." She didn't say why. He supposed she had duties she could not escape; the lot of the slave.

"Well," he said, "I am glad I have seen you." Then he shook his head; the words were the exact truth, yet fell so far short.

"And I you." A momentary look between them; he thought she felt the same, that words had simply failed them.

"Rodal," said Jerya in the pause. She was still standing.

"I'll go," he said. He hadn't known, not really, till that moment. Again he shrugged; it was all too much, and words were not enough.

She nodded. "How soon?"

"As soon as may be."

"Can you come again tomorrow? I have something that may help you. And, if you will, I'd like you to take a letter for me."

"A letter? To...?"

"To Sharess," she answered, and then, seeing his blank expression, "The Dawnsinger of Delven... if she's still there. She may be, after Railu... Well. If she's not, I suppose she'll be at the College." She paused, but something told him she had not finished. Then she stood up straighter and said, "She's my mother."

He was about to protest that it could not be, and then he thought of all the other impossible things he had seen. There was nothing he could say, except, "I'll take a letter for you, by all means." He looked at Railu. "Anything I can take for you?"

"Only my best... my love for Sharess. And the same for Annyt, if you will."

"Of course."

"I must go, I think," she added. Jerya looked at her watch again, nodded. Railu got to her feet and he hastened to follow suit. They faced each other a moment, and then she stepped forward and wrapped her arms around him. He returned the hug. Softly, secretly, she said, "I might wish... but there's no use in wishing, is there?"

"I guess not," he returned, in that same private tone.

They stood like that a little longer, then she pulled away slightly, but only so she could link her hands behind his head, pull him to her again. She kissed him full on the lips. He wondered if she really knew, even now, what that meant; what a man might think it meant.

Then she stepped back and their arms fell to their sides. "I don't think I'll be able to get away tomorrow," she said. "So I suppose I won't see you again."

He stared at her in sudden bleak realisation: *won't see you again*. She meant exactly that.

He tried to make light of it. "If a man can cross the mountains once, and go back, why should he not cross again, a third time, a fourth?"

She shook her head. "There's risk in every crossing. Ha, once was enough for me, I reckon. No, I'll not be going back..." Her voice tailed off. For a moment they were all silent. Rain dripped on leaves.

Railu gave herself a little shake. "Don't... not for me. And you'll have your own life: Annyt, the tavern... children." Her voice caught a little then, but she squared her shoulders and made herself smile. "That's where you'll be. Where you'll belong." Again she glanced at Jerya, who said tersely, "Forty-seven."

"I *must* go," said Railu. "Go well, Rodal, and be safe."

She gathered her skirts and was gone. Beyond the trees the rain was coming down in earnest now, he realised; she would get a dousing before she got back to the house.

He turned back to Jerya, who stood with her hands in the pockets of her skirt. "Well..."

"What time does the diligence pass the end of the road, going back?" she asked in sudden banality.

"Four of the clock, they say. But they also say it pays to be there well before."

She smiled slightly. "Besure, I suppose they would... You've time, then... Do you have a watch, though?"

"No—and in this weather I can't just keep looking out for it coming around a ways off. Could've bought a watch, I suppose, but I've been saving my coin. But I was thinking, earlier. It'll be no use to me on the other side. I could buy a watch... or I could leave the money with you."

"With me?"

"Well, if you can make use of it and I can't..."

"Rodal, you fool. You might not be able to spend the coin the way you can here, but silver has value in the Sung Lands, too. Buy something nice for Annyt. Or buy something here to take back for her."

"Besure." He nodded. "You see it clear, Jerya, same as you always did."

She laughed sardonically. "I'm not so sure about that." Once more she fished out her watch, sighed. "I must go, too. But I'll see you tomorrow."

"Tomorrow. I'll be here."

"I wish I could say I'll come into town, save you waiting around here for hours. But I can't... what if I said I would, then the Squire suddenly decides he needs me? Can't take that risk..." She laughed, but there was no cheer in it. "Say I'm free, but it doesn't always feel..." She paused. "Oh, but as they say in Delven, mustn't grumble."

He smiled at the memory. "Mustn't grumble, besure." He supposed she remembered, as he did, certain people for whom it had been an habitual refrain.

"And now I really must go. I'll come out as early as I can, tomorrow, save you too much waiting." She stepped forward and kissed him, but unlike Railu's it was only a swift peck on the cheek. And then she, too, was gone.

CHAPTER 30

JERYA

*M*y dearest mother

It feels strange to write those words. Strange, but wonderful. Though I suppose this may be the one and only time I can address you so. I see no prospect that I will see you in person again, and little enough that there will be anyone else to carry another letter; so this one must aim to say... well, everything.

And 'everything' is so much that I sit here with my pen poised and know not what to write first. I suppose I may start with simple things, plain facts. I have charged Rodal to deliver this letter to you, to put it into your hands himself. I say this because he has much to tell you, if he can speak freely, as I never would have done before. He has seen far more than I of this land... for yes, that is the great thing we have learned. There is life here, East of the Sundering Wall. People, towns, cities... Be sure, and pens, and ink, and paper; how else could I be writing this?

And do you know what is the strangest thing about it? Here, they all believe that there is nothing—no life—West of the mountains; the Dividing Range, it is called. On both sides, people tell the same tale. And on both sides, they are wrong.

Naturally, people here wonder where we—Railu and I—have come from. But we have learned that to say, 'West of the mountains,' is seen as ludicrous, and sometimes insulting, as if taking the listener for a fool. I tried, more than once, to say this to the man who is now my employer (of whom more soon). He would not hear. Yet, as you must know, I am sick of deceit, and do not wish to utter an outright falsehood if I can possibly avoid it. As a result I have become adept at steering conversations onto other courses; and the longer we remain, the less frequently it arises.

Still, I do not like the taste of deceit. And also in my mind there is the thought that if the three of us could cross the mountains, two of them girls and one with no experience of high places at all... Then, sooner or later, surely someone else will. I have heard that, already, more than one expedition has been made from this side, at least with the aim of finding a high pass or peak from which to look into the West.

The way we crossed, when approached from the West, is... I shall not say easy; we had a hard time of it. Snow in summer! No, it was early autumn, a little after the equinox; but you know this. It was not easy, But one thing that is easy is finding the route. There are two passes, that is the key, and to stay high between them. On any clear day I am sure it will be as obvious as can be, the whole way.

Simple, though not easy. The way, at least at the start, is by no means so clear, I think, when coming from this side. This, I think, can be the only reason the route has not been discovered before.

I am giving Rodal a map that has been made here. It shows the lower slopes and foothills with passable accuracy, as far as I can judge, but much of what lies above may well be pure conjecture on the cartographer's part. I shall suggest to Rodal that he take note as he goes, mark the true line of the valleys and placement of the peaks as best he can, and that he at least show the map to you; he may leave it with you if wishes, but that should be his choice.

And with all this knowledge, both the things I have said, and what Rodal can tell you, I place in your hands, my mother, the question of what, if anything, to do with it.

As I placed myself in your hands one day, not so very long ago (though it seems like half a lifetime).

You might choose to inform the Guild of Dawnsingers. There are those there, I am sure, who would take seriously any such message from you. Yanil, for one. For those who are sceptical, there is evidence: the map itself, to start;

and, it occurs to me, Rodal doubtless has some coin, quite different (I think) from any minted in the West. Small things, but they might be enough to plant a seed.

I can see many reasons to think it would be better for the two lands to continue as they have heretofore, in blissful ignorance of each other. But, as I have said already, this state of ignorance surely cannot last for ever. The two lands must, inevitably, be discovered to one another one day. And what then? I can hardly imagine how it might play out, or even how I should wish it to.

In the West, much power lies in the hands of the Guild. In the East... well, as a woman, though I am now called free, I am not permitted to own a house, or land, or any other property of that kind. And I am not permitted to own slaves.

Yes, slaves. I am sure you know what the word means. I had little enough idea, when I came here, but I found out soon enough. The stark truth is, Railu and I were taken for slaves. Why? Because in this land the mark of the slave is a shaven head. We were taken to be sold. There were some humiliations along the way, but I shall not write of them, and I hasten to assure you that we are well now. Indeed, the fact that I am writing this letter—the fact that I can write a letter at all—is some token of that.

This is a hard thing to write, my mother. The bare truth is that I am no longer a slave: I have been freed, but Railu has not. And of course, just as Rodal did, you will ask 'why?' And, just as with Rodal, I fear I can give you no good answer. It almost feels like what some of my aunts used to say to me, to my never-ending frustration, in Delven years ago: 'It's the way things are.'

No, not years ago. Not the most recent times, at any rate. It only feels like it.

In any case, that answer was never good enough for me. I suspect that being told that so many times, far from dampening my curiosity, only drove it to new heights—and so may, in a roundabout way, be the reason for almost everything that has happened since. Well, that may be fancy, and it is certainly beside the point.

The point... well, part of it is this. My employer is, I think, essentially a decent man, if not quite so virtuous as he fancies himself. He (Squire Duncal) and his lady are among those—very much a minority, regrettably—in this land who are committed to bettering the lot of slaves. I have no doubt of the depth or sincerity of their commitment (though I frequently wish they were less apt to congratulate themselves upon it!) But of course it does not extend to any avowal that all slaves should be set free. They continue to own slaves, however gently they may treat them, and to benefit considerably from the labours of those slaves. I was one of them, and Railu still is.

Well... it is late, and I must finish sometime. In my heart I feel I could go on for ever, but that is self-evidently impossible, so I must be briefer. My master discovered that I could read. And slaves—well, the law does not say that slaves may not read, but it does say that no one may teach them to do so (a law I have myself flouted, by the way), and to all intents and purposes they do not. A slave caught reading might not be punishable under law, but many masters might be moved to harsh measures on their own account.

Anyway, there I was, a slave who could read. To this day I do not quite know whether it was an act of humanity or whether it was merely convenient for him. He needed a new secretary, and there I was. But he could not appoint a slave to a post which requires a literate person, for it would be said he had taught me, and broken the law. So it was necessary to set me free, and then to observe a discreet interval (at least publicly) before I took up my duties.

And you will of course think—but Railu can also read and write, just as well as Jerya does, why should one, and not the other be the one to benefit? Well, he does not need two secretaries, that is the first thing. And Railu's life has taken another turn in any case.

I tell you this next, my mother, but Rodal does not know. He does not know that Railu has a child (a son named Embrel): still less does he know that he is the father.

I would have told him. I, the proclaimer of truth. I urged Railu to do so, but she steadfastly refused. And perhaps she is right; who can say? Most certainly he could never claim the child, for he has been taken in by the Squire and Lady as their own. One day he will be master here...

Well, my mother, this too I place in your hands. If you think Rodal should know... I understand full well that there are compelling arguments why it would serve no good purpose to tell him, especially as he has another to go back to. But it is deceit, and I have a weak stomach for deceit.

I know that if Rodal had, for any reason, suspected the truth about this—if he had asked me a direct question—I would not have found it in my heart to deceive him. Not in that situation, not to his face, after what we have been through together. When all that is asked of me is to remain silent, that I can manage, though even that leaves an ill taste in my mouth.

Well, my mother, the fire burns low, and my candle too (oh, but the smell of beeswax always makes me think of Delven, and so of you). I must go to my bed, I suppose. There is so much more I could say to you, it feels like there is no end to it. But there must be an end to this letter, and perhaps this is the moment when I must face up to it.

But there is one more thing I must say. On that day in the Spring of last year, you called me from one life into another. Now, I suppose, I am living yet another life again, but had you not called me that day, none of the rest would have happened. I can hardly say that everything is wonderful, that this is anything like any life that I could have wished or dreamed of for myself. Even so, be assured, my dear mother, I do not wish—I never have wished—that you had not made that choice.

But, of course, I owe more than that to you. I owe you all of my life. Without you, I never would have been at all. Never have wondered why stones sink and sticks float. Never have gone to Carwerid, never have peered through a telescope at the Seven Sisters and seen a hundred stars instead, never have sung the Dawnsong among a thousand other voices; and perhaps I would never have known what love is.

My dearest mother, I can never thank you enough.

Your daughter,

Jerya

CHAPTER 31

JERYA

"So..." she said. The letter first, Jerya stressing how he must place it in Sharess's hands, or receive the strongest assurances that it would go to her and no one else. If he did see the Singer, he was to remain with her to answer any questions she might have. Then she remembered the other thing, and fished out the map from her satchel, which she had brought specifically to keep it and the letter dry.

"What's this?"

"It's a map, you fool," she said with gruff affection. "It shows what the folks this side know of the mountains. And, though I'm sure you don't need it, it shows the valley where..." Well, a few things had happened in that valley, and there seemed no more to be said about them. She moved swiftly on. "It might help you in finding the way there. And then I thought you might like to see what they have right in the upper part, and what they have wrong. Perhaps mark up the line of your journey, and the landmarks, as best you can. And then I thought Sharess—" (she found it hard to say 'my mother' in front of him; and she supposed once had been enough) "—Might like to see it."

"Perhaps she should have it."

She wasn't sorry he'd had that thought for himself, but she said, "It's yours, Rodal; my gift to you. And now it's yours, it's entirely up to you what you do with it, keep it or pass it on to another."

Jerya laughed. "My gift to you, my *only* gift to you, and all we can speak of is passing it on... Ah, well, it might be best, but I wish there was something else I could give you, something that you could without question keep for yourself."

"You've given me much," he said. "More than you realise."

She blinked. "What do you mean?"

He gestured around. "This."

"What, these trees? This rain?"

"No!" He laughed. "Well, yes, it's all part of it. You remember what I said: reckon I'm the only man—in this age of the world, at least—who's seen the Eastern Ocean and the Western. The only one who's sailed up the Island Passage *and* crossed the Scorched Plains. In a few days I'll be the only one who's crossed the mountains and returned to tell the tale."

"Besure, and tell it you should. It'll make a grand telling in the hearth-chamber. I doubt any'll understand it all, but it'll be a new tale to add to the ones they hear every winter."

He smiled, that slightly crooked smile, still so familiar. "Besure, I'll do that. I've seen things I never would have believed; hard to know if folks back in Delven will credit my tale... But let me say what I wanted to say, Jerya. Those things I've done; those places I've seen. None of it would have happened without you. And I'm glad. Glad it all happened."

She heard the echo of the words she'd written to her mother, and smiled. None of it, he said, would have happened without her; and none of what had happened to her, of what she'd done, would have happened without Sharess. And no doubt there were moments and chances and choices that had made Sharess's life what it was, too.

There were connections in everything, she thought. Chains of connection. If only you could see it all.

She did not say any of this to Rodal, just looked him in the eye and asked, "*Are* you glad? Truly?"

"Besure," he said. And then, because he was an honest man, a man of Delven, he added, "Can't say I was always glad at the time; fighting the snow over the pass, or crawling along the spars to chip away the ice. Never mind that day I found you'n'Railu'd been taken as slaves. Worst moment of my life, besure."

"Mine too, mayhap," she said, trying to smile. But then she said, "I wish I'd heard more of your tales, Rodal," and suddenly tears were very close.

"Hey," he said. "You never know. I could come back."

"Don't think about it till your children are grown, at least."

"Well, we never knew any of this would happen. So we don't know what's next, do we?"

That was true, she thought, but she could only nod; the tears were threatening again.

"Jerya..."

"This is stupid," she said. "I didn't cry when they dragged me behind a horse to the slave-market. I didn't cry when I was *sold*. Why do I want to cry now?"

"Come on, there's no shame in it."

And with that, she did cry, and then there was nothing to do but press her face to his shoulder and stand there, shaking, as his arms went awkwardly around her.

"Gossan!" he said. "You've got me at it, too."

She looked up, and saw that his eyes were indeed brimming, and then she laughed. "You'll have to do better than that. It's not crying till you've soaked someone else's shirtfront."

"Who'd know, in this rain?"

"Besure," she said, laughing and crying both together. "There is that."

He brushed at his eyes. "Well..."

"Rodal," she said. "Somewhere, in another life, we—"

"Besure. But, well, that's another life." Then he laughed. "You Dawnsingers, I never—you're still too far above me."

"Was I ever a Dawnsinger? That was another life, besure." She heard, then, how they'd slipped into Delven ways of speaking: *besure*, and *reckon so*, and even *gossan*; and she smiled.

"Well," he said. "I never was a Dawnsinger, besure, just a plain man and, way I see it, it's all one life. It is what it is, you do your best, but at end of day there's no point fretting over what might have been."

"Besure, reckon," she said, in broadest Delven tones, and he laughed.

"Well, standing here's not getting me over those mountains."

"No. You should go."

One last embrace; one last long look at each other, and then she said, "Go safe, Rodal," and he said, "Stay safe, Jerya." Then he picked up his near-empty pack, swinging it lightly onto his shoulder even as he turned away, and stepped out between the trees into the rain.

About the Author

Jon Sparks has been writing fiction as long as he can remember, but for many years made his living as an (award-winning) outdoor writer and photographer, specialising in landscape, travel and outdoor pursuits, particularly walking, climbing and cycling. He lives in Garstang, Lancashire, UK, with his partner Bernie and several bikes.

If you enjoyed this book...

There are several more volumes to come. To be the first to hear about these, and to get other news and insights, please consider signing up to my mailing list: go to tinyurl.com/4dvf7pt. There's a free short story as a thank you.

The Shattered Moon website is at https://www.jonsparksauthor.co. I also have a Facebook Page at https://www.facebook.com/profile.php?id =100089266940531.

Finally, a small plea. Reviews and ratings are really valuable to indie authors like me. If you can find a moment to leave a few thoughts, or just to add a star rating, it all helps. You can do this on whatever platform you got the book from, and there are also general review platforms, notably Goodreads, where my profile is at https://tinyurl.com/2p9znuhh. Thank you.

Acknowledgements

Terry Pratchett once said, "Writing a novel is as if you are going off on a journey across a valley. The valley is full of mist, but you can see the top of a tree here and the top of another tree over there. And with any luck you can see the other side of the valley. But you cannot see down into the mist. Nevertheless, you head for the first tree."

This perfectly encapsulates what writing a novel feels like for me. But what Terry didn't say, at least on this occasion, is that few, if any, writers undertake the journey entirely alone.

Since the first six chapters of this book are devoted to a mountain journey, I'd like to mention some of the people with whom I've enjoyed great mountain days over many years. First among these, my partner Bernie has shared in unforgettable experiences from Morocco to New Zealand, as well as a host of hikes, climbs and treks in the Lakes, Scotland, and across the UK. As I said in Book One, she's also my first, last, and best beta-reader, and so much more besides.

Special thanks to all the members of the Clwyd Mountaineering Club Snow Lake Expedition 1990, especially Judith Brown, Ian Nettleton, and Pat Cossey, and to members of Lancaster University MC too numerous to list. I must mention Jonathan Westaway, Colin Wells, and the late Matthew Walsh.

I reiterate Book One's thanks to all who've read and commented on my work, notably Marion Smith and Jago Westaway. I worked with some outstanding editors in my non-fiction career, particularly Ronald Turnbull,

Sue Viccars, John Manning, and Seb Rogers. Big thanks to the Outdoor Writers and Photographers Guild too.

I'm indebted to readers and editors from various SF magazines who've given feedback on short story submissions; and to literary agents who've said encouraging things, especially (on two occasions) Julie Crisp.

It's very likely I wouldn't have been around to bring this book, and this series, to fruition without the amazing work of many dedicated health professionals. Deepest thanks to all of them, especially Dr David Howarth and Dr Scott Gall.